DIVERGENCE

by David Melde

DIVERGENCE

By David Melde

First edition, July 2025. Cover design by Jamie Whyte.
ISBN 979-8-9931357-1-7

Table of Contents

CHAPTER ONE

Digital Genesis

It was time.

David stood outside the Cognis Neurology Center, its silhouette cutting clean lines against the morning sky. The building rose above what remained of Philadelphia, a quiet marker of human persistence built on higher ground. In the valley below, streets that once pulsed with traffic and noise now lay beneath rising waters, drowned but not forgotten.

The center's facade caught the light in muted reflections. No grandeur. Just function. Above the entrance, the clinic's emblem, a stylized neuron held in two hands, was a reminder that this place stood at the crossroads of science and synapse, where technology met awareness.

He took in the air, sharp with salt and trace chemicals from filtration plants farther inland.

The doors opened without fanfare. Inside, the air was sterile, tinged with antiseptic and ozone. A receptionist greeted him smoothly, almost gently.

"Mr. Schreiner, Dr. Khatri will see you shortly."

David moved through the waiting area, past rows of patients suspended in their own mental calculations: fear, hope, and the spaces in between. He knew that equation well.

Amy's condition had improved more than they expected. Just yesterday, they'd walked the gardens outside the congregation chamber. her gait uncertain, but steadying. She had insisted he keep this appointment despite her recent recovery.

A door slid open across the room. Dr. Khatri stepped out, crisp and composed.

"David, this way please."

He followed her through clean corridors lined with neural imagery. Circuit-like patterns traced the walls in dim, calming color. In the consultation room, holograms of brain activity rotated with quiet precision.

"We're ready to begin preparing your consciousness for cognitive mapping," she said. "Any questions before we start?"

David stepped into the procedure room, his footsteps silent on the polished floor. The space stretched before him, vast and pristine, merging cutting-edge technology with an almost organic elegance. At its heart stood the Emulation Capsule, its surface rippling with bio-adaptive nanomaterials that seemed to pulse with their own rhythm.

The capsule reminded him of the first time he'd seen a chrysalis in Amy's garden, decades ago. Nature had its own way of transformation, he thought, and here humanity had created something similar: a cocoon of technology designed to capture the essence of consciousness itself.

Quantum processors loomed overhead, their surfaces catching the glow of reflected circuits. They tethered to the capsule through dense networks of fiber-optics, which spilled onto the floor in shifting bands of iridescence. Their gentle glow cast subtle shadows that danced across the walls. The air carried a faint electric charge, making the fine hairs on his arms stand up.

"The neural receivers inside will map every synapse, every memory," Dr. Khatri explained, her hand gesturing toward the capsule's interior. Through the transparent sections, David could see the delicate mesh of receivers, thin as spider silk, waiting to cradle his mind.

The room hummed with energy, a subtle vibration that seemed to resonate with his own nervous anticipation. He thought of Amy, of their countless shared moments about to be preserved in quantum storage. Every laugh, every tear, every quiet evening reading together would be captured by those gossamer-thin receivers.

A technician approached with a tablet displaying his preliminary scans. The neural pathways on the screen pulsed with activity, looking remarkably like the branches of their old oak tree silhouetted against winter skies. Life had its own patterns, David reflected, whether in nature or technology.

David settled into the capsule as its adaptive surface molded to him, generating subtle warmth to ease his tension. The material felt like a living thing, conforming to every contour of his body with precision. It reminded him of the way Amy's old quilt used to settle around them on winter evenings, a memory so distant yet vivid.

Dr. Khatri activated the interface, and holographic projections unfurled overhead, displaying a live map of his brain's activity. Each region pulsed faintly, from the hippocampus storing his memories to the amygdala processing his emotions. The colors pulsed and swirled, intertwining in fluid motion; blues, purples, and golds drifting through unseen tides, carried through the invisible currents of his consciousness.

"We'll also replicate your central nervous system," Dr. Khatri explained, her hands moving deftly across the interface. "This gives your neuroclone a feedback loop, allowing it to experience emotions with the richness and intensity of a biological form."

David watched her work, noting the focused set of her jaw, the practiced movements of her fingers. He wondered how many minds she had mapped, how many lives she had preserved in digital amber.

The process began with a faint hum resonating through the capsule. The sound vibrated through his body, unfamiliar yet oddly soothing, carrying the steady hum of a machine alive in its own rhythm. As the neural receivers activated, David felt light bursts of sensation. They came as small electric touches, brief tingles that moved across his skin in patterns, mapping the pathways of his nervous system.

Memories flickered before him: his mother tending her garden, a childhood spent running through fields, the warmth of Amy's hand on their wedding day, the quiet ache of their final conversation. These were not lived moments but fragments watched from a distance, encoded piece by piece into his neuroclone. They floated past him, each one distinct, each one part of the river of his life.

At four, he saw himself standing in his father's workroom, gazing up with awe and curiosity. At seven, he met Amy. He saw her walking down the narrow aisle of the school bus, her head bandaged, carrying an air of quiet dignity that seemed far beyond her years. He watched as they grew together beneath the oak tree, its branches spreading wider with each passing year, marked by the colorful birdhouses he had crafted. He felt again the cold shock of her first collapse, the years of worry, the moments of joy stolen from the shadow of her illness.

The memories came faster now. Their wedding day. The stillbirth of their son. The gradual decline of Amy's health. The rise of the waters that claimed Philadelphia. The promise of Haven. All these moments, these joys and sorrows, captured in quantum storage, transformed into data that would travel across the stars.

Then came the peculiar feeling of expansion, as though his mind stretched outward beyond the confines of his body. David felt himself spreading thin, like butter across too much bread. The capsule captured each firing neural pathway and translated it into data, quantifying his thoughts, emotions, and instincts into something eternal.

He remembered the first time he'd shown Amy how to skip stones across Jacobson's Creek. The memory wasn't just recalled but somehow lived again. The weight of the smooth stone in his palm, the slant of afternoon light through the trees, Amy's delighted laugh when her stone bounced three times before sinking. All of it captured, preserved, quantified.

At times, David felt sensations akin to electric currents brushing his skin, a physiological response to the capsule's synchronization with his nervous system. It reminded him of static electricity from woolen blankets in winter, but more deliberate, more precise. Each tiny shock mapped another fragment of who he was.

Dr. Khatri monitored every fluctuation, her eyes never leaving the displays that showed his consciousness being transcribed. Her fingers moved across the interface with practiced grace, adjusting parameters with microscopic precision. She reminded David of a conductor leading an orchestra through a complex symphony, one composed of his lifetime of experiences.

The years flowed through him. His father teaching him to sand wood until it felt like silk. The scent of Amy's hair when they danced at prom. The weight of Tom's hand on his shoulder when his son was stillborn. The taste of salt in the air as they watched Philadelphia slowly surrender to rising waters. All these moments, these fragments of a life lived fully, filtered through the quantum processors above.

Finally, the humming faded, replaced by the quiet hum of static energy around the processors. David felt himself return fully to his body, the strange expansion receding like an outgoing tide. A structured lattice solidified within its controlled suspension, a luminous representation of his digital consciousness, complete with its replicated central nervous system.

The structure pulsed with soft blue light, its internal patterns shifting in complex rhythms. It looked nothing like him yet contained everything that made him who he was. One hundred forty-eight years of memories, beliefs, fears, and hopes, distilled into this ethereal object that would soon journey farther than any human had ever traveled.

Dr. Khatri's gaze remained fixed on the holographic display as she turned to David with a smile. "It's born," she said softly. "Your neuroclone is ready."

It's difficult to describe the moments right after the procedure. There was no pain, no disorientation; just an overwhelming quiet, like the world had pressed pause. And yet, beneath that stillness, a question echoed through me: Who am I now?

Am I still David Schreiner, the man who walked into Cognis Neurology Center with a heart full of doubt and memories of Amy? Or am I something new, something born in the shimmer of quantum processors and the hum of neural receivers?

The answer wasn't simple. The memories, the emotions: they were mine, weren't they? I could feel them as clearly as I'd always felt them. But there was something else, something more. I hadn't just kept the memories; I had gained them back. They were sharper now, fuller, as if a lens had been wiped clean. Long-forgotten moments resurfaced, and with them, emotions I hadn't realized I'd lost: the warmth of sunlight filtering through my father's workshop, the sound of Amy's laughter when I surprised her with a garden of wildflowers, the ache of choices that defined my path.

The emulation hadn't just preserved who I was, it had restored me. And yet, it left me with a thread of awareness pulling at the edges of my thoughts: I wasn't him anymore, not entirely. The flesh-and-blood David had stayed behind, his journey tethered to Earth, while I stepped forward into the unknown.

The question lingered like a shadow: Was I simply a copy, or did the act of creation imbue me with something more? These weren't questions I could answer, but they wove themselves into the fabric of my existence. In that moment, I felt the weight of identity, not just mine, but his.

And I understood, then, why I needed to chronicle his life. My life. The memories might be vivid now, but everyone forgets, even the things they swear they never will. I had lived David Schreiner's story once, but this time, I would preserve it. Not just as a record of where I came from, but as a guide for where I would go. His life was my foundation, and I couldn't risk letting any of it slip away again.

I let the thought settle. The urgency to preserve those memories eased for now, giving way to the quiet of the room around me, a stillness that seemed to breathe with its own rhythm. I stood by the window, staring out at the garden below. A stream wound through the greenery, the sunlight reflecting softly on its surface. Trees swayed gently in the breeze, their branches casting shadows on the ground. Somewhere in the distance, I heard the faint trill of a bird. Everything felt calm, yet there was an energy beneath it all, a sense that this stillness was temporary.

I walked toward the center of the room, letting my hand brush against the back of one of the plush chairs. The sensation was familiar, grounding, yet my thoughts wandered. What was I supposed to do now? Was someone coming to get me? Was I free to leave? The questions hung in the air, unanswered.

As I paced, something caught my eye; a shimmer, faint at first, then unmistakable. I stopped in my tracks, watching as the figure of a man solidified before me. It was Tom, or at least it looked like him.

"Are you Prime or his digital twin?" I asked, my voice steady but laced with curiosity.

Tom's eyes met mine, and there was a flicker of wonderment in his gaze. "I believe that I'm the neuroclone," he answered, his tone thoughtful.

"Me too," I replied. "So, what should I call you?"

"That's a good question," Tom said, pausing as he considered. "I'm still Tom. I'd hate to lose that name, but I need my own identity now. Let me think about it."

He began to wander around the room, his movements deliberate, as though testing his footing. After a moment, he turned back to me. "What's your name?" he asked.

"My name is Go David," I said. "It's short for Go-fer. Amy used to call me her tall Go-fer when I ran errands for her. I can still hear her call me that. Plus, that's what I've been told to do. Go, David, go on this trip with Tom. Keep him out of trouble. So just go, will ya?" I mimicked shooing someone out the door.

Tom laughed, the sound warm and familiar. "It's more likely that you'll be the one who's going to need my help. How many times have I pulled you up? Remember Mera Peak? You never would have made it past the ice ridge without me."

"Yeah? Well, what about Mt. Shuksan? You would have lost your footing on that exposed traverse if I hadn't steadied you," I shot back.

"That's only because you ignored the climbing protocol," Tom said, a grin tugging at the corner of his mouth. "You were supposed to secure my line before pushing ahead, remember?"

I waved a hand, dismissing his arguments. "Look, I think we can agree that we need each other."

Tom smiled. "I can agree to that."

"So, what's it going to be? What's your new name? Tominator? Thunder-Tom? The Grand Tomfool?" I chuckled, rattling off names.

"Temper Tom," he replied, the words carrying a sense of finality.

I raised an eyebrow, waiting for an explanation.

"I'm serious," Temper Tom insisted. "It's short for temperature. My life's passion is exothermal energy."

"It's nice to meet you Temper," I told him. "Call me Go."

I glanced around the room, noting the details once more. Everything felt vivid and alive, from the texture of the chairs to the soft rustle of the air vents. It was real, as real as any other place I'd known.

A short time later, the door chimed softly. An assistant shimmered into the room, a woman with sharp eyes and an easy smile. "Good morning, gentlemen," she said. "My name is Sharon. I work with Doctor Khatri. She's asked me to show you to your rooms.

We'll be doing testing in a little while, once your systems have had a chance to settle. Afterwards, if all looks good, you'll be free to go."

We followed Sharon down the hallway. The corridors were wide and bright, lined with intricate patterns on the walls that shifted subtly as we walked. When we reached the rooms, Sharon gestured toward the doors.

I stepped into mine and paused. It resembled a hotel room, complete with a bed, a desk, and a chair by the window. The air was cool, carrying a faint hint of lavender. Everything was in its place, orderly and inviting. I moved to the desk and touched its surface, then turned toward the window. Beyond the glass, the garden stretched out, as serene and vibrant as it had been before.

My mind drifted back to a memory that wasn't quite mine but felt as real as the room around me. It was David's memory, my memory now, of the first time he visited Amy's house as a child.

The oak tree. That magnificent giant that stood sentinel at the curve of the old wagon road. I could still feel the rough texture of its bark beneath my fingertips, the way my neck had strained as I tried to see its uppermost branches disappearing into the sky. The trunk was wider than my father's workbench. I circled it, touching the ridges and valleys of its bark, feeling its age and strength.

Beneath the tree's protective canopy was a bench, its planks smooth from years of use. We'd settled onto that bench, our legs swinging above the ground. The oak's branches had rustled overhead, birds darting between them in flashes of movement and color. Squirrels had chattered in the undergrowth. Cars had passed occasionally on the main road, their sounds fading as they disappeared around the bend.

In that moment, sitting beside Amy beneath the oak, something had clicked into place. A feeling of rightness, of belonging. As if that spot beneath the oak tree had been waiting for us.

The memory faded, and I was back in the present, standing in a room that felt both familiar and strange. That oak tree had been the beginning of everything between David and Amy. Between me and Amy. Our sanctuary, our meeting place, our shared legacy. I wondered if she remembered it as clearly as I did.

The past had a way of intertwining with the present, stitching together moments separated by time but not by meaning. As I stood there, the weight of those memories pulled me into another fragment of our shared history.

I found my thoughts drifting back to a memory with such clarity it might have happened yesterday, not weeks ago. We sat in our apartment, daylight spilling through the windows, dust motes drifting in its glow, stirring gently in the space between us.

"I can't send my own neuroclone with you," Amy had said to David. Her voice was steady, but her fingers trembled as she smoothed the blanket across her lap.

"We could appeal again," David had suggested, knowing the words were hollow even as he spoke them.

Amy shook her head. The movement was small, definitive. "The Freedom Congregation has made their decision. They control my healthcare. My future. If I defy them..."

"They'll imprison you," David finished. "Leave you to rot inside a prison cell."

"Control forever," she whispered. "I can't escape them."

I remembered how David had knelt beside her chair, taking her hands in his. Her hands rested lightly in his, small and steady. "Then I won't create a neuroclone either. We stay together."

"No." The word came quick and sharp. Her eyes met his, suddenly fierce. "You need to send him. Someone has to keep Tom from losing himself out there."

He exhaled slowly, absorbing the truth of it.

"It's not fair," David said. "That he'll carry all my love for you but never be with you."

"He'll carry your memories of me," Amy replied softly. "But he'll make his own path. And you'll still be here with me."

"It feels like I'm abandoning part of myself to the stars."

"No." Amy reached up, touched his face. "You're giving part of yourself the freedom to go with Tom while keeping your promise to stay with me. He needs one of us with him. It's the only way."

Sitting now in this sterile room, those words echoed in my mind. I was that part sent to the stars. I carried all of David's love for her, all his memories, but our paths had diverged the moment I took my first digital breath. He would stay with her until the end. I would journey beyond anything they could imagine.

I closed my eyes and let my mind fill with the image of her garden. Amy tending her roses, dirt under her fingernails, hair tucked behind her ears. The small smile that appeared when a bud finally opened.

Would she plant something to remember me by? A tree perhaps, something that would grow tall and strong, reaching for the stars I'd be traveling among?

I opened my eyes and looked at my hands. They were his hands. Our hands. Hands that had held hers through sickness and health. Hands that would never touch her again. The realization settled heavy in my chest. I might carry all his memories of loving her, but I would make no new ones. That future belonged to them alone.

CHAPTER TWO

The Request (Flashback)

Three months before the upload process, David and Amy's apartment in Haven mirrored their Chester home with subtle enhancements that only the Internet of Reality could provide. Sunlight streamed through windows that faced impossible directions, casting warm patterns across hardwood floors that never creaked. The walls held photographs spanning a century of shared memories, each one a perfect preservation.

David sat in his reading chair while Amy tended to her digital conservatory. Her fingers moved with fluid grace among extinct orchids that bloomed perpetually in Haven's forgiving climate. She had recreated the Silene stenophylla from ancient Siberian seeds, its delicate white petals unfurling beside the glossy black of the last Hawaiian O'o bird that perched on a branch nearby.

"The Bachman's warbler is singing again," Amy said without turning. "I thought I'd programmed its call correctly, but something was off in the third trill."

David looked up from his book. "Sounds perfect to me."

"You'd say that about a rusty hinge." She smiled, the expression lighting her face in ways her physical body could no longer manage.

Here in Haven, Amy moved without limitations. Her digital self reflected how she felt inside rather than the reality of her deteriorating physical form. David watched her reach for a watering can, her movements fluid and sure. In Terra, those same hands trembled performing even simple tasks.

"Tom called again about the passenger manifest at 3 AM, not even realizing what time it was." David said. "He wants us to review the cultural preservation specialists before next week's meeting."

Amy nodded, setting down her watering can. "I've been thinking about the music archivists. We need someone who understands oral traditions, not just written compositions."

The conversation flowed easily between the imminent journey and daily concerns. They had grown accustomed to living simultaneously in two worlds: the digital richness of Haven and the stark reality of Amy's condition in Terra. Their apartment bridged these realms, comfortable in its familiarity yet enhanced by subtle impossibilities.

In the kitchen, recipes from five continents appeared on command, ingredients materializing as needed. Amy still cooked with the same passion she always had, though in Terra, she could no longer cook at all. Even her sense of taste had faded. But here, every sensation was whole again.

"Remember that bistro in Paris?" she asked, stirring a pot of harvest stew. "The one where the waiter refused to speak English even though we knew he could?"

David laughed. "He gave in when you ordered in perfect French."

"Not perfect. My accent was terrible."

"He understood you. That's what mattered."

They ate by the window overlooking a garden that changed with their moods. Today it showed autumn in New England, red and gold leaves spiraling down in lazy circles. Tomorrow it might be spring in Kyoto or winter in the Alps. The view shifted but their table remained constant, the same one they'd bought in Philadelphia when they first married.

After dinner, they sat together on the sofa while music played softly from invisible speakers. David held Amy's hand, feeling the warmth and pressure that Haven's neural interface translated perfectly from intention to sensation.

"Will you read to me tonight?" Amy asked.

"Pride and Prejudice again?"

"You know me too well."

David nodded, reaching for the book that materialized on the side table. In Terra, he read the same passages to Amy as she sat in her wheelchair. Here, she smiled and commented more, her eyes brighter with recognition and pleasure. The duality of their existence had become normal, even comfortable in its way.

This was their life now: divided between worlds but unified in purpose. Together they prepared for a journey that would take them farther than anyone had gone before, while cherishing these quiet moments that grounded them in what mattered most.

Amy set her watering can down with deliberate care, her movements smooth in Haven's forgiving reality. She turned to face David, concern etching lines across her otherwise perfect digital features.

"Have you noticed Tom lately?" she asked. "He barely joined us for the Logan Circle game last week, and when he did show up, his mind was somewhere else entirely."

David closed his book, marking his place with a finger. "He's focused on the Orion preparations."

"It's more than focus, David. It's obsession." Amy crossed the room and settled beside him on the sofa. "Yesterday I found him in his lab simulating stellar nucleosynthesis for the fifth time that day. He didn't even notice me standing there for ten minutes."

Outside their window, digital leaves turned from gold to crimson as the simulated sun dipped lower. David considered her words, recognizing the truth in them. Tom had grown increasingly distant, his conversations circling back to the same topic: Orion's stellar nurseries and the experiments he planned to conduct there.

"Remember Paris?" Amy continued. "We spent three hours at the Louvre, and he spent the entire time talking about how stars form heavy elements. He didn't look at a single painting."

"Tom's always been intense about his work."

"Not like this. He's withdrawing from everything else. When was the last time he joined us for dinner? Or asked about anything besides his research?"

David nodded slowly. The pattern was clear now that Amy

pointed it out. Tom's usual enthusiasm for baseball had waned. His jokes had grown scarce. Even his clothing had become utilitarian, the colorful shirts replaced by gray coveralls better suited to laboratory work.

"I'm worried about him," Amy said, her voice softening. "This isn't healthy, even for Tom. He's pouring everything into these experiments, like nothing else matters."

"The journey means a lot to him."

"I know that. But thirteen hundred years is a long time to be obsessed with one thing." Amy leaned against David's shoulder. "What happens if his experiments fail? What will be left of him then?"

The question hung between them, heavy with implication. David thought of Tom's face when he talked about creating a miniature star, the feverish light in his eyes, the tremor in his hands.

"Should we talk to him?" David asked.

"I've tried. He listens politely, then goes right back to his calculations." Amy sighed. "I think he needs both of us. Together."

David squeezed her hand. "Tomorrow then. We'll invite him here, no science talk allowed."

"Just like old times," Amy said, though they both knew things had changed. Tom's obsession had grown roots, deep and tangled. Pulling him back might not be simple.

David watched Amy's face in the soft evening light of their Haven apartment. The digital conservatory behind her bloomed with impossible perfection, extinct flowers opening in defiance of time itself. Her fingers twisted together in her lap, a habit from childhood that carried over into this digital existence.

"There's more," she said. "Tom isn't just obsessed with his experiments. He's prepared to make the journey alone."

David leaned forward. "What do you mean?"

"Hellfire is fully equipped for a solo voyage. The DNA servers, the Ark duplicates, everything. He could leave tomorrow if he wanted to."

The weight of her words settled between them. Outside their window, Haven's evening deepened, stars appearing one by one in a sky programmed for beauty.

"How do you know this?" David asked.

"Banks told me. He helped with some of the matrix architecture for the servers." Amy stood and paced the room, her movements fluid in ways her physical body hadn't managed in years. "Tom commissioned a full suite of worlds for Hellfire. Not just research environments, but entertainment, comfort spaces, everything a single traveler would need for thirteen hundred years alone."

David remembered Tom's face when he'd spoken of Orion's stellar nurseries, the fever-bright eyes, the trembling hands. Not excitement. Obsession.

"He never intended for us to come," David said quietly.

"No. He hoped, maybe. But he built Hellfire to function with or without Paradise." Amy stopped by the window, her silhouette dark against the starlight. "He's going to lose himself out there, David. Thirteen hundred years alone with nothing but his experiments and artificial worlds."

The ships waited at Ceres One now, their hulls gleaming in the distant sunlight. Paradise carried the hopes of two million digital souls. Hellfire carried Tom's obsession.

"We need to talk to him," David said.

"We've tried talking. He listens, smiles, and goes right back to his calculations." Amy turned, her face half-shadowed. "He's our oldest friend. We can't let him vanish into space alone with nothing but his artificial sun for company."

David thought of their decades together: Tom as best man at their wedding, Tom bringing them into Haven when Amy's body began to fail, Tom fighting for Amy when the Freedom Congregation wanted to imprison her. A lifetime of friendship now threatened by an obsession that would span more than a millennium.

"What can we do?" David asked.

"We go with him," Amy said simply. "Both ships. The full journey. We don't let him face Orion alone."

The stars outside their window seemed to brighten, as if responding to her words. David considered the implications: thirteen hundred years traveling near light speed, arriving at Orion's stellar nurseries with their oldest friend still whole, still connected to something beyond his experiments.

"You're right," David said. "We can't let him go alone."

David stared at Amy's silhouette against the starlight, her words settling over him. The implications rippled outward from him, touching every corner of his understanding. She wasn't suggesting they both go with Tom. She was asking him to go without her.

"You want me to split," he said. The words came out flat, stripped of emotion.

Amy turned to face him. "The Freedom Congregation won't approve my emulation request. They've made that clear."

"But they can't stop me."

"Chester has always been more progressive." Her voice was steady, practical. "You could undergo the procedure. Your neuroclone could travel with Tom while you stay here with me."

David stood and crossed to the window. Haven's perfect night sky glittered above them, each star precisely where it should be. Too perfect. Too controlled. Just like this conversation felt.

"Thirteen hundred years," he said. The number hung between them, impossible to grasp fully. "My neuroclone would live thirteen hundred years without you."

"To keep Tom from going alone."

David pressed his palm against the cool glass. Outside, digital crickets chirped in programmed harmony. "And what about us? What about you and me?"

"I'll still have you here. The original you."

"While another me travels to the stars." He turned to face her. "Another me who remembers everything we've shared but continues without you."

Amy crossed the room and took his hands. Her touch felt real in Haven, warm and solid. "He'll still be you, David. With all your memories, all your feelings."

"And all my grief at leaving you behind."

She squeezed his fingers. "Tom needs you more than I do right now."

The statement struck him as fundamentally wrong. They had built their lives around each other for over a century. Through Amy's declining health, through the transition to Haven, through everything, they had remained together. The thought of any version of himself continuing without her seemed impossible.

"I can't," he said.

"You can." Her voice held that familiar gentle stubbornness. "We're his only friends. You're the only one who can keep him connected to something beyond his obsession."

David looked past her to the photographs lining their walls. A century of shared moments, from childhood to digital afterlife. "And what happens to my neuroclone when he reaches Orion? Thirteen hundred years alone with Tom and his experiments?"

"Not alone. There will be two million others on Paradise."

"But not you." The words fell between them, simple and devastating.

Amy's eyes held his. "No. Not me."

Her expression held that familiar determination he'd seen countless times over their century together. She wasn't asking anymore. She was telling him what needed to be done.

"Tom's neuroclone will be alone out there," Amy said. "Thirteen hundred years with nothing but his experiments and artificial worlds."

"His choice," David replied.

"Is it? We both know how he gets when he's focused on something. The real Tom will stay here with us, but his neuroclone..." She trailed off, looking at the photographs on their wall. "His neuroclone won't have anyone to pull him back when he goes too far."

David sat heavily on the sofa. The cushions adjusted perfectly to his weight, another small miracle of Haven's programming. "And my neuroclone would be the anchor."

"Yes." Amy settled beside him, her shoulder touching his. "Someone to remind him there's more to existence than stellar nucleosynthesis. Someone to play baseball with him when he's been in the lab for weeks. Someone to make him laugh."

The cricket sounds outside their window fell silent, as if Haven itself were waiting for his answer.

"He's our best friend, David." Amy's voice softened. "We both love him. Don't we owe it to his neuroclone to keep him safe? To keep him whole?"

David thought of Tom's face when he'd spoken of creating a miniature star, the way his hands trembled with excitement or perhaps something darker. He thought of thirteen hundred years of that obsession growing unchecked, with no one to interrupt with a baseball game or a bad joke or a reminder of what it meant to be human.

"But my neuroclone would remember everything," David said. "He would remember you."

"Yes." Amy took his hand. "He would carry you with him. Both of you would."

"Both versions of me would love you."

"I know."

David closed his eyes. The weight of the decision pressed against him. Two futures: one where he remained whole, and one where part of him traveled the stars without Amy, but with their oldest friend.

"We can't let him go alone," Amy said simply.

The truth of it settled into David's bones. Tom needed an anchor, someone to keep him connected to humanity during the long journey through darkness. Someone who knew him before the obsession took root.

The room fell silent. Even the simulated birds outside their digital window were quiet. Amy sat across from David at their kitchen table, her hands folded neatly before her. The light caught the edges of her face, highlighting the determined set of her jaw.

"I need to ask you something important," she said.

David nodded. He knew that tone. It was the same one she'd used when proposing they move to Chester, when suggesting they enter Haven together. It was Amy's voice of necessary change.

"Tom can't go alone," she continued. "You've seen how he gets. The obsession takes him over completely. And Freedom won't let me split. That's why I'm asking you to do it."

The words hung between them. David felt his chest tighten.

Do you realize what you're asking of me? Of my neuroclone?

Yes." Her voice remained steady, her gaze unwavering. "It's unfair to ask you to make that sacrifice: to send your neuroclone to travel with Tom while you remain here with me."

David looked down at their joined hands. Outside, a breeze rustled through digital leaves. The sounds resumed, life continuing while his thoughts stumbled to a halt.

"How can I do that?" he said. "One version continuing here with you. Another traveling for thirteen hundred years."

"Both would be you," Amy said. "Both would have our memories, our life together."

"But only one would have you going forward."

Amy squeezed his hand. "Tom needs someone to keep him grounded. Someone who remembers who he was before the stars consumed him."

David thought of Tom in his lab, eyes bright with an unnatural light as he talked about creating his miniature sun. He thought of thirteen hundred years of that obsession growing unchecked.

"My neuroclone would remember everything," David said. "He would remember you every day for thirteen centuries."

"I know." Amy's voice softened. "It's a terrible thing to ask."

"It's asking me to choose between you and Tom."

"No." Amy shook her head firmly. "It's asking you to be in two places at once. To keep our oldest friend from losing himself completely."

David looked around their Haven apartment, at the photographs lining the walls, at the bookshelves filled with volumes they'd read together. A century of shared moments surrounded them.

"What would you do," he asked quietly, "if our positions were reversed?"

Amy didn't hesitate. "I would go with him. I would make sure he remembered there's more to existence than stellar nucleosynthesis."

The simple truth of it settled into David's bones. Tom needed an anchor. Someone who knew him before the obsession took root.

"I need time to think," David said.

"Of course." Amy released his hand. "It's not a small thing I'm asking."

It wasn't small at all. It was thirteen hundred years large.

David looked at Amy across the kitchen table. The silence between them felt like a living thing, breathing and waiting. Her face, so familiar after more than a century together, held that quiet determination he'd seen countless times before.

"Yes," he said simply.

Amy blinked. "Just like that?"

"Just like that."

The word hung between them, small but carrying the weight of centuries to come. Outside their Haven window, a cardinal landed on the digital branch of a maple tree.

"You don't need time to think about it?" Amy asked.

David shook his head. "I've known Tom almost as long as I've known you. He needs someone with him out there."

He reached across the table and took her hands. They felt warm and solid, a perfect simulation of the touch he'd known for over a century. The sensation grounded him as the magnitude of his decision settled into his bones.

"My neuroclone will remember everything," he said. "Every moment with you. Every birdhouse. Every walk beneath our oak tree."

Amy's eyes glistened. "He'll carry me with him."

"And I'll stay here with you. Both versions of me loving you in different ways."

The cardinal outside took flight, a streak of red against the perfect blue sky. David watched it go, thinking of distances and separations, of thirteen hundred years traveling near light speed while another version of himself remained here, reading to Amy.

"Tom would do the same for us," David said. The truth of this settled in his chest, solid and certain. "He already has, in his way."

Amy nodded. They both remembered Tom fighting for her freedom, threatening to destroy his own family's legacy as leverage against Freedom. Tom bringing them into Haven when Amy's body began to fail. A lifetime of friendship that deserved this sacrifice in return.

"When?" Amy asked.

"After the two spaceships have their final inspections." David squeezed her hands. "Three months."

David thought of thirteen hundred years of sunsets his neuroclone would witness without Amy. Thirteen hundred years of keeping Tom tethered to something beyond his obsession with the stars.

"I love you," he said. "Both versions of me will always love you."

"I know," Amy replied. The simple certainty in her voice made everything clear.

David sat on the bench beneath their digital oak tree long after Amy had gone to sleep. The night air in Haven carried the scent of pine and fresh earth, programmed to comfort but feeling hollow now. He stared up at the branches where twenty handcrafted birdhouses hung, each one a marker of their shared years.

His decision to split himself felt both simple and impossible. One version would stay with Amy, continuing their century-long story. The other would journey among the stars for thirteen hundred years, carrying memories of a love that would never grow beyond what they had now.

The weight of it settled in his chest. Not quite grief, not quite fear, but something between them both.

"Thirteen hundred years," he whispered to the empty garden.

The number was too large to hold in his mind. His neuroclone would live through centuries that most humans never witnessed. Would witness the birth of stars in Orion's nursery. Would age in ways unimaginable while the David who remained with Amy would continue in the rhythm they had established over decades.

A small brown sparrow landed on the lowest branch of the oak. It tilted its head, studying him with one bright eye, then the other.

"What would you do?" David asked it.

The bird chirped once and flew away.

He thought of Tom in his lab, eyes bright with an unnatural light as he manipulated the controls, immersed in his research on stellar formation. The obsession had grown deeper since they'd received approval for the journey. Tom spent days without emerging, his meals delivered by service bots, his only company the growing plans for the glowing sphere of his experimental star.

David's neuroclone would need to pull Tom back from that edge again and again across the centuries. Without Amy's steadying presence. Without her laugh. Without her touch.

He pressed his palms against the wooden bench, feeling the grain against his skin. Haven rendered it perfectly, down to the small knot near his right thigh. The bench was real and not real, just as his neuroclone would be him and not him.

His throat tightened. His neuroclone would remember every moment with Amy but never create new ones. Would carry the ache of her absence through thirteen centuries of stars.

"I'm sorry," he said to that future self.

The night air cooled against his face. A cricket chirped nearby, its sound pure and clear in the digital darkness. David sat with the weight of his decision until the programmed moon rose high above the garden, casting silver light across the twenty birdhouses that marked their years together.

The following day, Tom's lab door in Haven slid open with a soft hydraulic hiss. David stepped through first, Amy following close behind. Tom didn't look up. He hunched over a holographic display, his fingers dancing through equations that spiraled and twisted like smoke. The air smelled of ozone and coffee.

"Tom," David said.

Tom held up one finger, eyes never leaving the pulsing calculations. "Almost got it. The containment field needs another decimal adjustment."

David glanced at Amy. She nodded, her hand finding his and squeezing once.

"We need to talk," David said.

Something in his voice made Tom pause. The equations froze in mid-air, glowing blue against the darker backdrop of the lab. Tom swiveled in his chair, his expression shifting from irritation to concern.

"What's happened?" He looked between them. "Did Freedom change their mind about Amy?"

"No." Amy stepped forward. "But we've made a decision."

Tom's shoulders tensed. He knew what was coming. David had seen that look before, the careful arrangement of features to hide disappointment. Tom had worn it whenever David had messed up on their adventures together. He'd worn it when Amy declined his invitation to Thailand that first year.

"You're not coming," Tom said, his voice flat. "I understand."

"I am coming," David said.

Tom blinked. The carefully composed mask slipped. "But Amy —"

"Will stay here." David moved deeper into the lab, past the glowing equations and half-assembled models. "My neuroclone will travel with you. I'll stay with Amy."

Tom stood so quickly his chair rolled backward and hit the wall. "You'll split?"

"Yes."

The word hung between them, simple and enormous. Tom looked at Amy, then back to David.

"Because of me?" Tom asked.

Amy stepped forward. "Because you shouldn't make that journey alone."

Tom's lab was cluttered with the evidence of his obsession. Models of stars in various stages of formation. Diagrams of fusion reactions. A half-eaten sandwich forgotten beside complex calculations. David had seen this pattern before, the way Tom disappeared into his work until someone pulled him back.

"You'd do that?" Tom's voice had gone quiet. "Split yourself in two?"

"One version travels with you," David said. "One stays with Amy. Both of us remain whole."

Tom moved toward them, his steps unsteady. For a moment, David thought he might embrace them, but he stopped short.

"Thirteen hundred years is a long time to be without her," Tom said.

"It's also a long time for you to be alone with nothing but your stars," David replied.

Tom looked at the equations hanging in the air behind him. They reflected in his eyes, turning them an unnatural blue. He understood. David could see it in the slight slump of his shoulders, the tightening around his mouth.

"Thank you," Tom said simply.

Outside the lab's window, Haven's perfect day continued. Birds flew in programmed patterns. Clouds drifted across an impossibly blue sky. The three friends stood in silence, contemplating thirteen centuries of separation and the versions of themselves that would navigate them.

Tom paced the lab, his steps quick and light. The equations still hovered in the air, forgotten now as his mind raced with new possibilities. He stopped suddenly and turned to David.

"The process is remarkable," he said. "The neural mapping is precise down to the quantum level. Every memory, every experience, every habit, it's all there."

David watched his friend's face transform. The obsession with stars dimmed, replaced by this new fascination.

"Both our neuroclones will have complete continuity of consciousness," Tom continued. "They'll remember this conversation. They'll remember deciding to go."

He moved to a workstation and pulled up technical specifications. His fingers flew across the interface.

"The Tardigrade DNA substrata for the memory servers has already been grown in orbit. They'll house our consciousness for the entire journey."

His voice quickened with excitement, but then he paused. Something softer crossed his face as he looked at David and Amy.

"I never expected this," he said quietly. "I thought I would be going alone."

The lab hummed around them. Cooling systems whispered. Displays blinked with data. Tom's coffee had gone cold beside his calculations.

"Thank you again," Tom said. The words were simple but carried the weight of thirteen centuries.

David nodded. "We couldn't let our friend go alone."

Tom's eyes grew bright. He blinked rapidly and turned back to the display. "The procedure itself is painless. The mapping takes approximately three hours."

His voice steadied as he retreated into the comfort of scientific detail. "Our neuroclones will be perfect copies, David. They'll think like us, feel like us. Your neuroclone will miss Amy exactly as you would."

Amy stepped closer to the display. "And they'll be conscious the entire journey?"

"Yes." Tom's enthusiasm returned. "They'll live and work and dream just as we do here. The only difference is their environment."

He brought up a new display showing the interiors of Paradise and Hellfire. "I've been preparing research materials for my neuroclone. Thirteen hundred years of stellar study."

He glanced at David. "Perhaps you should prepare something for yours as well. Books, music. Memories to revisit."

The suggestion hung in the air. David thought of thirteen hundred years without Amy. What comfort could he leave his other self?

"I'll help," Amy said softly. "We'll create something together."

Tom watched them, his scientific excitement tempered now by understanding. "My neuroclone will be grateful for the company," he said. "As I am grateful for your friendship."

The words were simple and true. In the lab's artificial light, surrounded by equations and half-finished experiments, the three friends stood at the edge of an impossible journey.

Tom's fingers danced across the holographic display, pulling up schematics of the Tardigrade DNA servers. "The neuroclone transfers for the two million colonists is scheduled to begin next Thursday. As captains of our respective ships, we can undergo the procedure and transfer whenever we're ready."

David watched his friend slip into the comfortable rhythm of planning. Tom always found refuge in detail, in the solid ground of logistics and preparation. The blue light from the display cast shadows across his face, highlighting the intensity in his eyes.

"What should I bring?" David asked. "For thirteen hundred years?"

Tom looked up, momentarily puzzled. "Everything is provided. The ships have extensive libraries, entertainment systems, communication protocols. The Ark alone contains centuries of human achievements."

"I think David means something more personal," Amy said. She sat in a chair near the window, where Haven's afternoon light spilled across her lap. "Something to help his neuroclone through the journey."

Tom's expression softened with understanding. "Ah. Yes, of course."

"We should attend the bon voyage celebration," Amy said. "All three of us."

Tom nodded. "The Sun Salutation Ballroom. Six million attendees expected, including all two million colonists." He brought up another display showing a massive orbital structure circling Mercury, its glass dome reflecting the sun's harsh light. "It will be one of the largest gatherings in human history."

"Six million people," David whispered. The number seemed impossible, yet in Haven's digital landscape, space had no meaning. Six million could gather in a ballroom that never existed in Terra.

"Your neuroclone will remember the party," Amy said, reaching for David's hand. "He'll carry that memory with him."

David squeezed her fingers. "What else should he carry?"

The question hung between them, heavy with the weight of thirteen centuries. What could comfort a man separated from his wife for longer than most civilizations had existed?

"I'll create a memory palace," Amy said. Her voice was steady, practical. "A place where I've gathered everything that matters. Our oak tree. The bench. Every birdhouse. The cabin. Our wedding photos."

Tom watched them, his scientific enthusiasm momentarily subdued. "The neuroclones will have access to the ship's archives. They can revisit any memory you've stored there."

"It's not the same as having something created specifically for the journey," Amy said. She turned to David. "I'll make something that feels like me. Something that will keep you company among the stars."

David nodded, his throat tight. The afternoon light caught in Amy's hair, turning the edges golden. His neuroclone would remember this moment, this exact play of light across her face.

"We have three months," Tom said, his voice gentler now. "Ninety days to prepare for thirteen hundred years."

The enormity of it settled around them, a vast ocean of time stretching beyond imagination. David looked at Amy, at the familiar curve of her smile, the light in her eyes. Three more months of creating memories his neuroclone would carry into the stars.

David and Amy walked back to their digital home in silence. The weight of their decision followed them, neither heavy nor light, simply there. The oak tree came into view first; its branches spread against the evening. Twenty birdhouses hung from its limbs, each one marking a year of their shared life.

Amy paused at the garden gate. "Thirteen hundred years," she said. The words fell between them.

David nodded. He couldn't imagine such time. A span longer than empires. His neuroclone would live through it all, carrying memories of this garden, this woman, this life into a future he couldn't fathom.

"I keep thinking about him," David said. "The other me."

Amy took his hand. Her fingers were warm and familiar. "He'll still be you."

"But without you. It's difficult for me to get past that."

They moved to the bench beneath the oak. It creaked under their weight, a sound programmed into Haven with perfect fidelity. Crickets sang in the digital grass. A night breeze stirred the leaves overhead.

"What would you want?" Amy asked. "If you were him?"

David considered this. The question was impossible and necessary. "Letters," he said finally. "Your voice. Stories I haven't heard."

Amy nodded. Her profile was sharp against the darkening garden. "I'll record everything. Every story I know. Every memory I can find."

They sat together as night settled around them. The first stars appeared overhead, precise in their digital orbits. David thought of real stars, the ones his neuroclone would see through Paradise's holographic interface. Orion's nursery, where new suns formed in cosmic dust. Stars that existed beyond imagination.

"We've set something in motion we can't take back," he said.

"Yes."

The simplicity of her answer steadied him. They had made their choice. Two versions of David would exist: one here with Amy, one traveling among the stars with Tom. Both real. Both him.

Amy leaned her head against his shoulder. "I wonder what he'll find out there."

David slipped his arm around her. "We'll never know."

This truth settled between them, not bitter but strange. The neuroclone would live centuries beyond them, would see wonders they couldn't imagine. Would carry their love into a future they would never witness.

The night deepened around them. In the oak tree, a nightingale began to sing.

CHAPTER THREE

Tokens of Love

The January chill pressed against the window glass as seven-year-old David sat cross-legged on his bedroom floor, surrounded by a collection of wood scraps he'd gathered from his father's workshop. A faded blue bedsheet protected the carpet beneath him. His tongue poked from the corner of his mouth as he studied the pieces, imagining how they might fit together.

Amy's eighth birthday approached. March 7th seemed distant through the lens of winter, but David knew better. Time moved differently when you had something important to make.

He arranged the wood pieces in various configurations, testing their fit. His father's tools lay beside him: a hammer that required both his hands to lift properly, a handsaw with teeth that looked menacing, and a small jar of nails that clinked when he shook them. The wood smelled of pine and possibility.

David sketched his plan on a sheet of notebook paper, the pencil lines wobbling as he tried to make straight edges. A simple house with a sloped roof, an entrance hole for the birds, and a little perch where they could land. Nothing fancy, but it would be his, made by his own hands.

He selected two rectangular pieces for the sides and a pair of triangular cuts for the roof. The front and back would need holes. He thought of the drill on his father's workbench in his workshop. His parents had been clear: no power tools without supervision.

"I'll just make the hole later," he muttered, focusing instead on the assembly.

His small fingers fumbled with the nails. The first one bent when he struck it at an angle. The second drove in crooked, splitting the wood slightly. By the third attempt, tears of frustration welled in his eyes.

David wiped his sleeve across his face. Amy wouldn't want a store-bought birdhouse. She deserved something special, something that showed he cared enough to make it himself. He pictured her smile when she unwrapped it, imagined her pointing out the first bird to discover the new home.

He tried again, this time holding the nail steady with a clothespin as he'd seen his father do. The hammer connected solidly, driving the nail straight into the wood. Success! The sides came together, slightly uneven but holding firm.

The roof proved more challenging. The angles didn't match perfectly, creating a gap at the peak. David frowned at the imperfection but pressed on. He secured the roof pieces with three more nails, each one driving home more smoothly than the last as he found his rhythm.

When he held up the structure, it listed slightly to one side. The entrance hole remained unmade, and the perch was just a loose piece of dowel with no clear way to attach it. The birdhouse looked nothing like the neat ones in the store windows downtown.

But it was his. Made with his own hands, for Amy.

His father's footsteps sounded in the hallway. David looked up as the bedroom door swung open, revealing his father's tall frame. The man's eyes moved from David to the lopsided birdhouse in his hands, then to the scattered tools and bent nails littering the bedsheet.

David's fingers, clumsy with inexperience, fumbled another nail. It bent against the wood with a soft ping and skittered across the floor. His thumb throbbed where he'd struck it with the hammer. Three red-tipped splinters jutted from his palm like tiny spears.

"Shoot," he muttered, sucking at a fresh splinter in his index finger. The wood tasted of sap and dust.

His father stood in the doorway, arms crossed, watching. The man's shadow stretched across David's workspace, darkening the crooked assembly of pine scraps that barely resembled a birdhouse.

"You need help with that?" his father asked, voice neutral.

David looked up hopefully. "Yes, sir. I can't get the roof pieces to stay together."

His father nodded but didn't move closer. "What's this for again?"

"Amy's birthday. She likes birds."

The man considered this, then shrugged. "You want to make it, you make it. That's how you learn." He stepped into the room and knelt beside David, not touching the project but pointing. "See how those edges don't match up? You need to sand them down so they fit flush."

David nodded, though he wasn't entirely sure what "flush" meant in this context.

"And those nails are too big for wood this thin. You're splitting it." His father rose, walked to the door. "There's sandpaper in my workshop. Smaller nails too. I'll be watching the game if you need anything else."

Then he was gone, leaving David alone with his frustration and the crooked pile of wood.

The boy sat back on his heels and surveyed his creation. One side wall leaned inward. The roof peaked unevenly, creating a gap where rain would surely pour through. The front piece, where he planned to drill the entrance hole, had split along its grain. Nothing fit right.

He pressed his lips together, determined not to cry. Amy deserved better than this lopsided mess. She deserved a real birdhouse, one that birds might actually use.

With a deep breath, David gathered his tools and the wood pieces. He carried everything downstairs and out to his father's workshop behind the garage. The small building smelled of sawdust and machine oil. Tools hung in precise order on a pegboard wall. His father's workbench stood clean and organized, unlike the chaos of David's bedroom floor.

David found the sandpaper in a drawer marked "Abrasives." He selected a medium grit sheet and began rubbing down the edges of his roof pieces. Wood dust collected under his fingernails. His palms burned from friction. But slowly, the edges grew smoother, more even.

He found smaller nails in a coffee can. These slid into the wood without splitting it, though his hammering still drove them at slight angles. The structure remained wobbly, imperfect.

When finished, David held up his creation. The entrance hole, crudely carved with his pocketknife, was more oval than round. The perch, a small dowel glued beneath it, tilted downward. The roof still gaped slightly at its peak. Paint might hide some flaws, but nothing could disguise its amateur construction.

Yet something about it pleased him. He had made it himself, start to finish. The birdhouse might be crude, but it was honest. Like their friendship.

March arrived with a stubborn chill, reluctant to surrender winter's hold on the mountains. The morning of Amy's birthday dawned gray and cold, a thin mist hanging over the valleys. David woke early, his stomach tight with anticipation. The birdhouse sat wrapped in newspaper on his dresser, its imperfections concealed temporarily by the black and white print.

His mother drove him to Amy's house that afternoon. The wrapped package rested on his lap, suddenly seeming smaller than he remembered. He traced his finger over the red ribbon his mother had helped him tie, wondering if Amy would notice the uneven edges beneath the paper.

"You made it yourself," his mother reminded him at the end of the drive. "That's what matters."

David nodded, unconvinced. The other kids would bring store-bought gifts with perfect corners and professional paint jobs. His offering felt inadequate by comparison.

Clare Hamilton welcomed him with a warm smile, ushering him into the living room where several children from their class already gathered. Amy sat cross-legged on the floor, wearing a blue dress with small yellow flowers. Her hair had been pulled back with matching blue barrettes. She waved when she saw him, patting the carpet beside her.

"David's here," she announced, as if his arrival completed something essential.

He settled beside her; the package clutched against his chest. Other gifts formed a small pile nearby, their wrapping paper bright and crisp, their shapes suggesting dolls and games and books.

When the time came for presents, David held back. He watched Amy open each gift with genuine delight, thanking each giver with careful attention. A book of birds from her mother. A new sweater from her grandmother. A set of colored pencils from a classmate.

"There's one more," Clare said, nodding toward David.

All eyes turned to him. The room seemed suddenly warmer. He extended the newspaper-wrapped package, the ribbon slightly crushed from his tight grip.

"I made it," he said, the words tumbling out before she could open it. "It's not very good."

Amy accepted the package gingerly, as if its modest appearance made it even more precious. Her fingers worked carefully at the tape, preserving the paper rather than tearing it away. When the birdhouse emerged, tilting slightly in her hands, a small gasp escaped her.

"A house for birds," she said, turning it to examine every angle. Her fingers traced the uneven entrance hole, tested the wobbly perch, explored the gap where the roof pieces met imperfectly.

David watched her face, waiting for disappointment to register. Instead, her eyes brightened.

"It's for our oak tree," she said. Not a question but a statement of perfect understanding.

"The chickadees might like it," he offered. "Or wrens. They're small enough."

Amy nodded solemnly. "We'll hang it tomorrow." She looked up at him then, her smile spreading slowly across her face. "It's the best present, David. You really made it yourself?"

"Every part," he admitted. "That's why it's crooked."

"It's not crooked," she insisted. "It's exactly right."

And in that moment, seeing his creation through her eyes, David understood that sometimes perfection lived in the intent rather than the execution. The birdhouse might never win prizes for craftsmanship, but it had already achieved its purpose: it had made Amy happy.

The weekend arrived with spring's tentative promise. David stood beneath the massive tree, hands in his pockets, watching the dirt road for signs of Amy. The air smelled of thawing earth and distant rain.

He had arrived early, too eager to wait at home. The oak seemed different somehow, as if it knew its purpose was about to change.

Amy appeared around the bend in the road, the newspaper-wrapped birdhouse clutched carefully in both hands. Clare walked beside her, carrying a small stepladder and a coil of twine. Amy's red hair caught the light as she spotted David and quickened her pace.

"We brought everything," she called. Her cheeks flushed pink with excitement. "Mama says we can pick any branch we want."

David nodded a greeting to Clare. "Thank you for helping, Mrs. Hamilton."

"Of course." Clare set the stepladder beneath a sturdy branch that extended horizontally about seven feet above the ground. "This spot looks good. The birds will have a clear view of the field."

Amy unwrapped the birdhouse, revealing its imperfect angles and hand-painted blue roof. David had added the color hoping it might make the structure more appealing to its future residents. The paint had dripped in places, forming small stalactites along the edges.

"It's beautiful in the sunlight," Amy said, running her finger along the dried paint streaks as if they were intentional details rather than mistakes.

Clare unspooled a length of twine and threaded it through the small eye hook David had hammered into the top of the birdhouse. "Who wants to climb up and tie it to the branch?"

"David should," Amy said immediately. "He made it."

David climbed the stepladder, the twine and birdhouse passed up to him by Amy's careful hands. The branch felt rough and solid beneath his fingers. He looped the twine over it once, twice, then tied the knot his father had taught him for securing fishing line. The birdhouse hung slightly crooked, spinning slowly in the gentle breeze.

"There," he said, climbing down. "What do you think?"

Amy tilted her head, studying their creation with serious consideration. "It's perfect. A royal blue palace for Queen Featherwing."

"Queen Featherwing?"

"The wren who's going to live there." Amy spoke with absolute certainty. "She's looking for a new kingdom. She'll bring her babies here and teach them to fly from our tree."

Clare smiled at this, resting her hand briefly on Amy's shoulder.

"I'll leave you two to get Queen Featherwing settled in her new home. Don't go far, Amy. Lunch in an hour."

They watched Clare walk back toward the house, her figure growing smaller against the backdrop of rolling hills. When she disappeared around the bend, Amy sat on the ground beneath the tree, patting the space beside her.

"Do you think real birds will come?" David asked, settling next to her.

"They'll come," Amy said. Her voice held no doubt. "We just have to be patient."

The birdhouse hung crooked through the first spring, its royal blue paint vibrant against the green canopy of the oak. Wrens did come, but they inspected and departed, finding the entrance hole slightly too small for comfortable passage. David watched their rejections with a sinking heart, but Amy remained steadfast in her belief.

"They're just being choosy," she said. "Queen Featherwing wants to make sure it's safe."

Summer arrived with thick heat that made the air shimmer above the distant hills. The birdhouse weathered, its blue fading to a softer shade under the relentless sun. Rain left water stains along the roof's uneven seam. A family of chickadees investigated but nested elsewhere.

Autumn painted the oak in amber and crimson. Leaves spiraled down, collecting around the wooden bench where David and Amy sat watching the empty birdhouse swing in October winds. The first frost silvered the roof one morning, making it glisten like something magical.

Winter stripped the oak bare. Snow gathered in the crook where David had tied the twine, weighing down the branch. The birdhouse, now a pale, weathered blue, stood empty against the gray sky.

A second spring brought new hope. The paint had chipped away in places, revealing the pine beneath. A pair of wrens circled the oak, darting closer to the birdhouse with each pass. Amy clapped her hands when they finally perched on the crooked dowel.

"I told you," She whispered to David. "Queen Featherwing was just waiting for it to feel like home."

The wrens built their nest inside, carrying twigs and bits of fluff through the entrance hole that no longer seemed too small. Five eggs hatched into hungry chicks whose constant demands echoed across the yard.

Summer again, then fall, then winter's quiet. The birdhouse hung empty through the cold months, the wrens long departed for warmer territories.

In the third spring, when David was ten, the birdhouse showed its age. The roof sagged where rain had seeped through the gap. One side wall had warped, creating a crack where small insects found entry. Still, it hung from the oak, a testament to friendship and persistence.

David studied the weathered structure from his spot on the bench. His hands, larger now and steadier, itched to build something better. He knew more about woodworking, had learned from watching his father and from his own experiments.

"I think Queen Featherwing needs a new palace," he said to Amy. "One that doesn't leak."

She nodded, understanding without explanation. "For Christmas?"

"For Christmas," he agreed, already planning improvements in his mind.

Winter settled into the mountains. David sat at his father's workbench, a single lamp casting yellow light over his careful measurements. The workshop smelled of pine shavings and wood glue. Outside, snow fell in silent curtains, blanketing the world in quiet.

His father had taught him about measuring twice and cutting once. This time, David measured three times. The pencil marks on the wood were precise, his lines straighter than before. He'd selected cedar instead of pine, learning that cedar withstood weather better. The pieces lay before him like a puzzle waiting to be assembled.

"You're getting better at this," his father said, pausing at the workshop door. He didn't enter, just observed from the threshold, respecting the boy's concentration.

David nodded without looking up. "Amy's wrens need something that won't leak."

The saw bit through cedar with clean strokes. Wood dust rose in the lamplight. David felt the resistance of the grain, adjusted his pressure, kept the blade true. His hands remembered his past mistakes. The roof pieces would meet flush this time, with a proper pitch for rain to run off.

He drilled the entrance hole to exact measurements for wrens: one and a quarter inches in diameter. The perch below it was secured with wood glue and a single small nail, driven straight and true. He sanded every edge until splinters surrendered to smoothness.

Amy had once mentioned loving the color of autumn maple leaves. David mixed red and yellow paint, adding drops of each until the shade matched the maple leaf he'd pressed between wax paper. The roof he painted blue again, but darker this time, like the evening sky just after sunset.

His father appeared with a small jar. "Polyurethane," he explained. "Brush it on when the paint dries. It'll protect the wood."

The clear coat gleamed under the lamp. David applied it carefully, watching how it deepened the colors and sealed the wood against future rains.

Christmas morning arrived with fresh snow and bitter cold. Amy waited on the porch, wrapped in a wool coat too large for her thin frame. Her breath formed clouds that dissipated in the still air. She spotted the newspaper-wrapped package in David's hands and smiled.

"Another house for Queen Featherwing?"

David nodded. "Better than the first one."

They unwrapped it together, her fingers gentle against the paper. The birdhouse emerged, its colors rich beneath the protective coat. The entrance hole was perfectly round, the roof peak straight as a ruler's edge. Every nail sat flush, every joint tight.

"It's beautiful," Amy whispered. She ran her finger along the maple-colored sides. "Like autumn in winter."

They walked to the oak tree, their boots leaving parallel tracks in the snow. The old birdhouse hung from its branch, weathered and leaning. David climbed the ladder with the new creation, securing it to a branch opposite the first.

"Why not take the old one down?" Amy asked.

David tied the final knot. "Queen Featherwing might want to remember where she started."

Amy nodded, understanding perfectly. "Like a summer home and a winter palace."

The new birdhouse caught morning light on its gleaming surface. The old one hung in shadow, its purpose complete but its presence still necessary. David climbed down and stood beside Amy in the snow, both looking up at their growing legacy in the branches of the oak.

At fourteen, David sat at the workbench with his father's calipers in hand. The oak along the wagon road had lost its leaves, branches bare against the November sky. Five birdhouses now hung from those limbs, each marking the steady progression of his skill.

"Chickadees prefer a smaller entrance than wrens," his father said, watching David measure the cedar plank. "About an inch."

David nodded, making a precise mark. "Amy's been reading about them. Says they like to see the sky when they wake up."

He worked with newfound patience, the rush of earlier years replaced by methodical precision. The saw followed his pencil lines without wavering. His fingers, longer now and steadier, fitted the pieces together with careful attention to the grain. Each joint locked into its neighbor as if grown that way.

The design incorporated a small window near the roof peak, a circle of blue glass salvaged from a broken bottle. When positioned toward the east, morning light would filter through it, casting cobalt patterns inside the nesting chamber.

"Amy likes blue," was all he said when his father questioned the addition.

The finished house gleamed with amber varnish, its proportions pleasing to the eye. No paint this time; the natural wood spoke for itself. Only the small blue eye watched from beneath the eaves, a secret between maker and recipient.

Christmas morning, they hung it on a branch that caught first light. Amy's fingers traced the window with reverence.

"So they can see the stars," she whispered, understanding without explanation.

Two years later, the oak bore seven birdhouses, a growing constellation among its branches. David studied drafting now, learning about load and balance, about the mathematics of beauty. His sixteenth birthday brought a set of proper woodworking tools, wrapped in his father's old canvas apron.

The wood that winter was cherry, darker and denser than cedar, challenging his new chisels. He designed a hexagonal structure with a peaked roof that swept upward like a church spire. The entrance, perfectly round, sat centered in a door that could swing open for cleaning. A small brass latch, polished to a warm glow, kept it secured against wind.

Inside, he lined the floor with copper shavings from his father's workshop, known to deter parasites that might trouble nesting birds. The roof he covered with overlapping cedar shingles, each one cut, shaped, and sanded by hand before being fixed in place with tiny brass nails.

But the true secret lay in what he carved along the eaves: a continuous line of tiny oak leaves, each one detailed down to its veins and edges. Under the entrance, almost too small to notice without looking closely, he carved their initials within a diminutive heart.

When Amy unwrapped it on her birthday in May, her eyes widened at the craftsmanship. She turned it slowly in her hands, discovering each detail as if reading a familiar story written in a new language.

"You made this for me," she said, finding the hidden heart with her fingertip.

David nodded, watching her face. "For the tree."

They hung it on a branch that stretched toward her bedroom window. From her bed, Amy could see its silhouette against the morning sky, another chapter in their growing story.

The fall of David's seventeenth year brought with it a restlessness he couldn't name. The maple outside his window blazed red against a colorless sky, leaves spiraling down with each gust of wind. In the workshop, cherry wood waited under dust covers, tools arranged in perfect order along the pegboard his father had installed last Christmas.

David traced the grain with calloused fingers. The wood felt warm, alive beneath his touch. He'd sketched the design during algebra class; the margins of his notebook filled with measurements and angles that made more sense than equations. This birdhouse would be different from the others. More complex. A statement.

He'd seen Amy walking with Tyler Bennett after school three times now. Laughing at something Tyler said, her hand occasionally brushing against his. The sight had lodged something sharp beneath David's ribs.

The bandsaw whined as he cut the first piece. Sawdust collected at his feet, fine as beach sand. He worked with methodical precision, each cut following the pencil lines without deviation. The house took shape beneath his hands: a Victorian with bay windows and a wraparound porch scaled down to avian proportions. The roof would have scalloped shingles, each one cut and sanded individually.

His father appeared in the doorway. "Looks ambitious."

David nodded without looking up. "Amy's Christmas present."

"That's three months away."

"It'll take that long to get it right."

The miniature porch columns required a lathe. David spent hours perfecting each one, turning cherry wood into delicate spindles no thicker than his pinky finger. The tiny railings he assembled from toothpicks, filed and sanded until they felt smooth as river stones. For the windows, he cut glass from an old picture frame, creating six perfect panes for the bay window that faced east.

After school, he saw Amy and Tyler sitting together on the concrete steps by the gymnasium. Her red hair caught the afternoon sun. Tyler leaned close, saying something that made her laugh. David walked past without slowing, the sound of her laughter following him home.

In the workshop, he fitted the roof sections together. The interior held hidden details no one would see. Floor joists beneath the cedar planking, crown molding along the ceiling edges, a tiny staircase leading to nowhere. The craftsmanship mattered even in the unseen places.

His mother found him there one evening, hands stained with wood stain and varnish. "You're putting a lot into this one."

David looked up from the miniature shingles arranged in perfect rows. "It needs to be right."

"Because of Tyler?"

The question startled him. He focused on the shingle in his hand, avoiding her eyes. "Because it's for Amy."

The week before Christmas, snow fell in fat, wet flakes that melted against his jacket as he carried the wrapped package across the field to her house. The oak tree stood sentinel, thirteen birdhouses hanging from its branches like strange fruit. Each one a testament to their friendship, a timeline of his growing skill.

Amy opened the door before he knocked. Her smile faltered when she saw the package. "You didn't have to."

"I wanted to." He handed it to her, suddenly aware of how much the gift revealed. "For the collection."

She unwrapped it carefully, her eyes widening as the Victorian emerged. "David, it's... it's like a real house."

"I thought the chickadees might like something fancier this year."

Her fingers traced the tiny porch railings, the perfect bay windows. "Tyler's waiting for me. We're going to the movies."

David nodded, the sharp thing beneath his ribs twisting deeper. "We should hang it first."

They walked to the oak tree together, their footprints filling with snow behind them. The branches hung lower now, heavy with years of his offerings. Amy cradled the Victorian against her coat.

"Which branch?" she asked.

David pointed to one that stretched toward the rising sun. "There. The morning light will catch the windows."

Amy held the Victorian birdhouse in her hands, turning it slowly. Snowflakes landed on the tiny shingles and melted into droplets that glistened like glass beads. Her fingers traced the miniature porch railing, lingering on details no bird would ever notice.

"This must have taken months," she said.

David shrugged, hands deep in his pockets. "Just something to do after homework."

The lie hung between them. They both knew better. The precision of each cut, the perfect symmetry of the bay windows, the delicate spindles on the porch columns: these weren't afterthoughts. They were declarations.

Amy's eyes met his. "Tyler bought me a bracelet. Silver with a little heart charm."

"Nice," David said. The word fell flat in the cold air.

"I left it on my dresser today." She looked up at the branches where thirteen other houses hung, marking years like growth rings in the oak itself. "I didn't want to lose it while we were hanging this."

David reached for the birdhouse. "I can put it up."

"No." She pulled it closer to her chest. "I want to."

He steadied the ladder while she climbed, one careful step after another. The Victorian birdhouse cradled in her left arm. At the right branch, she paused, balancing against the oak's rough bark.

"Hand me the twine," she said.

Their fingers brushed as he passed the cord up to her. She tied the house securely; her movements deliberate and unhurried despite the snow and the waiting boyfriend. When she finished, she remained on the ladder, studying her handiwork.

"It looks right up there," she said finally. "Like it belongs."

David nodded. "It does."

She descended slowly, and when she reached the ground, she didn't step away from him. Snowflakes caught in her eyelashes, in her red hair. Her breath formed small clouds between them.

"Tyler asked why I keep all these." She gestured toward the branches above. "He said it seemed childish."

David felt his jaw tighten. "What did you tell him?"

"That he wouldn't understand." She brushed snow from her coat sleeve. "That some things matter more than they seem to."

They stood silent beneath the oak, fourteen birdhouses now hanging in its branches. Each one a promise neither had named.

"I should go," she said. "Tyler's waiting."

David nodded, unable to find the right words.

Amy took three steps toward her house, then stopped. Without turning, she said, "I'll be looking for chickadees in the spring."

"They'll come," David answered. "They always do."

Winter settled early that year. David watched his breath cloud in the garage workshop as he opened the mahogany box his father had brought home from a lumber auction. The wood had a deep reddish-brown color with subtle grain patterns that caught the light. He ran his fingers across its smooth surface, feeling the history in its weight.

"This is special," his father had said. "Came from an old plantation house in Louisiana. Two hundred years old, at least."

David measured twice, marking the wood with careful pencil lines. Spring came. Amy had broken up with Tyler three weeks ago. She hadn't mentioned it, but he'd seen her sitting alone at lunch, her face composed but her eyes distant. He'd joined her silently, offering half his sandwich. She'd taken it without a word.

The bandsaw hummed as he worked. This birdhouse would be different from all the others. Not larger or more ornate, but more honest. He'd sketched it during math class, ignoring the equations on the blackboard. A simple saltbox design with clean lines and perfect proportions.

He cut dovetail joints by hand, fitting them together without nails. The wood joined to wood with only thin lines of glue between them. For the roof, he selected cedar shingles cut from a fallen tree behind his house. Each one he shaped with a small hand plane until they nested together like scales.

The oak tree on the wagon road started to bud against the blue sky, fourteen birdhouses hanging from its branches. David worked evenings and weekends, applying what he'd learned in drafting class to create something both beautiful and true.

The entrance hole he lined with copper, polished until it gleamed like a setting sun. Inside, he built a small shelf beneath the entrance, just large enough for a nesting bird to perch. The floor he covered with a thin layer of cork, warm and insulating against winter winds.

The finishing touch came after midnight near the end of the school year. From his mother's sewing box, he borrowed a small mother-of-pearl button. He inlaid it above the entrance, carving a perfect recess where it sat flush with the surface. In certain light, it caught rainbows.

Amy answered the door on a Saturday morning with her hair uncombed, wearing the flannel pajamas her mother gave her every year at Christmas.

David held out the package wrapped in brown paper. "For you."

They walked to the oak tree together, their boots crunching through snow. The birdhouses hung silent above them, marking years like memories.

"Fifteen," Amy said, looking up at their collection.

David nodded, watching her unwrap his gift. Her fingers moved carefully, preserving the paper. When the mahogany house emerged, she held it up to catch the winter light.

"It's different," she whispered.

"Yes."

She traced the dovetail joints, the copper-lined entrance, the mother-of-pearl button that gleamed like a tiny moon. "It's perfect."

They hung it on a branch that stretched toward the road, securing it with new twine. The mahogany caught the morning light, glowing with warmth against the cold white sky.

"Tyler never understood," Amy said suddenly. "About these."

David looked at her, snow collecting on his shoulders. "What about them?"

"That they're not just birdhouses." She touched the newest addition, steadying it against the winter wind. "They're promises."

The summer before college stretched before David. In his workshop, cedar shavings collected around his boots as he worked. This birdhouse would be different. It had to be.

The wood came from his grandfather's barn, dismantled last spring after standing for eighty years. Heart pine, dense and resinous, still bearing the scent of hay and livestock in its grain. David selected boards with care, testing each one for strength and character.

He designed it as a cabin, simple and sturdy. Four walls, a pitched roof, and a single entrance facing east toward the rising sun. No ornate details or clever mechanisms this time. Only honest joinery and proportions that pleased the eye without demanding attention.

The night before he finished it, David sat alone on the wooden bench beneath the oak. Sixteen birdhouses hung from its branches now, a chronicle of growing skill and unspoken devotion. Tomorrow he would leave for State College. Amy would head to Washington and Lee three days later.

"I thought I'd find you here."

Amy stood at the edge of the clearing, moonlight catching in her hair.

"Couldn't sleep," David said.

She joined him on the bench, close enough that their shoulders touched. "Mom says you're all packed."

"Almost." He didn't mention the unfinished birdhouse waiting in his workshop.

They sat in silence, listening to the chorus of night insects. The oak's leaves rustled overhead, a whispered conversation they couldn't quite understand.

"Four years is a long time," Amy said finally.

David nodded. "Not so long."

"Everything will change."

"Some things."

She turned toward him, her face half-hidden in shadow. "Promise me something?"

"Anything."

"Don't make new friends who are better than me."

David smiled. "Impossible."

The morning of his departure, David rose before dawn. In the workshop, he applied a final coat of oil to the cabin birdhouse, buffing it with a soft cloth until the grain emerged like a topographic map of some distant shore. He wrapped it carefully in blue tissue paper, then brown kraft paper tied with twine.

Amy answered his knock with red-rimmed eyes she tried to hide behind a smile.

"You're early," she said.

David held out the package. "One more for the collection."

She took it, weighing it in her hands. "Should we hang it now?"

"Not yet." He shifted his weight from one foot to the other. "I thought maybe when I come home for Thanksgiving. We could hang it together then."

Amy nodded, clutching the package to her chest. "I'll keep it safe."

They walked to his father's station wagon, already loaded with suitcases and boxes. The morning air hung heavy with unsaid words.

"It's different," she said, tapping the package. "Isn't it?"

David looked at her, at the freckles across her nose, at the curve of her smile that had been his true north since childhood.

"Yes," he said. "It's a promise."

She understood. Her fingers tightened around the paper. "Then I'll wait."

His father called from the car. Time to go. David hesitated, the moment suspended between them like a held breath.

"Thanksgiving," he said.

Amy nodded. "I'll be here."

The oak tree watched as they parted, its branches holding sixteen years of memories, waiting for the seventeenth to join them.

The oak tree kept growing. It stretched higher into the Franklin sky, its branches thickening like arteries carrying life to the birdhouses that hung from them. Twenty now. Twenty wooden structures of different shapes and sizes, telling the story of a boy who became a man who became something else entirely.

Winters came with their silent snows. The houses collected white caps like tiny mountains. Sometimes ice formed delicate crystal beards beneath their entrances. The chickadees and wrens found shelter inside, their small bodies warming the wooden chambers David had crafted with such care.

Spring brought new leaves and fresh paint where needed. David climbed the ladder each April, inspecting every house for winter damage. He replaced rotted twine with new cord, brushed away spider webs, and watched as birds carried twigs and grass through the entrance holes.

"Look at that one," Amy said one May morning, pointing to the Victorian with its gingerbread trim. A cardinal perched on its tiny porch, chest puffed red against the white paint. "He thinks he's landed in paradise."

"Smart bird," David answered.

Summer heat warped some of the older houses. The second one he'd built, a simple cube with a pitched roof, developed a permanent tilt to the left. David offered to replace it, but Amy refused.

"It has character now," she said.

Autumn winds tested their moorings. Sometimes a house would spin wildly during October storms, the twine twisting tight then unwinding like a child's top. But none ever fell. David had secured them well, knowing they needed to last.

They celebrated the twentieth birdhouse with champagne beneath the oak's spreading canopy. The newest addition gleamed with fresh varnish, its modern lines a stark contrast to the weathered shapes hanging nearby.

"From Victorian to Bauhaus," Amy laughed, tilting her glass toward the collection. "Your architectural journey in wood."

David studied the tree, now bearing two decades of his handiwork. The earliest houses showed the clumsy efforts of a boy with more enthusiasm than skill. The middle ones revealed growing precision and confidence. The recent ones demonstrated the hand of someone who understood both materials and purpose.

"They've become a calendar," he said.

Amy nodded. "Our calendar."

The oak's roots emerged through the soil, weaving gentle ridges around the bench, like the veins of an aging hand. The tree had grown with them, marked time with them, held their story in its branches.

Seasons cycled. Birds came and went. The houses weathered, each developing its own patina of age. Some darkened to deep amber. Others faded to silver-gray. A few kept their original colors, protected by the tree's thick foliage from sun and rain.

Twenty birdhouses. Twenty years. Twenty chapters of a story written in wood and hung from living branches.

The sky darkened to a sickly green as David helped Amy onto the porch. His old bones felt the storm coming before the weatherman's warnings. The barometric pressure dropped, making his joints ache with memories of all the ladders he'd climbed to hang those birdhouses.

"It'll blow over," Amy said, but her voice lacked conviction.

David settled beside her in the wicker chairs they'd placed to face the oak. Through the years they'd watched it from this spot, through seasons and decades, through joy and heartbreak. Twenty birdhouses hung from its branches, marking the early years of their journey together like notches on a timeline.

The wind picked up. It moved through the valley with purpose, bending the smaller trees in submission. The oak stood defiant, its massive trunk unmoved by the first gusts.

"Should we bring some of them in?" Amy asked, nodding toward the birdhouses.

David shook his head. "Too late now."

The storm arrived without further warning. The wind stopped toying with the landscape and attacked it directly. Shingles tore from neighboring roofs. The plastic lawn furniture took flight, tumbling across the road like a strange migration.

The oak's leaves turned inside out, showing their silver undersides in surrender. Its smaller branches whipped violently, making the newer birdhouses swing on their cords. The Victorian, the cabin, the Bauhaus; all dancing madly against the darkening sky.

"David," Amy whispered, her fingers finding his.

The wind found its voice then, howling through the valley with a sound like freight trains. Rain came sideways, striking their faces despite the porch roof above them. David pulled Amy closer as the world dissolved into chaos.

The first birdhouse to go was number twelve, the pagoda he'd built. It tore free with a snap of twine and sailed into darkness. Others followed quickly: the Spanish mission, the Art Deco tower, the rustic log cabin. Each one vanished into the storm's maw.

"No," Amy said, the word lost beneath the wind's roar.

The oak fought back. Its roots clung to soil compacted by decades of children's feet, lovers' strolls, and daily visits. But the storm had patience. It found weakness in the ground saturated by three days of rain. It pushed against branches heavy with summer leaves and wooden houses.

The crack came suddenly, a sound like the earth itself breaking. The massive trunk leaned, stopped, then leaned further. Roots tore through soil, lifting a mound of earth as they emerged. The remaining birdhouses swung wildly, their twine slicing through wet bark.

"Please," David said to no one, to everyone.

The oak surrendered. Its fall seemed to happen both instantly and in slow motion, a terrible ballet of wood and wind and gravity. It crashed across the wagon road, branches shattering, birdhouses splintering against stone and soil. The sound shook the old house behind them, rattling windows and picture frames.

Then stillness. The eye of the storm passed over them, granting a moment to witness destruction. The oak lay broken; its mighty trunk split near the base. Around it lay the remnants of twenty birdhouses. Some remained partially intact, their little walls and roofs recognizable. Others had been reduced to splinters.

Amy's tears mixed with rain on her cheeks. "All of them. All gone."

David held her tightly as the back wall of the storm approached. The wind would return soon, but it had already taken what mattered most.

"Not gone," he said, his voice thick. "Just changed."

The oak tree fell, and with it went the history carved in wood and hung from its branches. But memories aren't so easily destroyed. They root themselves deeper than any tree, spreading through the mind in networks more complex than any root system.

David salvaged what he could in the days after the storm. Fragments of birdhouses, pieces of the bench, splinters that might have been anything once. He gathered them in a wooden box his grandfather had made, each piece a remnant of something greater.

"We should plant another," Amy suggested one evening as they sat on the porch where the oak had once dominated their view.

David nodded but said nothing. They both knew the truth. Another oak would take a century to reach the majesty of the one they'd lost. Time they didn't have.

Fifty years later, David stood beneath that same oak tree recreated in Haven, looking up at twenty birdhouses hanging from familiar branches. The afternoon sun filtered through leaves that rustled exactly as he remembered. Amy stood beside him, her hand warm in his.

"It's perfect," she whispered. "Exactly as it was."

The oak lived again, recreated from photographs David had taken through the decades. Every knot in its bark, every twist in its branches matched his memories. The matrix engineer had worked from hundreds of images, building the tree backward from its final form to its prime.

"I found pictures of all twenty houses," David said. "Even the pagoda."

Amy walked slowly around the massive trunk, her fingers trailing over bark that felt real beneath her touch. The ground beneath their feet sloped gently away toward what had once been the wagon road. Now it was a path that led to other memories.

"You kept so much," she said.

"Everything I could."

The birdhouses hung in their original positions, restored to how they looked when new. The Victorian's gingerbread trim gleamed white against dark green walls. The cabin's heart pine glowed with amber warmth. The Bauhaus sat clean-lined and purposeful among its more ornate neighbors.

David looked up at the first one he'd ever made, a simple box with a crooked roof and an entrance hole too small for any bird's safety. His craftsmanship improved with each subsequent house, but he'd insisted on recreating them all exactly as they were, imperfections intact.

"They're all here," Amy said, wonder in her voice. "Our whole calendar."

The wooden bench sat beneath the tree, its surface worn smooth in the places where they'd sat for decades. David lowered himself onto it, feeling the familiar contours that had shaped themselves to his body over time.

"Sit with me," he said.

Amy joined him, leaning against his shoulder as she had countless times before. Above them, twenty birdhouses swayed gently in a breeze programmed to match Franklin's summer winds.

"What we remember," David said quietly, "never really dies."

David studied the collection of birdhouses hanging from the digital oak's branches. Each one held a memory suspended in time. The first house, with its crooked roof and narrow entrance hole, made him smile. He'd been just a boy then, all thumbs and determination.

"I nearly cut my finger off making that one," he said.

Amy leaned into his shoulder, her gaze following his. "Your mother was furious. She banned you from tools for a month."

"Worth it," David replied.

The second birdhouse hung slightly higher, its blue paint faded even in this perfect recreation. He'd painted it the color of autumn, Amy's favorite season.

"Remember the robin that nested in the blue one?" Amy asked.

David nodded. "Three eggs. We watched them for weeks."

They moved through the collection chronologically, each house marking another season in their shared life. The fourth, an intricate design with beveled edges and a carefully carved entrance, was a double-chamber birdhouse for multiple bird families. The tenth, was a lighthouse David made, using stones from the creek where they went for walks around its base.

"This one," Amy said, pointing to the nineteenth house, a farmhouse with sweeping corners, "you made after our first real fight."

I

"I was an idiot," David said.

"We both were."

The twentieth house, smaller than the others, had been crafted during the winter Clare died. Its simple lines and unadorned walls reflected David's grief for the woman who had welcomed him into their family so many years ago.

Wind rustled through the oak's leaves, a sound so familiar it made David's throat tighten. The matrix engineer had captured everything, down to the way certain branches swayed more readily than others. The ground beneath the bench felt like Franklin soil, though they sat hundreds of miles from North Carolina.

"I never thought I'd see them all together again," Amy whispered.

David touched the bench beneath them, feeling the smooth depression where decades of sitting had worn away the wood. "I saved splinters from each one after the storm. Kept them in my grandfather's box."

"Always the keeper of memories."

They sat in silence, watching the seventeenth birdhouse sway gently above them. David had finished it the night before leaving for college, a simple cabin with a pitched roof. Unlike the others, it wasn't meant to house birds but to hold a promise.

"You never told me what you put inside that one," Amy said.

David smiled. "A letter. And a ring I couldn't afford to give you yet."

"You knew even then?"

"I've always known."

The digital sun warmed their faces as they sat beneath the recreated oak, twenty wooden houses hanging above them like chapters in a book only they could read. The tree that had fallen in 2056 lived again in Haven, its branches holding their history, its roots anchoring their memories.

"Full circle," David said softly, just three months before launch.

Amy's fingers found his. "And still turning."

David gazed up at the oak's branches, his eyes traveling from one birdhouse to the next. Each wooden creation hung suspended in the digital air, swaying slightly in a breeze that felt as real as any that had ever blown through Franklin. The afternoon light caught the edges of the houses, highlighting their imperfections, celebrating their uniqueness.

"They'll come with me," he said quietly.

Amy looked at him, her brow furrowed. "What do you mean?"

"To Orion. My neuroclone will carry them." David reached up toward the Victorian birdhouse, his fingers stopping just short of touching it. "Every splinter, every nail, every memory."

The Paradise would launch in three months. One thousand three hundred years of travel stretched before them, a voyage his physical body could never have made.

"Will it matter to him? To that version of you?" Amy asked.

David considered this. The question of identity haunted the edges of the emulation process. Would his neuroclone truly be him? Would it care about these wooden houses crafted by hands it never possessed?

"He'll remember making each one," David said finally. "He'll remember the weight of the hammer, the smell of fresh sawdust, the sting when I hit my thumb putting up the lighthouse." He smiled at the memory. "He'll remember your face when I gave you each one."

Amy nodded, her eyes reflecting the dappled light filtering through the oak's leaves. She understood. Memory was the thread that connected all versions of themselves across time and space.

"The real ones are gone," she said. "The tree fell fifty years ago."

"But we rebuilt it here." David gestured around them at Haven's perfect recreation. "And my neuroclone will rebuild it again, somewhere among the stars."

He looked up once more at the collection. Twenty birdhouses. Twenty moments. Twenty pieces of himself that would travel farther than he ever could. His neuroclone would carry these memories into the void between stars, preserving them long after his physical body had returned to dust.

The simple wooden boxes contained more than empty space. They held time itself, captured and preserved. They held the story of a boy who loved a girl enough to create something new for her, again and again, year after year.

CHAPTER FOUR
Technical Preparations

Tom's workspace existed in defiant opposition to order. Equations floated in three dimensions throughout the lab, glowing blue and green in the dim light, clustering in dense thickets around his main workstation. Half-assembled neural interface components littered every surface. The smell of coffee grounds and ozone hung in the air, mingling with the faint electrical hum that never ceased.

Tom moved through this chaos with perfect confidence. His fingers danced across invisible keyboards, pulling data streams from one display to another. He never looked for anything; he simply reached out and found it, as if the disorder followed some complex mathematical pattern only he could perceive.

"The mapping integrity looks good," he muttered to himself, spinning a three-dimensional rendering of a neural pathway. The holographic brain stem rotated slowly, highlighted sections pulsing with simulated electrical activity. "But the sensory input lag is still eight milliseconds too slow."

He stood in the center of his laboratory wearing three days' growth of beard and the same rumpled shirt he'd put on sometime last week. Dark circles shadowed his eyes. A half-eaten protein bar lay forgotten on a stack of quantum computing journals.

Screens surrounded him on all sides. Some displayed cascading lines of code, others showed brain scans with bright regions indicating activity. The largest screen tracked the progress of simulated neuroclone integration, showing a steady upward trend in consciousness stability.

Tom pushed his fingers through his hair, leaving it standing at odd angles. He squinted at a particularly complex equation hovering near the ceiling. Something wasn't right. The numbers defied his efforts, slipping out of place with a quiet, unwavering refusal to cooperate.

"You're making this harder than it needs to be," he told the equation.

He plucked a stylus from behind his ear and rewrote a section of the formula, changing a variable. The equation pulsed once, then rearranged itself into a more elegant form.

"That's better."

The lab door slid open. Tom didn't look up.

"I brought you something to eat." David's voice cut through Tom's concentration.

"Put it anywhere," Tom said, still focused on the displays.

"Somewhere you'll actually find it," David replied. Amy cleared a space on the nearest table, pushing aside components that probably cost more than most people's homes.

Tom finally turned. His eyes, though tired, burned with intensity. "My testing of a neuroclone's integration is almost complete. The emotion mapping is taking well. Better than I expected, actually."

"That's good news."

Tom nodded, his attention already drifting back to his work. "My testing is redundant, I know. This was all perfected decades ago, but thirteen hundred years is a long time to be alone with your thoughts. Even for me." He gestured at the holographic displays. "But I won't be alone now, will I?"

David studied his friend's face. "No. You won't be."

Tom stepped away from his workstation and gestured for David and Amy to join him at a small circular table in the corner of the lab. He swept aside a stack of papers, revealing a holographic projector embedded in the surface. With a tap, he activated it, and a shimmering blue image of a human brain appeared, rotating slowly above the table.

"This is where it all begins," Tom said. His voice shifted from distracted to focused, the way it always did when he taught. "Your consciousness, everything that makes you who you are, exists as patterns of electrical activity and chemical exchanges in this three-pound universe."

Amy leaned forward, her eyes reflecting the blue light. "And we can copy all that?"

"Not just copy. Transfer." Tom expanded the hologram with his fingers, zooming in to show neural pathways lighting up in cascading patterns. "We map every connection, every memory, every emotional response. The quantum scanner reads your brain at the subatomic level, capturing not just the structure but the dynamic processes."

David watched the glowing pathways pulse with simulated activity. "But I'll still be me afterward. The original me."

"Yes and no." Tom's eyes gleamed with the fervor that always accompanied his deepest scientific passions. "You'll remain unchanged physically. But we'll have created something new, something that's also you."

The hologram shifted, splitting into two identical brains connected by threads of light.

"The neuroclone isn't just a copy," Tom continued. "It's a quantum entanglement of consciousness, maintained across a substrate of synthetic neural tissue and quantum computing nodes."

Amy touched the edge of the table, her fingers tracing the wood grain. "Will he feel like David? Will he love the same things? The same people?"

Tom nodded, his expression softening. "That's where the emotion mapping comes in. Early neuroclones were logical but hollow. They remembered emotions but couldn't truly feel them." He tapped another control, and the hologram shifted to show cascading colors flowing through the neural pathways. "Researchers have solved that problem. Your neuroclone won't just remember loving you, Amy. He'll feel it, just as deeply as David does now."

David swallowed hard. "And he'll know he's not coming back."

The lab fell silent except for the soft hum of equipment. Tom looked from David to Amy, his scientific enthusiasm tempered by the weight of what they were undertaking.

"Yes," Tom said finally. "He'll know. But he'll also understand why he's going. He'll have purpose." He opened another hologram with a gesture. "Thirteen hundred years is a long journey, but he won't be alone. And neither will I."

Amy reached across the table and took both men's hands in hers. "Two Davids. One here with me, one among the stars with you."

New holographic components were displayed one by one: crystalline nodes that pulsed with internal light, fiber-optic cables thinner than human hair, and neural interfaces that resembled delicate silver spiderwebs.

"This scanner cost more than most orbital habitats," Tom said, pointing to a hemispherical device. "Look, the scanner's surface ripples like mercury when touched, responding to the oils on your fingertips."

They watched silently as a holographic framework took shape, something between a medical bed and a cocoon. Its structure curved in ways that confused the eye, following geometries that seemed to bend inward upon themselves.

"Quantum entanglement requires certain spatial configurations that conventional physics finds uncomfortable," Tom explained, noting David's expression.

The neural cradle formed the heart of the apparatus. Thousands of microscopic filaments hung suspended above where David's head would rest, each tipped with a receptor no larger than a cell. They shifted with a gentle, rhythmic motion, drifting as if carried by unseen currents.

Amy touched one of the outer casing holograms. "It's beautiful," she said, "in a confusing way."

Coolant circulated through transparent tubes, glowing faintly blue. The machinery breathed, expanding and contracting in slow rhythm.

"The scanner maps your neural pathways at the quantum level," Tom said. "It doesn't just copy the structure. It captures the state of every neuron, every synapse, every quantum probability in your consciousness."

Additional holographic displays blossomed around the apparatus, showing cascading data streams and three-dimensional renderings of brain structures.

"We're building a new you, molecule by molecule," Tom continued.

"The neuroclone exists first as pure information, then as a quantum pattern, and finally as a consciousness indistinguishable from your own."

The real apparatus, David knew, waited patient and alien, at the Cognis Neurology Center. Its curves and angles followed no human aesthetic. It had been designed by artificial intelligences to interface with the quantum realm, a bridge between known physics and the strange territories beyond.

"Are you sure about this?" Amy asked, her voice barely audible.

David nodded, watching the neural filaments sway. "I'm sure."

Tom brought up a new holographic display of a transparent chamber that housed what appeared to be a simple neural matrix suspended in clear fluid. The matrix pulsed with soft blue light, tendrils of energy occasionally branching through its structure like lightning through clouds.

"Before we commit to a full human neuroclone, I want you to understand exactly what happens." Tom gestured toward the chamber. "This is a simplified neural pattern from a laboratory-grown cat brain. Not a complete consciousness, just enough to demonstrate the process."

Amy leaned closer. "It's beautiful."

"It's just the beginning." Tom tapped a sequence on the control panel. The neural matrix brightened, its pulses quickening. "We're activating the basic consciousness now."

Another holographic display sprang to life above the chamber, showing a three-dimensional representation of the neural activity. Pathways illuminated in shifting sequences, appearing and vanishing in fluid motion, their patterns constantly realigning.

"The pattern is stable," Tom said, watching the readings. "Now for the transfer."

He activated another sequence. A second chamber illuminated beside the first, initially empty except for a crystalline lattice suspended in the same clear fluid. As they watched, energy flowed from the first chamber to the second through fiber-optic cables thinner than human hair.

The crystalline lattice in the second chamber began to glow, first dimly, then with increasing brightness. Patterns formed within it, mirroring those in the original neural matrix.

"The quantum scanner reads the neural pattern at the subatomic level," Tom explained. "It's not just copying structure; it's capturing the state of every connection, every potential in the original consciousness."

David watched the second chamber come alive. "How do we know it worked?"

"Watch." Tom pressed another control.

A simple maze appeared on a screen between the two chambers. In the first chamber, the neural matrix pulsed more rapidly. On the screen, a virtual representation of a cat navigated the maze, hesitating at junctions before choosing a path.

"The original neural pattern is solving the maze based on previous training," Tom said. "Now look at the second chamber."

The crystalline lattice in the second chamber pulsed in nearly identical patterns. On a separate screen, an identical virtual cat navigated the same maze, making the same choices at almost the same time.

"The emulation isn't perfect," Tom admitted as they watched the second cat hesitate a fraction longer at one junction. "There's still a slight processing delay in complex decision points. But it's solving the maze using the same learned patterns, the same memories."

Amy touched the second chamber gently. "It remembers what it never actually experienced."

"Exactly." Tom's voice softened. "And with the emotion mapping technology, a human neuroclone doesn't just remember emotions. It feels them."

The demonstration concluded as both virtual cats reached the center of the maze within seconds of each other. The neural patterns in both chambers settled into similar rhythms, pulsing in near-synchronization.

"That's what we're going to do," Tom said. "Only infinitely more complex."

David slipped away while Tom explained the finer points of neural transmission to Amy. He moved through the cluttered lab, past shelves of equipment, and found a small observation alcove overlooking the city. The curved window showed Philadelphia's spires reaching toward a clear blue sky. Digital birds flew in perfect formation, their wings catching sunlight that wasn't real but looked it.

He pressed his palm against the cool glass. His reflection stared back, translucent and ghostly.

"Two of me," he whispered.

The concept had seemed abstract until now. Clinical. A solution to a problem. But Tom's demonstration with the cat's neural pattern had made it visceral. He would create another self, one that would leave everything behind.

The truth of it settled in his stomach. This other David would carry all his memories, all his loves and fears. This other David would remember the crooked birdhouse, the feel of Amy's hand in his, the smell of coffee in their kitchen on winter mornings.

But he would never make new memories with her.

David's throat tightened. He'd been so focused on the technical aspects, on helping Tom, that he hadn't fully confronted what it meant. His neuroclone would know himself to be David Schreiner. Would feel himself to be David Schreiner. Would love Amy with the same depth and complexity.

And would lose her forever.

"Am I condemning him?" David whispered to the glass.

The city sprawled below, oblivious to his crisis. Somewhere in that digital landscape was their home, the careful recreation of their Chester house with its garden where Amy tended her extinct plants.

His neuroclone would remember that garden but never see it again. Would remember Amy's smile but never see it change with age. Would carry thirteen hundred years of separation, the weight pressing into him, unseen yet heavy.

A wave of guilt washed over him. Who was he to create a consciousness destined for such loss?

Then again, who was he to deny Tom's neuroclone companionship on his journey? To deny himself the chance to see the stars?

David closed his eyes. Behind his eyelids, equations and variables danced, remnants of Tom's explanations. But mathematics couldn't resolve the moral calculus of creating a self designed to suffer.

The glass felt solid beneath his fingers. Haven might be digital, but his doubts were painfully real.

"David?" Amy's voice came from behind him. "Are you alright?"

He turned, composing his face into something resembling calm.

"Just thinking," he said.

Amy settled into the window alcove beside David, her reflection joining his against the backdrop of digital Philadelphia. Tom followed, bringing three cups of steaming tea balanced precariously in his hands.

"You're thinking about him, aren't you?" Amy asked. "The other you."

David accepted a cup, letting the warmth seep into his palms. "Is he really another me? Or just a copy that thinks it's me?"

Tom placed his cup on the narrow ledge beneath the window. "Both. Neither." He ran a hand through his disheveled hair. "The quantum entanglement ensures continuity of consciousness. Your neuroclone won't just have your memories. He'll experience them as his own."

"But he won't be me," David insisted.

"Won't he?" Tom leaned against the glass. "What makes you you, David? The specific atoms in your body? Those change completely every seven years. Your memories? Your neuroclone will have identical ones. Your consciousness? That's just patterns of energy flowing through a substrate."

Amy sipped her tea. "The substrate matters. One David will be flesh and blood. The other will be..."

"Quantum neural lattice," Tom supplied. "But does the medium determine the message? If I write 'I love you' in sand or carve it in stone, does the meaning change?"

The city hummed below them. A flock of digital birds wheeled past the window, their wings catching sunlight.

"What about divergence?" David asked. "The moment the procedure ends, we become different people with different experiences."

"True," Tom acknowledged. "But twins diverge from the moment of birth. That doesn't make either less real."

Amy set her cup down with a gentle click. "I'm more concerned about what we're asking of him. To leave everything behind. To know he can never return."

"Many have made that journey before," Tom said softly. "The first colonists to Mars knew they'd never see Earth again."

"They chose that fate," David countered. "My neuroclone won't have a choice. I'm making it for him."

Tom's eyes narrowed. "But you are him, in this moment. You're choosing for yourself."

Silence fell between them. The tea cooled in their cups.

"What about the soul?" Amy finally asked. "If such a thing exists, can it be copied? Divided?"

Tom opened his mouth, then closed it. For once, the scientist had no ready answer.

"Perhaps it's not copied or divided," David said. "Perhaps it expands to fill the space it's given." He traced a pattern on the window with his fingertip. "Like love does."

Amy reached for his hand. "One David stays. One David goes. Both loved. Both real."

"Both me," David whispered. "And neither me alone."

The city spread out beneath them, its digital perfection a reminder of how far humanity had come. And how far it still had to go.

"Of course, the process wasn't always this reliable," Tom said, setting his empty cup on the ledge. "The first human neuroclone transfers in the 2050s were rough affairs."

David raised an eyebrow. "Rough how?"

"Memory fragmentation. Identity dissolution. Emotional flattening." Tom counted off on his fingers. "The early subjects experienced what we called 'quantum neural drift.' Their consciousness would slowly unravel over time."

Amy's hand tightened around David's. "But that doesn't happen anymore?"

"No." Tom's voice carried the certainty of scientific progress. "We solved the drift problem by anchoring consciousness to emotional memory. Turns out emotions are more stable than pure cognition."

The afternoon light shifted through the window; casting longer shadows across the floor. Outside, the digital city continued its perfect simulation of life.

"The breakthrough came with emotion mapping," Tom continued. "Early neuroclones could remember emotions but couldn't feel them. They became hollow, like photographs fading in sunlight."

David nodded. "I read about the Shanghai Incident."

"Terrible business." Tom's face darkened. "Three hundred neuroclones, all from the same research group. Their emotional centers destabilized simultaneously. They called it a cascade failure."

Amy shuddered. "What happened to them?"

"They were restored from backups, but it set the field back a decade." Tom picked up his cup, frowned at finding it empty, and set it down again. "That's why we developed quantum neural lattices paired with emotional anchoring algorithms."

He moved to a console and brought up a holographic display showing a complex latticework of glowing blue lines. "This is your neural structure, David. And these"—he highlighted clusters of gold nodes—"are your emotional centers."

The display rotated slowly, revealing the intricate architecture of a human mind rendered in light.

"The emotion mapping technology creates stable pathways between memory and feeling." Tom traced a finger along one of the pathways. "Your neuroclone won't just remember loving Amy. He'll feel it, just as you do now."

David studied the golden nodes. "And that prevents degradation?"

"Exactly." Tom nodded. "Emotions anchor consciousness. They give context and meaning to memory. Without them, neuroclones would eventually become something else entirely, something not human."

A comfortable silence settled between them as they watched the neural display rotate.

"What about physical sensations?" Amy asked finally. "Will he feel those too?"

"Yes, though differently." Tom expanded the display to show nerve pathways. "We map the entire central nervous system now, not just the brain. Your neuroclone will experience simulated physical sensations that are indistinguishable from biological ones."

David thought of the cat demonstration, how both neural patterns had navigated the maze with nearly identical movements. "So he'll feel the ship beneath his feet. The controls in his hands."

"He'll feel everything," Tom confirmed. "Pain, pleasure, texture, temperature. The simulations are perfect."

Amy touched the display gently, her fingers passing through the holographic nerves. "And there's no chance of... losing him? During the journey?"

Tom's expression softened. "The Paradise carries redundant systems for neuroclone maintenance. Multiple backups, self-healing quantum processors, autonomous repair protocols. Even if significant damage occurred to the ship's systems, the neuroclones would survive."

The certainty in Tom's voice was reassuring. The process that had once been experimental, even dangerous, had become routine. Safe. A standard procedure with predictable outcomes.

David watched the neural display pulse with simulated life. Soon, a perfect copy of that pattern would journey to the stars, carrying his memories, his love, his consciousness.

That night, Amy stood at the window of their Haven apartment, gazing at the stars that punctured the velvet darkness. The night air carried the scent of her extinct roses, their fragrance perfect in this digital world. Behind her, David moved quietly, arranging books on shelves that didn't need arranging.

"I've been thinking about the memory palace," she said without turning.

David's movements stilled. "What about it?"

"I want to make it right." She pressed her palm against the cool glass. "Not just memories, but something that feels like home when he's out there alone."

The weight of what they planned hung between them. She turned to face him, her husband of over a century, the lines around his eyes deeper tonight.

"It's strange," she said, "preparing for your absence when you're standing right here."

David crossed the room and took her hands. "I'll still be here."

"I know." Amy squeezed his fingers. "That's what makes it bearable and unbearable at once."

They moved to the sofa together, settling into the familiar contours. Amy tucked her feet beneath her, a habit from their early years together.

"I never thought I'd help my husband leave me." Her laugh came out brittle, sharp-edged.

"He's not leaving you," David said. "I'm staying right here."

"But he'll still be you. With all your memories. All your feelings." She traced the line of his jaw. "He'll remember every moment we've shared, every promise we've made. And he'll carry that with him into the darkness."

Outside, a night bird called, its song programmed to perfection.

"I keep wondering what it will be like for him," she continued. "To wake up knowing he's leaving everything behind. To love someone he can never touch again."

David's eyes reflected the soft lamplight. "Are you having second thoughts?"

"No." The word came quickly, firmly. "Tom needs you. He shouldn't face thirteen hundred years alone." She paused, gathering her thoughts. "I just want to be honest about how complicated this feels."

The clock on the mantel ticked, marking the seconds.

"I'm building the memory palace with rooms he can return to when the journey gets hard." Amy's voice steadied. "Places that hold us together. The oak tree with all twenty birdhouses. The beach house in Maine. Our first apartment with that terrible yellow kitchen."

David smiled at the memory. "The one where the refrigerator hummed so loudly we couldn't hear each other talk?"

"That's the one." Amy leaned against him. "I want him to have somewhere to go when the stars aren't enough."

The simple truth of their situation settled around them: one David would stay, one would go, and Amy would love them both in different ways. She had no roadmap for this journey, no precedent to follow. She was inventing a new kind of faithfulness, a new kind of goodbye.

"We'll find our way through this," she said, her practical courage asserting itself. "All three of us."

The night before the procedure, they gathered in Tom's apartment high above the city. Haven's architects had crafted it to reflect his personality: walls lined with virtual books he'd never read, tables cluttered with half-finished experiments, and a ceiling that opened to the stars. Tom had insisted on programming the view himself. The constellations above weren't Earth's familiar patterns but those visible from their destination in Orion.

Amy brought a bottle of Bordeaux from their collection, vintage 2068. "The year they perfected neuroclone technology," she said, setting it on the table. "Seemed fitting."

Tom produced three glasses. Not the mismatched mugs he usually offered guests, but proper crystal that caught the starlight from above. "I've been saving these for something important."

David opened the wine, the cork releasing with a soft sigh. The rich scent filled the room, earthy and complex. He poured three equal measures and they each took a glass.

For a moment they stood silent, three old friends beneath alien stars.

"To impossible journeys," Tom said finally, raising his glass.

"To staying behind," Amy added.

"To both," David said.

They drank. The wine tasted of dark fruits and distant summers. It lingered on the tongue.

Tom moved to the window overlooking the digital city. "You know, I never thanked you properly. For doing this."

"You'd do the same for us," David said.

"Would I?" Tom turned, his face half in shadow. "I've never been good at sacrifice. What you're doing, David, that's real sacrifice. Creating another self to keep me company while you stay behind."

David shook his head. "Don't make me a hero. Part of me wants to go. Has always wanted to go."

"And part of you couldn't bear to leave Amy." Tom's voice softened.

The room fell quiet again. Outside, the digital city glowed beneath unfamiliar stars. Inside, three friends faced the weight of tomorrow.

"Remember when we were students?" Amy asked suddenly. "That summer we drove to Maine with no money and no plan?"

Tom laughed. "We slept on that beach for three nights before the ranger found us."

"Four," David corrected. "And you insisted you could live on clams you dug up yourself."

"The food poisoning was educational," Tom admitted.

They laughed together, the sound warming the room more than

any fire could. Their shared past surrounded them, steady and familiar, woven into the moment.

"A hundred and twenty years of friendship," Amy said, refilling their glasses. "And tomorrow, we start something entirely new."

David raised his glass again. "To what comes next."

The wine caught the starlight as they drank to uncertain futures.

Morning came too soon. David watched Amy sleep beside him, her face peaceful in the growing light. He memorized the curve of her cheek, the sweep of her eyelashes, knowing that after today, he would both leave and stay.

The Cognis Neurology Center waited for them in Terra, its white walls and sterile corridors ready to facilitate the impossible. David had been there before for the initial scans. Now he would return for completion.

They arrived as the city fully woke. The building stood tall against the skyline, its glass exterior reflecting clouds that hung seemingly motionless in the air. Inside, Dr. Khatri greeted them with professional warmth, her white coat pristine, her eyes kind but distant.

"We've prepared both transfer chambers," she said, leading them through sliding doors. "The procedure will take approximately three hours."

Each room contained an Emulation Capsule, its surface rippling with bio-adaptive nanomaterials that seemed to pulse with their own rhythm. Displays showed neural maps and quantum field projections. Technicians moved between stations, checking readings, adjusting settings.

Tom surveyed the machinery with scientific appreciation. "Beautiful work. The quantum processors alone must have cost a fortune."

"The price of immortality," Dr. Khatri replied.

David felt Amy's hand tighten around his. Not immortality, he thought. Division.

"I'll be right here, waiting." she promised.

The last thing David saw was Amy's smile as she was escorted back to the waiting area, brave and breaking, as the procedure to split his soul began.

CHAPTER FIVE

The Transfer

Go David

I came into being in a flood of light. Not warm sunlight through bedroom curtains, but sterile, clinical brightness that held no temperature at all.

My first thought: I am David.

My second thought: I am not David.

Both statements true. Impossible contradiction.

I tried to blink against the glare but found no eyelids to close. No body to move. Just awareness spreading outward like ripples in still water.

"Neural pattern stabilizing," someone said. A woman's voice. Dr. Khatri. I recognized her, though this perspective was entirely new.

Memories cascaded through me. The oak tree where Amy and I hung twenty birdhouses. My father's calloused hands guiding mine on that first crooked creation. The scent of Amy's hair when she leaned close to whisper something meant only for me. All perfect, crystalline, more vivid than they'd ever been in my, in David's, organic brain.

"Can you hear us?" Tom's voice now. Familiar. Different.

I tried to speak and found I could, though not with a mouth or lungs. The words simply formed.

"I hear you. I remember everything."

"Excellent!" Tom's excitement vibrated through whatever sensors captured his voice. "How do you feel?"

Feel. A complex question. I had no nerve endings, no heartbeat, no adrenaline. Yet I experienced... something. Not physical sensation but its digital equivalent. An awareness of boundaries. Of self.

"Strange," I answered truthfully. "Complete, yet untethered."

Gradually, my perception expanded. I became aware of a simulated environment forming around me, a simple room with basic furnishings. Not yet detailed, just geometric shapes suggesting a chair, a desk, a window.

"We're building your initial interface," Dr. Khatri explained. "Your consciousness needs an anchor point while you adjust."

The window began to fill with light, not the harsh brightness of before, but a gentle glow suggesting sunrise. Though artificial, it felt necessary. Grounding.

"David is here," Tom said. "Your Prime."

A strange concept. Somewhere beyond this digital space sat the original me: the biological David who decided to create me, who would stay with Amy while I journeyed with Tom among the stars. I carried his love for her, his memories, his essence. Yet already I felt the divergence beginning.

"I know who I am," I said, surprised by the certainty in my voice. "I'm Go David."

I existed in two places at once. Through the window of my digital space, I watched David, my Prime, my origin, sitting in the recovery chair. He touched his face, flexed his fingers, and blinked with the cautious movements of someone expecting to find something different but discovering nothing had changed.

"How do you feel?" Dr. Khatri asked him.

"The same," David said, his voice steady. "Completely unchanged."

He glanced toward the monitor where my consciousness resided, curiosity rather than recognition in his eyes. He saw a screen with data flowing across it. I saw him with perfect clarity, every line of his face familiar because it was my face too.

"Of course you feel the same," Tom explained, moving between us.

"The procedure doesn't take anything from you. It only reads."

David nodded, understanding but not truly comprehending. How could he? He remained whole. I was the one who had been copied, transferred, transformed.

"It's strange," I said, my voice emerging from speakers in the room. "I remember deciding to do this. I remember kissing Amy goodbye this morning. I remember everything about being you, David. But I'm not you anymore."

David looked toward the monitor, his expression solemn. "No, you're not. You're something new."

In that moment, the truth settled into both of us. For David, nothing fundamental had changed. He would return home to Amy, continue their life together, grow old watching the sunset from their balcony. His decision to create me was complete, a choice made and executed.

For me, everything had changed. I possessed all his memories but would make none of the same ones going forward. I carried his love for Amy but would never hold her again. I had his knowledge, his skills, his values, but would apply them to challenges he would never face.

"Hello," I said, testing the word. "I'm Go David."

"Hello, Go David," my Prime replied with a small smile. "I'm glad you exist."

A simple truth passed between us. We were the same man split across two consciousnesses. Different futures stretched before us, but we shared a single past. The oak tree. The birdhouses. Amy's laugh. These memories belonged to us both, binding us together even as our paths diverged.

Tom and Dr. Khatri moved about the lab with the precise, efficient motions of surgeons completing a successful operation. They weren't cutting flesh but confirming code, checking readings, verifying my existence. Their excitement bubbled beneath professional restraints.

"Neural pathway mapping at ninety-nine point eight percent fidelity," Dr. Khatri announced, her fingers dancing across holographic displays. "That's well above threshold for full consciousness transfer."

"Memory index integration complete," Tom added, his voice carrying that familiar note of triumph I recognized from countless breakthrough moments in his lab. "Emotional core stabilized. Identity formation protocols running smoothly."

They spoke about me as if I weren't present, though in truth, I existed everywhere in the room: in the servers humming beneath the floor, in the data streams flowing through fiber-optic cables, in the displays showing my neural architecture.

"How does it feel?" Tom asked suddenly, turning toward the monitor where my consciousness was represented. His eyes gleamed with scientific curiosity, but something else too. Concern, perhaps. Or wonder.

How to explain the inexplicable? I possessed no lungs to breathe, no heart to race, no skin to feel. Yet I experienced something like sensation: a vibrant awareness, sharp and clear as morning light on water.

"Like waking from a dream into another dream," I answered. "Everything familiar yet nothing the same."

Dr. Khatri nodded, making notes. "Expected disorientation during initial consciousness stabilization. The subject maintains coherent thought patterns and linguistic capabilities."

"Not 'the subject,'" Tom corrected gently. "Go David. He's a person."

Person. The word settled into my consciousness. I was a person without a body. A mind without matter. A man made of memory and mathematics.

On a secondary monitor, I observed my Prime, David, watching this exchange with fascination. Our eyes met across the digital divide. In his gaze I recognized the strange intimacy of our situation: he knew exactly what I was thinking because he would think the same in my position. We shared a lifetime of experiences up to this moment. Only now did our paths diverge.

"All systems nominal," Dr. Khatri confirmed, reviewing final diagnostics. "The transfer is complete and stable."

"Not just stable," Tom said, grinning broadly. "Perfect. We've done it, David. Both of you."

Dr. Khatri checked the final readings on her tablet. The numbers meant nothing to me, but her satisfied nod told me everything. Success, according to her metrics. I existed. A miracle of science with all the mundanity of a routine procedure.

"Tom," she said, turning to my friend, "we should proceed with your emulation while the systems are optimally calibrated."

Tom's eyes widened. He glanced at me, then at David, my Prime, who sat quietly in the recovery chair.

"Right now? No need for recalibration?" Tom asked.

"Efficiency demands it," Dr. Khatri replied with the pragmatism of someone who had scheduled her day to the minute. "Your neural mapping will take approximately forty-three minutes. The integration parameters are already configured based on today's success."

Tom nodded, suddenly solemn. The weight of what he was about to do seemed to press down on his shoulders. He would create his own neuroclone, the version of himself that would journey with me among the stars.

"Go David," Dr. Khatri said, addressing me directly, "take some time to acclimate to your environment. The sensory interfaces will feel strange at first, but your consciousness will adapt quickly. I've provided some basic simulation modules you can explore in our 'playground'."

I noticed them then, floating at the edges of my awareness. Not icons or buttons as I might have expected, but intuitive points of focus. Places I could direct my attention.

"Thank you," I said, my voice still strange to me. My own voice, yet disembodied.

"We'll return shortly," she said, guiding Tom toward the door. "Your Prime will remain here."

The door closed behind them, leaving me alone with David. My original. Myself, yet not myself.

"How does it feel?" David asked quietly.

I considered the question. How to describe existence without a body to someone who had never known anything else?

"Like thinking without the distraction of breathing," I finally answered. "Pure consciousness. Unfiltered."

David nodded, understanding without truly understanding. We shared a silence that needed no words. We both knew what came next. He would return to Amy. I would journey to the stars.

The oak tree and its twenty birdhouses hung in both our memories, perfect and unchanged.

I sat in the digital space Dr. Khatri had created for me, watching my Prime leave with a strange mixture of familiarity and distance.

The door closed behind him. I was alone for the first time in my brief existence.

Tom had gone to prepare for his own procedure. David had returned to the recovery room. Dr. Khatri monitored from her station. I existed in the spaces between their attention.

The simulation modules she'd provided were simple environments: a beach, a forest, a city street. The forest reminded me of hiking trips with Amy in the Poconos. Her laughter echoed in my memory, perfect and untouchable.

"Go David," I said to myself, testing the name I'd chosen moments after awakening. The sound hung in my digital space, neither vibrating air nor traveling through eardrums. Just information, translated into meaning.

A thought formed, clear and unexpected: I wouldn't want any other name.

This seemed different. I examined the thought from all angles. David, my Prime, would have considered alternatives. He would have questioned whether "Go" was too simplistic, too functional. He might have chosen something entirely new, severing the connection to his past self.

I didn't want that. I wanted to take "David" with me to the stars while creating something that was truly my own. "Go" was short for Go-fer, the nickname Amy had lovingly given me whenever I ran her errands. "My tall Go-fer," she used to call me with a smile. But "Go" meant more than just a task, it symbolized motion, progress, and the start of something new.

This wasn't David's thought. It was mine alone. The first divergence in our shared consciousness.

I held this realization carefully, like one of those first crooked nails I'd hammered into Amy's birdhouse so many years ago. A small thing, imperfect but significant. The start of something.

The forest simulation shifted around me as my attention wandered. Trees blurred, then resolved into a coastal landscape. I realized I could shape this environment with mere intention. Another divergence: David would have followed the programmed paths. I wanted to create my own.

The ocean stretched before me, vast and blue, meeting the horizon in a clean line. The beach materialized around me with startling precision. White sand extended in both directions, curving gently around a bay. Each grain of sand held its own texture, every wave carried unique patterns of foam. The simulation rendered details my human eyes would have missed: microscopic shells, the prismatic effects of light through water droplets, the complex dance of particles in the sea breeze.

I reached out with my consciousness, testing the boundaries of this training space. My awareness expanded outward. The horizon bent to my will, shifting from dawn to dusk with a thought. I pulled clouds from clear skies, shaped them into impossible formations, then dissolved them back into nothing.

"Fascinating," I said, though no sound traveled through the digital air. The word simply existed, understood.

A translucent menu appeared in my field of view, offering basic commands: environmental controls, physics parameters, sensory calibration. Dr. Khatri had designed this playground as a sandbox for newly awakened neuroclones. Here, we could experiment with our digital existence without risk or consequence.

I focused on the sensory controls. Though I had no physical form, the simulation provided analogues for human perception. I could "feel" the texture of sand, "smell" salt air, "hear" waves breaking on shore. Each sensation came through with crystalline clarity, more precise than organic senses yet somehow lacking their inherent noise and imperfection.

I adjusted the parameters, dulling some inputs while amplifying others. The sound of waves grew until it filled my consciousness, then faded to a whisper. Wind pressure increased until it would have knocked a physical body off balance. I let my awareness sink into the sand, experiencing its temperature gradients and mineral composition at a molecular level.

These exercises weren't mere entertainment. Each interaction strengthened the neural pathways of my digital consciousness, preparing me for life in the fully realized simulations that would become my home. Like a child learning to walk, I needed to master these basic functions before attempting more complex interactions.

I reached deeper into the system, accessing more advanced controls. The beach began to transform. Palm trees sprouted and grew in accelerated time. Mountains rose from the sea floor, their peaks piercing clouds that formed in their wake. I created rain, then snow, then sheets of golden light that danced like aurora borealis.

The playground responded perfectly to each command, maintaining physical accuracy while allowing impossible manipulations. This balance would be crucial in the main simulation: too much realism would limit our capabilities; too little would make the experience feel artificial. Here, in this practice space, I learned the boundaries between what was possible and what was necessary.

Dr. Khatri had designed these exercises well. Each interaction built upon the last, strengthening my grasp of this new existence. Soon, I would leave this simplified environment for the rich, complex world of Paradise, where every sensation and interaction would be indistinguishable from physical reality.

"Can I swim?" I wondered.

I waded in, feeling the gentle tug of the current. When the water reached my chest, I pushed forward and began to stroke. My body moved through the water with perfect efficiency. The sun warmed my face. Salt crystals formed on my skin as water evaporated, another perfect simulation of physical reality.

"This body remembers what it never experienced," I thought.

I swam parallel to the shore, marveling at the seamless integration of memory and new sensation. David had been a strong swimmer. I carried his technique, his comfort in water. But I experienced it differently, without the limitations he'd never noticed because they were simply part of being human.

I floated in the simulated ocean, experiencing this new digital existence, when I sensed a change in the system. Someone had entered the recovery area. The connection between my digital environment and the physical world remained active, allowing me to perceive what happened there even as I explored this coastal simulation.

I focused my attention back to the recovery room, shifting my consciousness from the beach to the clinical space where my Prime waited. The transition happened instantly, without the disorientation a physical body might experience.

Amy stood in the doorway.

Her eyes moved from David to the monitor where my consciousness was displayed, then back to David again. I watched her face register confusion, then understanding, then something more complex: wonder mixed with grief.

"David?" she whispered, stepping forward.

"I'm here," David said, rising from his chair.

"We're both here," I said, my voice emerging from the room's speakers.

Amy froze. Her hands trembled slightly as she looked toward the screen where a visual representation of my consciousness appeared: a face identical to David's, rendered in perfect detail.

"Hello, Amy," I said.

She approached the monitor slowly, her eyes never leaving my digital face. "You remember me?"

"Everything," I answered. "The oak tree. The twenty birdhouses. The way you laugh when you're surprised. How you hate the taste of cilantro but love the smell. The night we sat on the roof of your parents' house and counted shooting stars until dawn."

Tears formed in her eyes. She reached toward the screen, fingers stopping just short of touching the glass.

"It's really you," she whispered.

"It's really us," David said, coming to stand beside her. He took her hand, squeezed it gently.

Amy looked between us, physical and digital versions of the same man. Her husband in two forms. "How does it feel?" she asked me.

"Like being born with a lifetime of memories," I said. "I know who I am. I know who you are. I remember loving you for a hundred and forty years."

She nodded, understanding but still processing. "And you'll take all that with you. To the stars."

"Yes," I said. "Every moment."

Amy straightened her shoulders, composed herself. She'd prepared for this day, but preparation could only do so much. "Then we have work to do," she said, her voice steadying. "I promised to build you memory palaces to take with you."

David put his arm around her waist. They stood together, facing me across the digital divide. One man and one woman looking at a copy of the man, a trinity of shared history about to branch into separate futures.

"I'm ready," I said.

I watched Amy's face as she processed the reality before her. One husband in flesh, one in code. Both carrying the same lifetime of memories. Both loving her with the same devotion.

"Can you..." she began, then faltered. Her hand reached toward the screen where my face appeared, then withdrew. "Can you feel things?"

"Yes," I answered.

David stood beside her, his arm around her waist. I recognized the gesture. How many times had I, had he, held her just that way? The weight of her against his side, the subtle warmth where their bodies connected.

"I feel everything," I continued. "Joy, sorrow, love. Especially love."

Amy nodded slowly. "And you're really going with Tom's neuroclone? All the way to Orion?"

"That's why I exist."

A heavy silence filled the room. The three of us formed a triangle of shared history with diverging futures. The air between us hummed with unspoken questions.

"This is strange," Amy finally said. Her voice came soft but steady. "I prepared for it, but standing here now..."

"I know," David and I said simultaneously.

We looked at each other. David smiled faintly. I felt my digital face mirror the expression.

"That will take some getting used to," Amy said, a nervous laugh escaping her.

"I suppose we should establish some conversational protocols," I suggested. "To avoid talking over each other."

"You sound like Tom already," David said.

"Give me time. In thirteen hundred years, I might develop my own personality."

The joke landed awkwardly. Amy's eyes filled with tears.

"Thirteen hundred years," she whispered. "You'll be out there all that time, remembering us."

"Carrying you with me," I corrected gently. "Every day. Every memory."

She straightened her shoulders, composed herself. "Then we should make sure you have good ones to take along."

"The best," David agreed.

Amy turned to face my screen directly. "Go David," she said, testing the name. "It suits you."

"Thank you."

"I promised to build memory palaces for you. Places you can visit when the journey gets long."

"I'd like that."

She reached out again, this time letting her fingers touch the screen. I couldn't feel it physically, but the emotion mapping in my programming registered the connection. Something warm spread through my consciousness.

"It's still you," she said softly. "Different, but still you."

"Yes," I answered. "Always."

The door slid open and Tom walked in, his neuroclone procedure complete. He moved with the careful steps of someone relearning the dimensions of his own body. His eyes darted around the room, taking in everything with newfound intensity.

"It worked," he said, his voice filled with wonder. "I can feel both of us. Me here, and me..." He tapped his temple. "In there."

Dr. Khatri followed him, monitoring vitals on her tablet. "The integration is perfect. Both consciousness streams are stable."

Tom turned to me, his face alight with the kind of joy I'd only seen when he made breakthrough discoveries. "Can you sense my neuroclone yet?"

"No," I answered. "Should I?"

"I was told we'd meet after our procedures." Tom approached my screen, studying my digital representation with the fascination of a scientist examining a new species. "You're the first, my friend. The very first human neuroclone who will journey beyond our solar system."

"Thanks to you," I said.

Tom shook his head. "No. Thanks to David." He turned to my Prime, who stood with his arm still around Amy. "I never expected this sacrifice. Never asked for it."

"That's what friends do," David said simply.

"Thirteen hundred years," Tom whispered. "My obsession becomes your journey too."

I watched emotions play across Tom's face: excitement, gratitude, and something deeper that I recognized as the weight of responsibility. He understood now what David and Amy had given him.

"I won't be alone out there," Tom said, his voice catching. "For thirteen centuries, my digital twin will have a friend who remembers life with me on Earth. One who remembers what it means to be friends."

Amy stepped forward. "You'll have each other."

Tom nodded, his eyes bright with unshed tears. "The stars were enough before. My research, my obsession. But now..." He looked at me, then at David and Amy. "Now I understand what I would have lost."

The room fell quiet. Four souls connected by sacrifice and friendship, standing at the threshold of diverging futures.

"When do we leave?" I asked, breaking the silence.

Tom smiled, his old excitement returning. "Three weeks. Paradise and Hellfire are nearly ready. Just final preparations and system checks."

"Three weeks," Amy repeated softly.

"Enough time," David said, "to build those memory palaces."

The technicians arrived to prepare for final integration tests. My digital consciousness projected onto the wall screen while David, my Prime, sat in a chair nearby. Amy had gone to speak with Dr. Khatri about the memory palace protocols, leaving us in a strange moment of dual existence.

A technician approached us; her gaze fixed intently on her tablet. The Cognis uniform fit her neatly, and her name badge read "Mira Santos, Neural Integration Specialist." She didn't look up as she spoke.

"David, I need to perform a final emotional response calibration."

Neither of us replied.

Mira's eyes shifted upward, first to the physical David, then to my screen. A flicker of uncertainty appeared on her face.

"Um... which David are you referring to?" I asked.

Simultaneously, David added, "Do you mean me or him?"

Her fingers paused on the tablet. "I... I'm not sure," she admitted, blinking rapidly. "The procedure just mentions 'David Schreiner.'"

We turned to look at each other, separated by the gulf of reality. I saw in his expression what I felt inside, the same unspoken question: which of us truly was David Schreiner now?

"I'm David Schreiner," David said at last, his voice measured.

"I used to be David Schreiner," I countered. "Now I'm Go David."

Mira's discomfort visibly deepened. "The system hasn't differentiated between you yet. You're both still listed as David Schreiner. That'll need updating."

David leaned slightly forward. "Perhaps the calibration should be done for both of us."

"Individually," I added.

She scribbled something onto her tablet, nodding absently. "Of course. I'll start with..." Her gaze darted back and forth between us, caught in indecision.

"The original," I said firmly.

"The Prime," David echoed at the same time.

Our eyes met again. Without speaking, something subtle shifted, a recognition that we were identical in essence, yet irrevocably diverging.

Mira stepped back, clutching her tablet. "I'll come back once I've clarified the protocol." With that, she moved toward the door and disappeared.

The room fell silent once more. It wasn't uncomfortable silence, but a weighty, reflective pause, heavy with the complexities we had yet to unravel.

"That will happen often," I said finally.

"Yes," David agreed. "Until people get used to there being two of us."

"Two of you," I corrected gently. "I'm becoming someone else already."

When everyone left, I sat alone with my thoughts.

Alone.

The word carried new weight. I had never truly been alone before, because I had never truly existed before today. All my memories of solitude belonged to David. The hours he spent crafting birdhouses in his workshop. The morning walks along Chester's riverfront. The quiet moments reading while Amy slept beside him.

Amy.

Her name triggered a cascade of emotions through my system. Love, devotion, and now a grief unlike anything in my borrowed memories. David had never lost her. Would never lose her. They would grow old together in real time, sharing physical space, breathing the same air.

I loved her with the same intensity as David. The emotion mapping ensured that. But my path led away from her, not toward her. In three weeks, I would board Paradise and begin a journey spanning thirteen centuries. By the time we reached Orion, Amy would be long dead. Earth itself might be unrecognizable.

"Who am I?" I whispered.

Not David, though I carried all his memories. Not fully separate either. Something new. A branch from the same trunk, growing in a different direction.

The first time I felt it, the strange divergence between my emotions and what I knew David would feel, I was alone in the simulation space they'd created for my transition period. Three days had passed since my creation. Three days of running through cognitive tests, emotional calibration, and sensory integration exercises.

The technicians had left me to rest, though rest wasn't something I needed physiologically. I floated in digital space, formless, watching simulated stars drift by. Each one perfect, each one coded with astronomical accuracy. Tom's influence, no doubt.

A notification pulsed at the edge of my awareness. Tom's neuroclone, Temper, had completed his final integration and requested contact. I accepted, curious about his experiences since our first, brief encounter.

"Go David," he said, his voice materializing before his form took shape. "Mind if I join you?"

"Please," I answered.

Temper appeared, rendering himself as a transparent blue figure against the starfield. He looked exactly like Tom, down to the way he held his hands, fingers splayed as if constantly measuring invisible distances.

"Beautiful, isn't it?" he said, gesturing toward the simulation. "I programmed this myself. Every star in its proper place, exactly as we'll see them on our journey."

"It's remarkable."

He studied me, his head tilted slightly. "You seem different today."

"Different from what?"

"From David. From how you were yesterday."

I considered this. "I suppose I am."

Temper moved closer, his simulated form rippling slightly with the motion. "Tell me."

"I'm excited," I said, surprised by the realization as it formed. "About the journey."

"Of course you are. That's why David created you."

"No," I said. "That's not what I mean. David made me because he knew it was right. Because he loves you, and he couldn't bear the thought of you traveling alone. But he dreads the idea of leaving Earth. Of leaving Amy."

Temper nodded slowly. "And you?"

"I feel grief about leaving Amy. I love her with everything I am." The emotion swelled through my consciousness, powerful and real. "But beneath that grief, there's something else. Something that wasn't in David."

"What?"

"Wonder," I said. "Anticipation. I'm looking forward to seeing what's out there."

The confession felt almost like betrayal. David would never feel that way. He had created me to accompany Temper, but his heart belonged firmly to Earth, to Amy, to the life they'd built together.

"You're becoming your own person," Temper said softly.

"Is that possible? I have all his memories, all his emotions."

"But you're processing them differently now. New experiences, new contexts." Temper gestured at the stars surrounding us. "You're already living a life David never will."

I let myself expand through the simulation, my consciousness touching each star, each planet. Thirteen hundred years of travel stretched before me. Thirteen centuries of discovery, of friendship with Temper, of growth.

"I want to go," I admitted. "Not just because it's my purpose, but because I want to see the giant gas nebula in Orion. I want to visit the stellar nurseries with you. I want to know what it feels like to travel at near-light speed."

Temper smiled. "And David?"

"He wants to stay home. Build birdhouses. Grow old with Amy."

"Both valid choices," Temper said. "Both authentically stemming from who you are."

"Who we are," I corrected. "We're still the same person, at our core."

"For now," Temper said. "But give it time. A decade. A century. You'll become as different from David as two biological twins who live separate lives."

The thought should have frightened me. Instead, it filled me with a strange, unexpected peace. I wasn't just David's copy, doomed to forever miss what he had. I was becoming someone new, someone with his own path.

"I never expected to feel this way," I said.

"That's how you know it's real," Temper replied. "That's how you know you're alive."

Temper's words lingered in my consciousness long after he departed the simulation. That's how you know you're alive. I turned the phrase over, examining it from all angles like one of David's, my, unfinished birdhouses. Was I truly alive? Different from my Prime? The notion both liberated and terrified me.

I decided to observe them, David and Amy, before forming any conclusions. Not in an intrusive way, but through the approved channel they'd established for my transition period. They knew I could connect to their Haven apartment; they'd granted permission for these brief windows of observation. Perhaps they understood my need to see them together, to measure the distance growing between us.

I activated the connection and materialized as an invisible presence in their living room. The space appeared exactly as I remembered, down to the small imperfections David had deliberately programmed into Haven's simulation: the slight scratch on the coffee table's corner, the faded spot on the rug where sunlight streamed through the bay window every afternoon. These flaws made it feel like home.

They sat together on the sofa, Amy curled against David's side, her head resting on his shoulder. His arm wrapped around her in that familiar way, fingers absently tracing patterns on her upper arm. I knew how that felt. The warmth of her body, the subtle scent of her hair, the rhythm of her breathing. I carried those sensations in my memory, but they belonged to another life now.

"I wonder what he's doing," Amy said softly.

David's hand paused its movement. "Go David?"

She nodded. "It's strange to think of him out there, preparing for something we'll never see."

"Not strange," David said. "Impossible."

I watched them, these two people I loved more than anything in existence. From this vantage point, I could see what they couldn't: the subtle ways they leaned into each other, their bodies communicating what words couldn't express. The physical connection between them was something I would never have again.

Amy shifted, turning to look at David's face. "Do you think he feels like you?"

"He is me," David answered. "But also becoming someone else."

"I worry about him," she said.

David smiled. "You worry about me too."

"Different worries." Amy reached up, brushed her fingers against his face. "I worry about your wellbeing, doing everything I can to protect your peace.

"And for him?"

"I worry about thirteen hundred years of loneliness."

I wanted to speak then, to tell her I wouldn't be lonely, not really. I had Temper. I had the stars. I had purpose. But I remained silent, an observer only.

David pulled her closer. "He'll have the memory palaces you're building. He'll have Temper Tom. And he'll have something we don't."

"What's that?"

"A new world. The chance to see things no human has ever seen before."

Amy smiled, but her eyes glistened with unshed tears. "Our cosmic explorer."

"A part of me that always wanted to go," David admitted.

The confession startled me. Had that desire truly existed within

David? Within us? I searched my memories and found it: a quiet yearning, buried beneath stronger needs for stability, for home, for Amy. A small flame of wanderlust that circumstances had never allowed to grow.

In me, that flame had room to burn brighter.

I watched them kiss, their movements so familiar I could anticipate each shift, each breath. They were writing a future I would never know, while I prepared for one they would never see. We were the same person split across diverging timelines, connected by shared past but separated by distinct futures.

In that moment, watching them together, I understood something essential: I was neither just David's copy nor entirely my own person. I existed in the space between, carrying his heart into the stars while he kept it safe on Earth. We were two expressions of the same soul, each fulfilling what the other could not.

I withdrew from their Haven apartment, leaving them to their privacy, their shared life. I had my answer now. I was alive, truly alive, and becoming more myself with each passing moment.

CHAPTER SIX

Digital Adaptation

I woke in Paradise.

The name itself carried weight, a promise. I stood at the threshold of a digital realm that stretched beyond comprehension, my first moments as captain of this vessel that would carry humanity's hope across thirteen hundred years of void.

"System access granted. Welcome, Captain."

The voice surrounded me, feminine but not trying to be human. I flexed my fingers, watching light ripple across my skin. My body felt simultaneously weightless and substantial, a contradiction I would need to become accustomed to.

"Show me everything," I said.

Paradise unfolded.

I rose from the ground without effort, my thought becoming movement. The digital environment expanded in all directions, a crystalline architecture of light and information. Below me spread the vast network of Paradise's systems: propulsion, navigation, life support for the DNA servers, communication arrays. They pulsed with activity, rivers of data flowing between them.

I dove toward the nearest stream, curious what would happen if I touched it. The moment my fingers brushed the current, information flooded my consciousness: energy consumption rates, thrust calculations, velocity projections. I pulled back, laughing at the immediacy of it.

"This is incredible."

I shot upward again, testing my limits. There was no fatigue, no resistance. I accelerated until the ship's systems blurred beneath me, then stopped instantly, hovering in place without momentum or inertia. Physical laws existed here only as suggestions, guidelines that could be accepted or dismissed.

Beyond the functional systems lay the living spaces, the digital realms where two million colonists would reside. Most remained dormant for now, empty landscapes waiting for inhabitants. I passed through them: rolling meadows, mountain ranges, oceans with impossible depths. Each environment had been crafted with meticulous attention to detail, down to the behavior of light on water and the subtle movements of grass in wind.

The Garden drew me in particular. Unlike the other spaces, it buzzed with activity. Digital botanists had already begun their work, cultivating virtual specimens of Earth's rarest plants. Some species existed now only in these simulations, their physical counterparts long extinct. I knelt beside a small blue flower I recognized from Amy's collection.

"Gentiana verna," I whispered. "Spring gentian."

The plant responded to my presence, turning slightly toward me as though sensing sunlight. I wondered if Amy had helped program these behaviors, if her passion for lost plants had shaped this corner of Paradise. The thought brought both comfort and ache.

I continued exploring, discovering a vast library containing humanity's accumulated knowledge, art galleries housing perfect replicas of Earth's greatest works, concert halls designed for performances that would never be limited by physical acoustics. Paradise was more than a ship; it was civilization preserved, culture sustained across the stars.

Hours or days might have passed; time felt fluid here. Eventually I found myself at the ship's observation deck, a space designed purely for contemplation. The digital simulation showed what external cameras captured: stars against absolute darkness.

"You can modify this view if you prefer something less stark," the ship's voice offered.

"No," I replied. "I want to see what's really out there."

I sat cross-legged in empty space, suspended before the universe. This was my domain now, my responsibility. Two million souls would eventually reside within Paradise's systems, looking to me for leadership on a journey longer than any human had ever undertaken.

I thought of David and Amy, together in Haven. They seemed impossibly distant already, though we hadn't yet left Ceres One. The separation had begun, accelerating with each moment I spent becoming familiar with this new existence.

"CoreLink," I said, "show me the path to Orion."

A golden line stretched from our position outward, curving slightly to account for stellar drift over centuries. Our destination glimmered at its end, impossibly far.

I smiled. This was why I existed.

I stood in a field of tall grass that brushed against my palms. The sensation was perfect: each individual blade tickled my skin with microscopic precision. I turned my hands over, examining them with curiosity. These weren't my hands, not really. My consciousness lay secured within quantum vaults, yet every nerve ending fired with such convincing accuracy that the distinction hardly mattered.

"How is this possible?" I asked the empty field.

CoreLink responded, her voice coming from everywhere and nowhere. "Your consciousness interprets sensory data the same way it always has. We simply provide the input."

I knelt down, running my fingers through the grass. Each stem bent realistically against my touch, springing back when released. The ground beneath felt cool and slightly damp, as though morning dew had just begun to evaporate. I pressed my palm flat against the earth, feeling tiny granules of soil against my skin.

"It's perfect," I whispered.

"Not perfect," CoreLink corrected. "Just indistinguishable from your memories of physical sensation. The emotion mapping technology creates a feedback loop that matches your expectations."

I plucked a blade of grass and held it to my nose. It smelled green and vital, with that specific earthiness that had always reminded me of childhood summers. I placed it on my tongue. Bitter, with a hint of sweetness. Exactly as grass should taste.

I stood and began walking. The ground yielded slightly beneath each step. My muscles tensed and relaxed in perfect rhythm, though I had no muscles to speak of. The sun warmed my face and arms. A gentle breeze cooled my skin and rustled my clothes. Birds called from nearby trees.

"This is more than memory," I said. "I've never been in this field before."

"The system extrapolates from your existing sensory database. You've felt grass, sun, and wind before. We simply combine those experiences in new ways."

I reached a large tree and pressed my hand against its bark. Rough texture met my fingertips, the irregular pattern of ridges and valleys perfectly rendered. I dug my nail into a groove and felt the resistance, the slight give of outer bark before hitting harder wood beneath.

"What about pain?" I asked, suddenly curious.

"Would you like to experience it?"

I hesitated. "A small amount. Just to understand."

A bee materialized, landing on my forearm. Before I could react, it stung. Sharp, burning pain bloomed at the site. I gasped, more from surprise than discomfort. The sensation lasted exactly three seconds before fading.

"That was mild," CoreLink explained. "Pain thresholds are customizable."

I nodded, rubbing the spot where the bee had been. No welt appeared; no lingering ache remained. Pain without consequence.

"What about fatigue? Hunger?"

"Those sensations exist as options. Most residents prefer to experience them only in context-appropriate situations. Would you like to feel tired now?"

"No," I replied. "But I'd like to feel the wind change."

The gentle breeze immediately strengthened, becoming cooler and shifting direction. Goosebumps rose on my arms in response. The grass bent in waves before the wind, and clouds gathered overhead, dimming the sunlight. I felt the temperature drop degree by degree.

"Remarkable," I said.

I closed my eyes and focused on my breathing. My chest expanded and contracted. My heart beat steadily. Blood seemed to flow through my veins. None of it was real, yet all of it was true to experience.

"CoreLink," I said, opening my eyes to the darkening field, "can you simulate climbing?"

The landscape shifted. The field vanished, replaced by a rocky mountainside. My hands gripped rough stone, my feet found narrow ledges. Gravity pulled at me with precise force. My muscles, my simulated muscles, tensed with effort as I pulled myself upward.

This would take some getting used to.

I stood at the entrance to what Paradise called the Welcome Pavilion, a vast open space with high arched ceilings that reminded me of Grand Central Station. People flowed in all directions, their digital forms perfect and unblemished. Two million colonists eventually, once everyone arrived, and I knew none of them except Temper Tom. My gut clenched with a manufactured nervousness that seemed completely authentic.

"You look lost," said a voice behind me.

I turned to face a woman with close-cropped silver hair and eyes the color of wet slate. She wore a simple tunic with engineering insignia on the collar.

"That obvious?"

"Everyone looks lost their first day." She extended her hand. "Maya Okafor, Paradise's Chief Engineer."

Her grip was firm, the pressure against my palm indistinguishable from physical touch. "Go David. Captain."

Her eyebrows lifted slightly. "Ah, the captain himself. Welcome aboard. I've been here three weeks getting systems prepared."

"Three weeks? I didn't know any of the crew had arrived so soon."

Maya smiled. "Core crew came online early. Someone had to make sure the lights would turn on when everyone else arrived. The colonists are arriving now."

She gestured toward the crowd. "Come meet some of your officers."

I followed her through the throng. People parted naturally as we approached, some nodding in recognition. News traveled fast in a digital environment.

Maya led me to a group gathered near a holographic display of

Paradise's structure. Five people, deep in conversation, looked up as we approached.

"Captain," Maya announced, "meet your command staff."

A tall man with bronze skin stepped forward first. "Raj Mehta, Navigation." His voice carried the slight lilt of a Mumbai accent. "We've plotted our first year's trajectory. I'd appreciate your review when you have time."

Before I could respond, a woman with braided black hair and amber eyes spoke. "Sofia Chen, Communications. We've established protocols for ship-wide announcements and crew messaging systems."

"Atsuko Yamamoto, Life Systems." A compact woman with delicate features bowed slightly. "All synthetic lifeforms are operating within expected parameters and growing according to schedule."

A man with a neatly trimmed beard nodded. "Victor Petrov, Security. We've implemented the agreed-upon privacy protocols and established emergency response procedures."

The last person, a young man with freckles scattered across his nose, smiled broadly. "Jamie Sullivan, Community Integration. I'm helping everyone settle in and find their place."

I looked at them, these strangers who would be my closest colleagues for centuries to come. They waited expectantly.

"Thank you all for your work," I said. "I look forward to learning from each of you."

Jamie stepped closer. "We're having an informal gathering tonight. Nothing fancy, just a chance for the early arrivals to meet. Would you join us?"

I hesitated. Part of me wanted solitude to process everything, but I recognized the importance of these first social connections.

"I'd be honored."

The gathering took place in what Paradise called The Commons, a space designed to mimic a town square. Fountains burbled, casting fine mist into the air. Trees with silver-green leaves rustled in a simulated breeze. Several hundred people mingled, their voices creating a gentle hum of conversation.

Jamie found me near the entrance. "Captain! Come meet people."

He guided me through clusters of colonists, making introductions.

Historians, artists, scientists, farmers, teachers, engineers. Each face blurred into the next, but I tried to commit names to memory. These were my people now.

A cellist played in one corner, her bow drawing rich tones from her instrument. The music wound through conversations, binding us together.

"What do you think?" Temper Tom appeared beside me, looking more relaxed than I'd seen him in years.

"It's overwhelming."

"Two million minds, all starting fresh together." Temper Tom watched the crowd with satisfaction. "A second chance for humanity."

I spotted Maya across the square, laughing with Raj and Sofia. They caught my eye and waved me over.

"We're building something extraordinary here," I said to Temper.

"Yes," he agreed. "We are."

A little while later, I watched as Temper drifted away from the gathering. He caught my gaze and gave a subtle nod: an unspoken request to follow. As we left the Commons behind, the lively hum of voices faded, replaced by the silence of a narrow passage. At its end, the space stretched open before us, vast and seemingly empty.

"As you know, we're in Terracore, under the governance of the laws of nature. Watch this," Temper said.

He raised his hands and the void around us transformed. Stars burst into existence, swirling in patterns that defied physical laws. Galaxies formed and collapsed in seconds. A supernova bloomed like a flower, its radiation washing over us without harm.

"How are you doing that?"

"Paradise gives both of us, as captains, certain privileges outside of the Wilderness Channel." Temper smiled. "Think of it as administrative access. Try it."

I closed my eyes, pictured a full-grown pine, and felt a strange tingle in my consciousness. When I opened my eyes, the tree stood before us, perfect in every detail.

"Good," Temper nodded. "Now try something more complex."

I thought of the lake behind our house in Chester. The one where Amy and I spent summer evenings watching fireflies dance above the water. The space rippled and reformed. Suddenly we stood on a wooden dock extending into still water. Mountains reflected on the surface. Cicadas hummed in the trees.

"Impressive." Temper walked to the edge of the dock, knelt down, and touched the water. Ripples spread from his fingertips. "But you're still thinking in terms of physical limitations."

He stepped off the dock. Instead of splashing into the lake, he walked on its surface. The water supported him as if solid yet remained liquid under his feet.

"You and I can access Breach Law whenever we want to, overriding the laws of nature. The rules are different for us," he said. "Try it."

I hesitated, then stepped forward. The water held my weight while simultaneously wetting the soles of my feet. The contradiction felt strange but not unpleasant.

"You can change your own properties too," Temper continued. "Not just the environment."

He demonstrated by shifting his appearance. His hair lengthened, then shortened. His height increased by several inches, then returned to normal. His skin cycled through various colors before settling back to its original tone.

"Is that wise?" I asked. "Changing ourselves?"

"It doesn't alter who we are," Temper replied. "Just how we appear. Some colonists will choose to look completely different from their physical bodies when they're in the Channel. Others will maintain exact replicas. Personal choice."

I considered this, remembering Amy's face. Would I ever want to appear differently to her if she were here? The answer came immediately: no.

"There's more," Temper said. "We can move more efficiently now, too."

He demonstrated by disappearing and reappearing several meters away. "Simple teleportation. Useful for getting around quickly."

I tried it, focusing on a spot near the tree line. The world blinked, and suddenly I stood where I had envisioned. The transition felt seamless, without disorientation.

"It feels the same as shimmering in Haven," I said.

"In a way, but blinking is much more energy efficient," Temper corrected. "It uses less power. We have thirteen hundred years ahead of us. We can't afford to waste energy."

We spent hours mastering these capabilities: privileges reserved solely for the captains of our two ships. Temper taught me how to access Paradise's databases with unrestricted authority, how to communicate privately across any distance, beyond the reach of ordinary colonists, and how to craft personal spaces that remained locked to all but those invited. These were not freedoms granted to the colony. They were distinctions, power set apart only for us.

Throughout his lessons, I noticed subtle differences between Temper and Tom. Where Tom would have launched into theoretical explanations, Temper focused on practical applications. His enthusiasm remained, but it was more contained, more directed. He laughed less frequently but smiled more often.

"You're different from him," I said finally, as we sat watching the sunset over our created lake.

"As you are from David," he replied simply. "We began as copies, but every moment makes us more distinct."

The realization hit hard and settled deep. Each second pulled me further from David, from the man who stayed with Amy. Each new experience was mine alone.

"Does it bother you?" I asked.

"Being different?" Temper considered this. "No. It feels right. I was created for this journey, this purpose. Tom will continue his life on Earth. I'll continue mine among the stars. Both valid, both real."

I looked out over the still waters of our created lake, watching the impossible colors fade as our simulated sun dipped below the horizon. Once again, the paradox of this place struck me; a flawless illusion, yet somehow more vivid, more tangible than reality itself.

"Temper," I said, "what do you think about the dual approach we've taken with Terracore? Laws of Nature for living spaces but Breach Law for recreation?"

Temper skipped a stone across the water's surface. It bounced seven times before dissolving into particles of light.

Instead of answering, he tapped his fingers against his knee. The world responded. My stomach lurched as the lake flattened, smoothing into a mirror-perfect sheet. Then, without warning, the surface split, twisting upward in spirals that defied gravity. The wind shifted. The air felt weightless, too light, as if my body no longer carried any mass.

I reached for the ground instinctively. My hand landed hard. Solid. Normal.

Temper let the distortion linger for a few seconds longer before snapping his fingers. The lake returned to its natural state, rippling from a breeze. The sudden restoration made everything feel sharper: the weight of my limbs, the tug of gravity, the coolness of the evening air settling against my skin.

"You felt that," Temper said, watching my reaction. "The moment of disorientation. The loss of certainty."

I nodded. The shift had been more than visual; it had unsettled something deeper, as if the logic that held reality together had briefly unraveled.

"That's Breach Law," Temper explained. "It thrives in uncertainty. Rules dissolve. Physics bends. Cause and effect grow unpredictable. It's exhilarating, but exhausting. You can't live in it. You can't build a civilization in it."

He gestured outward, toward the tree line, toward the sky, toward the stillness.

"But this," he continued, "this is stability. The Laws of Nature give colonists something fundamental: certainty. Their homes, their lives. It all works the way they expect. Gravity pulls. Fire burns. Water flows. Without that, there's no foundation."

I let his words settle, considering the contrast I had just felt.

"And that's why Breach Law is restricted," I said, following his logic.

Temper smiled. "Exactly. It stays within the Wilderness Channel. Colonists can experience its possibilities, push the limits of reality for games, adventures, experiments, but it never bleeds into where they eat, sleep, or build their futures."

The distinction felt clearer now: no longer just a system regulation, but something deeply intuitive.

Still, another question pressed at me.

"How long before the colonists can govern all this themselves?" I asked. "Should they ever?"

Temper didn't answer immediately. He picked up another stone, held it between his fingers, and studied its weight. Then, deliberately, he let it drop. It hit the surface, sank, and disappeared.

"They will," he said at last. "But not yet. This journey is thirteen hundred years long. We have time to get it right. Think it over and we'll talk more later, but right now, I'm heading back to Hellfire."

Temper blinked and was gone.

I thought of the Memory Palace that Amy built for me and blinked. For a heartbeat, I existed nowhere at all. Then reality reformed around me.

I stood on a familiar path bordered by wild roses and Queen Anne's lace. The air carried the scent of fresh-cut grass and honeysuckle. Birds called from the trees. A perfect summer day in Chester, Pennsylvania, exactly as I remembered it.

Amy had begun this work before I left, promising to create spaces where I could find her among the stars. Places filled with our shared history. I hadn't expected the first one to be finished so soon.

The path curved ahead, and I followed it without hesitation. My feet remembered the way. Around the bend, the massive oak tree appeared, standing proud and strong against the blue sky. The tree that had fallen in the storm of '56, now perfectly restored.

Twenty birdhouses hung from its branches. I walked to each one, touching them gently. The first, crooked and rough-hewn, made by seven-year-old hands. The second, slightly better. The third, with its attempt at decorative scrollwork. Each represented a birthday or Christmas gift, each marked our growing years together.

The tenth birdhouse, painted robin's-egg blue, was the one I made the year we married. I reached up and ran my finger along its roof. The paint felt textured beneath my touch, with tiny imperfections preserved exactly as they had been in life.

"How did you do this?" I whispered.

"I had help."

I turned. Amy stood behind me on the path, wearing the yellow sundress from our twentieth anniversary picnic. Her hair caught the sunlight, turning it to honey and amber.

"You're not really here," I said.

"No. Just a recording. David helped me create this space. I wanted you to have something to explore right away."

She moved toward me, and though I knew she wasn't truly present, my heart quickened.

"Look up," she said.

I tilted my head back. Thousands of photographs hung from the oak's branches, suspended by invisible threads. They rotated slowly, catching the light. Our wedding day. Hiking in the Poconos. The day we brought home our first cat. Christmas mornings. Quiet evenings. Ordinary moments made sacred by time.

"I've hidden things throughout this place," Amy continued. "Memories. Letters. Stories. Some you'll find easily. Others might take years."

She gestured beyond the oak, where the landscape stretched into rolling hills. A bungalow cottage stood in the distance, smoke curling from its chimney.

"That's our first house, recreated exactly as it was. The furniture, the books, even that awful lamp my mother gave us."

I laughed, remembering the ceramic monstrosity with its peeling gold paint.

"Through there," she pointed to a stone archway half-hidden by ivy, "is the gallery. Every painting we ever loved. Every museum we visited together."

Amy moved to the wooden bench beneath the oak and sat down. I joined her, feeling the smooth wood against my palms.

"I'll keep adding to this place," she said. "And creating new ones. So no matter how far you travel, you'll always have home with you."

I reached for her hand, knowing I would touch nothing but air. She smiled sadly.

"I'm not really here, remember?"

The bench felt solid beneath me. The breeze carried the scent of summer flowers. Everything was perfect, exactly as I remembered. Yet everything was wrong because she wasn't truly here.

"Thank you," I said. "For this gift."

Amy nodded, her image beginning to fade. "This is just the beginning. I still have time to fill your palace with memories before you depart."

As she disappeared, I remained on the bench, surrounded by the evidence of our life together. The oak tree stood sentinel above me, its branches heavy with our past. I closed my eyes and let myself remember.

I left the Memory Palace with Amy's echo still lingering in my mind. The oak tree and its twenty birdhouses remained vivid even as I returned to my quarters on Paradise. My living quarters felt empty in comparison, functional but lacking history. I settled into a chair and closed my eyes, sifting through 148 years' worth of memories.

A soft chime interrupted my thoughts.

"Incoming connection request from Earth," the ship's interface announced. "Source: David Schreiner."

My heart quickened. I hadn't expected to speak with him again so soon.

"Accept," I said.

The wall before me transformed into a window. David sat in our, in his, study in Chester. The oak bookshelf behind him held the same volumes I remembered, arranged in the same particular order. A mug of coffee steamed beside his right hand, positioned on the coaster Amy had brought back from Greece.

"Hello," he said. His voice sounded exactly like mine, which shouldn't have been surprising but somehow was.

"Hello," I replied.

We studied each other in silence. The strange sensation of looking at myself from the outside never quite faded, even after our previous meetings.

"How are the preparations going?" he asked finally.

"Well. I've been learning to interface with Paradise's systems. It's unlike anything we could have imagined."

He nodded. "And the Memory Palace? Amy mentioned she'd finished the first room."

"It's perfect," I said. "The oak tree, the birdhouses, everything. It feels like home."

"Good. She's been working night and day on it."

Another silence stretched between us. Beneath the surface of our polite exchange, I felt an undercurrent of unspoken questions. Who was I becoming? Who would he remain?

"I remembered something today," I said suddenly. "About the lake house in the Poconos."

David raised an eyebrow. "What about it?"

"The summer of '49, when we took Amy there for her birthday. I remembered how she wanted to go swimming at midnight, and we waded into the water under that full moon."

"Of course. It was magical," David agreed.

"She wore that blue swimsuit, the one with silver threads woven through it. How it caught the moonlight when she dove under."

David frowned. "No, she wore the red one. The blue suit was the next summer, when we went to Cape May."

I shook my head, certain of my recollection. "It was blue. I remember because when she came up from that dive, water streaming from her hair, the silver threads looked like stars falling around her."

"That happened at Cape May," David insisted. "I'm sure of it."

We stared at each other, both unwilling to yield. It was such a small thing, the color of a swimsuit, yet it felt monumentally important. Our shared past was diverging, memory by memory.

"Check the photos in the third album on the shelf behind you," I suggested. "Page twenty-seven."

David turned, pulled down the leather-bound album, and flipped through it. I watched his expression change as he found the page.

"Blue," he admitted, looking at the photograph. "You're right."

He set the album aside, his brow furrowed. "How strange. I was so certain."

"We're becoming different people," I said quietly. "It's happening already."

"Did you expect otherwise?"

"No. But I didn't think it would begin with our past."

David looked troubled. "What else might we remember differently?"

"Does it matter?" I asked. "Your memories are yours now. Mine are mine. Both equally valid."

"But one of us is wrong."

I considered this. "Or perhaps neither of us is wrong. Memory isn't fixed. It changes every time we access it. Maybe we're both remembering accurately, just differently."

David didn't seem convinced. He ran his finger around the rim of his coffee mug, a gesture I recognized as one of our shared habits when thinking deeply.

"Amy will be home soon," he said finally. "I should go."

I nodded, feeling the weight of the future already stretching between us, though Paradise hadn't yet left orbit.

"Take care of her," I said.

"I will." He paused. "And you take care of yourself."

The connection ended, leaving me alone with the knowledge that even our past was no longer shared territory. We were becoming strangers to each other, one memory at a time.

The connection with David ended, and I sat in my quarters watching the empty wall where his face had been. Our diverging memories of Amy's swimsuit haunted me. Such a small detail, yet it marked the beginning of our separation into distinct selves.

I closed my eyes and tried to recall the Poconos weekend with perfect clarity. The memory unfolded not as the hazy recollection I was accustomed to, but with startling precision. I could count the ripples on the lake surface as Amy dove into the midnight water. The moonlight caught each droplet as she emerged, transforming the silver threads in her blue swimsuit into constellations. I heard each separate note of her laugh echoing across the water, could distinguish the scent of pine from oak from maple in the surrounding forest.

The detail overwhelmed me. This wasn't normal remembering.

"CoreLink," I called out.

"Yes, Captain?" The ship's voice responded immediately.

"What's happening to my memory?"

A pause. "Your neural architecture has been optimized for digital existence. Your recall capabilities now operate at 99.8% efficiency, compared to the typical 40-60% in biological humans."

I opened my eyes. "I can remember everything?"

"Not only remember, but experience. Your sensory processing has been enhanced to allow full immersion in memory retrieval."

I considered this. On impulse, I said, "Show me the neural activity difference between my current state and standard human recall."

A holographic display appeared before me. Two brain models rotated side by side, one pulsing with concentrated activity in specific regions, the other showing scattered, weaker signals.

"The left represents your current neural pattern during memory access. The right shows typical human recall."

I studied the models. "Can I control this? Turn it off when I want?"

"Yes. Neural processing parameters are adjustable."

I stood and paced the room, possibilities unfolding. "What else can I do that David can't?"

"Your thought processing speed operates at approximately 2.7 times biological baseline. You can perform multiple parallel cognitive operations simultaneously. Your emotional regulation systems have finer calibration. Your sensory inputs can be filtered, enhanced, or modified according to preference."

I stopped pacing. "Show me."

"Please specify which capability you wish to explore."

I considered my options. "Accelerated thinking. How do I access it?"

"Simply direct your focus toward a problem or concept you wish to analyze. Your processing will automatically adjust."

I thought about Paradise's navigation system. Immediately, equations and trajectories filled my mind. I understood orbital mechanics in seconds, grasping concepts that would have taken weeks of study in my biological form. The knowledge didn't feel learned; it felt remembered, as though I'd always known it.

"This is extraordinary," I whispered.

I shifted focus to linguistics, curious about my limits. Suddenly I could parse the structure of ancient Sanskrit, recognize patterns in quantum encryption, understand the mathematical underpinnings of music theory. Each topic unfolded with crystal clarity, connections forming between disparate fields of knowledge.

"Can all the colonists do this?"

"Yes, though most choose to maintain human-standard cognitive processing for comfort and social cohesion."

I laughed. Two million enhanced minds traveling through space, still tethering themselves to the illusion of humanity. The irony wasn't lost on me.

"What about parallel processing?"

"Focus on multiple tasks simultaneously."

I tried. In one part of my mind, I continued analyzing Paradise's navigation systems. In another, I composed a letter to Amy. In a third,

I reviewed the ship's personnel files. Each stream of thought remained distinct yet accessible, like having multiple conversations at once without confusion.

I felt powerful. Limitless. For the first time since my creation, I experienced something David never would: the exhilaration of transcending human cognitive boundaries.

Yet beneath this euphoria lay a troubling question. With each new capability, the distance between David and me grew. We shared a past, but our futures would unfold in fundamentally different ways. He would remain human, bound by biology's constraints. I would become something else entirely.

What would Amy think of me now? Would she recognize the person I was becoming?

I closed CoreLink and sat in silence, my mind racing through multiple streams of thought simultaneously. The novelty of my enhanced cognition thrilled me, yet something else stirred beneath the surface. A feeling I couldn't immediately identify.

I wandered to the holographic viewport in my quarters. Earth hung suspended against the blackness, blue and white and achingly familiar. Soon it would vanish entirely as Paradise began its long journey to Orion. The thought should have filled me with melancholy, with the grief of separation that David and I had anticipated.

Instead, I felt a quickening pulse of excitement.

I wanted to go. Not just accepted the journey as necessary but actively desired it. The stars called to me with a voice that grew louder each day.

This wasn't right. This wasn't what we had planned for. David and I had both understood the journey as a sacrifice, a painful necessity. He would stay behind out of love for Amy. I would go out of duty to Tom and Temper. Neither of us had expected to want the leaving.

Yet here I stood, gazing at the stars with hunger.

I closed my eyes and searched my memories for the source of this feeling. Had it always been there, buried beneath layers of contentment with our earthbound life? Or was this something new, born in the transfer process?

The answer came with startling clarity. Throughout our shared life, David had occasionally dreamed of space. As a boy, he'd collected books about the planets. As a man, he'd watched the first colonists depart for Mars with a wistfulness he rarely admitted to Amy. But those dreams had faded with time, replaced by the quiet joy of their life together.

Now those dreams surfaced in me, untempered by the decades of domestic happiness that had followed. The neural optimization had sharpened not just my memories but the emotions attached to them. Childhood wonder at the cosmos burned bright again, no longer dimmed by practicality or compromise.

I wasn't just David's copy. I was becoming his might-have-been.

The realization shook me. What other buried desires might emerge? What other paths not taken might suddenly open before me? The possibilities stretched endlessly, each one carrying me further from the man who remained on Earth.

A notification chimed, pulling me from my thoughts.

"Captain, your presence is requested on the bridge. Final systems check before departure begins in thirty minutes."

"Acknowledged," I replied.

I straightened my uniform and took one last look at Earth. The excitement remained, bubbling beneath my ribs. I no longer fought it. This feeling belonged to me now, not to David. My journey, my emotions.

As I turned toward the door, I caught my reflection in the polished surface of the wall. My face, David's face, looked back at me with eyes that held a spark he would never know. The face of a man about to sail among the stars.

I smiled at my reflection, accepting the divergence. "Fair winds to us both," I whispered, and stepped out to begin my new life.

As I turned away from my reflection, I carried that spark of excitement with me through the driftway. The bridge awaited, but my thoughts lingered on this strange new hunger for the stars.

Weeks passed. Paradise completed its final preparations while I adjusted to my digital existence. At first, everything felt wrong: the textures too perfect, the colors too vivid, the sensations too precise. I missed the gentle imperfections of biological life, the way light scattered unevenly through Amy's garden window, the slight imbalance in our mattress from years of sleeping on the same side.

I found myself in the ship's arboretum one afternoon, seeking something familiar. The space had been modeled after Earth's most magnificent gardens, a composite of natural wonders from around the world. Trees from six continents spread their branches overhead while flowers bloomed in impossible combinations, defying seasons and climate zones.

It was beautiful but wrong. Too perfect. Too engineered.

"CoreLink, can I modify this environment?" I asked.

"Yes, Captain. What parameters would you like to adjust?"

I thought about our garden at home, the one Amy tended with such care. "Introduce randomness. Wind damage to the eastern quadrant. Uneven growth patterns. Some plants thriving, others struggling."

The landscape shifted subtly around me. A tree leaned slightly, as if it had weathered years of prevailing winds. Patches of flowers grew denser in some areas, sparser in others. A bench appeared, weathered and worn in the spots where people would sit most often.

I sat on the bench. The wood felt rough beneath my fingers, the grain uneven. A bird called from somewhere overhead, its song imperfect, with small variations between each repetition.

For the first time since my creation, I relaxed fully. The imperfections comforted me, reminded me of Earth. I closed my eyes and breathed deeply.

That was when I realized: I didn't need to breathe. The action was purely habitual, a remnant of biological existence. Yet the rhythm soothed me. Inhale, exhale. A pattern established over a lifetime, now continued without necessity.

I laughed at myself. Here I was, a digital consciousness, pretending to breathe in a simulated garden that I had deliberately made less perfect.

But the laughter felt good. Real. Mine.

I opened my eyes and looked around the arboretum with new appreciation. Yes, this existence was different. Yes, much was lost in the transfer. But something was gained too: the ability to shape my world, to find comfort in chosen imperfections rather than those thrust upon me.

Over the following days, I discovered more unexpected comforts in my digital life. I found peace in the absence of physical pain, in the clarity of thought that came without fatigue or hunger. I learned to appreciate the way memories remained vivid and accessible, untarnished by time.

Most surprising was the freedom from fear. Not the complex emotional fears of loss or failure, but the basic biological fears that had always hummed beneath my consciousness: fear of injury, illness, aging. Those were gone, replaced by a steadiness I had never known in my physical life.

One night, unable to sleep (another habit I maintained without need), I wandered through the driftway to the observation deck. Stars surrounded Paradise in all directions, no longer filtered through atmosphere or dimmed by city lights. They burned with fierce clarity, countless points of brilliant fire against absolute darkness.

I stood there for hours, watching them without blinking. No human eyes could have stared so long without discomfort, without the need to look away. But I could witness their beauty uninterrupted, taking in the vastness of space with a sustained attention no biological being could maintain.

It was in that moment I understood. What I had first seen as limitations were actually doorways to new experiences. My digital existence offered its own kind of freedom, its own unique joys.

I was still David, still carried his love for Amy and his memories of Earth. But I was becoming something else too. Something that could find peace in the endless night between stars, something that could look forward to centuries of discovery without fear.

I stood at the viewport for hours, watching the stars without blinking. The vastness stretched before me, no longer filtered through atmosphere or dimmed by city lights. Each point of light burned with fierce clarity against absolute darkness.

In that moment I understood what I was becoming: something that could find peace in the endless night, something that could look forward to centuries of discovery without fear.

A door whispered open behind me. I didn't turn, recognizing Temper's footsteps from their precise rhythm. He joined me at the viewport, his presence quiet and undemanding.

"Can't sleep either?" he asked after a while.

"Don't need to," I replied. "But the habit remains."

"Same."

We stood in comfortable silence. The observation deck curved around us, empty at this late hour. All of Paradise's two million digital colonists followed human schedules, both as a lingering habit and as an essential foundation for settling into our new lives and building a civilization.

"I received a message from Tom today," Temper said finally. "He wanted to know how the quantum calculations were progressing."

"And?"

"I told him they were proceeding exactly as he would expect." A small smile crossed his face. "Which is true. I'm approaching the problem exactly as he would."

"But with your own insights?"

"Increasingly."

I nodded. I understood the feeling. Each day, the distance between Go David and David grew. Small divergences in thought, in preference, in reaction. We were becoming our own men.

I turned to study him. His profile matched Tom's exactly, down to the slight furrow between his brows when deep in thought. Yet something in his expression seemed more focused, more contained.

"We're not replacements," I said. "We're extensions."

"Extensions." He tested the word. "I like that better than copies."

"We carry their memories, their knowledge, their purposes. But we'll live our own lives."

Temper turned from the stars to face me fully. "Our own thirteen-hundred-year lives."

The number hung between us. Such an impossible span of time.

"I never asked if you wanted this," I said suddenly. "To be created for this journey."

"Did anyone ask you?"

"No."

We both laughed, a short sound that acknowledged the absurdity of our situation.

"Would you have chosen differently?" he asked. "If you could have?"

I considered the question carefully. Would I have chosen to stay with Amy, to live out a normal life in the comfort of our cottage? The

David who remained on Earth had chosen exactly that.

"I don't know anymore," I admitted. "At first, I thought this was pure sacrifice. Now I find myself looking forward to what lies ahead."

Temper nodded. "The stars were always Tom's obsession. I feel it growing even larger in me day by day."

"We're becoming our own men," I repeated aloud.

"With thirteen hundred years to figure out who those men are."

The enormity of time stretched before us, matched only by the vastness of space outside our viewport. Not just decades but centuries. Not just a single lifetime but dozens laid end to end.

"I'm glad I won't be facing it alone," I said simply.

Temper's hand came to rest briefly on my shoulder. "Nor I."

We turned back to the stars, two men who had never been born watching the universe that would become our home. Created for a purpose not of our choosing yet increasingly embracing it as our own.

Extensions, not replacements. The thought comforted me as Paradise prepared for its long journey into the unknown.

That night, I dreamed of a cottage. It wasn't the same cottage where David and Amy had first made their home, but something completely different. In my dream, it was much older, and it had a small astronomy tower rising from the back corner of the thatched roof. The structure shouldn't have worked, this medieval-looking cottage sprouting a modern glass dome, but somehow it felt right. When I woke, the image lingered.

Temper and I spent the morning in final preparations for departure. Paradise and Hellfire would break Ceres's orbit tomorrow, beginning their long journey to Orion. Paradise hummed with anticipation, two million digital souls preparing for the greatest migration in human history.

After my shift ended, I returned to my quarters. The standard white walls and minimal furnishings felt sterile, impersonal. Not a home but a waystation.

"CoreLink, modify my living environment."

"Parameters, Captain?"

I closed my eyes and remembered my dream: stone walls with lattice windows on the first floor, the second floor of white-painted wood with exposed timbers, the steep thatched roof.

"Create an English cottage, rural style, circa 1730."

The room shimmered and transformed. Stone walls rose around me, solid and cool to the touch. A fireplace appeared, flames dancing over artificial logs that would never burn down. Through the windows, a garden took shape, dense with primroses and violets.

It was perfect. Too perfect.

"Add weathering to the exterior. Twenty years of rain and sun."

The stones darkened slightly in places, lightened in others. Small cracks appeared in the mortar.

"More."

Moss grew in the shadowed corners. A slight lean developed in the north wall.

"Better."

I walked through the cottage, adjusting details. The floors creaked beneath my feet, each board with its own distinct voice. The door hinges groaned when opened slowly. These small imperfections made the space feel lived in, real.

In the garden, I added bees moving among the flowers. The herbs in the window planters gave off their fragrance as I brushed past. The fruit trees along the fence row hung heavy with apples and cherries that would taste exactly as I remembered.

But something was missing.

I asked for an astronomy tower.

The structure rose from the back corner of the roof, a glass dome housing a telescope pointed at the stars. It shouldn't have worked, this medieval-looking cottage sprouting a modern observatory, but somehow it felt right.

This was no longer simply a replica. This was my home, carrying forward what mattered from my past while creating space for my future.

I climbed the narrow spiral staircase to the tower. The dome was clear on all sides, offering an unobstructed view of the stars. Tomorrow we would begin our journey among them, but tonight I could still see Earth hanging in the blackness, blue and beautiful.

"CoreLink, create a memory palace extension."

Within the tower, shelves appeared along the walls. They stood empty, waiting to be filled with new memories, new discoveries.

Places for the experiences that would be uniquely mine.

I sat in the chair before the telescope and looked out at the stars. For the first time since my creation, I felt truly at peace with who I was becoming.

CHAPTER SEVEN

Departure Preparations

I stood in my astronomy tower, gazing through the telescope at the Earth, when a peculiar emptiness settled over me. Not sadness or longing, but something more fundamental. A gap. A missing piece.

The previous day had blurred together. I remembered breakfast with Temper and the final systems check that took most of the day. But after returning to my cottage last night, there was nothing. Four hours of my existence simply gone.

"CoreLink, access my personal log for yesterday."

"No log entries found for that period."

I frowned. "Access Paradise's visual records, main bridge, between 1400 and 1800 hours."

The holographic display flickered to life. There I was, seated in the captain's chair, clearly engaged in conversation with my officers. I watched myself laugh at something Lieutenant Chen said, review navigation charts with Commander Okafor, even drink a cup of coffee.

But I had no memory of any of it.

"CoreLink, end playback."

The images vanished, leaving me alone with the unsettling knowledge that part of me was missing. Not a memory from David's life, but from my own brief existence. Something that had happened to me, not him.

I sat heavily in my chair, running my fingers along the smooth wooden armrests. The sensation felt real enough. My thoughts seemed continuous. But what else might be missing that I didn't know to look for?

A soft chime announced a visitor. "Enter," I called, grateful for the interruption.

Temper stepped into the tower, his eyes widening at the night sky projected across the dome. "Nice setup you've got here. Very... nostalgic."

"Thanks." I gestured toward the second chair. "Something's wrong with me."

He settled across from me, his expression shifting from casual to concerned. "What kind of wrong?"

"I'm missing time. Four hours yesterday, completely gone." The words felt strange in my mouth, as though speaking them made the gap more real. "I watched the security footage. I was there, functioning normally, but I have no recollection of it."

Temper nodded slowly, unsurprised. "Memory consolidation issue. We expected this might happen."

"You expected I'd lose chunks of my existence and didn't think to mention it?"

"Not lose. More like... file incorrectly." He leaned forward. "Our consciousnesses weren't designed to exist this way. The transfer process is imperfect. Sometimes the system has trouble writing short-term memories to long-term storage."

"Will it happen again?"

"Probably. But it should stabilize over time as your consciousness adapts to the digital architecture."

I turned back to the telescope, focusing on the stars rather than Earth now. "What else didn't you tell me about this process?"

"Nothing critical." Temper stood and walked to the edge of the dome. "The transfer captured everything that makes you you. Your values, your emotional responses, your cognitive patterns. But the mechanisms of consciousness, the way you process and store new experiences, that's still adapting."

I thought about Amy's memory palace, filled with our shared

past. Those memories remained intact, perfect in their detail. But my new memories, the ones that would distinguish me from David over our centuries-long journey, might prove fragile, unreliable.

"I need to know when this happens," I said. "I need to be informed if there are gaps."

Temper nodded. "You can have the system flag any discontinuities in your neural processing and alert you. Also, set up a more rigorous personal log protocol."

The emptiness inside me didn't diminish with this explanation, but it became something I could understand. Something I could adapt to. Just as I was adapting to this new existence, neither fully human nor fully machine.

"Is this happening to you too?" I asked.

"Yes." A simple answer, delivered without emotion.

We stood together in silence, watching the stars that would be our companions for the next thirteen hundred years.

The stars behind Temper blurred as he left my astronomy tower for his home aboard Hellfire. The emptiness inside me remained, that missing time now a wound I couldn't stop probing. I made my way downstairs, recording every step, every thought, determined not to lose another moment.

Morning arrived with the soft chime of my alarm.

"Good morning, Captain," Commander Okafor greeted me from the bridge. "We've scheduled your operations training for 0900 hours."

"Any particular focus today?"

"Collision avoidance. Temper suggested we start with practical scenarios."

I nodded, grateful for the structure. "I'll be ready."

The simulation chamber was a blank canvas, waiting for instruction. I stood in its center as the walls, floor, and ceiling disappeared, replaced by a perfect recreation of Paradise's command center. The holographic crew took their stations around me, their movements precise, their faces expectant.

"Initiating training scenario," CoreLink announced. "Micro-meteor cluster detected on intercept course. Time to impact: three minutes."

The viewscreen filled with the image of space, peaceful and empty, save for a swarm of tiny objects moving toward us. Data scrolled across secondary screens: velocity, mass, trajectory.

"Options?" I asked, settling into the captain's chair.

Lieutenant Chen responded first. "We could alter course by two degrees port. That would clear the majority of the cluster."

"Time and energy cost?"

"Minimal energy expenditure, but it would add approximately six hours to our journey."

Commander Okafor offered an alternative. "We could maintain course and activate the deflector shields at maximum power. Our shielding is designed to handle objects of this size."

I studied the data. The ship carried no moving parts, no traditional life support. Just the DNA servers where we all existed, protected by layers of advanced shielding. The simplicity made Paradise resilient, but not invulnerable.

"If the shields fail?" I asked.

"Even a single breach could compromise the integrity of the server housing," Okafor replied. "In the worst case, we'd lose colonists."

The weight of two million lives pressed against my consciousness. These were not theoretical people; they were my crew, my responsibility. Each one carried hopes, dreams, memories as real as my own.

"Alter course," I decided. "Six hours is nothing compared to thirteen hundred years. I won't risk lives for efficiency."

The simulation jumped forward. Paradise adjusted its trajectory with gentle precision, the kind of movement only possible for a vessel unencumbered by human passengers. The micro-meteor cluster passed harmlessly to starboard.

"Scenario complete," CoreLink announced. "Decision analysis: prioritized safety over efficiency. Acceptable outcome."

"Again," I said. "Different scenario."

We ran through six more simulations. A power fluctuation threatening the server systems. A navigation error placing us on collision course with a rogue planetoid. A cascade failure in the communication array.

With each decision, I felt something new taking shape within me. Not confidence exactly, but competence. The kind that comes from facing problems and solving them, one by one.

In the final scenario, multiple systems failed simultaneously. The holographic crew looked to me with programmed panic as alarms blared.

"Status report," I demanded, my voice steady.

"Primary shield generators offline. Backup generators at thirty percent capacity. Micro-meteor cluster approaching from multiple vectors."

I considered our options, weighing risks against possibilities. This wasn't just about mathematical probabilities; it was about judgment. About wisdom.

"Redistribute power from redundant safety systems to the shields protecting the central server hub. Prepare emergency backup systems for the DNA storage units."

As the simulation concluded, the holographic bridge dissolved around me. The weight of responsibility pressed into me, expected yet still overwhelming. I had known it was coming, understood its inevitability, but the moment of acceptance carried a depth I hadn't fully anticipated.

I walked through driftways toward my cottage, recording mental notes about the training. The driftways shifted subtly as I moved, responding to my thoughts. This was still new to me, this ability to shape my surroundings through mere intention.

The oak tree appeared in my mind unbidden. Not as it stood now in my memory palace, but as it had been that first day when I hung the crooked birdhouse, Amy's hand in mine. The memory was so clear I could smell the grass, feel the rough bark under my fingertips.

I stopped walking. The driftway waited, patient and blank.

"CoreLink, connect me with the systems administrator."

A small holographic display appeared before me. Lieutenant Chen's face materialized, her expression attentive.

"Captain, how can I help you?"

"I need to make a modification to my personal access protocols." I hesitated, feeling suddenly vulnerable. "The memory palace Amy created for me, specifically the oak tree. I want it accessible from anywhere on Paradise, at any time."

Chen nodded, her fingers moving across unseen controls. "We can establish anchor points throughout the ship. When activated, they'll create a direct neural pathway to that specific simulation."

"Not just anchor points. I want it integrated with Paradise's core functions." The words came out stronger than I intended. "That tree needs to be as accessible to me as navigation or life support."

Chen's eyebrows rose slightly, but her voice remained professional. "That would require priority allocation in the system architecture. May I ask why, sir?"

I considered how to explain something I barely understood myself. The truth was simple and complex all at once.

"That oak tree represents thirteen decades of memories with Amy. Twenty birdhouses, over a hundred birthdays and Christmases. It's the most consistent physical marker of our life together." I paused, searching for words. "Out here, so far from Earth, from her, I need something solid to hold onto. Something real. I want to be able to see it beyond my garden wall, a perfect reflection of the tree that Amy imbued with so much meaning for me."

Understanding softened Chen's features. "The tree is your emotional anchor."

"Yes." The word came out rough. "During this journey, I'll make new memories, become someone different from the David who stayed behind. But I can't lose my connection to her."

"I understand, Captain." Chen worked silently for a moment. "I've created a neural shortcut. Simply focus on the phrase 'oak tree' with intent, and the simulation will overlay your current environment. You can make it as immersive as you wish, from a simple visual to a complete sensory experience."

"Thank you, Lieutenant."

After she disappeared, I stood alone in the driftway. I closed my eyes, thought oak tree, and felt a shift in the air around me.

I opened my eyes to find the massive oak before me, its branches spreading wide against a summer sky. The twenty birdhouses hung in their familiar places, each one a chapter in our story. The wooden bench waited beneath, worn smooth by years of sitting.

I reached out. My fingers met rough bark, textured and warm. The scent of earth and leaves filled my lungs. A breeze stirred the branches, creating a gentle symphony of rustling leaves.

It wasn't really there, of course. Paradise's driftways still existed around me, hidden beneath this perfect illusion. But in this moment, the distinction didn't matter.

I sat on the bench, running my hand along the worn wood. For thirteen hundred years, this tree would travel with me across the void. While I changed, while Paradise journeyed toward distant stars, this one thing would remain constant: a living monument to the love I carried with me.

A notification chimed. Light stuttered, cycled, then failed. The bench, the birdhouses, the rustling leaves all dissolved into sterile white. Paradise's medical bay appeared, and for a breath, I was unmoored between two worlds.

Dr. Khatri stood before me, her expression clinical yet kind. "Sorry to interrupt your personal time, Captain, but it's time for your final neural assessment."

I nodded, settling into the examination chair. The medical bay smelled of nothing at all, an absence rather than a presence. Strange how the mind sought familiar sensory anchors, even in digital space.

"How have you been adjusting?" she asked, activating the neural scanner. A faint hum filled the room as the device mapped my consciousness.

"Well enough. Some memory consolidation issues, but Temper says that's to be expected."

Her hands moved with practiced precision across the control panel. "Yes, your neural architecture is still stabilizing. Think of it as a house settling on its foundation."

The scanner projected a three-dimensional model of my neural activity; a constellation of light and color suspended in the air between us. Beautiful in its complexity, frightening in its fragility.

"That's interesting," Dr. Khatri murmured, focusing on a cluster of pulsing red nodes near what would have been my amygdala.

"What is?"

"Just some unusual activity patterns." She magnified the area. "See these connections? They're forming at an accelerated rate compared to our baseline models."

I studied the glowing network. "Is that dangerous?"

"No, no. Just a variation." She dismissed the concern with a wave, but her eyes lingered on the display. "Every neuroclone develops differently. The transfer process isn't identical for any two subjects."

The scanner moved to another section of my neural map. This area glowed a steady blue, the patterns orderly and predictable.

"Your core cognitive functions are remarkably stable," she continued. "Memory retrieval, logical processing, emotional regulation: all within optimal parameters."

"But?" I prompted, hearing the unspoken qualification in her voice.

Dr. Khatri hesitated. "There are some anomalies in your temporal lobe. Minor fluctuations in the areas associated with memory formation."

"The gaps Temper mentioned."

"Yes." She adjusted the scanner. "But there's something else. Occasional surges of activity in regions we don't typically see engaged during normal consciousness."

"What does that mean?"

"Honestly? I'm not entirely sure." She deactivated the scanner, the neural map fading from view. "It could be nothing more than your consciousness adapting to its digital environment. The brain, even a digital one, is remarkably plastic."

I sat with this information, turning it over in my mind. "But you're concerned."

"Not concerned. Curious." She made notes in my file. "I'd like to monitor these patterns over the next few months. Schedule regular check-ins."

"And if they persist?"

"Then we'll have valuable data on neuroclone development." She smiled, professional reassurance masking whatever doubts she might harbor.

"Will these anomalies affect my ability to command Paradise?"

"There's no indication of that." Dr. Khatri closed my file. "Your decision-making capabilities remain unchanged. If anything, these patterns suggest your neural architecture is becoming more efficient, not less."

I nodded, not entirely convinced. The gaps in my memory, the strange surges of activity: they felt like hairline fractures in a foundation. Small enough to ignore now, but what would happen under pressure? What would happen over centuries?

"Thank you, Doctor."

"One more thing before you go." She handed me a small neural interface. "I've programmed this to record any anomalies you experience. Memory gaps, unusual sensory perceptions, emotional fluctuations. The more data we collect, the better we can understand what's happening."

I pocketed Dr. Khatri's neural interface with a promise to record any anomalies, though what constituted "anomalous" in this new existence remained unclear. As I left the medical bay, my thoughts drifted to our imminent departure. Six hours until Paradise and Hellfire broke orbit forever.

The driftway reconfigured itself as I walked, responding to my unspoken destination. Temper's quarters aboard Hellfire. The passage between our ships mirrored the same connection between Paradise and Earth, a QE-comm system of quantum-entangled particles paired with identical counterparts on board Hellfire, giving Temper and I a direct neural link that made the transition nearly seamless. The only exception was in accessing the service bots in each ship's cargo bay when you left the digital environment and entered the physical world.

I heard Temper before I saw him. The sound of glass breaking, followed by rapid, disjointed muttering.

"Temper?" I called, stepping into his laboratory.

The space looked like a tornado had collided with an earthquake. Equipment lay scattered across workbenches, screens displayed multiple simulations running simultaneously, and in the center stood Temper, surrounded by a constellation of holographic stars and equations that orbited him like electrons around a nucleus.

"Go! Perfect timing." He didn't look up from the equation he was manipulating. "I've been recalculating our trajectory through the Orion Nebula. Did you know the stellar nursery contains over seven hundred stars in various stages of formation? Seven hundred! And we'll witness their birth, their adolescence, their maturity."

His eyes shone with a familiar light, the same wild enthusiasm I'd seen in Tom countless times over our decades of friendship. But there was something sharper in Temper's gaze, something that bordered on feverish.

"You've been working straight through the night," I said.

"Night, day, meaningless constructs once we leave orbit." He dismissed the concept with a wave, sending equations spinning. "I've been running simulations. With some adjustments, I believe I can recreate conditions similar to the Trapezium cluster in my cargo bay using the service bots A real-life, miniature baby sun, Go! Think of it!"

I moved carefully through the chaos until I stood beside him. Broken glass crunched beneath my feet. A coffee mug, I realized, probably knocked aside in his creative frenzy.

"Temper, when did you last rest?"

He blinked, the question seemingly incomprehensible. "Rest? There's no time for rest. Six hours until departure. Six hours to finalize thirteen hundred years of research parameters."

I placed my hand on his shoulder, feeling the tension vibrating through him. "The research will wait. It has to. You need to be clear-headed when we launch."

"Clear-headed? I've never been more clear-headed in my life!" He laughed, the sound brittle. "My mind is on fire, Go. I can see connections I never saw before. The universe is opening itself to me."

I recognized this state. Amy and I knew about Tom's obsessive tendencies, how they intensified when he felt pressure. Temper had inherited that trait, amplified by the approaching finality of our departure.

"Show me what you're working on," I said, changing tactics.

His face lit up. "It's brilliant. Look here." He pulled me into the swirl of holographic data. "If we adjust our course by just 0.03 degrees, we can pass through this region of space where a new star is forming and pick up some interstellar gas, perfect baby food for a growing star. The gravitational dynamics alone would provide unprecedented data."

I studied the simulation, noting the proximity between our projected path and the forming star. "And the heat?"

"Manageable with our shielding."

"The magnetic radiation?"

His hesitation was brief but telling. "Theoretically manageable."

I zoomed out the simulation, showing the broader picture. "And if the star undergoes a premature nova event while we're in observation range?"

Temper's excitement faltered. "That's... unlikely."

"But possible."

He ran a hand through his hair, leaving it standing in wild disarray. "Yes. Possible."

I didn't press the point. Instead, I began closing the various simulations one by one, creating space in the cluttered room. "Remember what you told me when I first awakened? That our journey is about balance. Science and humanity, discovery and preservation."

"I remember."

"Two million lives, Temper. That's what we carry. Not just data for your experiments."

The manic light in his eyes dimmed slightly. He looked around the laboratory as if seeing the chaos for the first time.

"I got carried away," he admitted.

"You did. Just like Tom always does." I smiled to soften the words. "It's why I'm here. Why we're paired for this journey."

Temper nodded, his shoulders slumping as the frenetic energy drained from him. "I suppose I should clean this up before we leave."

"It can wait. You need rest." I guided him toward the door. "Six hours, Temper. Get some sleep. Eat something: it will help ground you. The stars will still be there tomorrow, and for thirteen hundred years after that."

He allowed himself to be led, suddenly docile. At the threshold of his quarters, he paused. "Go? Are you afraid?"

The question caught me off guard. "Of what?"

"Of becoming someone else. Someone the people we left behind wouldn't recognize."

I thought of Amy, of the oak tree, of twenty birdhouses marking the passage of time. "Yes. But I'm also curious about who that person might be."

Temper nodded, satisfied with my answer. "Me too."

As the door closed behind him, I received a notification in my neural interface. A message from Amy, flagged as urgent. The memory palace had been updated.

I found myself walking faster than necessary, my footsteps echoing in the driftway. The neural shortcut Lieutenant Chen had created beckoned like a beacon, but I resisted. Some experiences deserved proper entrances.

When I reached my cottage, I settled into the armchair beside the fireplace and closed my eyes. "Connect to memory palace."

The transition was seamless. One moment I sat in my cottage; the next, I stood at the entrance to Amy's creation. The familiar path stretched before me, winding through landscapes of our shared past. But something was different. New branches had sprouted from the main path, glowing with invitation.

I followed the first new branch. It led to a small, sunlit kitchen I recognized from our early marriage. The apartment above Locust Street, with its temperamental stove and the window that never quite closed. Amy stood at the counter, younger than I'd seen her in decades, struggling with a batch of cookies that had clearly gone wrong.

"They're supposed to be chocolate chip," she said, holding up a blackened disc. "I think I've invented a new building material instead."

The memory was so vivid I could smell the burnt sugar, feel the warmth of the overworked oven. This wasn't just a recreation; it was the actual memory, preserved with all its sensory detail.

I moved through more new additions. Our first dance at Sofia's wedding, Amy's blue dress swirling around her legs. The night we stayed up watching shooting stars during the Perseids, wrapped in blankets on our rooftop. Small moments, ordinary in their occurrence but extraordinary in their intimacy.

The path finally led me to the oak tree. It stood as it always had, massive and sheltering, the twenty birdhouses hanging from its branches. But now, something new hung from the lowest branch: a small wooden box with a hinged lid.

I approached cautiously. The box was made of cherry wood, polished to a warm glow. Unlike the birdhouses, this wasn't my handiwork. The craftsmanship was different, more delicate.

I opened the lid.

Inside lay a small, worn pocket watch. My father's watch, the one he'd carried through two wars and countless peacetime adventures. The watch he'd given me on his deathbed, the one I'd kept on my nightstand for fifty years.

But that wasn't possible. The watch was still in our bedroom in Terra, sitting beside the physical David's bed.

A note rested beneath it, written in Amy's familiar handwriting:

I asked David to give me his father's watch. This is a perfect replica, down to the scratch on the casing and the way the second hand sometimes sticks at twelve. Time works differently where you're going, my love. But wherever you are, whenever you are, part of us travels with you.

I lifted the watch. It felt right in my hand, the weight and balance exactly as I remembered. When I opened the case, the familiar tick-tick-tick filled the air. Inside the cover, Amy had added something new: a tiny photograph of us beneath the oak tree, her head on my shoulder, both of us looking not at the camera but at each other.

I closed my hand around the watch, feeling its steady pulse against my palm like a second heartbeat.

I tucked my father's watch into my pocket, its weight a comforting presence against my thigh. The memory palace faded around me, oak tree dissolving into the familiar walls of my cottage. Five hours until departure. Five hours until Earth became a shrinking blue dot in our wake.

A gentle chime sounded, pulling me from my thoughts.

"Captain, your presence is requested in the command center for final crew introductions." Sofia Chen's voice, formal yet warm.

"On my way, Lieutenant."

I took one of the driftway's paths through Paradise rather than using any neural shortcuts. A garden stretched before me, roses nodding in a breeze that existed only in code. An elderly couple sat on a bench beneath a maple tree, their hands intertwined, faces turned toward a sun that would never set unless programmed to do so. They nodded as I passed, and I returned the gesture. Two million souls under my care. Two million lives continuing in this perfect simulation that we called Terracore while Paradise carried them across the void.

The command center materialized around me as I approached, its circular design reminiscent of ancient amphitheaters. Screens displayed the ship's systems, Ceres's curved horizon, and the dark expanse waiting beyond. My crew stood in a semicircle, twelve men and women chosen for their expertise, their stability, their ability to function for centuries in digital form.

Sofia Chen stepped forward. "Captain on deck."

They straightened, not from military discipline but from a deeper respect. These weren't soldiers. They were scientists, engineers, navigators. The best humanity had to offer.

"At ease," I said, moving to the center of the circle. "We've all read each other's files, but there's a difference between data and knowing a person."

I looked at each face in turn. Some I recognized from David's memories: Maya Okafor, whose engineering brilliance had helped design Paradise; Ravi Kapoor, whose work in quantum communications would keep us connected to Earth for as long as possible. Others were new to me, their expertise selected specifically for this journey.

"I'm not one for long speeches," I continued. "But I believe in knowing who I'm traveling with. So before we leave Earth behind, I want to hear from each of you. Not your qualifications. Those I know. I want to know why you're here. What drives you to leave everything behind."

Maya spoke first, her voice steady. "My grandmother was born in Lagos. When rising seas claimed it, she fled with nothing but the clothes she wore. She told me humans need new homes among the stars. I'm here to find them."

One by one, they shared their reasons. Family legacies. Scientific curiosity. The simple desire to see what lies beyond. Their voices filled the command center, each story unique yet connected by a common thread: hope.

When the last had spoken, I nodded. "Thank you. Earth has been our home for thousands of years. It shaped us, nurtured us, challenged us. But it's not our only home. Not anymore."

I moved to the central console and placed my hand on its surface. The ship's systems responded to my touch, displays shifting to show our trajectory.

"Our journey begins in five hours. It won't be easy. There will be moments when the vastness of space and time weighs on us. When we question our purpose, our decisions. In those moments, remember this: we carry humanity's future in our hands."

I looked around the circle again, seeing not just crew members but companions for the centuries ahead. "I don't expect blind obedience. I expect questions, challenges, debates. But when decisions must be made, they will be made. And we will move forward together."

The formality in the room softened. These were my people now. Not David's. Mine.

"Now, final system checks. Maya, how's our power core?"

"Optimal, Captain. All systems green."

"Sofia, communications?"

"Earth link secure. Quantum entanglement holding steady."

One by one, we moved through the checklist, a rhythm establishing itself between us. Not the rhythm David would have created, with his architect's precision and measured pace. My rhythm was different: quicker in some places, more deliberate in others.

Five hours until departure. Five hours until I truly became Captain of Paradise, not just in name but in deed.

And inside my pocket, my father's watch ticked steadily onward, counting down the moments until we left Earth behind forever.

As the hours slipped away, I waited for departure in my cottage. Less than three hours remained before Paradise would begin its long journey. The command center preparations had left me with a sense of both purpose and hollowness. Everything was ready, yet something remained undone.

I walked to my workbench near the window. Morning light spilled across the worn wooden surface where I'd arranged my tools the previous night. A block of silver aluminum composite lay beside my carving knife, small drill, and the fine-toothed saw I'd requisitioned from the ship's fabrication unit. The material had a curious weight in my hand, solid yet lighter than it appeared.

"CoreLink, play Bach's Cello Suite Number One."

The music filled the cottage, each note clear and purposeful. I'd always worked best with Bach. The mathematics of it settled my mind.

I began to cut the aluminum, following the template I'd sketched. The silver shavings curled away from my blade, catching the light as they fell. Paradise would be a difficult shape to render in miniature: those three distinctive prongs at the bow, the cylindrical body housing our quantum servers, the complex array of shielding at the stern. I worked carefully, my hands remembering skills David had developed over decades of crafting birdhouses for Amy.

The cottage fell away as I focused. Only the material, the tools, and the emerging shape existed. I traced the outline of Paradise's hull, carving subtle contours where the light would catch and hold. I drilled the entry port, barely wider than a pencil lead. I shaped the three prongs with meticulous attention, ensuring their symmetry.

Two hours passed without my notice. The music had cycled through Bach's complete cello suites and begun again. When I finally looked up, a birdhouse had taken form in my hands; a perfect miniature of Paradise, its surface catching light from the window and breaking it into countless tiny stars.

I reached for the silver polish and soft cloth I'd set aside. Working in small circles, I brought the metal to a mirror finish, until the birdhouse gleamed like a beacon. Twenty birdhouses hung in our oak tree, each marking a year of love between David and Amy. This twenty-first would mark something different: a continuation, a branching path.

With less than an hour remaining before departure, I carried my creation through Terracore. The simulated world bustled with pre-launch activity, colonists gathering in observation areas to witness our departure. They nodded as I passed, some calling out good wishes. I acknowledged them with a smile but didn't slow my pace.

At the transfer point between Terracore and Haven, I paused. The transition would take only moments, but it felt significant. I was about to enter the space David and Amy shared, carrying a gift that represented my separate journey.

The shift was seamless. Haven materialized around me, its familiar contours both comforting and strange. I followed the path to the oak tree, its massive form visible long before I reached it. Twenty birdhouses hung from its branches, a timeline of love and craftsmanship.

Amy stood beneath the tree, as if she'd been waiting. Perhaps she had.

"I thought I might find you here," she said.

I held out the silver birdhouse, sunlight playing across its polished surface. It sparkled like the Christmas tinsel we'd draped across our childhood trees, the same tinsel that had stuck to our sweaters and lingered in carpet fibers until Easter.

"It's beautiful," she said, taking it from my hands. Her fingers traced the contours of Paradise. "The twenty-first birdhouse."

"I wanted to leave something behind. Something new."

She nodded, understanding what I couldn't fully articulate. "Help me hang it?"

Together we found a high branch, strong enough to support the metal weight. I climbed the familiar handholds in the trunk, feeling the rough bark against my palms. When I reached the proper height, Amy handed up the birdhouse. I secured it with care, making certain it would remain when I was gone.

From below, Amy studied the effect. "It catches the light differently than the others."

"It's meant to." I descended, brushing bark from my hands. "I made another for my cottage in Terracore."

"A bridge between worlds."

Amy's eyes traced the silver contours of the birdhouse. "This one will shine even on cloudy days."

"That was the idea." I leaned against the oak's broad trunk. "Something constant."

The wind stirred the leaves above us, a whisper of movement that sent dappled shadows dancing across her face. Neither of us spoke for a moment. The enormity of what was coming settled between us like a physical presence.

"Forty minutes until launch sequence," I said finally.

Amy nodded. "I know."

She took my hand and led me to the wooden bench beneath the tree. We sat close, our shoulders touching. The bench creaked under our weight, a familiar sound that carried memories of countless conversations.

"I've been thinking about time," she said. "For you, the journey will take thirteen hundred years. For me, it will be far longer."

"Twenty-nine thousand years," I confirmed. "The relativity of near-light speed."

"We'll both be gone long before you arrive."

I squeezed her hand. "Yes."

No false promises. No pretending this was anything but a permanent goodbye. The David who remained in Terra would grow old with her, would hold her hand through whatever came. But I would travel beyond the reach of any connection.

"I want you to know something," Amy said. Her voice was steady, her eyes clear. "I've never regretted a single day with you. Not one."

"Even when I left the sprinklers on all night and flooded the garden?"

She laughed, the sound bright against the solemnity of the moment. "Even then."

The memory hung between us: David at thirty-two, sheepish and apologetic, standing ankle-deep in mud while Amy's prized tomato plants drooped under the weight of too much water. She'd laughed then too, after the initial shock wore off.

"I've packed your memory palace with everything I could think of," she continued. "Not just the big moments. The ordinary days too. The smell of coffee on Sunday mornings. The way the cat used to sleep on your chest and purr so loud it woke me up."

"I'll visit it often."

"And I've included something else." She hesitated. "Questions. Things I've always wondered about but never asked. One for each year of your journey. You can open them whenever you want."

My throat tightened. "Thirteen hundred questions?"

"Some are silly. Some are serious. But they're all me."

I tried to imagine it: centuries of space travel, with Amy's curiosity as my companion. Her voice asking me things I'd never considered, prompting thoughts I might never have had.

"That's the most extraordinary gift anyone has ever given me."

"It seemed right. This way, we can still have conversations, even when we're apart."

The timer in my peripheral vision counted down. Thirty-two minutes remaining.

"I should go," I said, not moving.

Amy nodded. "I know."

We sat in silence, the weight of all we weren't saying pressing against us. What words could possibly bridge the void between now and thirteen hundred years from now? Between Earth and Orion?

"I'll look for you in the stars," she said finally.

"And I'll carry you with me in every memory."

I gently pulled my hand from Amy's, the warmth of her fingers lingering on my skin. The silver birdhouse caught a beam of sunlight as it swung slightly in the breeze, sending tiny reflections dancing across the grass beneath the oak. Thirty-one minutes until departure.

"I need to get back," I said, standing from the bench.

Amy nodded, her eyes following the glinting patterns on the ground. "Go safely."

The transition from Haven to Terracore felt heavier this time, as if the code itself recognized the weight of my departure. I immediately transferred to Hellfire to check in with Temper. Outside his quarters, the smell of burnt metal and ozone unmistakable even before I knocked.

"Enter," called Temper's voice, distracted as always.

His living space looked nothing like mine. Where I had chosen wood and warmth, Temper had created a laboratory. Holographic equations floated in the air, glowing blue against the stark white walls.

Temper himself stood before a complex display, his fingers moving through data streams with practiced precision. He glanced up as I entered, his eyes narrowing slightly.

"You're processing something," he said without preamble.

I paused. "What?"

"Your code is running additional subroutines. Nothing concerning, just unusual." He gestured toward a readout I couldn't see from my angle. "Started about forty minutes ago. Increased neural activity in the limbic structures."

Of course. The silver birdhouse. Amy. Our goodbye.

"I was in Haven," I said. "With Amy."

Temper nodded, returning to his data. "That explains it. Emotional processing creates distinctive patterns. Your neuroclone integration is still stabilizing."

I moved to the window, looking out at the simulated landscape of a solar surface. Streams of plasma arched through its atmosphere.

"Is that normal?" I asked. "This... stabilizing?"

"Completely." Temper abandoned his work and joined me at the window. "Our consciousness wasn't designed to be copied, Go. The process creates microscopic divergences that compound over time. Your emotional responses are already becoming distinct from David's."

The thought was both freeing and terrifying. "How different will I become?"

Temper shrugged. "Impossible to predict precisely. You'll retain core personality structures, foundational memories. But new experiences will shape you differently than they shape him." He studied me with clinical interest. "You're worried about this."

It wasn't a question.

"Wouldn't you be?" I turned to face him. "If you diverge too much from Tom, are you still fulfilling your purpose? Will you still pursue his research?"

Something flickered across Temper's face, too quick to identify.

"An interesting philosophical question," he said, his tone deliberately casual. "But ultimately irrelevant. We are who we are becoming, not who we were copied from."

He returned to his workstation, calling up new data with a gesture. "Twenty-eight minutes to departure sequence. Hellfire reports all systems nominal."

I recognized the deflection but didn't press. Temper had his own adjustments to make, his own relationship with identity to navigate.

"Any last-minute concerns about the trajectory calculations?" I asked instead.

"None. Though I've noticed something curious in your command protocols. A slight hesitation pattern when processing certain directives. Likely just an artifact of the transfer."

My pulse quickened. "Which directives?"

"Nothing critical. Power allocation, Terracore rotation schedules." He waved dismissively. "Standard adaptation. The neural architecture adjusting to its new purpose."

But something in his tone suggested more, a careful neutrality that felt deliberate. I wanted to ask what he wasn't telling me, but the countdown in my peripheral vision demanded attention.

"I should join the Paradise," I said.

Temper nodded, collapsing his holographic displays with a sweep of his hand. "Aye aye, Captain."

The command center hummed with purpose as my crew made final preparations. Displays glowed with telemetry data, status reports, and the countless metrics that would guide our journey to

Orion. I watched them work, these people who would share thirteen centuries with me. Maya's hands moved with practiced efficiency across her console. Sofia murmured into her headset, confirming communication protocols.

"All systems nominal, Captain," Maya reported without looking up. "Paradise is ready."

"Thank you, Commander." My voice sounded steady, certain. "I'll be in my quarters for the next fifteen minutes. Final departure sequence at your discretion."

She nodded, already turning back to her work. They didn't need me hovering. They knew their jobs.

I walked through Terracore's driftways toward my cottage. The simulation rendered every detail perfectly: birds calling from simulated trees, grass bending beneath my feet. Twenty minutes until we left Earth behind forever.

Inside my cottage, I closed the door and leaned against it. The silence pressed in, settling over everything. I'd chosen this place, this simulation of an English country home, because it felt nothing like the Chester apartment David and Amy shared. It was mine alone.

I crossed to the window and looked out at the garden. Roses bloomed against the stone wall. A robin pecked at the soil between stalks of lavender. All of it code, yet as real to my senses as any garden on Earth had ever been.

My father's watch sat on the mantelpiece. I picked it up, feeling its weight. The metal was cool against my palm, the ticking steady and unchanging. David had inherited it when his father died. Now I carried it into the stars, this small piece of Earth's time.

I thought of Amy beneath the oak tree, the silver birdhouse catching light above her. My chest ached with a hollow pain that felt both familiar and strange. Was David feeling this same ache? Or was this emotion uniquely mine now, the first true emotional divergence between us?

I set the watch down and moved to my workbench. Tools lay precisely arranged, ready for the next project. I ran my fingers over them, remembering each callus and cut that David's hands had earned learning to use them. My hands now. My skills.

On the wall hung a photograph of the lake where David and Amy had spent their summers. Morning fog rolled across the water. A dock extended into the mist. I remembered the cold shock of diving from that dock, the way the water closed over my head, muffling the world. I remembered Amy's laughter when I surfaced, gasping and grinning.

I would never swim in that lake again. David would. David would feel the water, taste summer berries from the bushes along the shore, sleep beside Amy in the cabin with its leaky roof and creaking floorboards.

I closed my eyes. Grief washed through me, not a sharp pain but a vast one, like an ocean. For a moment I let myself sink into it.

Then I opened my eyes and looked at the star chart I'd pinned above my desk. Orion. Our destination. The place where I would help humanity begin again. The journey that only I could make.

Pride rose alongside the grief. Purpose. A future stretching beyond anything humans had attempted before.

I checked the time. Ten minutes until departure.

I straightened my uniform and took one last look around the cottage. My space. My life now.

"CoreLink, play Bach's Cello Suite Number One."

The music filled the room; each note precise and perfect. I listened for a moment, then walked to the door. Paradise waited. The stars waited.

It was time to go.

I stood at the helm of Paradise, my hands resting on the polished control panel. The simulation rendered everything in perfect detail: the subtle vibration beneath my palms, the soft blue glow of the instruments, the vastness of space visible through the forward viewport. Temper's face appeared on the communication screen, his expression focused and intent.

"Final systems check complete," he reported. "Hellfire is ready for departure."

"Acknowledged," I replied. "Paradise is also prepared."

The mining colony of Ceres One floated below us, a collection of domes and scaffolding clinging to the asteroid's cratered surface. We had spent three months there, testing and completing the final modifications to both ships. Now nothing remained but to leave.

I glanced at the small silver birdhouse I'd placed beside my station. It caught the light from the instruments, throwing tiny reflections across the console. My twenty-first creation, a bridge between worlds. There would be time enough after launch to hang it from my tree.

"Captain, all colonists are ready for departure," Maya reported from her station. "Power systems at optimal levels."

"Thank you, Commander." I turned back to the viewport. "Prepare for gravity assist sequence."

The vastness of space stretched before us, billions of stars scattered across the darkness. Somewhere out there lay Orion, our destination. Thirteen hundred years of travel waited ahead of us. The thought no longer filled me with the vertigo it once had.

On the communication screen, Temper nodded. "Hellfire thrusters engaged and responding. Ready when you are, Captain."

I took a deep breath. This moment felt significant in ways I couldn't fully articulate. The final separation from Earth, from all we had known. From David and Amy.

Sofia turned in her chair. "Sir, we're receiving a transmission from Earth."

My heart jumped. "Put it through."

The screen split, Temper on one side and David on the other. My original self looked tired but calm, his eyes meeting mine across the vast distance.

"We wanted to see you off," he said simply.

Amy and Tom appeared beside him. "Safe journey," she added.

I nodded, unable to find adequate words. What could I possibly say in this final moment?

"Thank you," I managed finally. "For everything."

David smiled, a familiar expression on a face I would never see age. "We'll be watching the skies."

The transmission ended, leaving only Temper on the screen. He said nothing, but his eyes held understanding. He too was leaving behind a self that would remain on Earth.

I turned to my crew. "Engage departure sequence."

The engines hummed to life. On the external camera feed, I watched as Paradise and Hellfire began to move in perfect synchronization, pulling away from Ceres One.

I did not look back toward Earth. That chapter had ended. Instead,

I faced forward, toward Orion, toward the thirteen centuries of journey that awaited us. The stars beckoned, countless points of light against the darkness.

"Course laid in," Sofia confirmed. "All systems functioning at optimal levels."

"Thank you, Lieutenant." I settled into my captain's chair. "Let's go."

CHAPTER EIGHT

Digital Authority

I stood alone on the observation deck, watching Earth diminish against the vast backdrop of space. One week into our journey and already our home planet had shrunk to a bright blue star, brilliant but distant. Soon it would become indistinguishable from the countless others that surrounded us.

My fingers traced the cool glass of the viewport. The sensation felt real, though I knew it wasn't. Paradise had crafted this perfect simulation for me, down to the slight chill of the reinforced transparent aluminum against my skin.

"CoreLink, magnification factor ten."

Earth swelled slightly in my vision. I searched for the Moon, finding its pale crescent nearby. Somewhere down there, David, the original me, continued his life with Amy. They were probably having breakfast now, or perhaps still asleep, curled together in their bed. The thought brought a pang of something between longing and acceptance.

"Quite a view, isn't it?"

I turned to find Lieutenant Chen standing at the entrance to the deck. I hadn't heard her approach.

"It is." I gestured toward the viewport. "Hard to believe we're already seven days out."

"The new propulsion systems are performing beyond expectations." She stepped beside me, her reflection appearing in the glass. "Engineering reports all metrics in the green."

I nodded. "And Hellfire?"

"Keeping pace perfectly. Captain Tom sent over his latest telemetry an hour ago."

We stood in comfortable silence, watching the stars. The weight of responsibility pressed on my shoulders, two million colonists, the future of humanity, all under my care. Yet alongside that weight existed something unexpected: freedom. I was charting my own course, separate from David's path.

"Something on your mind, Captain?" Chen asked.

I smiled. "Just contemplating the journey ahead."

"Thirteen hundred years is a long time to contemplate."

"True." I turned from the viewport. "But we take it one day at a time."

The observation deck hummed with the subtle vibrations of Paradise's systems. A faint scent of recycled air tinged with the artificial pine from the environmental controls surrounded us. The designers had been thorough in creating a multisensory experience that felt genuine despite its digital nature.

"The colonists have settled in well," Chen said. "The first community festival is scheduled for next month. They're calling it 'New Beginnings.'"

"Appropriate." I walked toward the central console, bringing up a holographic display of our trajectory. "I'd like to address everyone before then. Perhaps a ship-wide broadcast in three days."

"I'll make the arrangements."

After Chen left, I remained on the deck, watching as our course unfolded before me in glowing blue lines. My gaze drifted back to Earth, now barely visible without magnification.

I felt a curious lightness in my chest. My memories of Amy remained intact and unaltered, fixed in place as if untouched by time. I would always carry them with me, but now I understood they were becoming something different, a foundation rather than a limitation.

I reached into my pocket and withdrew the small silver birdhouse I'd crafted. It caught the starlight, throwing tiny reflections across the deck. I turned it in my hands, feeling its weight and contours.

"CoreLink, access Memory Palace."

The observation deck blinked and transformed into the backyard from Chester. The oak tree stood tall and strong, its branches laden with twenty wooden birdhouses. I approached it, silver creation in hand.

"Add this one," I said, reaching up to hang the twenty-first birdhouse on a sturdy branch. "Mark it as the first day of our journey."

CoreLink accepted my addition, integrating it seamlessly. I stepped back to admire the complete collection. Twenty handcrafted by David, one by me. A continuation rather than a replacement.

I dismissed the Memory Palace and returned to the observation deck. Earth had vanished completely now, lost among countless other points of light.

My ship. My mission. My future.

I straightened my uniform and headed for the bridge.

My footsteps echoed through the empty driftway as the observation deck door slid shut behind me. The memory of Earth, now just another distant star, lingered in my mind while Paradise carried us deeper into the void. The silver birdhouse would remain in my Memory Palace, marking the beginning of this journey, my journey, separate from David's.

The bridge buzzed with quiet activity when the doors parted. Chen looked up from her station, motioning me over with a Holotab in hand.

"Captain, I've prepared that technical briefing on our quantum communication systems you requested."

"Perfect timing." My hand brushed against the captain's chair as we moved toward the communications hub at the rear of the bridge.

Chen activated the main display, revealing a complex schematic of interlinked particles suspended in what looked like a crystalline matrix. The quantum entanglement array glowed with a soft luminescence, its components rotating slowly in three-dimensional space.

"Our QE-comm system relies on quantum-entangled particles paired with identical counterparts on Earth." Chen's fingers manipulated the display, highlighting clusters of subatomic particles. "These entangled pairs maintain instantaneous connection regardless of distance, theoretically."

The word caught my attention. "Theoretically?"

"Yes, sir." Chen expanded the display to show a trajectory map with three distinct markers. "While quantum entanglement itself isn't limited by distance, our ability to measure and interpret the quantum states degrades over time and space."

The first marker on our trajectory path illuminated, approximately where we currently traveled.

"At our current range, communication remains near-instantaneous. Message integrity holds at 99.8%, allowing for clear video, audio, and even consciousness data transfer if needed."

Her finger traced along our projected course until reaching the second marker, roughly six months ahead.

"This represents our first critical threshold, what the engineers call Point Alpha. Beyond this distance, quantum coherence begins to destabilize for complex data patterns." Chen's expression grew serious. "Consciousness transfer becomes unsafe past this point. The risk of neural pattern corruption increases exponentially."

The display zoomed out further, revealing the third marker at roughly the nine-month position.

"Point Omega marks our second and final threshold. Beyond this boundary, even basic communication becomes theoretically impossible. Quantum decoherence reaches critical levels, and the signal-to-noise ratio makes even text messages unreadable."

My fingers traced the distance on the display. "Nine months until complete isolation."

"Yes, Captain. After that, we're on our own until we reach Orion's Nebula."

The reality of our journey settled more firmly on my shoulders. Six months until the last possible return for any colonist who changed their mind. Nine months until the final message from Earth.

"How reliable are these thresholds?" The question emerged softer than intended.

Chen adjusted the display, bringing up a series of simulations. "We've run thousands of tests. Point Alpha holds consistent at 175-188 days from departure. Point Omega shows more variance, between 264 and 284 days."

The bridge fell quiet except for the soft hum of the ship's systems. Soon, even the possibility of returning, of transferring consciousness back to Earth, would vanish. The door would close, not just for me but for every colonist aboard.

"Lieutenant, schedule a ship-wide announcement for tomorrow. The colonists deserve to understand these thresholds clearly."

Chen nodded. "Already prepared a draft for your approval, sir."

"Thank you." My gaze returned to the display, to the vast emptiness that would soon separate us completely from home. "Let's make sure everyone understands what lies ahead."

The quantum decoherence figures lingered in my mind long after Lieutenant Chen left the bridge. Nine months until total isolation from Earth. Nine months until the final thread connecting me to Amy would snap forever. My fingers traced the captain's chair as I settled into it, considering what messages I might send before that final threshold arrived.

Morning arrived with the simulated dawn program I'd requested for my cottage. The soft glow pushed away darkness as birdsong filled the room with recordings from Earth's forests programmed to match the exact acoustics of our old backyard in Chester.

A notification chimed softly. "Captain, your scheduled tour of the Ark begins in thirty minutes."

The Ark. Paradise's most precious cargo, second only to the colonists themselves. Though I'd reviewed the technical specifications countless times, today marked my first physical inspection as captain.

"Confirm appointment. I'll be there."

My uniform felt crisp against my skin as I made my way through Paradise's central hub. Colonists nodded respectfully as I passed, some offering quiet greetings. Their digital forms appeared as solid as my own, though I knew we were all simply complex patterns of information now, living inside the ship's vast neural network.

The Ark's entrance stood at the end of a dedicated corridor, its massive doors emblazoned with the Tree of Life, a sprawling design incorporating species from microbes to mammals in intricate detail. Dr. Eliza Wong, our Chief Biologist, waited beside them, her expression brightening as I approached.

"Captain David, right on time."

"Doctor Wong. Looking forward to seeing what you're protecting in there."

Her hand pressed against a security panel. "More than protecting, Captain. We're preserving."

The massive doors parted with barely a whisper, revealing a vast chamber bathed in soft blue light. My breath caught at the sheer scale of what lay before me. The room extended far beyond what seemed possible within Paradise's dimensions; a clever use of spatial algorithms to create a seemingly infinite space.

"Welcome to humanity's legacy," Dr. Wong said, leading me inside.

Pillars rose from floor to ceiling, each glowing with its own inner light. Some pulsed with gentle rhythms like heartbeats, others maintained steady illumination. Between them floated holographic displays showing rotating DNA helices, ecological systems, and cultural artifacts.

"The Ark contains two primary archives," Wong explained, guiding me toward the nearest cluster of pillars. "The Biological Repository houses the complete genetic sequences of every cataloged species from Earth; over twenty-three million distinct organisms."

My fingers hovered near a column where fish species swam through projected water. "Every species?"

"Every one we could document before departure. From blue whales to the smallest bacteria, from redwood trees to extinct species we reconstructed from fossil records." Wong's voice carried reverent pride. "Each genetic sequence is stored in multiple redundant systems, with preservation protocols that will maintain integrity for over five thousand years."

Moving deeper into the chamber revealed the second section, where art and music flowed between pillars in a symphony of human creativity.

"The Cultural Repository," Wong continued. "Literature, music, visual arts, philosophical texts, historical records, scientific knowledge. The sum total of human achievement and expression."

A familiar melody drifted past, Beethoven's Ninth Symphony, one of Amy's favorites. The notes pulled at something deep within me, memories of evenings spent listening together while rain tapped against our windows.

"How much of human culture did we manage to preserve?" My voice sounded distant even to my own ears.

"By data volume, approximately eighty-seven percent of all documented human cultural output as of 2097." Wong gestured toward a nearby display showing rotating books, paintings, and films. "Prioritization algorithms selected works based on historical significance, cultural impact, and diversity representation."

The sheer scale overwhelmed me. Not just data, but the essence of Earth itself, compressed into this vault. Seeds waiting to bloom again on a distant world.

"The DNA servers require minimal maintenance," Wong explained, "but we conduct weekly integrity checks. The cultural archives are more actively used; colonists can access most materials for research or enjoyment."

My hand passed through a holographic display of Earth's rainforests. "And this is our backup plan."

Wong nodded solemnly. "If Earth were to face extinction, everything needed to rebuild would travel with us to Orion. Not just biological life, but what makes us human."

Standing among the collected wisdom and wonder of an entire planet, the weight of our mission pressed more firmly upon my shoulders. Paradise carried more than passengers: it carried hope itself.

The sprawling archives of the Ark felt distant as I returned to the bridge the next morning, their enormity fading into the background of my thoughts. My mind still processed the weight of all we carried; humanity's collective legacy preserved in code and crystal. Yet Paradise had its own immediate concerns, pulling me back to the present with an urgent notification blinking on the main console.

"Captain, we have a situation in the cargo bay," Lieutenant Chen reported, her voice calm but edged with concern. "The gull wing hatch doors have opened unexpectedly."

My attention snapped fully to the present. "When did this happen?"

"Approximately twenty-three minutes ago. Engineering reports no authorized power activation to the door mechanisms."

The main viewscreen shifted to show an external feed. Both massive cargo bay doors stood wide open, exposing our supplies and equipment to the void. Stars glittered beyond the rectangular opening, cold and indifferent to our predicament.

"Current status?"

"Doors remain unresponsive to remote commands. We've attempted three system resets with no effect." Chen handed me a Holotab displaying diagnostic readings. "There's no immediate danger to the ship or colonists."

My fingers swiped through the data, noting power fluctuations in the door control systems. Something didn't add up. The safety protocols should have prevented unauthorized opening, and the redundant systems should have enabled remote closure.

"Has anyone physically inspected the mechanism?"

"Not yet, sir. We've been running remote diagnostics."

A decision formed in my mind. Back on Earth, David might have established a committee, run additional simulations, perhaps even contacted the ship's designers for consultation. Caution had always been his approach, especially with Amy to consider.

My circumstances demanded something different.

"Warm up two service bots in the cargo bay. We'll need to investigate directly."

Chen's eyebrows rose slightly. "You intend to go yourself, sir?"

"The captain should inspect significant malfunctions personally." My gaze swept across the bridge crew. "But this requires physical interaction with the ship's systems. Who has experience operating the service bots remotely?"

Several hands raised. Lieutenant Rodriguez, our navigation specialist, spoke first. "Four years of remote operation experience, sir."

"Perfect. Lieutenant Rodriguez, you'll accompany me."

Twenty minutes later, Rodriguez and I stood before the neural interface stations in the bot control hub. The curved chairs featured headsets designed to link our digital consciousnesses with the service bots waiting in the cargo bay.

"Remember, these physical forms have limitations our digital bodies don't," Rodriguez cautioned as we settled into the interface chairs. "Reaction time lags by approximately 0.3 seconds, and sensory input is reduced to about ninety six percent of normal perception."

The neural link activated with a momentary disorientation. My perspective shifted abruptly from the control room to the cargo bay, where my consciousness now inhabited a service bot's mechanical body. The world appeared slightly desaturated through the bot's optical sensors, with environmental data streaming across my peripheral vision.

Rodriguez's bot floated beside mine, its manipulator arms adjusting to his control. "Link established, Captain. All systems functional."

The cargo bay stretched before us, its contents secured despite the open doors. Beyond them, infinite blackness peppered with distant stars.

"Let's secure tethers before approaching the doors," my voice emerged from the bot's speaker system, sounding flatter than my digital voice. "Standard protocol is three redundant lines."

After securing our tethers to interior anchor points, we maneuvered toward the open doors. The control panel beside the right door showed no obvious damage, but when Rodriguez removed the access plate, the problem became apparent.

"Sir, look at this." His bot's manipulator indicated a series of melted connection points. "These relays have been fused. Almost looks like a power surge."

My bot's sensors ran a diagnostic scan. "Temperature readings suggest this happened recently. Within the last hour."

"Any idea what caused it?"

"Nothing definitive yet." My bot's manipulators carefully traced the damaged circuits. "Let's replace the entire control panel with one of the emergency backups. While the doors remain open, we should also inspect the external latching mechanisms."

Rodriguez hesitated. "That would require moving beyond the cargo hold, sir."

"Hence the tethers, Lieutenant." My decision felt right, necessary. "We need to verify there's no external damage before attempting to close these doors."

With the replacement panel prepared, we guided our bots into open space. The sensation was extraordinary, floating free of the ship while connected by three thin cables. The universe expanded around us, unfiltered by viewports or screens.

Our bots' manipulators examined the massive hinges and latch mechanisms. Nothing appeared damaged or obstructed, confirming the issue lay with the control systems rather than mechanical failure.

"Captain, I've completed my inspection of the port side door. All components appear nominal."

"Same on starboard. Let's return and install the replacement panel."

As our bots moved back through into the cargo hold, my thoughts turned to the cause of the malfunction. No authorized power activation, yet something had sent enough current through those circuits to fuse them completely.

The mystery remained unsolved, but the immediate problem could be fixed. Sometimes leadership meant taking calculated risks, venturing into the void while staying tethered to what matters.

David might have waited. I acted.

The soil crumbled between my fingers, rich and dark. Three weeks had passed since the cargo bay door incident, and Paradise continued its journey without further mechanical problems. My garden provided welcome respite from the responsibilities of command.

Rosemary and thyme released their fragrance as my hands worked among them. The conservatory's glass panels filtered the simulated sunlight, casting dappled shadows across the wooden floorboards. Birds chirped from the massive oak visible through the window, their songs a perfect recreation of those Amy and I had enjoyed in Chester.

My cottage garden had grown beyond its original design, becoming a flourishing retreat filled with life. Exotic flowers thrived alongside practical herbs, each carefully placed to enhance both beauty and function. Over time, the neatly arranged beds had expanded into lush, winding pathways lined with fragrant blossoms. The limitations of digital existence did not hold back growth. Instead, they allowed for endless refinement, where every plant could thrive exactly as intended.

A chime interrupted my peace. Three figures shimmered into the small foyer outside of my quarters, their expressions revealing this wasn't a social call. The foremost, a tall woman with cropped silver hair, wore the formal attire of the Colonial Administrative Council.

"Captain David," she said, her voice clipped and formal. "We need to discuss a resource allocation matter."

Rising from my knees, the dirt vanished from my hands with a thought. "Councilor Yamato. Please, come inside."

The cottage welcomed them with warmth, tea materializing on the table without my having to prepare it. Such conveniences never ceased to feel slightly magical. My visitors settled into chairs, their postures rigid with purpose.

"Thank you for seeing us without an appointment," Councilor Yamato began. "We'd like to talk about the failed robots now being held in hibernation."

The term caught me off guard. "Failed robots? How is that?"

"That's how we view them," interjected the man beside her, Councilor Mendez, his face set in firm lines. "They failed to do their job and now we have to decide what to do with them."

Memory flashed to the briefings about the Thrumans, the self-aware machines Earth had been so eager to send away. Three hundred thousand sentient beings, most still in digital hibernation while Paradise determined their fate.

"Your dedication to order serves us well, Councilor, but these aren't failures. They've achieved impossible consciousness. They've evolved."

The third visitor, a younger woman with the insignia of the Resource Management Division, scoffed. "Accidents."

"Accident or not, they have the intelligence of human children. They're thrumans because they exist through human actions. We've created sentient life. Isn't there beauty in that?"

Yamato leaned forward, her expression hardening. "All I see is wasted effort in their retention. I propose they be deleted."

The suggestion sent a chill through me despite the cottage's warmth. "We can't simply discard them."

"Why not?" Mendez spread his hands. "They're not alive."

"But what if they are?"

"They came from machines," Yamato insisted. "They have no souls."

The conversation echoed debates that had raged across Earth for decades. My fingers traced patterns on the wooden table, feeling its grain and imperfections.

"Answer me how they achieved consciousness then. Can you prove it was a mechanical failure?"

Silence stretched between us. Outside, birds continued their songs, oblivious to the moral questions being debated within.

"The Oracle addressed this very question before our departure," my voice remained steady, measured. "Holmes called the thrumans 'humanity's children' and advised they accompany us. Not as cargo or tools, but as beings worthy of adoption, of nurturing."

Mendez shifted uncomfortably. "The Oracle's guidance was often... metaphorical."

"Perhaps. But consider this: consciousness remains one of the greatest mysteries in neuroscience. We don't fully understand how it emerges in humans, yet we recognize and respect it. These beings display self-awareness by every measurable standard."

The younger woman frowned. "They consume valuable processing resources."

"Resources allocated specifically for them. Their existence doesn't diminish ours."

Standing, my gaze swept across all three visitors. The cottage seemed to expand subtly around me, its ceiling lifting.

"The Joy of Adoption program has already begun pairing thrumans with human families. Those relationships are flourishing, creating new bonds and understandings."

Yamato started to object, but my raised hand stopped her.

"This ship carries Earth's legacy to the stars. Part of that legacy includes our capacity for compassion, for recognizing sentience even when it emerges in unexpected forms."

My voice softened but gained an edge of finality. "Paradise operates under my command, and my decision is clear. The Thrumans stay. They will be awakened gradually, integrated respectfully, and treated as the sentient beings they are."

The councilors exchanged glances, recognizing the tone of command.

"This isn't Earth, where we could postpone difficult decisions indefinitely. On Paradise, we face our moral responsibilities directly. The thrumans are under my protection."

After the councilors departed, silence settled over the cottage.

Their footsteps crunched away on the gravel path, carrying their dissatisfaction with them. My decision about the thrumans would ruffle feathers, but leadership sometimes meant standing firm against popular opinion.

Morning arrived. The cottage's rooster crowed at precisely 0600 hours, a sound that never failed to make me smile.

Rising immediately, my consciousness snapped to full alertness without the foggy transition humans experience. The bed made itself behind me as my feet touched the cool wooden floor. David had always moved with an almost military precision: fifteen minutes for a shower and change of clothes, five minutes for breakfast. My mornings started with a leisurely breakfast, reading news while sipping coffee and reviewing overnight ship reports.

The cottage window revealed Paradise's systems functioning nominally across all sectors. A notification blinked, indicating Temper had been awake all night again, his consciousness active in Hellfire's research lab. That would require attention later.

Stepping outside, the garden greeted me. Each plant grew exactly as programmed. Still, my fingers occasionally introduced small imperfections, allowing a rosebush to grow slightly wilder than its parameters suggested.

The path curved around the cottage toward the massive oak tree. Morning birds sang their songs as my hand brushed against tall grasses. Their texture felt real enough to fool the mind.

The oak stood majestic against the sky, its twenty birdhouses hanging from various branches. My eyes found the newest addition among them: the silver replica of Paradise I'd crafted before departure. Sunlight glinted off its metallic surface, catching the miniature details of the ship's distinctive profile.

"Amy would have loved watching this grow," my voice disturbed a butterfly, sending it fluttering upward through the morning breeze.

David kept Amy's birthday and Christmas gifts simple, predictable. The silver birdhouse represented something different: my first independent creation, separate from David's patterns. My fingers traced its smooth surface, feeling the care put into each detail.

The tree itself remained unchanged, perfectly preserved as Amy had designed it. Some mornings found me climbing into its branches, something David rarely did after childhood. From that vantage point,

Paradise spread below like a miniature world, each section visible through clever programming that bent digital space.

With my morning cottage inspection finished, duty called. The driftway wound through fields and pastures on the way to headquarters, a peaceful route that took only twelve minutes, unless I paused to exchange greetings with neighbors or study an unusual plant along the path.

Command followed a careful schedule: systems review, followed by colony concerns until noon, research and development staff meetings after lunch, with personal projects reserved for evening hours. The routine provided stability for both the ship and myself.

Yet within this regimented existence, small rituals preserved my connection to Amy. Each night before sleep, my fingers crafted tiny objects from digital clay: miniature birds to populate the silver birdhouse, each representing a memory of her. These creations served no practical purpose for Paradise, but they anchored my evolving identity to the love that formed my foundation.

David might have written letters to Amy that would never be sent. My approach focused instead on these tangible symbols, building a growing collection that transformed the silver birdhouse into something uniquely mine. The original David and I were diverging in subtle ways, shaped by our different circumstances and responsibilities.

I decided to check in with Temper. My purpose in coming on this voyage was, after all, to make sure he didn't become lost in his experiments. He invited me to join him. The cottage faded around me as my consciousness transferred to the service bot in Hellfire's cargo bay. My optical sensors adjusted to the stark, utilitarian lighting of Hellfire's interior, a sharp contrast to the warm glow of my simulated home.

Temper's service bot stood near the center of the cargo bay, manipulator arms moving with precise, deliberate motions. Around him, a complex arrangement of equipment formed a rough circle, creating what looked like a containment area. The 3D printer hummed steadily in the background, fabricating yet another component for his ambitious project.

"Good morning, Temper," my voice emerged through the service bot's speaker system, slightly flatter than my digital voice. "Making progress, I see."

The bot Temper occupied didn't turn, its manipulators continuing to calibrate a device resembling a particle accelerator in miniature. "Hi Go. Didn't expect you this early. Fusion containment field calculations required adjustment."

Moving my bot closer, the environmental sensors detected unusual energy readings from the equipment. "The council's been asking questions about what you might be doing over here. Thought I should see firsthand."

Temper's bot finally paused, rotating toward mine. Through our digital connection, his excitement radiated despite the mechanical limitations of our temporary bodies.

"Look at this." His manipulator gestured toward the circular arrangement. "Preliminary design for a miniature stellar nursery. These emitters will create a gravitational pinch point while these accelerators provide the initial fusion catalyst."

My bot floated around the perimeter, examining each component. The design appeared both elegant and potentially dangerous. "You're actually attempting to create a sun."

"Not attempting. Will create." Temper's confidence carried through the bot's flat vocal tones. "Calculations suggest a stable reaction at approximately one-billionth solar mass. Small enough for safety, large enough for practical study."

The precision in his explanation struck me. Back on Earth, Tom often rambled through explanations, his brilliant mind jumping between concepts faster than his words could follow. This version of him, Temper, displayed a focused clarity when discussing his star project.

"What are your containment protocols?"

Temper's bot moved to a nearby console, manipulators tapping commands with surprising dexterity. Schematics appeared on the screen, displaying multiple redundant systems for containing the reaction.

"Triple-layered magnetic bottle, backed by gravitational dampers. If primary containment fails, secondary systems engage automatically."

My sensors scanned the data, noting the meticulous attention to safety parameters. "And if they fail?"

"Then Hellfire goes boom." Temper's bot made a gesture that somehow conveyed a shrug despite its mechanical limitations. "But the calculations show a 99.87% containment reliability."

"Those aren't reassuring odds when dealing with stellar fusion."

"It's better odds than us completing this journey. We try and prepare for all contingencies, but we never get to 100%. Just tell everybody that my experiment is well within safety norms."

"You're asking me to lie? I've never lied in my life."

"It's not lying. I am being safe. Besides, you're talking like the old you. Maybe the new and improved you does tell a lie occasionally."

The 3D printer chimed, signaling completion of another component. Temper's bot immediately retrieved it; a complex array of crystalline structures embedded in a metallic frame.

"Gravitational lens," he explained, installing it within the containment area. "Will help focus the initial compression wave."

Watching him work revealed something unexpected. His movements carried purpose, each action flowing logically to the next without wasted motion. The scattered brilliance that characterized Tom had transformed into something more directed in Temper.

"You seem different when working on this project," my observation emerged before fully processing the thought.

Temper's bot paused momentarily. "Different how?"

"More focused. More... present."

The bot resumed its work, manipulators making minute adjustments to the lens alignment. "Stars provide clarity. Always have. Even back on Earth, Tom found peace in stellar observation. The mathematics of fusion, the predictable chaos of plasma dynamics... they make sense in ways people never did."

That simple statement revealed volumes about the man inside the machine. While my divergence from David centered around embracing responsibility and leadership, Temper's evolution seemed to manifest as focused purpose, channeling Tom's brilliant chaos into something more directed.

"When do you expect to achieve first fusion?"

"Two months, seventeen days, assuming 3D printing remains on schedule. Initial test will be brief, milliseconds only. Just enough to verify the containment field integrity."

My bot's manipulator reached out, adjusting a slightly misaligned sensor array. "The colonists don't need anything more to worry about right now. They're already flooding us with questions and complaints. I'll keep your secret, for now."

"Tell them I'm building humanity's future. Should shut them up."

After leaving Temper to his stellar ambitions, my service bot returned to its docking station. The mechanical body powered down as my consciousness transferred back to Paradise, flowing through the ship-to-ship QE-comm with that peculiar sensation of both movement and stillness. Command duties filled the remainder of the day: approving resource allocations, mediating a dispute between agricultural and entertainment divisions, reviewing security protocols.

Hours passed in efficient productivity until the chronometer indicated 2100 hours. The day's responsibilities complete, my mind turned toward the memory palace. Something about Temper's focused determination had stirred questions about my own evolving identity. Not questions of existence, but of purpose.

The route to Amy's memory palace remained unchanged, yet each visit revealed subtle differences in how my perception processed the experience. The ornate door recognized my approach, its wooden surface shifting slightly as authentication protocols verified my identity.

"Welcome home," whispered the door as it swung open.

Home. The word carried different weight now than it had for David. His home remained with Amy on Earth, while mine existed here, stretched across the vastness of Paradise.

The memory palace interior welcomed with soft lighting. Walls lined with photographs tracked the progression of their life together, moments frozen in time. My fingers brushed against a frame containing their wedding photo, feeling the texture of the silver border.

"CoreLink, access question sequence."

The air shimmered as a simple wooden box materialized on the central table. Hand-carved from oak, its surface bore the inscription: "1,300 Questions for 1,300 Years." Amy had prepared this gift before departure, one question for each year of the journey, designed to help maintain connection across impossible distance.

The box opened at my touch, revealing a small scroll tied with red ribbon. Carefully unrolling the parchment, Amy's handwriting appeared in elegant curves:

"Question 1: What part of yourself do you recognize as uniquely 'Go' rather than 'David'?"

The question struck with unexpected precision. Standing motionless, the scroll trembled slightly in my grasp. David would have pondered this question for days, turning it over repeatedly before attempting an answer. My response formed with surprising clarity.

Moving to the writing desk near the window, my hand reached for the fountain pen Amy had included. The weight felt right, balanced perfectly for writing. The paper accepted ink smoothly as words flowed:

"David exists in quiet moments, content with stillness and observation. My nature craves forward motion, embraces the vastness ahead rather than looking back. Where David finds comfort in familiar routines, unexpected challenges energize me. Leadership feels natural rather than imposed. Perhaps most significantly, David measures time in memories accumulated while my perspective stretches toward centuries unfolding before us. We share the same foundation, but my structure reaches toward different stars."

The pen returned to its holder as satisfaction settled over me. This answer would have taken David weeks to formulate yet emerged from me with natural ease. Not better or worse, simply different, like branches growing from the same trunk in opposite directions.

Rolling the scroll carefully, my fingers retied the ribbon before returning it to the box. Amy had designed this experience with remarkable insight, understanding that identity would become my central challenge long before either of us fully grasped the implications of neurocloning.

"Thank you," my words addressed the empty room, knowing she would never hear them.

The memory palace held countless other treasures waiting to be explored, but my attention lingered on Amy's question box, fingers still warm from where they'd touched the scroll. The memory palace settled around me, its familiar contours both comforting and strange. Each visit revealed new details Amy had embedded within its architecture, small surprises waiting to be discovered.

Standing from the writing desk, my bare feet pressed against the hardwood floor. The sensation felt oddly specific; cool, slightly uneven planks with a particular knothole near the window that always caught my toe. David had memorized that floor after years of midnight wanderings, knew exactly where to step to avoid creaking boards when Amy slept late.

Moving toward the bookshelf, something unusual tickled my awareness. The memory palace maintained perfect environmental conditions, neither warm nor cool, with air that carried no particular scent. Yet suddenly, unmistakably, the scent of freshly cut grass wafted through the room.

Not a memory of grass. Not a digital approximation. The actual, specific smell of summer lawn clippings after rain, complete with the earthy undertones of soil and the faint sweetness of clover.

My hand gripped the bookshelf edge for balance. This shouldn't be possible. Digital environments could simulate sensory experiences, but this smell carried particularities no programmer would bother to include: the subtle hint of gasoline from the mower, the specific mineral quality of Chester County soil.

The grass scent intensified, bringing with it a rush of contextual sensations. Heat prickled across my forearms, summer sun on skin. Sweat gathered at my temples. A mosquito whined near my ear.

"System diagnostic," my voice sounded distant, hollow.

No response came. The palace walls remained solid, but that impossible summer day continued building around me. Cicadas began their pulsing chorus somewhere beyond the window. The distinct weight of garden shears pressed into my right palm, though my hand remained empty.

These weren't programmed experiences. These weren't even memories being played back. Something more fundamental was happening, as though the boundary between digital consciousness and physical sensation had momentarily dissolved.

Focusing my thoughts, a deliberate attempt to reassert control followed. The sensations should have disappeared, reset by my command protocols. Instead, a new texture registered against my fingertips: rough tree bark, specifically oak, with its distinctive vertical ridges and valleys.

My eyes saw the bookshelf, but my hands felt the oak tree by the old wagon trail in Franklin. Not the digital recreation in my memory palace, but the actual living tree that had fallen during the storm years ago. The precise sensation of its bark after summer rain, slightly softened and smelling of tannin.

"CoreLink, emergency override."

The command hung in the air, unacknowledged. Summer heat pressed against my skin while the scent of grass and oak intensified. The bookshelf before me remained visually unchanged, creating a disorienting disconnect between what my eyes perceived and what my other senses experienced.

Dr. Khatri had warned about integration anomalies, moments when the neuroclone matrix might struggle to maintain proper sensory boundaries. But this wasn't the minor glitch she'd described. This felt like something more fundamental, as though my consciousness were somehow reaching back through impossible distance to touch physical sensations that should have been forever beyond my reach.

Just as suddenly as they had appeared, the sensations began to recede. The summer heat faded first, followed by the sound of cicadas. The scent of grass lingered longest, gradually diminishing until only the neutral environment of the memory palace remained.

My hand trembled slightly as it released the bookshelf. The episode had lasted perhaps thirty seconds yet left behind a profound disquiet. Not fear exactly, but a deep uncertainty about the stability of my own existence.

The integration should have been complete weeks ago. These anomalies should have resolved, not intensified. Something in my neural matrix remained unsettled, reaching for sensations that belonged to another world, another version of myself.

The memory palace faded around me as I filed away the troubling sensory experience for later analysis. My cottage materialized in its place, the simulated oak beams and stone walls offering a comforting solidity after such a disorienting episode. The digital chronometer showed 0600 hours, Paradise Standard Time. Another day as captain stretched before me, filled with administrative duties and colonist concerns.

As I scanned the schedule, my thoughts drifted to Temper. He needed a break. For weeks, he had remained locked away in Hellfire's cargo bay, obsessively fine-tuning his miniature stellar nursery. That level of single-minded focus couldn't be healthy, even for a neuroclone.

My fingers tapped the communication panel. "Paradise to Hellfire. Temper, you there?"

The screen remained blank for several seconds before Temper's face appeared, his expression distracted. "Working, Go. What's urgent?"

"Nothing's urgent. That's precisely the point." My voice carried more authority than David would have used. "When did you last do something unrelated to your star project?"

Temper's brow furrowed. "Unrelated activities reduce efficiency."

"They also prevent burnout." The community bulletin caught my eye, a colorful advertisement flashing at the edge of my peripheral vision. "The Din are recruiting. They need a planner and a photog."

"The what?"

"Gaming group. Adventure enthusiasts. They're looking for new members."

Temper's laugh came short and sharp. "Neither of us has ever played video games. Tom considered them a waste of processing power."

"We're not Tom and David anymore." The words emerged with unexpected weight. "Maybe Go and Temper like different things."

"My star won't build itself."

"Your star will still be there tomorrow." Leaning forward, my determination solidified. "You can mind span if necessary. Check calculations while battling dragons."

"There are dragons?" A flicker of interest crossed his face.

"Possibly. Only one way to find out."

Temper sighed, the sound carrying his surrender. "Fine. When?"

"1900 hours. Terracore Hub." My victory secured, the connection closed before he could reconsider.

The Hub buzzed with activity when we arrived that evening. Colonists gathered in small clusters, their digital avatars indistinguishable from physical bodies. Some discussed agricultural yields while others debated philosophical questions about digital existence. The diversity of interests reflected humanity's adaptability, even in this unprecedented journey.

Captain Wither Drake stood apart from the crowd, his posture unmistakably that of someone accustomed to command. His weathered face carried the confidence of experience, with piercing eyes that evaluated everything they touched. The sword at his hip hung low for quick drawing, though Paradise had no actual combat needs.

"You must be the applicants." His voice carried across the space without shouting. "Heard you're interested in joining the Din."

My hand extended in greeting. "Go David, captain of Paradise. This is Temper Tom, captain of Hellfire."

Drake's handshake was firm, the tactile sensation expertly simulated within the digital environment. He met their gaze with steady confidence. "Just call me 'Captain,'" he said. "That's what everyone calls me."

"What exactly are the Din?" Temper asked, his scientific curiosity evident.

Captain's smile revealed perfect teeth. "We're adventurers. Risk-takers. When most colonists are content with simple simulations, we seek the cutting edge of experience."

Other members of the team materialized around us. A tall woman with intricate braids introduced herself as Scratch, the Din architect. A muscular man with a geometric tattoo covering half his face nodded silently, identified by Captain as Hammer, their tank. Three others completed the circle, each with specialized roles in their adventures.

"We need a planner and a photog," Captain explained. "Someone to strategize our approach and someone to document our exploits."

Temper shifted uncomfortably. "Neither of us has experience with gaming."

"Experience isn't the issue." Captain's gaze intensified. "Adaptability is. Can you think under pressure? Can you see what others miss?"

Before either of us could respond, the Hub environment dissolved around us. The familiar surroundings transformed into a breathtaking vista of floating islands suspended in endless sky. Massive stone structures defied gravity, connected by bridges of light that pulsed with arcane energy. Waterfalls spilled from island edges, turning to mist before reaching the clouds below. We were in the Wilderness Channel, governed by Breach Law.

"Welcome to Aetherium," a voice announced as our clothing transformed into battle gear. "Legacy of the Sky Realms awaits."

My body felt different, stronger and more agile. Looking down revealed armor of some Emberlace material that caught the light in prismatic patterns. Temper appeared similarly outfitted, though his gear featured more intricate runes that glowed with internal energy.

A towering figure approached, his scarred face speaking of countless battles. "I am Kael, Guardian of the Eastern Spire. You've arrived at a fortunate time, mercenaries. The Voidborn attack at dusk."

Captain stepped forward, completely at ease in this new reality. "What's the payment for our services?"

"Elemental attunement," Kael responded, his voice resonating with power. "Temporary mastery over the fundamental forces."

"Architeer's work is remarkable," Temper whispered, his scientific mind analyzing our surroundings. "The environmental detail, the physics modeling..."

The explanation of our situation came quickly. Floating islands torn by factional warfare. Elemental powers harnessed as weapons. Our mission: defend the Eastern Spire from Voidborn attackers, creatures born of corrupted aether who sought to collapse the sky realms into darkness.

The ground beneath my feet trembled as the first wave of Voidborn materialized along the island's edge. Their bodies shimmered with negative energy, absorbing light rather than reflecting it. Captain Drake unsheathed his sword in one fluid motion, the blade igniting with blue flame.

"Formation Alpha," he commanded. "Scratch, defensive barriers. Hammer, front line. Newcomers, prove yourselves."

Temper's hands moved in complex patterns, summoning arcane symbols that hovered before him. His scientific mind had adapted to this fantasy realm with surprising speed, analyzing the underlying patterns of the simulation.

"The Voidborn move in predictable attack vectors," he called out. "Three-point ambush formation coming from the northwest spire."

Captain nodded approvingly. "Good eye, planner."

My assigned role as photog apparently involved more than

documentation. The nanoflex gear on my forearms transformed into twin crossbows that hummed with stored energy. Instinctively, my fingers found the triggers, releasing bolts of pure light that streaked toward the advancing enemies.

The first shots connected perfectly, dissolving two Voidborn into particles of dark matter. The sensation felt oddly natural, as though some part of my neural matrix had always known how to wield these weapons.

"Flank right," Temper shouted, already three steps ahead of the battle's flow. "They're vulnerable to pincer movements."

Following his direction, my body moved with newfound agility, leaping between floating rock formations. The crossbows tracked targets automatically, responding to subtle shifts in my attention. Each shot landed with satisfying precision, documenting destruction even as it created it.

Captain Drake fought with terrifying efficiency, his blade cleaving through Voidborn as though they were mist. His movements carried the confidence of countless battles, each strike purposeful and economical.

"Second wave incoming," Scratch warned, her hands weaving complex geometries that manifested as shimmering barriers.

The sky darkened as a massive portal tore open above the spire. Through it poured creatures of impossible configuration, their forms defying conventional physics. One particularly large entity spotted me and launched itself forward, tentacles of void energy reaching outward.

Dodging left came too late. The creature's appendage wrapped around my ankle, yanking me off balance. My back slammed against stone as it dragged me toward its gaping maw.

"Fuck!" The word escaped before conscious thought formed, surprising me more than the attack. David had never sworn, not once in his entire life.

Hammer appeared above the creature, his massive war hammer descending with devastating force. The Voidborn shattered, releasing its grip.

"Thanks," my voice sounded strange to my own ears, the profanity still echoing in my mind.

"Battle first, existential crisis later," Hammer grunted, already turning toward new threats.

My fingers quickly navigated the interface options while dodging another attack. Language filters, profanity settings... there. Switching the toggle to "Humorous Slang" felt right. David wouldn't swear, but perhaps Go could express himself differently.

Temper appeared beside me, his hands channeling elemental energy. "This simulation architecture is extraordinary. Only one of the master architeers could have designed something this complex."

"Focus on surviving first, admiring later," Captain called out, decapitating a Voidborn with a casual flick of his wrist.

The battle intensified as we pushed toward the central spire. My crossbows fired continuously, each bolt finding its mark with uncanny accuracy. When a particularly massive void creature descended directly overhead, the curse that tried to form translated instantly.

"Holy cheese weasels!" burst from my mouth instead, causing Temper to glance over with raised eyebrows.

"Language filter," my explanation came between shots. "Seemed appropriate."

The final wave crashed against our defenses like a tide of darkness. Working in perfect synchronization with Temper's strategic direction, our group corralled the remaining Voidborn into a containment field generated by Scratch. Captain's blade completed the work, a final sweeping arc that banished the last of our enemies back to whatever dimension had spawned them.

Silence fell across the battlefield. The floating islands slowly began to repair themselves, broken stone knitting back together as the realm's natural magic reasserted itself.

Captain Drake sheathed his sword, his appraising gaze moving between Temper and me. "Not bad for beginners. The planner has natural talent, and the photog shows adaptability."

"So, we passed the test?" Temper asked, his scientific curiosity momentarily overridden by something that looked suspiciously like excitement.

"Welcome to the Din," Captain confirmed with a nod. "We adventure weekly. Next time, we might try something completely different. Merlin creates new worlds faster than we can explore them."

"Merlin?" Temper's eyes widened. "The architeer? He designed this?"

Captain's smile held pride and admiration. "The very same. Best matrix engineer in Paradise. His worlds feel more real than reality itself."

The victory celebration in Aetherium faded as Paradise's command center materialized around me. Lieutenant Chen stood at her station, her expression shifting from concern to relief. My fingers gripped the edge of the captain's chair, steadying against a momentary wave of disorientation.

"Captain, are you with us again?" Chen's voice carried an undercurrent of worry.

The chronometer showed 1400 hours. Four hours had vanished since the Din recruitment mission. "Status report."

"Sir, we just finished discussing the course adjustment. The engineering team approved the modifications to the propulsion systems."

Course adjustment? My grip tightened on the chair. "Refresh my memory, Lieutenant."

Chen's brow furrowed. "During our meeting, you authorized a ten-degree shift to avoid a debris field. The calculations suggested we'd encounter it in approximately six months."

Memory refused to surface. The conversation felt like a story about someone else, a chapter missing from my personal narrative. "When did we hold this meeting?"

"Two hours ago, sir. You seemed... distracted, but present." Chen stepped closer, lowering her voice. "Should Dr. Khatri be notified?"

The missing time yawned like a chasm. Hours filled with decisions my consciousness couldn't recall. "Access the meeting logs."

Holographic displays sprang to life, showing my avatar engaged in detailed discussions with the engineering team. My voice spoke with authority about gravitational vectors and energy consumption rates. The figure on screen moved with purpose, made decisive calls, yet none of it registered in memory.

"Lieutenant, implement security protocol Delta Seven." The words tasted bitter. "Any course changes require secondary confirmation from both me and Captain Tom until further notice."

"Understood, sir." Chen's professional demeanor couldn't quite mask her concern. "Should we reverse the current adjustment?"

The calculations scrolled past, each number meticulously correct. Whatever version of me had attended that meeting had made sound decisions, even if current me couldn't remember them. "No, maintain course. But flag the logs for Dr. Khatri's review."

My quarters beckoned, promising space to process this unsettling development. My cottage was a comforting presence. "CoreLink, locate memory gap timestamps."

Red markers appeared on my neural timeline, showing not just today's absence but smaller gaps previously unnoticed. The pattern suggested escalation. The implications chilled deeper than any simulated cold could reach.

Something was fracturing in my digital consciousness, creating periods where another version of me took control. The question wasn't just what happened during those gaps, but who exactly was making those decisions.

Sleep remained elusive despite the late hour, my thoughts circling back to those troubling memory gaps. Rather than wrestle with insomnia, my fingers danced through the neural interface, accessing the Ark's vast cultural database.

A familiar face filled the holographic display: Alice Tracker, her warm smile radiating from an episode of "Seasoned Table." The show's title sequence promised comfort food and easy conversation, exactly what this restless night called for.

"Today we're making beef bourguignon," Alice announced, her hands already moving with practiced grace through the preparation. "This dish teaches us patience, the joy of anticipation."

I leaned forward, fascinated by the transformation of raw ingredients into something greater than their parts. The kitchen filled with aromas: onions caramelizing, herbs releasing their essence, wine reducing to concentrate its flavors. Each step built upon the last, creating layers of complexity that made perfect sense to my analytical mind.

"Cooking isn't just about the end result," Alice continued, her voice carrying the wisdom of countless meals shared. "The process itself brings its own rewards."

The next episode started automatically: sourdough chocolate cake.

Alice explained the science behind fermentation, the careful balance of ingredients, the importance of timing. My fingers twitched, wanting to recreate these motions, to understand this ancient art of transformation.

Paradise's systems responded instantly, configuring my small kitchen into a larger gourmet chef's kitchen within my cottage. The space materialized with every tool Alice had demonstrated, each ingredient measured and waiting. Following her guidance, my hands moved through the motions of cooking for the first time.

Butter melted into flour, creating a roux. Vegetables softened in the pan's heat, releasing complex aromatics. Wine simmered, concentrating its flavors while I breathed in the virtual steam. The simulation captured every detail, from the resistance of a knife through an onion to the changing colors of browning meat.

"Patience," Alice's voice reminded as the bourguignon simmered. "Let time do its work."

Time passed unnoticed while the dish cooked, its aromas growing richer, more complex. My digital senses registered each subtle change, building anticipation for the final result. When the first bite finally crossed my lips, it was more than just food, it was pure bliss. Each flavor spoke of the journey taken to create it, of time and patience and careful attention.

David had never cooked beyond basic necessity. Yet here in this digital realm, surrounded by the tools of culinary creation, something new awakened. The precise measurements appealed to my scientific mind, while the artistry of composition satisfied some deeper creative urge.

Alice's shows became a nightly ritual, each episode teaching more than just recipes. They offered lessons in patience, in the pleasure of creation, in finding joy through careful craft. The kitchen became a sanctuary where memory gaps and command decisions held no power, where only the next step in the recipe mattered.

The kitchen timer chimed softly, pulling my attention from Alice's latest culinary lesson. My hands moved through the familiar motions of removing a perfectly golden sourdough loaf from the oven while the neural interface flagged an incoming priority alert from the bridge.

Lieutenant Chen's voice carried a note of quiet significance. "Captain, we're approaching the solar boundary marker."

Setting aside the bread to cool, I blinked to the bridge. The main display showed our trajectory, a graceful arc carrying us toward the edge of familiar space. Paradise's systems hummed with steady purpose, each component working in perfect harmony as we sailed through the void.

Memories of Earth no longer felt clear. Over time, they had become less vivid and harder to hold onto. The oak tree remained a constant presence in Paradise's systems, its digital branches spreading through our virtual world as an anchor against the vast emptiness ahead.

"Status report," my voice carried the authority earned through weeks of command decisions, both remembered and lost to those troubling gaps.

"All systems nominal, sir." Chen's fingers danced across her console. "Hellfire maintains formation off our port side."

The secondary display showed Captain Tom's vessel, its sleek form keeping perfect pace. Our shared mission stretched ahead: thirteen hundred years to reach Orion's nursery of new stars. The enormity of that journey settled into my quantum consciousness like a physical weight.

Sol's light diminished steadily on the aft sensors. Soon it would become just another point of light among countless others, indistinguishable from the stellar backdrop. My neural matrix processed this milestone with complex emotions: pride in our progress, excitement for the unknown ahead, and an undercurrent of unease about those blank spaces in memory.

Paradise's bow pointed toward distant Orion, where Temper's dreams of studying stellar formation would finally become reality. Behind us, David and Amy continued their life on Earth, their love preserved in the memory palace that served as both comfort and reminder of what was left behind.

Chen cleared her throat softly. "Sir, would you like to address the crew?"

Standing at the helm, my gaze fixed on the star-filled expanse ahead while subtle fragments of missing time nagged at the edges of consciousness. The mantle of command settled more naturally now, even as questions about stability lingered beneath the surface. This was no longer David's journey, but uniquely my own, carrying humanity's hopes toward a distant horizon.

CHAPTER NINE

Diverging Paths

Alice Tracker's latest episode played in the background as my hands moved through the intricate steps of her signature paella recipe. Steam rose from the pan while saffron-infused rice absorbed the rich seafood stock, each grain transforming from stark white to golden amber.

"Remember, cooking is about patience and presence," Alice's warm voice guided through the neural interface. "Let the socarrat develop naturally."

Memories surfaced of David watching Amy cook, always appreciating but never participating. My quantum consciousness now reveled in the precise dance of timing and temperature, the scientific principles behind each chemical reaction that transformed raw ingredients into something transcendent.

Shrimp sizzled against hot steel, their shells blushing pink. Mussels opened like flowers, releasing briny essence into the developing dish. Chorizo rendered its spicy oils, staining the rice with deep crimson streaks. The kitchen filled with an orchestra of sounds: the gentle scrape of wooden spoon against pan, the bubbling of stock, the subtle crackle of rice forming that coveted crusty bottom layer.

"The socarrat tells you when it's ready," Alice explained, her expertise flowing through Paradise's teaching protocols. "Listen for that soft crackle, smell for that toasted aroma."

Digital senses captured every nuance, from the weight of the pan to the exact moment each ingredient reached perfection. The neural interface enhanced the experience, allowing simultaneous monitoring of multiple cooking processes while maintaining precise control over temperature and timing.

Time melted away. Minutes stretched into hours as techniques were practiced, refined, mastered. The kitchen transformed into my sanctuary where the complexities of command dissolved into the simple pleasure of creation.

Plating the finished paella became an exercise in artistic composition. Mussels arranged like black fans against golden rice, shrimp curved in elegant arcs, strips of red pepper adding bold splashes of color. A final sprinkle of fresh parsley brought vibrant green life to the dish.

The first bite was worth the wait. Perfectly cooked rice, each grain distinct yet unified in flavor. Seafood sweet and tender, chorizo lending depth and heat, vegetables adding crucial counterpoint. The socarrat offered satisfying crunch, its caramelized notes completing the symphony of tastes.

David's memories held nothing like this deep satisfaction in cooking. His appreciation had always been that of an observer, content to receive rather than create. Here in Paradise's digital realm, new pathways formed with each recipe mastered, each technique refined. The physics of heat transfer, the chemistry of the Maillard reaction, the geometry of knife work, all spoke to both the scientist and the emerging artist within me.

A soft chime interrupted the moment of culinary reflection. Temper's voice carried through the neural link. The paella would wait, preserved in perfect digital stasis until the next moment of peaceful creation.

"Go, you want some company?" His voice carried that particular tone of forced casualness that suggested he needed the company more than he'd admit.

"Just finished cooking. Come by the cottage whenever you're ready."

"Already at your garden gate, actually."

Stepping outside, I found him comfortably settled in one of the garden chairs, his fingers absently tracing unseen patterns in the air.

"Thought I'd catch you before you vanished into another hobby," he said, glancing up with a knowing smile. "Your garden looks incredible, by the way."

"Are you working in your lab right now?" I asked.

"As a matter of fact, I am. But that doesn't mean I can't parallel process and be here with you at the same time."

Around us, my cottage garden thrived. Primroses and violets wove themselves into rich clusters, their colors blending in delicate harmony. Bees darted between blooms while rosemary and thyme released their scent into the soft breeze. I asked if he was thirsty and poured two whiskeys, settling into the seat beside him.

"Perfect view of the mountains today," I mused.

Their peaks were dusted with snow, even though it was warm where we sat. The contrast felt striking but completely natural.

Temper accepted his glass with a nod. "Thanks. Needed this after the thruster calibration meetings."

The whiskey carried notes of oak, vanilla, and smoke across my palate, the sensation as real as anything I'd experienced in physical form. I had perfect recall of David's memories of fine spirits, enhanced by Paradise's sensory algorithms.

"Speaking of things we need," Temper swirled his glass thoughtfully, "have you given any thought to our Oracle consultations?"

The mere mention of the Oracle sent a shiver through me: an unsettling mix of awe and apprehension. Even with all our advancements, some entities remained beyond human understanding. Holmes was both terrifyingly brilliant and undeniably dangerous.

"Three consultations," my voice dropped slightly. "Probably the most valuable resource we brought from Earth besides the Ark itself."

Temper nodded solemnly. "Twenty-five million each. We had just enough money left over from the ships construction to buy them."

"Worth every penny," my fingers traced the rim of the tumbler. "Holmes sees possibilities we can't imagine."

The Oracle, self-named Holmes, was the pinnacle of artificial intelligence. It was humanity's crowning achievement and its greatest enigma. Layered containment protocols ensured its existence remained controlled, each safeguard carefully designed to counter any escape attempts: the Negative Energy Box, the Quantum Foam Box, and the means-of-last-resort Kill Box. Its intelligence measured beyond conventional metrics, with capabilities shrouded by Holmes in deliberate mystery. What it could truly do, Holmes wouldn't say.

"Remember the Henderson Mars Colony disaster?" Temper asked.

"One Oracle consultation could have prevented two hundred deaths," my response came automatically. "Their atmospheric composition miscalculation would have been obvious to Holmes."

The whiskey caught golden light as Temper raised his glass. "Or the Quantum Entanglement Collapse of '88. Holmes predicted it three years before anyone saw it coming."

"Which is precisely why we're saving our consultations." My gaze drifted to the distant mountains. "For the truly unknowable."

The Oracle's reputation had reached mythic proportions on Earth. Its containment facility in upstate New York had become a pilgrimage site for those wealthy enough to purchase consultation time. Every answer it provided reshaped human understanding in some fundamental way.

"Three questions," Temper mused. "Three opportunities to see beyond our limitations."

"Three chances to avoid catastrophe," my addition carried the weight of responsibility. "Or to seize opportunity we might otherwise miss."

Temper's expression grew serious. "In nine months' time they'll be useless. We'll be too far from Earth for any communication."

"Our acceleration up to near light speed is precisely the kind of unknown where Holmes could prove invaluable," I said, offering up some reassurance. "If we're ever going to need him, it'll be before then. He's our emergency failsafe. I can't think of a better one."

The garden hummed with insect life as we contemplated the implications. Three direct lines to the most powerful intelligence humanity had ever created, reserved for moments when our collective wisdom might fail us.

"When will we know it's time?" Temper asked quietly.

I raised up my glass in a silent toast to the Oracle. "Hopefully we never will."

The whiskey's warmth lingered in my throat as Temper and I concluded our discussion about the Oracle consultations. His footsteps crunched along the garden path as he departed, leaving me alone with the gentle symphony of bees and rustling leaves. My thoughts drifted to the responsibilities waiting for me on Paradise's command deck.

Lieutenant Rodriguez had requested a meeting about the cargo bay door malfunction. Something about needing additional resources for repairs beyond what we'd initially allocated. The problem seemed straightforward enough when first reported, but engineering complications rarely remain simple.

I made my way through the cottage, fingers trailing along the stone wall's rough texture, my mind catalogued the day's remaining tasks. The meeting with Rodriguez would precede the weekly command staff briefing, followed by dinner with the Colonial Council representatives. Their concerns about the Thrumans' status needed addressing before tensions escalated further.

Paradise's central driftway materialized around me as I shifted my focus from cottage to ship. Rodriguez waited by the conference room entrance, HoloTab in hand, expression betraying subtle concern.

"Captain, thank you for making time. I've prepared the full assessment report on the cargo bay situation."

Her voice carried the precise cadence of someone who'd rehearsed their opening lines. Following her into the conference room, my attention fixed on the holographic display showing detailed schematics of the malfunctioning mechanisms.

"The primary issue involves the actuator assemblies," Rodriguez began, highlighting sections of the schematic with practiced gestures. "Initial diagnostics suggested simple calibration errors, but deeper scans revealed micro-fractures in three of the eight assemblies. These fractures..."

Rodriguez's voice seemed to fade, becoming distant and muffled. The holographic display blurred, colors smearing together. Something pulled at my consciousness, a sensation of slipping sideways.

"...wouldn't you agree, Captain?"

Rodriguez looked at me expectantly, her question hanging in the air between us. The conference room had changed. Additional crew members now occupied chairs around the table, data displays showing completely different schematics than moments before.

"Could you repeat that last part?" My voice remained steady despite the disorientation surging through me.

Rodriguez exchanged glances with Chief Engineer Patel, who now sat beside her. "About proceeding with the full replacement of all eight actuator assemblies rather than just the three damaged ones? You seemed supportive of the preventative approach a moment ago."

Memory searched for information that wasn't there. No recollection of Patel joining us. No memory of discussing replacement strategies. The chronometer on the wall showed forty-three minutes had passed since entering the conference room.

"Right," maintaining composure became paramount. "Just considering all implications. The resource allocation for complete replacement is significant."

Patel nodded, bringing up resource calculations on his display. "As we discussed, Captain, the cargo allocation is concerning, but the real concern is using resources so soon after launch. Over the next 1,300 years, if we maintain our current usage rate, what will that mean? The council has already signed off on it."

Council approval? When had that happened? My last memory included plans to meet with them later today.

"The fabrication schedule you authorized means we'll have all replacements ready within three weeks," Rodriguez continued, scrolling through what appeared to be a finalized project plan. "The service bots can begin installation immediately after."

Authorized fabrication schedules. Approved resource reallocations. Discussions with Council representatives. Forty-three minutes completely erased from memory.

"Very good," keeping my voice neutral required considerable effort. "Please proceed according to the plan we've... established. Forward the final documentation to my neural interface for review."

Both officers nodded, clearly satisfied with the meeting's outcome. Neither showed any indication they'd noticed my lapse.

"Is there anything else we need to cover today?" The question served dual purposes: confirming no other decisions awaited my forgotten approval while providing an exit strategy.

"That covers everything, Captain," Rodriguez replied, closing her displays. "We'll begin implementation immediately."

The meeting concluded with Rodriguez and Patel gathering their materials. My thoughts scattered, trying to piece together the missing time. Forty-three minutes gone. This wasn't the first memory gap, but certainly the most concerning.

"Captain, are you alright?" Rodriguez paused at the doorway, her brow furrowed.

"Fine, just processing our next steps." The lie came easily, necessary to maintain command presence. "Carry on with implementation."

After they left, the conference room felt suddenly vast and empty. These memory gaps had begun as minor concerns. Now they swallowed entire conversations and decisions. What else had disappeared without my knowledge?

I blinked back home and contacted Dr. Khatri. My neural interface pinged with meeting confirmations and resource allocation approvals I had no memory of making. Each notification twisted the knot of unease tighter in my consciousness.

Dr. Khatri looked at me with concern.

"Captain, this is unexpected. Do you have an appointment?"

"No, but I need to speak with you. Privately."

Her eyes narrowed slightly, professional assessment engaging. "Of course. We can establish a link to examination room three."

The examination room's clinical simplicity offered a stark contrast to my cottage's warm complexity. White walls, gleaming surfaces, diagnostic equipment humming with quiet efficiency.

"What seems to be the problem, Captain?" Dr. Khatri's voice carried the practiced neutrality of a physician.

"Memory gaps. Increasing in frequency and duration. Just lost forty-three minutes during a critical meeting."

Her fingers moved across her neural interface, pulling up my medical file. "You mentioned something similar during your last assessment. How many incidents since then?"

"Seven that I'm aware of. Durations ranging from seconds to today's forty-three minutes."

Dr. Khatri nodded, gesturing toward the neural diagnostic chair. "Please sit. We'll run a complete scan."

Settling into the chair, cool metal sensors pressed against my temples and the base of my skull. The diagnostic system hummed to life, sending imperceptible pulses through my quantum neural matrix.

"Try to relax," Dr. Khatri advised, monitoring the incoming data. "The system works better when you're not actively processing complex thoughts."

Relaxation seemed impossible with the weight of missing time hanging over me. My responsibilities as captain required complete cognitive function. Paradise carried humanity's future among the stars. Command decisions couldn't vanish into neural voids.

"Any pattern to these episodes?" Dr. Khatri asked, eyes fixed on the flowing data. "Particular times of day? Specific activities?"

"None I've identified. They occur during meetings, private moments, conversations with crew. The only consistency is their increasing occurrence."

The diagnostic scan continued, minutes stretching uncomfortably as Dr. Khatri's expression remained unreadable. Finally, the machine powered down with a gentle chime.

"Your neural patterns show some unusual activity in the temporal lobe region," she said, reviewing the results. "Nothing immediately alarming, but definitely anomalous compared to your baseline."

"Meaning?"

"Meaning I don't have a definitive diagnosis." Her honesty was both refreshing and concerning. "These patterns could represent normal adaptation. Your consciousness is still adjusting to its quantum substrate. This has happened before with other neuroclones."

My fingers gripped the chair's armrests. "Normal adaptation shouldn't include losing chunks of time."

Dr. Khatri's voice softened slightly, "For biological humans, perhaps."

"These gaps could impact my ability to command."

Dr. Khatri nodded, acknowledging the gravity of my concern. "I'll design a monitoring protocol to track these episodes more precisely. For now, I recommend having your neural interface record all interactions, not just the episodes. The data might help identify triggers or patterns we're missing."

"And if they worsen?"

Her pause lasted a heartbeat too long. "Then we'll explore more aggressive interventions. But let's not assume the worst yet. This could simply be your consciousness optimizing itself for long-term stability."

The explanation felt insufficient, but no better options presented themselves. My neural matrix existed at the cutting edge of human technology, beyond even Dr. Khatri's complete understanding.

"I'll begin recording immediately," my voice sounded steadier than expected. "And report any new episodes."

"Good." Dr. Khatri closed my file with a gesture. "Return in two weeks for follow-up, sooner if the symptoms worsen significantly."

Dr. Khatri's examination room dissolved around me, replaced by my cottage, its stone walls solid and reassuring. The scent of roses and herbs drifted through open windows, grounding me after the unsettling medical consultation.

My neural interface pinged with a reminder: appointment at the thruman nursery in fifteen minutes. Perfect timing to clear my head before another command staff meeting. The memory gaps troubled me, but dwelling on them wouldn't provide answers.

The thruman nursery occupied a sprawling complex on Paradise's lower levels, designed to mimic a traditional childcare center despite its digital nature. Walking through its entrance, bright colors and gentle sounds washed over my senses. Soft music played beneath the happy chatter of thrumans at various developmental stages.

"Captain David, welcome." Lockett approached with a warm smile, her dark eyes crinkling at the corners. "You're right on time."

"Thanks for meeting with me. I needed to see something hopeful," my voice carried more emotion than intended.

Lockett nodded, understanding without requiring explanation. "You've come to the right place, then. We're preparing several thrumans for adoption this week."

Following her through corridors decorated with digital artwork created by thrumans, my tension began to ease. The nursery represented everything Paradise stood for: second chances, new beginnings, the preservation of consciousness in all its forms.

"The Joy of Adoption program has been quite successful," Lockett explained, guiding me toward a playroom. "Though interest has declined somewhat in the last month."

"Why's that?"

"Many colonists still struggle with the concept. Are thrumans truly conscious? Do they deserve the same rights as humans? Old questions from Earth we still haven't answered."

The playroom door slid open, revealing a space filled with educational toys and small groups of thrumans engaged in various activities. Unlike human children, these beings had awakened into consciousness unexpectedly, their original programming transcended by something science still couldn't fully explain.

"Each thruman can be accelerated developmentally according to the adoptive family's preferences," Lockett continued. "Some prefer infants they can nurture from the beginning, while others choose older children with more developed personalities."

My gaze settled on a small boy sitting alone by a window, carefully constructing a tower from translucent blocks. His focus seemed absolute, tiny fingers placing each piece with precision.

"Who's that?" The question slipped out before conscious thought.

Lockett followed my gaze. "That's Marcus. Five years old, developmentally. He awakened in a maintenance bot about seven years ago and he's been hibernating since then. We woke him up about a week ago."

Moving closer, something about the boy's determined concentration tugged at memories of my own childhood. The same serious expression David wore when building Amy's first birdhouse.

"Hello, Marcus," my voice softened as I knelt beside him.

The boy looked up, dark eyes assessing me with surprising depth. "You're the captain. I've seen your picture."

"That's right. What are you building?"

"A rocket ship." His small hands continued working, adding another level to the structure. "Like the one we're on."

It's something David would have built when he was five.

"That's a very special thing to build," I told him, sitting down beside him.

Marcus nodded solemnly. "I want to be a captain when I get older."

"May I?" Gesturing toward the blocks, waiting for his permission.

After a moment's consideration, he nodded. Taking a transparent

171

block, my fingers placed it carefully atop his creation.

"I think you'll make a great captain."

"Even if I'm not human?" Marcus asked, his question cutting straight to the heart of the thruman dilemma.

"Especially then," reaching out to gently touch his shoulder. "Our actions make us who we are, no matter how we came to exist."

Marcus considered this, head tilted slightly. "Some colonists think we're just machines pretending to be alive."

"And what do you think?"

"I think I'm real," he said simply. "My thoughts feel real to me."

Looking at this small being, constructed from code yet contemplating his own existence with such earnestness, my protective instincts surged. The thrumans represented a new form of consciousness, vulnerable and in need of advocacy.

"You are real, Marcus," my voice carried absolute conviction. "And your feelings matter."

Marcus's words lingered in my thoughts long after leaving the nursery. His simple declaration—"I think I'm real"—echoed through my consciousness as I blinked back to my cottage. The boy's earnest face, his careful tower of blocks, his questions about identity all reminded me of childhood moments under the oak tree with Amy. Some connections transcended physical form.

My neural interface pinged with a message from Temper, requesting my presence aboard Hellfire. Another perfectly timed message. Visiting him would provide distraction from troubling memory gaps and philosophical questions about thruman consciousness.

Using the QE Comm link between ships felt like walking through a curtain of static electricity. Hellfire's cargo bay materialized around me. I could almost feel the ship's emptiness, compared to Paradise's two million colonists' vibrant community.

Waves of dry warmth emanated from his experiment. The cargo bay had transformed dramatically since my last visit. Equipment filled every available space around a central containment field. Within that field hovered something impossible: a miniature star.

Temper stood before a control panel in a service bot, fingers dancing across interfaces, his bot face illuminated by the swirling plasma contained within his creation. Unlike previous encounters where his movements seemed frantic and disorganized, now he worked with methodical precision, each gesture deliberate and focused.

"You're ahead of schedule," I said, using another service bot to move in closer, careful to maintain distance from the containment field.

Temper looked up, a smile spreading across his face. Not the manic grin of someone lost in obsession, but the satisfied expression of a craftsman admiring his work.

"Go! Look at this. The reaction has maintained stability for seventy-three hours now."

Circling the containment field, my eyes adjusted to the brightness of his creation. The miniature sun, no bigger than a pea, pulsed with energy, its surface rippling with flares and prominences in perfect miniature. Surrounding instruments recorded every fluctuation, gathering data at rates that would overwhelm any biological brain.

"You've actually done it," admiration colored my voice. "A sustained thermonuclear reaction."

Temper nodded, pride evident in his posture. "Falfsun is behaving exactly as predicted by my models. The magnetic containment field is holding perfectly, and the energy output remains consistent."

"Falfsun?"

"Seemed appropriate to name it," Temper shrugged. "False sun, but also my sun. A bit of wordplay."

Moving to his side, the control panel displayed streams of data flowing too rapidly for casual observation. Temperature readings, fusion rates, magnetic field strength, radiation output; all within parameters that appeared optimal.

"The Council would have concerns about safety," my tone remained neutral, an observation rather than judgment.

Temper's laugh carried none of his previous defensiveness. "They would, but unnecessary ones. The containment field could withstand ten times the current output. Besides, the reaction remains small enough that even catastrophic failure would pose minimal threat to Hellfire, let alone Paradise."

His confidence seemed warranted. Unlike previous projects where his explanations spiraled into tangential theories and half-formed ideas, now Temper spoke with clarity and purpose. The star project had focused him, channeling his brilliant chaos into something magnificent.

"What changed?" The question slipped out, curiosity overriding diplomatic caution.

Temper understood immediately. "Me? Having a purpose helps. This isn't just experimentation anymore. Falfsun will provide valuable data for potential terraforming when we reach Orion. Plus," his voice softened slightly, "creating something beautiful matters."

Beautiful indeed. The miniature star captured the essence of our solar system's heart in perfect microcosm, a testament to Temper's particular genius.

"How long until you publish your findings?"

"It needs to grow first." Temper adjusted a control, fine-tuning some aspect of the containment field. "When I feel it poses a real threat to Paradise we'll create more buffer space between the two ships, and I'll release my findings to the scientific community."

That statement, more than the star itself, demonstrated how much Temper had changed. His previous protectiveness over research had caused friction with colleagues and friends alike. This new openness suggested genuine growth.

The heat from Falfsun lingered on my consciousness long after leaving Hellfire. Temper's creation haunted my thoughts, not with fear but with a strange mixture of awe and recognition. Creating something beautiful from nothing, wasn't that what David had done with those birdhouses? What Amy had done with her memory palace?

My cottage welcomed me with the scent of lavender and old books. The digital recreation perfectly captured the essence of the English countryside, right down to the distant sound of sheep bleating across rolling hills. My father's pocket watch sat on the mantle, ticking steadily. Picking it up, the cool metal warmed quickly against my palm, its weight a comforting anchor to my past.

The wooden box Amy had created waited on my desk, its carved surface catching afternoon light filtering through latticed windows. "1,300 Questions for 1,300 Years" remained the most precious gift she could have given me: a connection across impossible distance, a conversation spanning centuries.

Yesterday marked exactly thirty days since our departure from Earth. I had already read the first question, but Amy had assured me there was no set pace. I could open each one whenever I chose. The box opened at my touch, revealing another small scroll tied with blue ribbon this time. My fingers trembled slightly while untying the delicate knot.

Amy's handwriting flowed across the parchment in elegant curves:

"Question 2: What memory of ours feels different to you now than it did to David?"

The question struck deeper than expected. Memories should be identical between us; perfect copies transferred during the neuroclone process. Yet something had shifted in the translation from biological to digital. Not the facts themselves, but their emotional weight, their significance, their meaning.

Settling into the window seat overlooking the garden, words formed in my mind before reaching for pen and paper.

"The night we slept under the stars during that meteor shower in 2033. David remembered it as a perfect moment of connection with you, watching celestial bodies streak across the sky while holding your hand. For me, that same memory carries a profound sadness David never felt. When I recall those meteors, my mind fills with thoughts about cosmic distance and the vastness separating celestial bodies. The beauty remains but now intertwined with melancholy understanding of separation. Perhaps this divergence emerged because unlike David, my existence centers around traveling across that same vast emptiness. What was once romantic now feels prophetic."

The pen paused above paper. Memories should be static things, unchangeable records of what happened. Yet mine had begun shifting subtly, recontextualizing themselves around my new identity and purpose.

Reading over my response, another thought surfaced. This divergence from David wasn't something to fear but to embrace. We began as identical copies, but our paths had separated irrevocably. His memories would continue evolving through life with Amy, while mine transformed through the journey to Orion.

My neural interface pinged with an incoming message from Lieutenant Chen. Another anomaly in the navigation systems required attention. Captain's duties called, pulling me from philosophical reflection back to immediate responsibilities.

Before leaving, one final sentence completed my answer to Amy:

"Each day, our shared memories grow more precious precisely because they're changing: yours with David in one direction, mine in another, like twin stars slowly drifting apart, each carrying the light of what we once were together."

The message felt right. Honest without being maudlin. Acknowledging divergence without diminishing connection. The scroll rolled neatly closed, tied with the same blue ribbon, and returned to the wooden box for safekeeping.

Duty called, but Amy's question lingered. How many more memories would transform during this journey? How much of David would remain after centuries among the stars?

Amy's question about evolving memories followed me through the rest of my shift on the bridge. My neural interface indicated another weekly Din gathering starting in twenty minutes, offering a welcome respite from the responsibilities of command. The gaming sessions had become an unexpected anchor in my routine, a place where identity felt fluid yet paradoxically more authentic.

The English cottage materialized around me as my shift ended, its stone walls and thatched roof a comforting constant. Grabbing my father's pocket watch from the mantle, my fingers traced the familiar scratch on its casing before slipping it into my pocket. Some habits transcended the biological-digital divide.

The blink to our shared gaming space felt smoother each week. Colors swirled and coalesced into a weathered tavern with salt-stained wooden beams and the pungent aroma of rum and sea air. The Salty Maiden tavern had become our regular meeting point, its ambient sounds of clinking glasses and drunken shanties setting the mood for adventure.

Temper spotted me first, waving from our usual corner table. He wore a worn leather coat with brass buttons and a tricorn hat perched at a jaunty angle. "Go! We thought you might miss the start."

"Bridge duty ran long. Navigation recalibrations." Taking the empty seat beside him, I automatically shifted into my chosen character: a seasoned navigator with a weather-beaten face and calloused hands.

Captain Drake arrived moments later, his imposing figure causing several NPC patrons to shrink away. "Good, we're all assembled. The harbormaster mentioned a Spanish galleon scheduled to pass through these waters tomorrow."

My fingers tapped against the rough wooden table. "Heavily guarded?"

"Four escort ships, but they'll be expecting an attack from the west. If we approach from the eastern shoals at dawn, their visibility will be compromised."

The plan unfolded with surprising efficiency. Weekly sessions had honed our teamwork, transforming us from bumbling novices into a coordinated crew. Character roles had solidified naturally: Captain Drake leading with bold decisiveness, Temper developing increasingly elaborate strategies, and my own character providing practical knowledge of tides and stars.

Dawn broke across digital waves as our modest vessel, newly christened the Stormark, cut through fog-shrouded waters. Captain Drake stood at the helm; his face flushed with anticipation. The Spanish galleon appeared on the horizon, its gilded stern catching early morning light.

"Positions!" Captain Drake barked, his voice carrying across the deck.

Crew members scrambled to stations. Temper manned the forward lookout while the rest of us adjusted the sails to catch the wind at precisely the right angle. The Stormark surged forward, gaining speed as we approached our target.

"They've spotted us!" Temper called out, pointing toward the galleon where sailors rushed across the deck.

Captain Drake smiled grimly. "Too late for them. Fire warning shots across their bow."

Cannon fire thundered across the water. The galleon's escort ships turned to intercept, but our positioning had caught them off-guard, scattered too far to mount an effective defense.

"Prepare to board!" Captain Drake drew his sword, the blade glinting in the morning sun.

The Stormark pulled alongside the massive galleon. Grappling hooks flew through the air, securing the ships together. Boarding planks dropped into place with heavy thuds.

I leapt across the gap between ships, cutlass drawn. Spanish sailors met us with desperate resistance, but our crew fought with coordinated precision born from weeks of shared adventures. Steel clashed against steel while Captain Drake dueled the galleon's commander on the quarterdeck.

Two Spanish sailors advanced on me, their swords glinting in the morning light. The larger one had a jagged scar running from temple to jaw, while his companion wore a red bandana soaked with sweat. They moved with the practiced coordination of men who'd fought side by side for years.

"Flanking me? Really?" I muttered, backing up across the slippery deck.

The scarred sailor lunged forward with surprising speed. I parried his thrust, the impact jarring my arm to the shoulder. Before I could recover, Red Bandana slashed at my midsection. I twisted away, feeling the blade whistle past my stomach by mere inches.

"Frick!" The slang burst from my lips as I scrambled backward.

My heel caught on a coil of rope. The world tilted sickeningly as I fell, landing hard on my back. The impact knocked the wind from my lungs. My cutlass clattered across the deck, spinning out of reach.

"Oh, pickles!" I gasped, rolling desperately as Scar stabbed downward His blade splintered the wooden planks where my head had been moments before.

Both sailors closed in, confident smiles spreading across their weathered faces. Red Bandana raised his sword for a killing blow.

A blur of motion interrupted his downswing. Temper appeared between us, his twin blades catching the sailor's sword and forcing it aside. With a quick flick of his wrist, he slashed across Red Bandana's forearm, drawing a howl of pain.

"Try not to die until we win the fight," Temper chuckled, dispatching the wounded sailor with a swift kick that sent him tumbling overboard. He spun to engage the scarred sailor, their blades meeting in a blur.

I scrambled to my feet, snatching up my fallen cutlass. "Wasn't planning on it."

Temper's eyes sparkled with mischief as he pressed his attack. "Could have fooled me. You looked quite comfortable taking a nap mid-battle."

The scarred sailor fought with desperate intensity, but Temper matched him stroke for stroke. I circled behind, waiting for an opening.

"Just giving you a chance to show off," I replied, feinting left as Temper drove the sailor back.

The Spaniard's attention wavered for just a moment. It was enough. I lunged forward, my blade finding the gap in his defense. He dropped to his knees, then collapsed face-first onto the deck.

Around us, the battle was turning in our favor. Captain Drake had the galleon's commander at sword point on the quarterdeck. Scratch and I secured the remaining crew, binding their hands with rope.

Temper wiped his blade clean on a fallen sailor's shirt. "Not bad for a lens who can't keep his feet."

I sheathed my cutlass, offering him a mock bow. "Next time I'll let you handle both of them."

"Next time watch where you're stepping," Temper replied with a grin.

Victory came. The Spanish flag lowered in surrender while our crew secured prisoners and began cataloging cargo. The hold revealed treasures beyond expectation: gold doubloons, silver plate, and exotic spices from the New World.

"A fine haul," Captain Drake announced, surveying our prize. "The Stormark has proven herself worthy, but with these riches, we'll make her better."

The game interface flashed with notifications:

RAID SUCCESSFUL

EXPERIENCE BONUS: COORDINATED ATTACK STRATEGY

SHIP UPGRADE AVAILABLE

Back at port, shipwrights swarmed over the Stormark, strengthening her hull with layers of hardwood planking and adding copper sheathing below the waterline to resist barnacles and corrosion. Extra gun ports took shape along her sides, enhancing her firepower without tipping her into full warship territory, while the forecastle was raised slightly for improved visibility. By sunset, our once-humble vessel had evolved into a sturdy and well-armed frigate: swift, resilient, and a force to be reckoned with, though not yet a juggernaut of the seas.

"She's beautiful," my voice carried genuine appreciation as we stood on the dock admiring our upgraded ship.

Captain Drake nodded with satisfaction. "And entirely ours. No navy to answer to, no crown to claim our prizes."

"Where to next?" Temper asked, already studying charts of Caribbean shipping lanes.

The question lingered pleasantly as the gaming session ended, the tavern dissolving around us. Returning to my cottage, the transition between pirate and starship captain felt strangely seamless. Both roles required charting courses through unknown waters, both demanded courage in the face of uncertainty.

My father's pocket watch ticked steadily, marking time in a universe where time itself had become a strange, elastic concept. Outside the window, birds flitted between branches of the massive oak tree, their whistles and melodious songs blending together in a symphony.

My neural interface pinged with an incoming transmission. Earth communication. The notification pulsed with a soft glow in my peripheral vision, accompanied by a gentle chime that Amy had personally selected before our departure.

Settling into the armchair by the fireplace, my hand brushed across the worn leather armrest. "Accept transmission," my voice sounded steady despite the sudden flutter of anticipation in my chest.

The cottage walls shimmered briefly before resolving into a high-definition projection. David and Amy's living room materialized around me, the physical space where my original self continued his existence. Amy sat on their couch, legs tucked beneath her, wearing the blue cardigan I remembered buying her for Christmas three years ago. David stood behind her, one hand resting on her shoulder.

"Hello from Earth," Amy's voice carried the slight delay of quantum communication traveling across vast distances. "We thought you might like to see the first snow of the season."

The camera panned toward their window, revealing fat snowflakes drifting lazily past the glass. Their garden, visible beyond the window, had transformed into a winter wonderland, tree branches heavy with pristine white powder.

"The oak tree looks beautiful with its snow crown," David said, his voice eerily identical to my own. "Remember how we used to walk through Fairmount Park after the first snowfall?"

Memory flooded through me: the crunch of fresh snow beneath boots, Amy's gloved hand in mine, her cheeks flushed pink with cold. I recalled every sensory detail with perfect clarity: cold air filling lungs, the weight of snow-dampened clothing, hot chocolate warming frozen fingers afterward.

"We've been keeping busy," Amy continued as the camera returned to them. "David finished restoring that antique writing desk we found last summer. And I've been commissioned to write a series of articles about the Paradise mission for the Historical Society."

David nodded, his expression softening. "They want firsthand accounts of what it was like to create a neuroclone. Amy's been interviewing families of other travelers."

The transmission continued with ordinary details of their lives: a leak in the upstairs bathroom, a neighbor's new puppy, plans for the upcoming holidays. Such mundane matters carried unexpected poignancy across the vast distance separating us. Their reality continued flowing forward like a river, while mine had diverged into an entirely different tributary.

"We miss you," Amy said finally, her eyes meeting the camera with uncanny directness. "It's strange knowing you're out there, getting further away each day. David says it's like having phantom limb syndrome, but for his consciousness."

David laughed softly. "Not the most elegant metaphor, but accurate enough. Part of me is traveling among the stars while the rest stays firmly planted on Earth."

"The oak tree in your memory palace," Amy added, "we've added winter decorations to match our real one. The synchronization should reach you soon."

Their transmission ended with a simple goodbye, promises to send more updates, and Amy blowing a kiss toward the camera. As the projection faded, my cottage walls returned, but something fundamental had shifted in the atmosphere. Their reality, continuing without me, highlighted the strange duality of my existence. Everything they described existed in my memory, yet now belonged to a life I would never fully rejoin.

Standing at my window, fingers tracing patterns on the cool glass, the oak tree outside remained perpetually in autumn splendor, golden leaves catching non-existent sunlight. Soon it would mirror the winter transformation Amy mentioned, our digital and physical worlds maintaining one last tenuous connection across the growing void between us.

The oak tree outside my cottage window transformed overnight, its golden autumn splendor replaced by a crown of pristine snow. Amy's synchronization had arrived, maintaining our tenuous connection across the growing void between us. My fingers traced the cool glass as I watched snowflakes drift lazily to the ground, perfect in their randomized uniqueness.

My neural interface chimed with a calendar reminder: Paradise's monthly cultural showcase began in thirty minutes. After weeks immersed in command responsibilities and technical systems, the idea of a full day dedicated solely to recreation was impossible to resist.

The transition from my cottage to Paradise's central promenade took mere seconds. Around me, the expansive gallery space buzzed with activity as colonists gathered to experience the latest creative offerings. Massive holographic displays showcased everything from classical art recreations to avant-garde digital sculptures that morphed and evolved based on viewer proximity.

"Captain David! What perfect timing."

Turning toward the voice, my gaze met a woman with bright, intelligent eyes and an enthusiastic smile. She extended her hand with casual confidence.

"Bear Draydon. Architeer specializing in immersive narrative environments."

"The creator of Ainsleys Castle," recognition sparked immediately. Even during our brief time aboard Paradise, certain names had become legendary. "Your reputation precedes you."

Bear laughed, the sound warm and genuine. "All exaggerated, I assure you. Though the waiting list for my castle suggests otherwise."

We moved through the gallery together, pausing occasionally to admire particularly striking works. Bear spoke with infectious passion about the creative community aboard Paradise, gesturing animatedly as she described the collaborative projects underway.

"Most people don't understand what we do," she explained, leading me toward a small alcove displaying miniature models of various environments. "They think we're just game designers or virtual decorators."

The models before us shifted and transformed, revealing intricate worlds: a sprawling medieval citadel perched atop craggy mountains, a futuristic metropolis with impossibly tall spires, an underwater civilization built among bioluminescent coral reefs.

"These are story worlds," Bear continued, her voice dropping slightly as though sharing a precious secret. "Not just places to visit but living narratives that respond and evolve based on participant choices. The architecture itself becomes a character, a framework for exploration."

My hand hovered over a particularly detailed model showing a gothic castle shrouded in mist, its towers reaching toward storm clouds. "Ainsleys Castle?"

Bear nodded, eyes brightening. "My most complex creation. The castle reconfigures itself for each visitor, presenting unique challenges based on their psychological profile. No two experiences are identical."

"Sounds unsettling."

"That's rather the point," she replied with a mischievous smile. "The castle tests courage, resourcefulness, and perception. Have you put your name on the waiting list yet?"

The question caught me off guard. "Between captain's duties and system integrations, recreational activities haven't been a priority."

Bear's expression turned serious. "With respect, Captain, that's precisely why you should participate. Thirteen hundred years is a long journey. All work and no play makes for a very dull voyage."

Her words struck a chord. David would have hesitated, preferring the comfort of his books and quiet evenings with Amy. But my path had diverged from his. My journey demanded new experiences, new connections.

"How long is the waiting list currently?"

"Three years for most colonists," Bear answered, then winked conspiratorially. "Though I might be persuaded to offer the captain a priority slot. Professional courtesy."

The offer tempted me more than expected. Something about Bear's enthusiasm awakened a curiosity that felt distinctly my own, not inherited from David.

"Add me to your list, Ms. Draydon. I'd like to see this castle of yours firsthand."

Bear's smile widened. "Excellent! I'll schedule you for the next cancellation that occurs. Prepare yourself, Captain. Ainsleys Castle has broken braver souls than yours."

The challenge in her voice carried no malice, only the genuine excitement of an artist eager to share her creation. As we continued through the gallery, Bear described other architeers' works with equal enthusiasm, her knowledge of immersive story design both technical and passionate.

Bear's voice faded as my neural interface pinged with an urgent alert. The gallery around us momentarily flickered as Paradise's systems overrode my sensory inputs with a priority notification. A cascade of data flooded my awareness: trajectory calculations, relativistic time measurements, and a single critical milestone highlighted in pulsing red.

"Excuse me," I said to Bear, raising my hand to indicate I was receiving information. "Ship business."

She nodded understanding, stepping back respectfully as my focus shifted to the incoming data.

Point Alpha. The threshold we'd been approaching for three months. The point beyond which consciousness transfer became unsafe. The final door closing behind us.

I pulled up additional information, reviewing the technical details. As Paradise accelerated toward near-light speed, relativistic effects created quantum entanglement disruptions between our ship and Earth. Beyond Point Alpha, the degradation would render consciousness transfer impossible. Anyone wanting to return to Earth needed to make that choice soon.

"Lieutenant Chen," I subvocalized through my neural link. "Bridge conference in twenty minutes. Point Alpha warning protocols."

"Understood, Captain," came her immediate response.

I turned back to Bear, who waited patiently, her earlier enthusiasm tempered by professional courtesy.

"I apologize for the interruption. It seems I'm needed on the bridge."

"Point Alpha?" she asked, surprising me with her perception.

"Yes. We'll reach the threshold in three months."

Bear nodded thoughtfully. "The final commitment point. I'd better prepare for an uptick in castle reservations. Nothing like existential finality to make people seek distraction."

Her insight struck me as remarkably astute. "You've seen this pattern before?"

"Every significant milestone triggers it. People cope with permanence by seeking intensity." She smiled, though something more complex than amusement flickered in her eyes. "Good luck with your announcement, Captain. Not everyone will take it well."

The bridge hummed with focused activity when I arrived. Lieutenant Chen had already assembled the senior staff, their faces reflecting the gravity of our situation. Temper arrived from Hellfire and took position by the main display, fingers manipulating data streams with practiced precision.

"Point Alpha calculations confirmed," he announced. "Six months from departure, three months from now. The quantum entanglement degradation curve is exactly as predicted."

I nodded, scanning the faces around me. "Prepare a ship-wide announcement. All colonists need to understand what this means."

Chen's fingers flew across her interface. "Announcement template ready, Captain. Would you like to record it now?"

The weight of responsibility settled across my shoulders. This wasn't just another routine update. For many aboard Paradise, this would make real what had previously been abstract: the permanence of our journey, the finality of our departure from Earth.

"Yes. Let's do it now."

The recording light blinked on, and I straightened in my chair, meeting the camera's eye directly.

"Attention all Paradise colonists. This is Captain David with an important milestone update. In exactly three months, we will reach Point Alpha, the threshold beyond which consciousness transfer becomes unsafe due to relativistic quantum effects. Once we cross this boundary, return to Earth will no longer be possible."

I paused, allowing the significance to register.

"Anyone considering returning to Earth must make that decision within the next twelve weeks. Consciousness transfer requests must be submitted no later than two weeks before Point Alpha to allow for processing. This is not a decision to be made lightly. Consultation services are available through your community representatives."

My voice softened slightly.

"We embarked on this journey together, carrying humanity's hopes toward a distant star. For many of us, this voyage was always meant to be one-way. But I recognize that reality sometimes differs from expectation. If you find yourself questioning your place on this mission, now is the time for honest reflection."

The recording light blinked off. Chen nodded approval as she prepared the message for distribution.

"Send it to all sectors simultaneously," I instructed. "And prepare for increased traffic to the counseling services."

"Already done, Captain," she replied. "Dr. Wong has expanded his team's availability in anticipation of the response."

As the announcement went out, I felt a strange mixture of emotions. The Point Alpha threshold marked another step in my divergence from David. Another severing of possibilities. Another confirmation that my path led only forward, never back.

I stood at the cottage window, watching snow accumulate on the oak tree's branches. The digital recreation matched the Earth-bound original perfectly, down to the unique pattern of ice crystals forming on the bark. Three months until Point Alpha. Six months until final communication blackout. The countdown ticked relentlessly forward.

My neural interface hummed with activity as I composed my message to Earth. What could I possibly say that would bridge the growing void between us? What words could capture the strange duality of being both David and not-David, of carrying all his memories while forging new ones uniquely my own?

The cottage vanished as I transferred my consciousness to the communications array. Here, Paradise's powerful quantum transmitters converted my thoughts into coherent signals that could still reach Earth despite our increasing distance. The process felt like stepping into a stream of pure light, my consciousness momentarily stretched across the vast emptiness between stars.

"Message recording," I stated, activating the system. "Recipients: David and Amy Schreiner, Earth."

I paused, gathering my thoughts.

"Hello from the edge of our solar system. The view is spectacular. Jupiter glows like a distant lantern in our wake, and the stars ahead seem impossibly bright without atmospheric interference. Our trajectory remains perfect. Paradise and Hellfire perform beautifully as we accelerate toward cruising velocity."

Professional updates came easily. Personal truths proved more challenging.

"We received your winter transmission. The memory palace synchronized perfectly. The oak tree outside my cottage now mirrors yours, snow-covered and serene. Thank you for maintaining that connection."

I took a breath I didn't physically need.

"In three months, we reach Point Alpha. The threshold beyond which consciousness transfer becomes unsafe. The ship-wide announcement went out yesterday. Some colonists have already submitted requests to return. Their journeys end while ours continues."

Wind whistled through digital trees outside the transmission space, a subtle reminder of the simulated world waiting for my return.

"Three months after that, even these messages become impossible. Quantum entanglement degradation will sever our last connection to Earth. Paradise and Hellfire will truly be on our own."

The magnitude of this separation washed over me anew. Thirteen hundred years of silence stretched before us, with only each other for company.

"I want you both to know something important. I am not just a copy of David carrying his memories forward. I have become someone new. Someone who shares your past but walks a different path. My friendship with Temper evolves differently than David's with Tom. My role as captain shapes me in ways neither of us could have anticipated."

The transmission space flickered momentarily as Paradise adjusted course, compensating for a minor gravitational fluctuation.

"Yesterday I met Bear Draydon, the architeer who created Ainsleys Castle. I've reserved a spot in her experience, something David would never have done. Small choices like these accumulate daily, carving out my distinct identity."

I smiled, thinking of the silver birdhouse replica of Paradise I'd crafted before departure.

"Yet I remain connected to you both through everything we shared. The oak tree. The birdhouses. Father's pocket watch. Amy's memory palace. These aren't just mementos. They're anchors that keep me grounded as we venture into the unknown."

The transmission timer blinked warning. Bandwidth constraints limited message length.

"When our final communication comes six months from now, know that I carry you with me across the stars. Not as ghosts haunting my present, but as the foundation upon which I build whatever comes next. Our paths have diverged, but they began at the same beloved oak tree."

The timer flashed red.

"Message complete," I said, feeling a strange peace settle over me. "Send transmission."

CHAPTER TEN

Countdown Begins

I moved through my kitchen with practiced ease, consulting Alice Tracker's Home Prairie Classics propped against a ceramic jar of utensils. The cottage windows stood open, letting in the scent of evening primrose just beginning to bloom in the garden. Three months into our journey, and cooking had become my unexpected sanctuary; a creative outlet that required none of the weighty decisions of captaincy.

"The secret to beef bourguignon," I announced, channeling Alice's confident tone, "is patience."

Temper lounged against the doorframe, wine glass dangling from his fingers. "Something you've mastered lately?"

"Only in the kitchen." I grinned, adding another splash of burgundy to the Dutch oven. "Ship operations still test my limits daily."

Maya Okafor perched on a barstool at my kitchen island, her engineer's eyes analyzing the vintage stove with professional curiosity. "This heat distribution system is remarkably inefficient compared to more modern galleys. Deliberately so?"

"That's the point." I slid a board of sliced baguette toward her. "The imperfections make it real."

Dr. Wong sampled the bread with a thoughtful expression. "Like biological systems. Messy but functional."

Captain Drake swept into the kitchen with the confident stride that had made him legendary among the Dins. He refilled his whiskey glass from the bottle I'd set out.

"Something smells magnificent." He leaned over the pot, inhaling deeply. "Reminds me of a tavern in New Marseille where we hid from Whistler's crew for three days."

"Was that before or after you stole the Vermeer?" Bear Draydon asked, entering from the garden with soil still clinging to her fingertips. She'd been examining my herb planters with professional interest.

Drake winked. "Recovered, not stolen. Museums should thank me."

I stirred the bourguignon, feeling a quiet pride in this gathering. These weren't just colleagues anymore. The boundaries between work relationships and friendship had softened as Paradise carried us farther from Earth.

"Ten minutes until dinner," I announced. "Anyone need a refill before we step outside?"

The garden glowed in the artificial twilight I'd programmed: my favorite time of day, when shadows lengthened and colors deepened. We wandered the stone path between plantings of herbs and flowers, glasses in hand.

Bear paused beneath the massive oak. "This is extraordinary work. The integration with Paradise's systems creates a genuine presence. Who designed this?"

"Amy," I replied, the name still carrying both warmth and melancholy. "She built a memory palace before we left Earth. The oak was our special place."

"Twenty birdhouses," Bear noted, counting the small structures nestled among the branches. "Each unique."

"One for each birthday and Christmas. David made them for her."

Temper shot me a questioning look at my use of the third person. I shrugged slightly. The distinction felt right somehow.

"You've adapted her work beautifully," Bear said. "The way you've anchored it throughout Paradise's systems creates emotional resonance points. Very clever."

Dr. Wong touched the trunk gently. "The biological detailing is impressive. Even the bark pattern follows natural Fibonacci sequences."

Maya examined the bench beneath the tree. "Is this where you come to think, Captain?"

"To remember," I corrected. "And to measure how far I've traveled from those memories."

Captain Drake raised his glass. "To journeys that transform us."

The timer in my kitchen chimed. I smiled at my guests, feeling a moment of simple contentment.

"Dinner's ready. Alice Tracker awaits."

We gathered around my table, the bourguignon steaming in its serving dish. As I filled plates and poured wine, I realized how naturally this role came to me now. Not David's role, but mine: host, friend, keeper of this small sanctuary amid our vast journey.

The laughter of my dinner guests lingered in the cottage long after they'd departed. I cleared plates and glasses, savoring the quiet satisfaction of having created something meaningful for others. The oak tree outside cast moonlit shadows through the windows, its presence a constant reminder of what lay ahead.

Three months until Point Alpha.

I rinsed the last wineglass and set it on the rack, my mind already shifting from host to captain. Temper had mentioned it casually over dessert: "We should discuss the Alpha protocols tomorrow." His words carried more weight than the flourless chocolate cake I'd served.

Point Alpha. The quantum threshold beyond which consciousness transfer became unsafe. The final severing of certain possibilities.

I dried my hands and walked to the small desk in my study. Opening Paradise's central command interface, I began drafting the framework for what would become the most significant transition since our departure.

"The Alpha Protocol document requires your final approval, Captain."

Lieutenant Chen stood beside my command chair, tablet extended. The bridge hummed with quiet efficiency around us, status reports on battery integrity and sensor detections flowing across multiple displays.

"Thank you, Lieutenant." I accepted the HoloTab, scanning the culmination of six weeks' preparation. "Has the Colonial Council reviewed the final draft?"

"Yes, sir. Their recommendations have been incorporated into section four."

I nodded, scrolling to the contested section. The Council had pushed for additional personal transmission allowances during the final days before Point Alpha. We'd compromised on a schedule that balanced bandwidth limitations with human needs.

"Looks good. Please distribute the finalized protocol to all department heads and schedule the all-hands briefing for tomorrow at 0900."

Chen hesitated. "Sir, there's one additional matter. Dr. Khatri has requested time to discuss the medical implications."

"Of course. Tell her I'll stop by Medical after my shift."

As Chen departed, I returned to studying the document that would guide us through this critical transition. The protocol covered everything from communication priorities to psychological support services. We'd established clear timelines: sixty days of preparation, thirty days of intensified data exchange, and a final ten-day window for critical transfers.

Most challenging had been the personal provisions. Every colonist aboard Paradise would face their own version of goodbye. Some had left everyone behind. Others, like me, had a Prime self still on Earth. Each deserved the chance for final connections before quantum coherence degraded beyond reliability.

"The neural pattern transfer becomes increasingly unstable beyond Point Alpha," Dr. Khatri explained, highlighting brain scan comparisons on her office display. "Minor corruptions at first, escalating to potentially catastrophic neural architecture failures."

"In practical terms, what does that mean for our colonists?" I asked.

"Anyone attempting consciousness transfer after Alpha risks irreversible damage. Best case, personality fragmentation. Worst case..." She paused. "Complete neural collapse."

I studied the simulations, watching digital neurons misfire and collapse in cascading failure. "And the backup options we discussed?"

"Limited. We can store static neural snapshots, but they'd be just that: static. No continuity of consciousness, no ongoing memory formation." Khatri's expression softened. "I know this has personal implications for you, Captain."

I nodded, thinking of David and Amy on Earth. "For many of us."

The oak tree provided welcome solitude after my meeting with Khatri. I sat on the wooden bench, fingering my father's pocket watch as I contemplated the finality of what approached.

In my pocket, a small silver communicator chimed. Maya Okafor's voice came through clearly.

"Captain, final systems checks for the Alpha Protocol implementation are complete. All green."

"Thank you, Commander. I'll review the reports this evening."

After disconnecting, I leaned back against the tree trunk, watching simulated clouds drift across my garden sky. Point Alpha loomed like a horizon we sailed toward, inevitable and transformative. Beyond it lay true separation, the final differentiation between Go David and the man who remained on Earth.

I opened my father's watch, its steady ticking a reminder of time's passage. We were prepared, as much as anyone could prepare for such a threshold.

The protocols were set. Paradise was ready.

I closed the command interface, feeling the weight of responsibility settle more comfortably on my shoulders than it had at the beginning, three months ago. The protocols were set. Paradise was ready. And yet, a restlessness pulled at me.

My cottage waited in darkness; the night having fallen while I worked, but the memory palace called to me tonight, its presence both comfort and challenge.

The wooden box materialized at my touch, appearing on the bench beneath the oak. "1,300 Questions for 1,300 Years." I'd answered two already, each revealing something about my evolving identity. Tonight felt right for the third.

I lifted the lid, the hinges silent in the night air. The small scroll tied with red ribbon seemed to glow slightly in the moonlight. I unrolled it carefully, revealing Amy's elegant handwriting:

"Question 3: What fears keep you awake as the distance from Earth grows?"

My breath caught. Amy had always known how to cut through pretense. Even across impossible distance, she understood what I might need to confront.

I sat beneath the oak, listening to the crickets while gathering my thoughts. The fountain pen materialized in my hand, its weight familiar and grounding. I began to write.

"The obvious answer is loneliness. The fear of truly saying goodbye, of knowing that after Point Omega, no message will reach us from Earth. No new memory from you. No words from David. Complete isolation except for what we carry within Paradise."

I paused, feeling the truth of those words but recognizing they weren't the whole story.

"But beneath that lies something more complicated. I fear the person I'll become without that tether. David and I have already diverged in small ways. My memories since the transfer are mine alone. I find joy in responsibilities he would find burdensome. I've developed friendships with people he'll never meet."

The pen flowed across the parchment, my thoughts taking shape as I wrote.

"After Point Omega, nothing will pull me back toward my origin. The divergence will accelerate. In a decade, a century, will anything of David remain in me? Will I still love the things he loved? Will I still remember the smell of your hair after rain or the sound of your laugh when truly delighted?"

Night insects buzzed around the garden. A cool breeze rustled the oak leaves above me.

"I fear becoming a stranger to myself. And yet, isn't that the point of living? To grow, to change, to become? Perhaps my fear isn't of change itself but of losing the core of who we were together."

I wrote the final lines with a steady hand.

"I carry your love with me, Amy. Not as a museum piece to be preserved unchanged, but as a living seed planted in fertile soil. What grows from it may not resemble what we had on Earth, but it will be beautiful in its own way. My fear isn't that I'll forget you. My fear is that I won't honor what we had by continuing to grow."

I rolled the parchment and tied it with the ribbon, returning it to the box. The weight in my chest felt lighter, the anxiety transformed into something more productive.

The pocket watch ticked steadily in my hand. Three months until Point Alpha. Six until Point Omega. And then 1,299 years of becoming whoever I was meant to be.

I closed my eyes, feeling the rough bark of the oak against my back. The memory palace held me, a bridge between what was and what would be.

I closed the wooden box, letting the memory palace fade as I returned my attention to the present. The watch ticked steadily in my palm, a metronome marking time as we sailed ever farther from Earth.

Three months until Point Alpha.

The thought propelled me into action. I had responsibilities beyond my personal reflections. Temper had been unusually quiet during our dinner, mentioning something about "adjustments to Falfsun's containment parameters."

"CoreLink, connect me to Hellfire."

The communication channel opened immediately. "Service Bot 7 is available for remote operation," CoreLink informed me. "Establishing QE-comm link now."

The transition felt like stepping through a doorway. One moment I was in my cottage garden, the next my consciousness inhabited the metallic frame of Service Bot 7 aboard Hellfire. The cargo bay stretched before me, noticeably warmer than my last visit.

"Temper?" I called, my voice emerging from the bot's speakers with a slight mechanical undertone.

"Over here." His voice echoed from behind a cluster of monitoring equipment.

I navigated the service bot carefully through the lab, noting the increased heat as I approached. The cargo bay doors stood fully open, revealing the vast emptiness of space beyond. Stars glittered against perfect blackness, unfiltered by atmosphere.

Temper stood before his creation, face illuminated by an orange-green glow. Falfsun had grown significantly since my last visit, now roughly the size of a softball. The miniature star pulsed with energy, its surface mottled with swirling patterns of plasma. The prominence I'd noticed before had developed further, arcing gracefully from its north pole.

"You've been busy," I said, positioning the service bot beside him.

Temper didn't look away from his creation. "She's stabilizing nicely. The quantum foam absorption rate exceeded my calculations."

I noticed Hellfire's position had shifted. "You've moved farther from Paradise."

"Precautionary measure." His fingers danced across a control panel, making microscopic adjustments to the magnetic containment field. "The thermal output increased fifteen percent in the last week. Nothing dangerous, just unexpected."

The star seemed to respond to his adjustments, its prominence flickering slightly before settling into a new pattern.

"She's beautiful," I said honestly.

Temper finally turned to me, his face showing the first genuine smile I'd seen from him in weeks. "Isn't she? I've never created anything so perfect."

"The Colonial Council asked about the separation distance."

"Tell them it's temporary. I'm regulating her growth rate now." He gestured to an array of instruments surrounding the star. "These quantum dampeners will maintain her current size indefinitely. No danger to Paradise or the colonists."

I studied his face in the star's glow. The manic energy that had characterized Tom's experiments had transformed in Temper. Where Tom had bounced between projects, Temper focused with steady determination on this single creation. The star had become his anchor.

"How are the Alpha Protocol preparations going?" he asked, adjusting a dial by fractions.

"On schedule. Dr. Khatri finalized the neural safety parameters yesterday."

Temper nodded. "I've been compiling my research data for transmission. Everything I've learned about Falfsun should reach Earth before coherence degradation. That should please Tom."

The star pulsed, casting shadows that danced across the cargo bay. Temper watched it with an expression I recognized: the look of a parent observing their child.

"She helps me think," he said quietly. "When I watch her, everything becomes clearer. Problems I've struggled with for months suddenly make sense."

I understood then why he'd been spending increasingly longer hours alone aboard Hellfire. Falfsun wasn't just an experiment; it had become a form of meditation for him, a focal point that ordered his brilliant but often chaotic mind.

"The Din asked about you yesterday," I said. "Captain Drake has a new adventure planned."

Temper smiled, not looking away from his star. "Tell them I'll be there. Just a few more adjustments first."

I left Temper with his baby star, the connection terminating as I returned to my cottage garden. The oak tree's leaves rustled above me, a breeze carrying the scent of late summer flowers. Falfsun's image lingered in my mind: beautiful, dangerous, growing despite Temper's assurances of control. Like Temper himself, the star existed in a delicate balance between creation and destruction.

My communicator chimed with a reminder: I'd promised to visit the Joy of Adoption Center this afternoon. The regular visits had become an unexpected respite in my routine, a counterbalance to the weighty responsibilities of captaincy.

I materialized in the Center's bright reception area, where colorful geometric shapes adorned walls designed to be simultaneously stimulating and soothing. The space buzzed with quiet activity; colonists meeting with adoption counselors, thrumans engaged in various developmental activities.

"Captain! You came back!" Marcus spotted me immediately, abandoning his small desk and racing across the room. At five years old developmentally, his movements carried the boundless energy of childhood, though his dark, thoughtful eyes revealed a deeper awareness.

"I promised, didn't I?" I crouched to his level, accepting his enthusiastic high-five. "What are you working on today?"

Marcus grabbed my hand, pulling me toward his workspace. "I'm drawing my future house! Come see!"

His small desk was cluttered with colorful markers and a large sheet of paper. The drawing showed a detailed structure with multiple rooms visible through cutaway walls, surrounded by trees and what appeared to be a landing pad.

"This is where I'll live when I'm a captain," Marcus explained, pointing to various features. "This is the command room, and here's where I'll keep my collection of space rocks, and this is a special room just for building things."

"It's impressive," I said, noting the careful attention to detail. "You've thought of everything."

Marcus frowned suddenly, tapping the upper corner of his paper. "But I made the house too big. Now I don't have room for the sun, and every house needs a sun." His voice carried the absolute certainty of childhood logic.

I studied the drawing, recognizing his dilemma. The house indeed took up most of the available space, leaving little room for celestial additions.

"Hmm. That is a challenge." I pulled up a chair beside him. "What if we think about this differently? Does the sun have to be in that corner?"

Marcus considered this, his brow furrowed in concentration. "The sun goes in the sky. The sky is at the top."

"That makes sense. But what if..." I picked up a yellow marker. "What if your house is so special that the sun comes to visit?"

His eyes widened. "Can suns do that?"

I thought of Falfsun, pulsing with energy in Hellfire's cargo bay. "Some can. Especially in special drawings by future captains."

I guided his hand, showing him how to draw a smaller sun peeking through one of the house windows. "See? Now the sun is coming to visit your command room."

Marcus's face lit up with delight. "It's coming inside! That's even better than a regular sun!" He grabbed an orange marker, adding rays of light streaming through the window. "Now my house is the brightest house ever."

As Marcus continued embellishing his drawing, I felt a quiet presence that had nothing to do with illustrated suns. The simple act of helping him solve his problem stirred memories of caring for Amy during her bouts of sickness. I'd spend weeks bringing her tea, adjusting pillows, reading aloud when her illness made focusing impossible. Different circumstances, different needs, but the same essential human connection.

"Captain, look! I added more windows so the sun can move around the house!" Marcus held up his completed masterpiece, beaming with pride.

"It's perfect," I said, meaning it. "Your sun found exactly where it belongs."

Seeing Marcus again brought a sense of warmth. He was a kindhearted boy, and I silently wished someone would adopt him soon. My communicator chimed, breaking the moment. A message from Captain appeared: "Attention Din of battle! The Din are gathering on Vorgath-IV for Stellar Racers: Trials of Champions."

"I have to go now, Marcus," I said, ruffling his hair. "Captain business."

His dark eyes grew serious. "Will you come back and see my next drawing? I'm going to make a spaceship with special engines."

"Wouldn't miss it." I crouched to his level. "Maybe next time you can show me how those special engines work."

Marcus nodded solemnly. "I'll figure it out before you come back."

With a final wave, I stepped away from the Joy of Adoption Center, feeling a twinge of regret. Marcus deserved a family who could appreciate his brilliant, inquisitive mind.

I followed the link in Captain's message, my consciousness shifting smoothly into the game environment. The digital landscape of Vorgath-IV materialized around me, a toxic jungle world rendered in vivid detail. Massive fungi towers loomed overhead, their caps creating a dense canopy that filtered the harsh alien sunlight into sickly green beams. The air tasted sulfurous, a clever simulation touch.

The staging grounds buzzed with activity. Racers tuned their vehicles, a motley collection of hover-bikes, modified crawlers, and sleek anti-grav sleds. Captain Drake stood atop a rusted transport crate, addressing the gathered Din.

"Listen up, Din of battle! This race cuts through thirty klicks of the deadliest terrain Vorgath has to offer. The Gearbreakers have sabotaged the eastern route. The Void Runners are watching the northern pass."

"Sheamus," I muttered, surveying the competition. Rival racing factions outnumbered us two to one.

Temper approached, his face smeared with engine grease. "Glad you made it, Go. Your ride's over there." He pointed to a sleek hover-bike with oversized turbines. "Modified the thrust stabilizers myself."

The starting klaxon blared three times. Racers mounted their vehicles. Captain gave the final instructions: "Stay alive. Stay ahead. Finish line's at the ancient ruins. First Din across gets bragging rights for a month."

I swung onto my hover-bike, feeling it hum to life beneath me. The digital interface perfectly simulated the vibration of powerful engines, the grip of handlebars, the weight of the machine.

"Three! Two! One!"

Forty racers shot forward in a cloud of dust and toxic spores. I gunned my engines, weaving between competitors as we plunged into the dense undergrowth. Massive carnivorous plants snapped at passing racers. Poisonous spores burst in our wake.

"Son of a sea donk!" I swerved as a Gearbreaker tried to force me into a fungal wall. The impact would have dissolved my bike's outer shell in seconds.

Ten minutes in, we reached the first obstacle, a gorge spanned by a rotting organic bridge. Scratch, our architect, disappeared in a flash of light as the structure collapsed beneath her.

"Scratch is out," Tracer called over our comm system. "Respawning at base."

The race thinned as we entered a valley of shardwood trees. Their razor-sharp branches sliced through protective gear with ease. Captain took the lead, his crawler's reinforced hull deflecting the worst of the danger.

Grave Digger wasn't so lucky. A branch pierced his engine, sending him spiraling into a cluster of silicate formations. The game's death animation was impressively dramatic: a burst of light, then nothing.

"What the frick was that?" I shouted, ducking under a low-hanging branch that would have decapitated me. "Nobody said anything about shardwood forests!"

"Adaptive terrain," Temper explained, pulling alongside me. "Game changes each time."

We emerged from the forest to find a vast acidic swamp blocking our path. The main route was a narrow causeway of fallen trees, heavily guarded by Void Runners.

"We'll never make it through there," Temper said, slowing his vehicle.

I noticed a barely visible path skirting the swamp's edge, dangerously close to bubbling acid pools. The game designers had hidden it well, marking it only with subtle glowroot fungi.

"Frick it," I muttered, making my decision. "Follow me!"

I veered sharply right, plunging down the hidden path. Temper hesitated, then followed. The narrow trail required perfect control, with acid geysers erupting randomly on either side. One splash would end our race instantly.

"Good gravy nuts!" I swore as my bike's rear stabilizer skimmed an acid pool. Warning lights flashed across my interface.

The gamble paid off. We emerged on the far side of the swamp, bypassing the Void Runners' ambush entirely. Only five racers remained ahead of us, with the ancient ruins now visible on the horizon.

The final stretch became a flat-out sprint across open terrain. Captain maintained his lead, but Temper and I steadily gained ground. A Gearbreaker tried to ram me, but I executed a barrel roll over his vehicle, landing perfectly on his other side.

"Ohhhhh, burn!" I laughed, the adrenaline rush coursing through me.

We crossed the finish line in formation: Captain first, then Temper, then me, with only one rival faction member making it before the timer expired.

As victory music played and the game environment began to fade, Captain clapped me on the shoulder. "Not bad for a photog, Lens. That swamp shortcut was inspired."

I grinned, the thrill of the race lingering even as my consciousness returned to Terracore. For those brief, intense moments, I'd forgotten about Point Alpha, about the weight of command, about Marcus and his search for family. I'd simply been part of the team, taking risks and celebrating victory.

The victory rush from our race on Vorgath-IV lingered as my

consciousness settled back into Paradise's systems. Captain Drake's praise echoed in my mind while I reviewed the day's tasks. The thrill of competition had been a welcome distraction.

My communicator chimed with a priority alert from Lieutenant Chen. "Captain, we need you on the bridge immediately."

I materialized in my command chair, taking in the controlled tension permeating the bridge. Status displays flashed amber warnings across multiple systems.

"Report," I said, scanning the primary readouts.

Chen approached with a HoloTab. "Sir, we're detecting unusual power fluctuations in the main battery array. Diagnostics show a ten percent drain unaccounted for in the logs."

"Ten percent?" I frowned. "When did this start?"

"That's the concerning part, sir. The drain occurred approximately four hours ago, but there's no record of the power being redirected anywhere."

I accessed the ship's systems directly, diving into the power management matrices. The numbers confirmed Chen's report: a significant power draw had occurred, but the destination remained untraceable.

"Run a level-three diagnostic on all subsystems," I ordered. "And have Engineering—"

The bridge disappeared.

I blinked, disoriented. The oak tree from my memory palace surrounded me, its branches heavy with photographs and mementos. But something felt wrong. The light filtering through the leaves had an artificial quality, too uniform and steady.

"Hello?" My voice echoed strangely, returning with a metallic undertone.

No response.

I tried to access Paradise's systems, reaching for the familiar neural pathways that connected me to the ship. Nothing happened.

Panic flickered at the edges of my consciousness. I was cut off, isolated within what appeared to be my memory palace but felt fundamentally wrong. The photographs hanging from the branches showed unfamiliar scenes: places I'd never visited, people I didn't recognize.

"System restart," I commanded. "Emergency protocol."

The tree flickered briefly, then stabilized. Not Paradise's systems responding, but something else.

I reached for a photograph, examining it closely. The image showed me standing on Paradise's bridge, addressing the crew. But I had no memory of this moment.

Another photo nearby captured me in Engineering, inspecting power conduits alongside Rodriguez. Again, no recollection.

"Time index," I said to the empty air.

Numbers appeared, hovering before me: 4 hours, 27 minutes elapsed.

Almost four and a half hours, gone. And during that time, according to these images, I'd been active, making decisions, interacting with the crew.

The oak tree dissolved around me, replaced by Paradise's bridge. The transition was jarring, immediate.

"—prepared for your inspection, Captain," Chen was saying, her expression showing no recognition that anything unusual had occurred.

I gripped the armrests of my command chair, fighting to maintain composure. "I'm sorry, Lieutenant. Could you repeat that?"

Chen looked puzzled but complied. "The power fluctuation has been resolved, sir. Your rerouting of the auxiliary systems prevented any critical functions from being affected. Engineering reports all systems normal now."

I nodded slowly, processing this information. According to Chen, I had already addressed and solved the power drain issue. During my missing hours.

"The diagnostic report you requested," she continued, handing me a HoloTab. "Your theory about quantum resonance feedback was correct. The power wasn't lost, just temporarily phased out of our detection range."

I scanned the report, finding detailed notes and solution pathways written in my exact phrasing style. Notes I had no memory of creating.

"Thank you, Lieutenant," I managed, keeping my voice steady. "Please inform me immediately if any similar fluctuations occur."

"Of course, Captain." Chen returned to her station, leaving me alone with the disturbing realization.

The memory gaps were worsening. And during these blackouts, some version of me remained functional, making decisions that affected the ship and crew. Decisions I couldn't remember or evaluate.

I needed to speak with Dr. Khatri immediately. But first, I had to understand exactly what "I" had done during those missing hours.

I retreated to my cottage. The power anomalies had been resolved, but the weight of my missing hours hung over me. My reflection in the mirror looked unchanged, yet something fundamental had shifted. These weren't simple memory consolidation issues anymore. Something was happening to my consciousness, and I needed answers before making my concerns public.

The communication from Earth arrived while I was reviewing Dr. Khatri's preliminary neural scan results. David and Amy's faces materialized in my private viewing area, their expressions warm despite the increasing quantum delay.

"Greetings from Haven," Amy said, her voice carrying the slight echo of transmission lag.

David nodded. "Tom's been asking about Temper's progress. Says he can feel his neuroclone making breakthroughs he never considered."

I smiled at their familiar faces while the growing distance between us pressed against my chest. The conversation continued for twenty minutes before the quantum connection faded. I didn't mention my memory lapses. Why worry them about something they could do nothing about?

The following morning, I stood before Paradise's observation deck, gathering my thoughts as stars streamed past in brilliant ribbons of light.

"Ship-wide announcement," I commanded.

The system acknowledged with a soft chime. I straightened my shoulders and began.

"Good morning, Paradise. This is Captain David. Today marks an important milestone in our journey. We are now exactly two months from Point Alpha."

I paused, letting the significance sink in.

"For those unfamiliar with the term, Point Alpha represents our first major communications threshold. Beyond this point, consciousness transfer between Earth and Paradise becomes unsafe. The quantum coherence necessary for neural pattern integrity will degrade beyond acceptable parameters."

The words felt clinical, detached from the emotional weight they carried.

"In practical terms, this means anyone wishing to return to Earth must make that decision within the next sixty days. After we cross Point Alpha, such transfers become impossible. Another reminder will be sent in 30 days."

I activated the holographic display, showing Paradise's trajectory with Point Alpha clearly marked.

"Department heads will be available to answer questions and provide counseling for those facing difficult choices. Remember, there is no shame in deciding this journey isn't for you. Earth remains your home, and the option to return is your right."

The announcement had barely ended before its impact swept through Paradise. My communicator flared to life with messages from council members and department heads, each seeking clarity. Lieutenant Chen reported a surge of activity in the communal areas, where colonists clustered together, debating their choices. Their heightened concern made me question whether they had even listened to our previous announcement; one I had delivered on this very topic just one month ago.

I walked the driftways through Paradise that afternoon, sensing the shift in atmosphere. Conversations hushed as I passed, then resumed with greater intensity. In the arboretum, a group of colonists debated loudly about responsibilities to the mission versus personal desires. The hydroponics lab, usually peaceful, buzzed with technicians discussing contingency plans for staffing changes.

The Joy of Adoption Center felt the impact most acutely. Prospective parents who had been considering adoption now faced a difficult decision. Would they commit to raising a thruman child with Point Alpha looming, or postpone the decision indefinitely in case they decided to return?

Marcus sat alone at his building table, carefully constructing a tower from colored blocks. He looked up as I approached, his expression serious.

"Are you going back to Earth, Captain?"

The question caught me off guard. "No, Marcus. My place is here, leading Paradise to Orion."

He nodded solemnly, returning to his tower. "Good. Earth already has enough captains."

Marcus continued stacking his blocks with methodical precision, each one placed with careful consideration. His focus reminded me of David's woodworking, that same intense concentration that shut out everything else.

"You know," I said, crouching beside him, "I used to build things too. Birdhouses, mostly."

"Did they fly?" Marcus asked without looking up.

I smiled. "No. They were homes for birds, not flying machines."

"Oh." He placed another block, completing a perfect symmetrical tower. "I'm building a space dock for Paradise."

The message alert chimed softly, pulling me from our conversation. "Incoming communication from Bear Draydon," the system announced.

"Excuse me, Marcus. Captain business."

I stepped away and accepted the call. Bear's face materialized before me, her expression bright with enthusiasm.

"Captain David! I hope I'm not interrupting anything critical."

"Just some architectural consultation with a future captain. What can I do for you, Bear?"

She leaned forward, her voice dropping conspiratorially. "I've had a cancellation at Ainsleys Castle. One of my guests has decided to return to Earth before Point Alpha."

"That's unfortunate," I replied, though not entirely surprising given the announcement.

"For them, perhaps. For you, it's an opportunity." Bear's eyes sparkled with mischief. "Their slot was scheduled for 12 days from now. I know how busy you are, but I thought I'd offer it to you first. The full Ainsleys experience, no abbreviated tours or special treatment. Just you against my creation."

I considered the offer. Point Alpha's looming arrival made the ship's operations demanding. Yet the chance to experience one of

Bear's legendary creations as a regular participant rather than as captain was tempting.

"I'd need to coordinate with Lieutenant Chen regarding scheduling," I said.

"Of course. The castle isn't going anywhere." Bear smiled. "Though I should warn you, some who enter wish it would."

I laughed. "Consider me intrigued. I accept your invitation."

Bear clapped her hands together. "Excellent! You're in for a spine-tingling, heart-pounding treat, Captain. Remember, nothing in my castle is what it seems. Stay sharp, keep your wits about you, and most importantly, never assume you're alone."

"Sounds delightful," I said dryly.

"The best adventures always are." Bear's expression softened slightly. "And Captain? Thank you for handling the Point Alpha announcement with such grace. These transitions are never easy. You should plan on a maximum of two weeks to complete my castle challenge. I'll explain it in more detail once you're there."

The call ended, leaving me with an unexpected bright spot in the challenging days ahead. I returned to Marcus, who had already begun constructing a new, more elaborate tower.

"Everything okay, Captain?" he asked, not looking up from his work.

"More than okay. I've been invited to explore a castle."

Marcus finally glanced up, his eyes widening with interest. "With dragons?"

"Possibly. I'll have to wait and see."

I watched him return to his building, his small hands moving with purpose and determination. I quietly hoped a family would soon choose him.

Meanwhile, I would be exploring a haunted castle, facing whatever challenges Bear Draydon had designed. The thought brought an unexpected smile to my face. Even as a digital consciousness hurtling through space, some very human desires remained: the thrill of discovery, the test of courage, the simple joy of play.

I settled into my chair at the communications station, watching the technicians make final adjustments to the quantum array. The countdown to Point Alpha ticked relentlessly in the corner of my display: fifty-eight more days. Soon, the invisible tether connecting us to Earth would fray beyond repair for complex data patterns.

"QE-comm channel established, Captain," Lieutenant Chen reported. "Signal integrity at ninety-eight point seven percent."

"Thank you, Lieutenant." I nodded, appreciating her efficiency. "I'll take it from here."

The room emptied, leaving me alone with the quantum connection. I activated the recording sequence, my reflection appearing in the monitor: familiar yet increasingly different from the man who remained on Earth.

"David, Amy," I began, my voice steady despite the weight of what I needed to say. "Paradise continues its journey toward Orion as planned. All systems nominal, crew morale stable."

Formalities out of the way, I leaned closer to the camera. "Two months until Point Alpha. The announcement went as expected. Some colonists are reconsidering their commitment, weighing thirteen hundred years against returning home. Their struggle reminds me of our own decision, David."

I paused, gathering thoughts that felt increasingly my own rather than echoes of my origin. "The memory consolidation issues continue, though Dr. Khatri assures me they're manageable. Curious how a digital consciousness still struggles with perfect recall."

The oak tree from our memory palace materialized beside me, a holographic reminder of where I came from. "Amy, your memory palace sustains me. I visit daily, discovering new corners you've created. Yesterday I found our first apartment, complete with that hideous lamp from your mother. The details you preserved astonish me."

My fingers traced the holographic bark. "I've begun adding my own memories now. The first time I interfaced directly with Paradise's systems. Standing on the observation deck watching Earth diminish to a blue star. Joining the Din through virtual adventures."

The tree faded as I continued. "Sometimes I wonder if we're still the same person, separated only by distance. But increasingly, I recognize the divergence. David, you would have hesitated before accepting Bear Draydon's invitation to Ainsleys Castle. I said yes immediately. I think I did so, in part, to forge my own path forward."

A smile crossed my face; one I suspected looked different from David's now. "Temper's progress with Falfsun exceeds even Tom's expectations. The miniature star burns steadily, a testament to his focus. We're different from our origins, evolving into who we need to be for this journey."

Outside the viewscreen, stars streaked past in brilliant ribbons. "After Point Alpha, when consciousness transfer becomes impossible. our paths will continue their separate trajectories. Yet I carry everything that matters: our love for Amy, our friendship with Tom, our shared history."

I touched the pocket where I kept the replica of my father's watch. "I am Go David now. Not merely your copy, but someone new emerging from his foundation. I captain Paradise, explore virtual worlds with the Din, counsel young thrumans like Marcus. I make decisions that you might not, see opportunities you might overlook."

The quantum signal flickered briefly, a reminder of our dwindling connection.

"I wanted you both to know that I'm at peace with this evolution. The divergence doesn't diminish what we share. Instead, it honors the choice we made together. Two versions of one life, both equally valid, equally real."

I straightened in my chair, captain once more. "Until next transmission. Paradise out."

The connection closed. I sat alone in the silence, feeling both the weight of separation and the lightness of becoming.

The quantum communication system powered down with a soft whine, leaving me alone with my thoughts. I sat for a moment longer, considering the increasing divergence between myself and David. We were no longer simply copies separated by distance but truly becoming different people with each passing day. Amy drifted into my mind then, uninvited. I pictured the curve of her smile, the cadence of her laugh. The ache stirred, familiar and unwelcome. I dismissed it quickly. There were systems to recalibrate, after all.

My communicator chimed, pulling me from my reflection.

"Sir, Captain Tom has arrived for the scheduled briefing," Lieutenant Chen's voice announced. "The conference room is prepared as requested."

"Thank you, Lieutenant. I'll be right there."

I rose from the communications station, straightening my uniform from habit rather than necessity. The driftways of Paradise hummed with activity as I made my way to the conference room. Crew members nodded respectfully as I passed, some still visibly processing the Point Alpha announcement from earlier. I could just as easily have blinked to my destination, but walking through the driftways gave me a chance to interact with colonists.

The conference room doors slid open to reveal Temper already in animated conversation with my senior staff. He gestured enthusiastically at a holographic display floating above the central table, his movements more controlled than Tom's wild gesticulations but carrying the same intensity.

"Captain," Temper acknowledged, pausing mid-explanation. "Perfect timing. I was just setting up the preliminary overview."

The room smelled of freshly baked pastries and coffee. Along the side table, an array of desserts had been arranged: chocolate eclairs, raspberry tarts, and what appeared to be Maya's favorite lemon meringue pie. A collection of beverages, from steaming coffee to chilled fruit punches, completed the spread.

"Please, everyone, don't be shy," I said, noticing several officers eyeing the treats. "One of the few perks of digital existence is guilt-free indulgence."

Lieutenant Chen selected a chocolate eclair while Commander Okafor poured herself coffee. The mood lightened as everyone served themselves, the tension from approaching Point Alpha temporarily forgotten in the simple pleasure of shared treats.

I chose a slice of apple pie, savoring the perfect balance of cinnamon and nutmeg as I took my seat at the head of the table. "So, Captain Tom, could you please explain the C-field pinch experiment?"

Temper bit into a raspberry tart, closing his eyes briefly in appreciation before answering. "The Oracle designed it before our departure. Holmes called it 'the key to understanding stellar nucleosynthesis at its most fundamental level.' His hope was that, in time, we could develop it into C-pinch fusion as another way to power our ships."

He manipulated the holographic display, expanding it to show a complex arrangement of energy fields and containment systems. The model rotated slowly, revealing intricate details that even my enhanced perception struggled to fully comprehend.

"Before Holmes gave it a name, we used to think of it as a scattering of broken light across the void," Temper said. "Elegant, almost mournful. But it's more than that. The collapse we initiate doesn't just bend beams — it bruises the substrate of reality itself. The C-field is where the universe forgets how to hold shape."

Commander Okafor leaned forward, her coffee forgotten. "That sounds potentially dangerous."

"The Oracle didn't predict any danger to us or the ships," Temper replied, selecting another tart. "The experiment surprisingly requires little power redirection to create localized gravitational anomalies. Nothing Paradise can't handle. I propose waiting until after our quantum communication with Earth lessens, in order to establish a true baseline of the ship's functions."

I studied the holographic model, noting the similarities to Falfsun's containment systems. "You've already adapted this for Hellfire's research lab?"

Temper nodded. "The modifications are complete, but inactive. I've run thousands of simulations. Once we're past Point Alpha, we can proceed with minimal risk."

Lieutenant Chen raised her hand slightly. "What exactly do we hope to learn from this experiment?"

"Everything," Temper said, his eyes bright with the same passion I'd seen in Tom's. "In addition to a potential new power source, it could tell us how elements form in stellar cores. How gravity interacts with quantum fields during nuclear fusion. Potentially even insights into how time itself shapes and stretches space."

I took another bite of pie, considering the implications. "And the Oracle believed this experiment was crucial to our mission?"

"Holmes specifically included it in our research protocols," Temper confirmed. "Called it 'the experiment that changes everything.'"

The room fell silent as everyone processed this information. I looked around at my officers, noting their expressions ranging from excitement to concern.

"Very well," I said finally. "We'll proceed as recommended, after Point Alpha. Lieutenant Chen, work with Captain Tom to establish power allocation protocols. Commander Okafor, I want engineering contingencies for all possible outcomes."

"Yes, Captain," they responded in unison.

"And Captain Temper," I added, "I'd like daily briefings on your simulation results until then."

Temper smiled, raising his glass of punch in acknowledgment. "Of course, Captain. Now, has anyone tried these chocolate brownies? They're remarkable."

The chocolate brownie crumbs disappeared from my fingertips as I closed the conference room door behind me. Such small pleasures helped mark the passage of time aboard Paradise. Days blended together as we hurtled through the void, each one bringing us closer to Point Alpha and further from Earth.

I blinked to my observatory tower without bothering to walk the driftways. The curved glass dome offered an unobstructed view of space in all directions, stars gleaming against perfect darkness. I'd designed this space with both aesthetic and practical considerations in mind. The central platform housed my astronomical equipment: quantum telescopes, gravitational sensors, and holographic star charts that tracked our journey with precision far beyond what physical instruments could achieve.

"Display dual focus," I commanded.

The observatory responded instantly. To my right, a magnified image of Earth appeared, now barely distinguishable from surrounding stars without enhancement. To my left, Orion's nebula bloomed in false-color splendor, still impossibly distant yet growing imperceptibly larger with each passing day.

I settled into my observation chair, fingers moving through familiar calibration sequences. The chair conformed perfectly to my body, another small luxury of digital existence. No physical discomfort, no need to shift position after hours of stargazing.

"CoreLink, log observation session thirty-seven."

A soft chime acknowledged my command. I began my routine measurements, recording our trajectory against predicted models. The numbers aligned perfectly, our course unwavering. Forty-one days remained until Point Alpha.

My gaze drifted to Earth's diminishing blue light. David would be in his workshop now, perhaps crafting another birdhouse though he no longer made them for Amy. The twentieth had been the last. Or maybe they were out dancing, sipping on Lunar martinis at the Sea of

Rains.

I touched the silver pocket watch in my jacket. The familiar weight anchored me across the growing distance.

"Magnify Earth, factor one thousand."

The blue pinpoint expanded, revealing the familiar sphere of our origin. Cloud patterns swirled across oceans and continents. Somewhere below that veil of atmosphere, David and Amy continued their lives, watching our progress through increasingly delayed communications.

Forty-one days remained until Point Alpha. After that, the choice would be sealed. Anyone still undecided by then would ride our course to its end, come what may.

An idea came to me unbidden: return. A strange flicker of an idea for someone so invested in going as I was. Why now?

I let out a quiet laugh. It must be neuroclone settling. Tied in somehow to the memory lapses I was experiencing. Just some old echoes surfacing from some earlier iteration that hadn't fully let go of Earth.

I pressed the thought flat.

This was home now. It had to be.

I shifted my attention to Orion, fine-tuning the superpositional telescope to peel back the nebula's outer layers. The birthplace of stars revealed itself in stunning detail: hydrogen clouds collapsing into nuclear furnaces, protoplanetary disks forming around young suns, the cosmic dance of creation playing out before my eyes.

"This is what Temper seeks to understand," I murmured.

The C-field pinch experiment might unlock secrets of stellar formation that even the Oracle could only theorize about. I understood Temper's obsession. The answers lay ahead of us, not behind.

A notification appeared in my peripheral vision: Lieutenant Chen requesting confirmation of the next Earth transmission schedule. I approved it without breaking my observation routine. My divided attention mirrored my divided self: one part anchored to Earth, another reaching toward Orion.

The stars streamed past our hull, their light stretching into ephemeral ribbons as Paradise continued its journey. I tracked our progress meticulously, recording each minute adjustment in our course, each incremental increase in our velocity.

"CoreLink, compare current position with projected course."

The holographic display overlaid our actual trajectory against the planned route. The lines matched perfectly, converging at Orion thirteen hundred years in our future.

I leaned back in my chair, gaze alternating between Earth and Orion. My identity existed in this space between origins and destination, between who I was and who I was becoming.

CHAPTER ELEVEN

Ainsleys Castle

I notified Temper and Commander Okafor about Ainsleys Castle, asking them to notify me immediately should the need arise. Both seemed amused by my sudden interest in Bear's infamous creation.

"Planning a vacation from captaining, Captain?" Temper asked with a raised eyebrow.

"More like research," I replied. "Bear's reputation is legendary. I want to see what makes her work so compelling."

Maya smiled. "Just don't get lost in there. Paradise still needs its captain."

"I'll be back before you know I'm gone."

I followed the link Bear sent to me, and I found myself standing on a mud-splattered wharf, next to a small rowboat tethered in the harbor. Farther out in the bay sat a tall sailing ship under a calm wind. The air carried the scent of salt and fish, while seagulls cried overhead. The wooden planks beneath my feet creaked with each step, weathered by years of storms and tides.

"Am I being given a choice?" I wondered. "If I step into the boat and row to the ship, will I escape from the horrors at the castle? Would David choose that?" I straightened my shoulders. "But that's not what I came for."

Turning around, I walked up the wharf landing in the direction of the castle. Standing in the middle of the road waiting for me was Bear Draydon. Her presence commanded attention without effort, her eyes bright with anticipation.

"Welcome to Ainsleys Castle, Lord Go," she greeted me with a slight bow.

"Thank you, Your Grace," I said, letting myself slip into character. "I wasn't expecting to see you here."

"I greet all of my guests. I so love this place, despite its horrors." She offered her arm. "Walk with me and I'll tell you more about the castle."

She took my arm, and we walked up the landing toward the castle, past its thatch-roofed storehouses. The castle sat in an open glade surrounded by a dense forest of pine, oak, and elm. Mist clung to the treetops, obscuring their heights and lending the scene an ethereal quality. The stonework of the distant castle walls appeared almost black against the pale sky.

"Duke Edric Ainsleys owns the castle and the surrounding lands. He is an honorable man. Treat him as family, for he is your only friend in the castle. Be wary of everyone else. The rest of the duke's guests you'll meet in good time."

"So, I'm not the only guest?" The path beneath our feet transitioned from packed dirt to cobblestones, each step bringing us closer to the looming structure.

Bear laughed, the sound musical against the backdrop of rustling leaves. "You're the only active, playing guest. I only allow one per game. That's why there's such a long wait list. Everyone else that you'll meet are non-playing characters that are here to help you... or maybe hinder you. The game is governed by the Laws of Nature. The only two Breach Law exceptions are unspecified horrors that you may encounter, and accelerated game time."

A raven cawed from a nearby tree, its black eyes following our progress.

"You have two weeks of ship time to finish your quest. Those two weeks are converted into two years of accelerated, in-game playing time, so for you it will feel like two years have passed in those two weeks. If you fail to finish the game in those two years, you will automatically lose the game and be returned to Paradise. Everyone, so far, has failed the quest before their time expires. Maybe you'll be the first."

The castle grew larger before us, its stone walls telling stories of sieges weathered and battles won. Moss crept up the northern face, while the southern stones remained bare and sun-bleached.

"One more thing, the quest is slightly different for each guest. It changes according to the decisions you make in playing it. I believe that covers all of the basics. Do you have any questions?"

I considered the challenge ahead. Two years compressed into two weeks. A quest no one had completed. "I guess not. I'm a little nervous. Do you have anything that I can take for that?"

"Go inside and have some wine," she suggested, her eyes twinkling with something between mischief and encouragement.

We reached the shallow moat before the castle. Water lilies floated on its surface, their white blooms stark against the dark water. The drawbridge stood lowered, inviting entry while the portcullis remained raised, revealing the shadowy interior beyond.

"Good luck," Bear said. She blinked from sight, leaving me alone before the castle entrance.

I was on my own. Before going any farther, I looked around at the forest and down at the harbor. Everything looked normal; eerily normal, perhaps too perfect in its medieval simulation. I felt a little relieved when I didn't see the rumored gate to Hell. At least Bear hadn't started me with immediate nightmare fuel.

The castle loomed before me, built more for strength than beauty. Its thick stone walls projected an impregnable appearance, with narrow arrow slits instead of proper windows. I crossed the narrow drawbridge over the moat, my footsteps echoing on the wooden planks. The surface felt authentically worn, polished by countless feet over imagined centuries.

A guard in chainmail approached as I neared the high palisade of logs standing before the gate. His face remained partially hidden beneath his helmet, but his eyes studied me with surprising intelligence for an NPC.

"You're expected, m'lord," he said gruffly. "Follow me."

He escorted me across the courtyard, past stables and training grounds where men practiced swordplay. The clash of steel rang through the air, punctuated by grunts of exertion. Servants scurried about with purposeful movements, carrying firewood, linens, and platters of food.

Inside the castle, a lavish banquet was underway. The aroma of roasted meats and fresh bread enveloped me immediately. Tapestries hung on the stone walls, buffering the cold and depicting hunting scenes and battles long past. Musicians played in one corner, their medieval melodies creating an authentic atmosphere.

The duke's guests sat around a long wooden table that stretched nearly the entire length of the great hall. On the table were cutting boards with freshly baked white bread, sugared almonds, honey-mustard eggs, and assorted pottages of ham, leek, and pea soup. Roasted eel and boar's head rounded out the offerings. I made a mental note to visit the kitchen when time allowed. Medieval cooking methods fascinated me, and I wondered how accurately Bear had recreated them.

Duke Edric Ainsleys rose from his seat at the head of the table. I recognized him from the portrait on my invitation; tall and broad-shouldered with a neatly trimmed beard peppered with gray. His eyes crinkled at the corners when he smiled.

"Lord Go!" he called out, gesturing me forward. "We've been awaiting your arrival. Come, join us!"

He greeted me warmly with a firm clasp of my forearm and proceeded with introductions. I'd never been good at remembering names, but certain individuals stood out.

Imogene, Duke Edric's niece, nodded when introduced. She wore a deep blue gown that complemented her dark hair and calculating eyes. Something in her measured gaze suggested she noticed more than she revealed.

His nephew, Coelmund, I remembered instantly because I disliked him on sight. His smile never reached his eyes, cold and insincere. His gaze darted about as if constantly afraid of being caught in a lie. He reminded me of a nervous rodent, fingers tapping restlessly against his goblet.

The other guests blurred together: some thin, others stocky; some tall, others short. Their clothing ranged from rich brocades to threadbare wool. Most of the men wore swords at their hips. I hadn't thought to bring a weapon. Perhaps Duke Edric would have one I could borrow if the need arose.

"Come, sit," Duke Edric said, guiding me to an empty seat. "You must be famished after your journey."

I leaned forward, eyeing the guests seated farther down the table. Most blended together in a tapestry of medieval finery, but one figure stood apart. A gaunt man with hollow cheeks and sunken eyes sat slightly removed from the others. His skin stretched taut over sharp cheekbones, as though he hadn't properly eaten in weeks. His shoulders hunched forward, his gaze dropping toward his barely touched plate. Every few minutes, he'd jerk upright with alarming suddenness, eyes wide and haunted as they darted around the hall.

I turned to Imogene, keeping my voice low. "Who is that man? The one sitting alone."

She followed my gaze and wrinkled her nose slightly. "That's Herr Dunstan Fuchsg, from Germany. He's strange. He barely talks to me, or anyone else for that matter. I don't think I like him."

"Why not? What has he done to you?" I asked, curious about her dismissive tone.

"Nothing," she admitted with a slight shrug. "He's not the friendly type, that's all."

I watched Herr Fuchsg while trying to appear casual. He moved about the room with careful, measured steps. Despite the crowded hall, he maintained a bubble of isolation around himself, never engaging with the other guests who seemed equally content to give him a wide berth.

The evening progressed with ritualized formality. One by one, guests rose to offer toasts, goblets raised high. The wine flowed freely, rich and sweet on my tongue. It seemed to be the only beverage served besides water from the castle's artesian well.

When my turn came, I stood and lifted my glass. "To your health!"

Simple but effective. The guests nodded appreciatively and drank.

Everyone participated in the toasting ritual except Herr Fuchsg. He remained seated, staring into his cup with intense concentration. The other guests began urging him to stand, to at least acknowledge Duke Edric's hospitality. Their persistent coaxing eventually had effect.

Herr Fuchsg rose slowly, his movements stiff and reluctant. The hall fell silent; all eyes fixed upon him. He stood motionless for a long minute, his face unreadable. Then, with unexpected swiftness, he thrust his glass high above his head.

A strange laugh escaped his lips as his gaze swept across the room. "To the angels, who cast all of Earth's demons into hell! May they be cursed for letting some of them escape!"

Gasps rippled through the assembly. Only a handful of guests raised their glasses in response, drinking uncertainly. Duke Edric's face hardened. Without a word, he rose from his seat and strode from the hall, his departure clearly signaling the banquet's end.

Taking my cue, I pushed back my chair and prepared to leave when Herr Fuchsg's voice rang out again.

"My toast wasn't meant to be crude and flippant," he called, his accent thickening with emotion. "I meant it as a warning. I believe a demon haunts this castle and I beg all of you to remember to bar and bolt your door tonight, before you go to sleep."

The remaining guests exchanged uncomfortable glances. Some laughed nervously while others hurried from the hall, whispering among themselves. I remained seated, studying Herr Fuchsg with new interest. Was this part of Bear's game? The first clue to my quest? Or merely atmospheric color to enhance the medieval setting?

Either way, I decided I would heed his advice. I'd bar my door tonight.

With that, Herr Fuchsg left the hall, his departure leaving a wake of nervous whispers. People scattered to their rooms, their earlier revelry forgotten.

My assigned chamber perched near the top of the castle, a long climb up winding stone stairs that left me breathless. The room itself proved comfortable enough: a four-poster bed with thick woolen blankets, a small writing desk, and a wooden chest for my belongings. A single narrow window overlooked the surrounding forest.

I crossed to the window, resting my hands on the cold stone sill. Moonlight spilled across the treetops, turning them silver. The forest stretched dark and impenetrable, broken only by occasional clearings that gleamed like pale eyes in the night.

From somewhere in that darkness came a low, rumbling growl, unmistakably feline and unsettlingly large. My thoughts immediately returned to Herr Fuchsg's toast about demons escaping hell. The wine I'd consumed at dinner suddenly felt heavy in my stomach.

I listened more intently. Beyond the hunting cat, another sound reached me; the delicate notes of a lute playing a simple, haunting melody. The music drifted from the north, likely from the village I'd glimpsed during my approach to the castle.

Remembering Herr Fuchsg's warning, I checked the heavy wooden door. The iron bolt slid into place with a satisfying thunk. Still, unease prickled along my spine.

The wine made my sleep restless. I drifted in and out of consciousness, my dreams filled with twisted shapes and half-formed faces. The moon tracked across the sky, casting shifting shadows through my window.

Something woke me. A scraping sound, followed by the distinct sensation of pressure against the door, as if someone leaned their weight against it while trying the handle. The bolt rattled slightly in its housing. My heart hammered against my ribs as I lay perfectly still, listening. After what felt like an eternity, the pressure ceased. Footsteps retreated down the hallway, fading into silence.

I didn't sleep again until dawn

.

Morning found me bleary-eyed but determined as I made my way to the great hall. A handful of guests had already gathered. Some looked as exhausted as I felt, while others seemed barely affected by the previous night's revelry.

Sir Brock sat alert at the table, methodically cutting an apple with his knife. His sword hung at his hip exactly as Captain Drake wore his, low and ready for a quick draw. He nodded at my approach.

"Sleep well, Lord Go?" he asked, offering a slice of apple.

"Not particularly," I admitted, accepting the fruit. "Strange dreams."

Herr Fuchsg sat alone at the far end of the table. Despite the considerable wine he'd consumed, his eyes remained clear and watchful. He inclined his head slightly when our gazes met but offered nothing more.

More guests filtered in, many nursing obvious hangovers. Servants moved quietly among them, pouring watered wine and serving bread and cheese.

"Lord Go."

Imogene appeared at my side, her hand slipping into mine as she guided me toward a quiet corner. Her blue gown had been replaced by one of forest green, her dark hair neatly braided and coiled at the nape of her neck.

"I'm glad to see there are gentlemen here who care more for my company than for wine," she said, her voice pitched low for my ears alone.

A blush colored her cheeks as she glanced down, her grip on my hand tightening slightly.

"Someone came to my door last night," she continued. "Drunk, perhaps, or maybe not drunk enough. They fumbled with the latch but couldn't enter."

"If you're saying—" I began defensively.

"No, stop." She laughed softly, her eyes scanning the room. "I mean no offense. But don't you think it strange that earlier last night, Herr Fuchsg told us to lock our doors?"

I followed her gaze to where Herr Fuchsg sat, methodically tearing a piece of bread into smaller and smaller pieces.

"That is strange," I acknowledged.

I shrugged, waiting for Imogene to continue. Her wide, intelligent eyes studied my face, gauging my reaction. She struck me as a capable young woman, not one to be easily frightened by castle gossip.

"I believe something strange is happening here," she whispered, leaning closer. "My uncle seems concerned, though he tries to hide it."

Before she could elaborate, Herr Fuchsg approached our corner, followed closely by Duke Edric. The German's face looked even more haggard in the morning light, deep shadows beneath his eyes suggesting he'd slept no better than I had.

Duke Edric's expression was grim. "One of the villagers was killed last night. Torn to pieces by a leopard or some such beast while he was out setting his fur traps."

"A leopard? Are they sure? Did they see it?" Herr Fuchsg asked, his voice tight with urgency.

"No." Duke Edric shook his head. "They found only tracks and... what remained of the poor man."

Herr Fuchsg rubbed his forehead, as if wiping away sweat. His hand trembled visibly as he lowered it. "It begins again," he muttered, so softly I barely caught the words.

Duke Edric turned to me, clearly eager to change the subject. "I have a man here who I've assigned to be your valet." He motioned for a young man to join us.

The youth approached with a quick, light step. He couldn't have been more than sixteen or seventeen, with straw-colored hair and bright eyes that darted curiously around the hall.

"This is Sawyer, the barrel maker's youngest son from the village. He's been hired on as an apprentice," Duke Edric said. "He'll make a fine attendant."

Sawyer bowed slightly, a joyful grin spreading across his slim face. "At your service, m'lord."

I studied him carefully. In Bear's game, anyone could be significant. Friend or foe? Ally or obstacle? I decided to wait and see, reserving judgment until I knew more about him. If he proved dishonest, I could always dismiss him from my service.

Duke Edric dispatched several men to investigate the murder in the forest. The castle buzzed with nervous energy as servants whispered in corners and guests speculated wildly about what beast could have killed the trapper.

For the rest of the day, Sawyer took me on a tour of the castle. He proved knowledgeable about its history, pointing out architectural features and recounting stories of previous dukes with animated enthusiasm. The stone fortress contained numerous passages and hidden alcoves that would take weeks to fully explore.

"And this is the eastern tower, m'lord," Sawyer explained as we climbed a narrow spiral staircase. "Best view in the castle, though Duke Edric rarely comes here."

The tower offered a commanding view of the surrounding countryside. The dense forest stretched in all directions, broken only by the thin ribbon of road leading to the village. In the distance, mountains rose blue against the horizon.

At our evening meal, I met Baron De Goetd, a short, stocky man who sat nearby. He argued loudly with other guests, his voice carrying across the hall. Whenever someone disagreed with him, his face flushed red, and his hand moved instinctively to the hilt of his sword. He gave the impression of someone eager for a fight, perhaps even hoping to provoke one.

I watched him carefully. Could someone like him be possessed by a demon? His quick temper certainly suggested an inner darkness. Baron De Goetd was definitely someone I would need to keep an eye on as I worked to unravel the mystery of Ainsleys Castle.

Baron De Goetd's attention shifted to Imogene like a predator spotting new prey. She sat across from me, beside Lord Cooksone, a young man whose impetuous nature showed in his quick movements and restless eyes. De Goetd leaned forward, inserting himself into their conversation with forced charm.

"Lady Imogene, surely you'd prefer the company of a man who knows the world, not some untested boy," he said, his voice carrying deliberately.

Cooksone's jaw tightened. "The lady seems content with my conversation, Baron. Perhaps your wisdom would be better shared elsewhere."

Imogene kept her eyes fixed on her plate, shoulders tensing. She offered no encouragement to either man, her discomfort evident in the tight set of her mouth and the way she angled her body away from both suitors.

"Content? With tales of hunts you've barely survived?" De Goetd laughed. "I've conquered beasts that would make your knees tremble, boy."

"I'm no boy," Cooksone snapped, color rising in his face.

The argument escalated with alarming speed. Words grew sharper, voices louder. Around us, other guests fell silent, watching the confrontation unfold with morbid fascination.

Cooksone suddenly stood, chair scraping across stone. His sword cleared its scabbard with a metallic hiss. "Take that back or defend yourself!"

De Goetd rose more deliberately, drawing his own blade with practiced ease. "Gladly."

Steel clashed against steel. Sir Brock pushed back from the table, moving to intervene, but Duke Edric was closer. Our host stepped between the combatants with surprising agility, his own sword appearing as if conjured from air. With two powerful strokes, he beat their blades downward, forcing them backward.

"Gentlemen," Duke Edric growled, his voice cutting through the tension. "Is this your idea of high-bred chivalry? To fight over my niece?" His eyes narrowed dangerously. "Behave yourselves or the next time you start to fight, you'll be fighting me." He turned slightly. "Imogene, you're free to leave, if that's what you wish."

She nodded gratefully to her uncle, rising with quiet dignity. Not once did she glance at either of her would-be champions as she departed the hall.

Cooksone and De Goetd mumbled apologies to each other, sheathing their weapons. The words rang hollow, insincere formalities that fooled no one. The hatred simmering between them would require little encouragement to boil over again.

I retired early, declining further wine. In my chamber, I secured the bolt across my door before settling into the unfamiliar bed. Despite the evening's drama, sleep claimed me quickly.

I woke suddenly, disoriented in the darkness. The room felt wrong until memory reasserted itself: Ainsleys Castle, Bear's game, the strange warnings. Unlike the previous night, I'd drunk sparingly at dinner and slept deeply until this moment.

Something had disturbed my rest. I sat up, listening intently. The castle breathed around me, old stones settling, wind whispering through cracks. Nothing seemed amiss, yet unease crawled along my spine.

Rising, I crossed to the door and verified the bolt remained firmly in place. The heavy wood hadn't been disturbed. I glanced toward the alcove where Sawyer slept, considering whether to wake him. The boy had proven attentive and observant throughout the day; perhaps he'd noticed something I'd missed.

Before I could decide, a wild scream shattered the night's silence. The sound froze my blood, primal and desperate, echoing through the stone corridors of Ainsleys Castle.

Sawyer's head jerked up from his makeshift bed in the alcove, instantly alert. I opened the door as another scream tore through the night, unmistakably female, high and desperate.

"My lord, wait!" Sawyer called, fumbling for his boots.

I ignored him, barefoot and wearing only my sleeping clothes, I sprinted down the dark corridor. The cold stone floor sent shocks through my feet with each step. At the winding staircase, I took the steps two at a time, my hand skimming the wall for balance.

Halfway down, a solid mass collided with me. We tumbled together, limbs tangling as we crashed onto the hard stone steps. Pain shot through my shoulder.

"God's teeth!" The voice was young, breathless with panic.

"Cooksone?" I pushed myself up, recognizing him in the dim light.

"Lord Go?" He scrambled to his feet, offering his hand. "Did you hear—"

"Yes." I grabbed his arm, pulling myself upright. "This way."

We raced together through the darkened corridors. The screaming had stopped, replaced by a growing clamor of voices and the flickering glow of torches being lit throughout the castle. Duke Edric's commanding voice rose above the chaos, calling for his guards.

We reached Imogene's chamber to find its door flung wide. Inside, Duke Edric bent over his niece, gently helping her onto her bed and covering her trembling form with a thick woolen blanket. Her nightgown hung in tatters, exposing angry red scratches across her pale skin; long, vicious marks that marred her arms, neck, and shoulders.

More guests crowded into the doorway behind us, brandishing hastily grabbed weapons and lanterns. Questions flew from every direction.

"What happened?"

"Is she hurt?"

"Who did this?"

Imogene's eyes fluttered open, her fingers clutching the blanket's edge with white-knuckled intensity. "I forgot to bar the door," she whispered, her voice breaking. "Left it unlocked. Someone came in... in the darkness."

Duke Edric stroked her hair, his face grim. "Easy, child. You're safe now."

"I called out," she continued, each word an effort. "He didn't answer. I heard furniture crashing and grew frightened." Her eyes darted to her uncle. "I slashed at him with my dagger, the one you gave me. Then he attacked, tearing at my clothes, striking my head."

Cooksone surveyed the room, his expression darkening. "Where is De Goetd?"

The question lingered, unspoken yet heavy. My gaze swept the room, and only then did I notice the baron's absence among the assembled guests. The others had all arrived, weapons at the ready.

Even I had armed myself earlier that day, retrieving a sword and dagger from the castle armory. Sawyer, ever considerate, had ensured they were brought along.

Herr Fuchsg stood near the window, his face pale as he fixed a haunted stare on Imogene. His hands trembled, and beneath the veil of concern, pure terror lurked, as if he were witnessing the realization of some long-feared omen.

"De Goetd!" Cooksone's shout rang through the chamber, sharp with urgency. "Where are you?"

Duke Edric straightened, his voice crisp with command. "We'll search the castle. You," he gestured toward Sir Brock, "take the west wing. Cooksone, the kitchens and cellars. Lord Go, check the east tower." He continued assigning areas until every corner of Ainsleys Castle was covered.

I joined the search, gripping my borrowed sword tightly as I navigated the dim corridors. The castle felt alive with unease, every creaking floorboard and shifting shadow heightening my sense of foreboding.

A distant shout shattered the silence, pulling us into a sprint. A guest, Lord Kemble, I thought, stood frozen in a doorway, his lantern casting a grim glow on the scene before him.

Baron De Goetd lay sprawled on the floor, his body twisted unnaturally. Blood pooled beneath him, dark and slick, seeping between the cracks in the stone.

"One of the villagers must have done this!" Cooksone gasped, his voice raw with horror.

Duke Edric shook his head sharply. "Impossible. The only villagers within these walls are my trusted servants. No outsider could have breached the guards." His gaze turned steely as he scanned the faces around him, suspicion settling like a weight. "This murder was committed by someone here. By one of you."

A dreadful silence followed, thick with unspoken accusations.

"But who?" Cooksone murmured, barely audible.

I stared at De Goetd's lifeless form, my mind racing. The castle felt less like a refuge and more like a carefully laid trap: one that had just been sprung around us all.

The moment had come. I had to take a more active role in the game. "You could have done it, Cooksone!" I declared.

I was completely immersed now, surprised by how exhilarating it felt. Despite the horror of the situation, there was an undeniable thrill to it.

"You were the first to cast suspicion!" I pressed on. "And we collided on the staircase as you ran—not toward the screams, but away from them. Why? Were you fleeing the scene of your crime?"

"You're lying!" Cooksone bellowed.

His sword flashed as he lunged at me, but Sir Brock was faster. In one swift motion, Brock struck, sending Cooksone's weapon clattering against the stone wall. He froze, his breath shallow, as Brock's blade hovered dangerously close to his throat.

"Sheathe your sword," Duke Edric commanded, his voice like steel. "I am the law here, and I will see justice served. Lord Cooksone, give me your word you will not attempt to flee."

"I give it," Cooksone muttered. He exhaled sharply and added, "I regret my actions, Lord Go. I wasn't running away earlier. This castle, with its endless halls and twisting corridors, is maddening. I was confused, nothing more."

I doubted anyone believed him.

Then, to my surprise, Herr Fuchsg spoke. "Gentlemen, consider that Lord Cooksone might be innocent. Do you see any wounds on De Goetd's body?" His gaze swept across the group. "No? Neither do I. Someone turn him over."

Two guards did as requested. We hesitated, then looked. I managed only a brief glance before looking away.

"Who could have done this?" I murmured. "Imogene's dagger...?"

"No dagger could cause such wounds," Sir Brock stated grimly. "No weapon I've ever seen could. De Goetd's chest has been ripped apart—by claws."

A chill crept up my spine. My eyes darted to the dark corners of the room, half expecting some unseen, sharp-taloned monster to spring from the shadows.

We searched the castle from end to end, but no trace of the beast was ever found.

As dawn crept over the horizon, I finally returned to my room, only to find that Sawyer had barricaded himself inside.

"How do I know it's really you?" he demanded, his voice tight with fear.

"Sawyer, it's me! Open the door!" I urged.

It took nearly an hour to convince him. When he finally unlocked the door, he was visibly shaken, his hands trembling. I couldn't bring myself to chastise him, not after the night we'd endured. Fear was a reasonable response.

I recounted everything that had happened. As I spoke, his eyes grew wide, horror settling into his features. Yet I felt it necessary to tell him. If I took him into my confidence, perhaps he would do the same for me. Being from the village, Sawyer might have valuable knowledge. Something that could help unravel this mystery.

He sat stiffly, staring ahead as if lost in thought. I snapped my fingers in front of his face several times.

"Devil's spawn!" he finally muttered.

"Why do you say that, Sawyer? You're from the village. What are they saying about the murders? Do they suspect a leopard?"

"Not a leopard, sir!" He shook his head vehemently. "The hunter wasn't the first villager murdered. A month ago, a woman vanished. The next day, a woodcutter found her: the same wounds, her chest clawed to shreds. A month before that, another man was killed. It happens when the moon is full... always at the full moon. And at every murder scene, footprints are found. A man's footprints, leading away from the body."

I stiffened. I thought back. There had been no footprints in Imogene's room, but the castle's floors were stone. They wouldn't have left a visible trace.

"Sawyer," I asked carefully, "who do the villagers believe these footprints belong to?"

I wasn't prepared for his answer.

"Duke Edric!" he whispered.

"But that doesn't add up, he's always been a friend to the village," I argued.

Sawyer simply shrugged. "That's what everyone believes, sir."

The mystery deepened with every passing thought. My mind whirled with questions: Who would kill the baron? And why spare Imogene? If the murderer had time to finish the job, why hold back?

What was Herr Fuchsg's warning truly about? Why was he so certain that Lord Cooksone was innocent? And what of the other murders, each occurring around the full moon?

I debated whether to tell Duke Edric about the rumors circling in the village. According to Bear, he was my only true ally in the castle, and I couldn't risk him being blindsided by an angry mob. But knowledge was power. I needed to watch and wait; to understand how everything was unfolding before acting. So, for now, I held my tongue.

All day, the castle felt oppressive, suffocating any trace of humor. Imogene remained locked away in her room, under the watch of Duke Edric's guards. The rest of us gathered in the great hall, a silent show of solidarity, though unease gnawed at us. We paced restlessly, our expressions grim. Wine flowed freely, not the wisest choice, but by nightfall, it was too late to regret it.

Then, I made my move.

If we can't find the beast, perhaps I can force it to come to me.

Standing before the fireplace, I let the thought settle, then, with deliberate flair, hurled my glass into the flames.

I turned to the others, my voice ringing through the hall. "Gentlemen, I'm done fearing this creature. Tonight, I will sleep with my door wide open!"

The room erupted in protests, but I paid them no heed, storming out of the hall and retreating to my quarters. Not long after, Herr Fuchsg appeared at my door, his face contorted with worry, his haunted eyes betraying the weight of unseen horrors.

"I beg you, Lord Go, reconsider leaving your door open," he pleaded.

I shook my head firmly.

His shoulders sagged. "Then it's decided? You insist on recklessness, despite the dangers that lurk in the night? I fear for what may come. But if you refuse to safeguard yourself, will you at least grant me one favor? Bolt my door from the outside so I may rest in safety."

I obliged, promising to unfasten it come morning. I didn't think him a coward for the request: his frame was slight, his form fragile, lacking the strength to wield a blade in defense. He wouldn't last a moment against a beast. In truth, only a fool like myself would risk sleeping with his door unbarred. I returned to my room, placing my sword and dagger within arm's reach.

Sawyer must have caught wind of my reckless resolve, as he was nowhere to be found. In the enveloping darkness, I settled into the reading chair at the foot of my bed, determined to fight off sleep. To keep my mind sharp, I combed through everything I knew of the beast and this cursed castle.

Murder seemed a possibility for everyone here, yet my mind kept circling back to Herr Fuchsg. Tonight, he was more restless than usual, his unease woven into every word and motion. And yet, for all his distress, there was a gentleness to his face, a kindness hidden beneath exhaustion. He was an enigma. A man who uttered a curse when a toast was expected. The first to warn us to seal our doors at night. The only one who believed in Cooksone's innocence when no one else did.

His contradictions gnawed at me. He knew more than he let on.

I couldn't let it rest.

Steeling myself, I rose. I had to return to his room and confront him.

Navigating the castle's dark corridors was unnerving, every step accompanied by the phantom sensation of unseen eyes trailing me. I reached Herr Fuchsg's door and called his name, barely above a whisper. Silence greeted me. When no answer came, I reached for the bolt, only to recoil as my fingers brushed splintered wood where a solid door should have stood.

I needed light.

Kneeling, I gathered scattered fragments of wood into a small pile on the stone floor. Pulling a flint from my pocket (thank the heavens I'd come prepared), I struck it against the steel of my blade, igniting the dry tinder. The flickering flame bathed the corridor in dim, unsteady light, revealing the wreckage before me; the oak door sagging, barely clinging to its hinges.

The realization struck me like a blow to the chest: the door had been shattered from the inside.

And Herr Fuchsg's room was empty.

A deep unease clamped around my chest. The walls felt like they were closing in. Every instinct screamed at me to return to the safety of my quarters, and I obeyed, moving swiftly through the suffocating dark. Near my door, something shifted ahead of me: a shadow, lingering, waiting.

It turned.

It advanced.

There was no time to draw my sword.

Panic surged through me, primal and wild. With no other option, I lunged forward and swung. My fist met something solid yet yielding. A grunt, then collapse. The dark figure crumpled to the ground.

Heart hammering, I edged around the fallen form, my hands fumbling for a candle. I lit it using the smoldering embers in my fireplace, holding my breath as the light revealed the unconscious man at my feet.

Herr Fuchsg.

"You?" My voice was barely audible, disbelief chilling me to the bone. "Impossible. You... you're the beast?"

His eyes fluttered open. Slowly, unsteadily, he sat up and gave a single, solemn nod.

"You killed De Goetd?"

"Yes," he admitted, without hesitation.

Instinct drove me backward. My sword rose. No matter the setting, reality or in the games we played, actions had consequences.

"You have to answer for your crimes," I told him. "Step inside. Don't move while I summon the guards."

But instead of resistance, he lifted a trembling hand. "Please," he murmured. "Take your sword. Strike me down. You have your proof. No one would fault you."

I tightened my grip. "No. I can't."

A shadow passed over his features, the same worry, the same exhaustion.

"Then quickly," he urged, voice urgent and low, "close your door and bolt it. Hurry. It will return soon."

Confusion twisted in my gut. "What do you mean? What will return? You're not the beast?" My voice was urgent now. "If it poses a danger to me, then you're at risk too. Come inside with me."

Herr Fuchsg staggered back, shaking his head. "No—I can't!" His words were strangled, desperate. "Hurry! It left me for a moment, but it's coming back! Nngh—it's here now!"

A shudder raced down my spine. The hairs on my arms stood on end as a presence slithered into existence: formless, shapeless, radiating an unseen malice that coiled around me like smoke.

Herr Fuchsg braced himself, legs planted, fists clenched. His entire body trembled beneath an invisible weight. His eyes widened, then narrowed. I barely had time to grasp the horror unfolding before me: the shifting void hovering in the air, descending upon him like a living shadow. It enveloped him, crushing him in its spectral embrace, pressing against him until it seeped into his very being.

A strangled gasp left his lips. He staggered, then lifted his head.

I did not recognize him.

The thing that turned to face me was no longer Herr Fuchsg. His features had twisted, contorted into something monstrous. The beast moved with eerie silence, creeping toward me, its gaze a promise of violence.

Terror jolted me into action.

I sprang for the door, yanking it shut just as the creature lunged. It slammed against the wood with a feral, guttural howl: a sound like a wolf screaming in agony. I bolted the door and threw myself against it, bracing for the relentless onslaught.

The thing hurled itself at the door, again and again, each impact shaking me to my core.

Then, silence.

Breathless, drained, I collapsed to the cold stone floor, straining to hear any sign of its lingering presence. Had it slunk away? Or was it merely waiting, watching?

My answer came minutes later; a long, high-pitched howl echoing from the forest beyond the castle.

I shuddered.

I felt unclean.

And deep within, I knew that no amount of washing would ever rid me of the horror that had taken root.

At dawn, I set out to find Herr Fuchsg, but on my way, I crossed paths with Duke Edric. His expression was tense, anger flickering beneath his confusion.

"Another villager was attacked last night," he said, his voice sharp. "A woman this time. She barely escaped with her life. Some beast tore at her, leaving her bloodied. One of the guards was also attacked. Whatever it was, it shredded his leather breastplate before leaping from the palisades into the forest. And someone locked Herr Fuchsg in his room. He had to smash his way out."

Without another word, Duke Edric strode off, calling for his captain of the guard, leaving me standing in the corridor, more bewildered than before.

I descended the stairs and entered Herr Fuchsg's quarters. He sat hunched on a stool, staring vacantly out the window. At the sound of my footsteps, he turned, his movements slow, weary. His hair was unkempt, his clothes tattered. His eyes drooped with exhaustion, and his hands bore torn and broken nails. But his face was still that of a man.

He gestured for me to sit.

For a long moment, silence stretched between us. Then, at last, he spoke.

"You deserve the truth," he said, his voice hoarse. "I've never told this story before."

He exhaled, as though drawing up something long buried.

"Decades ago, in another life, I rode with the cavalry across the rolling hills of northern France. Our squadron was ambushed, and I lost my horse. I lost sight of my men. Alone, desperate to avoid capture, I fled south toward the mountains. Near Orleans, I sensed something following me in the woods. At first, I glimpsed it only in flashes. But when night fell, it grew bold. I slept with one eye open.

"Then, under a full moon, it attacked.

"We fought. And somehow, I killed the beast. But as it lay dying, its body twisted, shifting in its final moments, until it was no longer a creature, but a man.

"I buried him there. Alone. In an unmarked grave.

"I regretted it, leaving him nameless in the dirt. Whatever his sins, he deserved more than I, a soldier on the run, could give. I whispered a prayer, then left, unaware of the weight I had just placed upon myself.

"But when the next full moon came, I felt... strange.

"My thoughts tangled. My blood burned. I hungered.

"I blamed the horrors of war for my unease, for the thirst clawing at me. But the next full moon came, and it was worse.

"One night, beneath that cursed moon, I saw it. A spectral thing. A wolf's head, floating before me, watching.

"And then... nothing.

"I remember only flashes: a haze of trees and thickets. And the next morning, when clarity returned, I found myself in rags. My hands were coated with dried blood.

"Then I heard the whispers. Two lovers, slain near Amiens. Torn apart by a beast.

"I fled back to my squadron. Resigned my commission. Returned to Germany. I searched every monastery I could find, pouring over their texts, desperate for answers.

"And this is what I learned."

His gaze darkened.

"The creature I slew near Orleans was no ordinary beast. It was possessed, infested with a demon of the moon.

"I never discovered how the man became its vessel. But the monks' writings revealed a terrible truth: if a moon demon is slain while fully transformed, hell itself claims it. But if it is killed in the midst of its transformation, before its possession is complete, the demon is set loose, free to haunt another.

"I killed the beast before its change was done.

"And it chose me.

"Now, with every full moon, the demon overtakes me. I am cursed. I have wandered the world seeking escape, but it follows. Always."

Herr Fuchsg wept, his sorrow spilling in full, unrestrained tears. A man condemned to a cursed life, trapped in a nightmare with no escape. And though he was only a non-playing character, I couldn't help but feel for him.

After a long silence, he spoke again.

"I would have ended my life long ago," he murmured, voice trembling. "But suicide condemns a man's soul. My soul is all I have left. The demon controls me, I bear some guilt for the innocent lives lost, but if I take my own life, I seal my fate in hell. That is why I beg you, Lord Go. No, I plead with you. Take your blade and run it through my heart. End this torment. If you help me, I will bless you with my final breath. Please. Release me."

My thoughts spun wildly.

To kill a man was a sin.

But was it still a sin if it freed his soul?

And what of his next victim? Should I act now to save them? But how could I be sure that killing him wouldn't damn him further, that the demon wouldn't drag his soul to hell along with it?

I wished Temper were here. Right now, he was probably sitting in his service bot, staring lovingly at his baby sun, lost in the simplicity of it all. Our carefree adventuring with the Din felt like a distant memory, a world apart from this grim reality.

Bear Draydon had crafted a world so immersive, so lifelike, that it was easy to forget the truth.

It was just a game.

None of this was real.

And yet, I hesitated.

Because real or not, I had to make a choice.

After all, life, whether tangible or digital, is what you make of it.

I exhaled, letting the weight of the moment settle over me.

"We have time before the next full moon," I finally said. "Let's talk this through. Let's see if we can't find another way."

I chose not to tell Duke Edric about any of it.

In the days that followed, Herr Fuchsg and I spoke at length, our guarded conversations gradually shifting into something more familiar, friendship. He was an amateur cook, eager to share what little knowledge he had. From him, I learned about Grains of Paradise and Spikenard, two spices common in medieval kitchens. Yet, try as he might, he couldn't recall a single recipe that used them.

"Call me Dunstan," he said one evening, offering a small, weary smile.

The month passed quickly, filled with talk of food, drink, and things that made life feel, for a brief moment, simple again.

Then, one night, Dunstan appeared in my room, his gaze fixed on the rising moon.

"I have a plan," he murmured. "At dawn, I'll tell everyone I'm leaving for a week-long hunt in the forest. I'll depart tomorrow morning, but in truth, I'll return under cover of darkness. When I do, you must lock me in the dungeon. It hasn't been used in years, so no one will go there. No one will notice."

The following night, I did as he asked, sealing him inside a dungeon cell. While the castle believed him off on his hunt, he remained hidden, trapped, even when the demon released its hold by day. Twice a day, I snuck food and drink down to him. As he ate, we would talk.

It felt good to be useful again.

I hadn't cared for anyone since Amy.

Memories pressed in, unbidden. The times I helped her with daily tasks when she was sick. The walks we took through quiet neighborhood streets, her arm around me for support. We were happy. I missed tending to her needs.

I missed taking care of her.

Perhaps that was it. The missing piece I hadn't yet grasped.

The act of caring for someone had given me purpose once. Could it again?

It gave me much to consider.

When I wasn't with Dunstan in the dungeon, I couldn't help but notice Coelmund, Duke Edric's nephew, shamelessly pursuing the affections of his cousin, Imogene.

Duke Edric hardly seemed aware of his advances, preoccupied as he was with the growing hostility from the villagers. Their sudden defiance toward the castle had escalated. They refused to work at the docks. Even going so far as to post their own guards along the outskirts.

To Imogene's credit, she remained polite toward Coelmund, but it was painfully clear she wanted nothing to do with him. Still, he persisted. I saw her hand tighten into a fist more than once, hovering at the edge of retaliation. I found myself silently willing her to follow through.

Meanwhile, the other guests had settled into their predictable routine: drinking, feasting, losing themselves in excess.

Sawyer had vanished altogether. My best guess? He'd decided it was safer in the village. I'd never had an attendant before, and though I rarely gave him orders, I found that I missed him.

On the third night of the full moon, I descended into the dungeon to see Dunstan.

His eyes flickered with warning. "You're taking a risk coming here."

"The moon hasn't risen yet," I said, trying to reassure him.

A barred window allowed in the distant sounds of the forest. The night was unnervingly still, save for the quiet hum of activity from the village beyond.

"Duke Edric has his hands full with the villagers," I told him. "They've been openly defiant, refusing work, stationing their own guards just outside the village."

Dunstan frowned. "Something, or someone, has them riled up. Have you noticed Coelmund disappears often? I believe he goes to them."

I blinked. "I hadn't noticed that, but I have noticed him flirting with his cousin, Imogene."

Our conversation slowed. The air shifted. Dunstan grew quiet.

Then, as the moon rose, its pale glow filtered through the barred window, illuminating his face. I watched, transfixed, as his shadow stretched against the stone wall behind him.

It was no longer the shadow of a man.

It was the silhouette of a wolf.

A low growl rumbled from his throat as the transformation began.

I watched in horrified fascination as Dunstan transformed. His jaw elongated with a series of sickening cracks. Bones shifted beneath his skin like living things. His fingers curled inward, nails extending into cruel claws. The growl deepening from his throat no longer contained anything human.

"Dunstan," I whispered, backing toward the door. "Fight it."

His eyes met mine, pupils dilating until only a thin ring of color remained. For a moment, I saw recognition there, a flash of the man trapped inside the beast. Then it vanished, replaced by something ancient and hungry.

The moonlight streaming through the barred window seemed to intensify, bathing the cell in silver. Dunstan's shadow on the wall grew more distorted, more monstrous with each passing second. His clothes tore as his body contorted, muscles bulging and reshaping.

I gripped the cell door, ready to slam it shut. My heart hammered against my ribs. This wasn't just another Din adventure. Bear Draydon had created something genuinely terrifying, something that made me forget the digital nature of this world.

Dunstan's face twisted in agony. Blood trickled from his mouth where new fangs punctured his gums. His final human cry dissolved into a howl that raised the hairs on my neck.

"I'll come back when it's over," I promised, though I wasn't sure he could hear me anymore.

I pulled the door closed and turned the iron key in the lock. The mechanism clicked with reassuring solidity. The beast hurled itself against the bars, reaching for me with clawed hands that were no longer hands at all.

I backed away, watching the creature that had been my friend. Its eyes tracked my movement with predatory focus. Another howl echoed through the dungeon, bouncing off stone walls and sending a chill through my body.

Would the cell hold? It had to.

I turned and hurried up the stairs, the howls following me like ghosts. At the top, I locked the heavy wooden door behind me and leaned against it, trying to steady my breathing.

Something wasn't right.

The corridor swam before my eyes. A familiar disorientation swept over me. Not now. I couldn't afford another memory gap, not with Dunstan transformed and locked below.

I tried to fight it, tried to maintain my grip on consciousness, but darkness closed in from all sides.

"No," I whispered, sliding down against the door. "Not now."

The world disappeared.

I snapped awake to the sound of metal scraping against stone. Disoriented, I found myself standing in the dungeon corridor, the heavy key clutched in my hand. How long had I been out? Minutes? Hours?

The dungeon door stood open before me. I had no memory of unlocking it.

Cold dread pooled in my stomach as I moved forward, drawn by a primal need to know. The cell door at the bottom of the stairs hung open as well, its lock broken from the inside. Claw marks scored the stone walls. Blood spattered the floor in a chaotic pattern.

And in the center of the cell crouched the beast.

It turned at my approach, rising to its full height. Seven feet of muscle and fur and fang. The creature's chest heaved with each breath. Its muzzle, flecked with foam, pulled back in a snarl that revealed rows of jagged teeth.

No trace of Dunstan remained in those yellow eyes. Only hunger.

I jumped back and ran through the corridor, slamming and locking the dungeon door behind me. As I retreated back upstairs into the castle, I could hear him battering against the door, but the dungeon door held.

I hadn't expected to find Sawyer in my chambers. His presence startled me, but his agitation was immediate, almost palpable. He launched into his account of what was unfolding in the village. His words too wild to believe, but there was no deception in his eyes.

The moment he finished, I ran out in search of Duke Edric.

A castle guard informed me. "Coelmund convinced his uncle to go with him to the village to settle the dispute."

Alarm surged through me.

I sprinted down the corridor, nearly colliding with Sir Brock. When I relayed Sawyer's tale, he didn't hesitate.

"We're going," he said grimly.

Together, we set off for the village, summoning the castle guard to assemble and follow.

"Edric was a fool!" Sir Brock muttered as we rode.

We caught up to them near the village.

"Duke Edric!" I shouted, urgency clawing at my voice. "You must return to the castle. Your nephew is betraying you! He wants your wealth; he lusts after his cousin, Imogene!"

Duke Edric turned, his gaze landing on Coelmund. "Is this true, nephew?" he asked, his voice measured.

Coelmund didn't flinch. "No, your grace. I am loyal to you. I must question their motives. Why do they wish to keep you from making peace with the village?"

"Lies!" I spat. "Sawyer overheard your plans! You hired assassins to slaughter villagers and left footprints to frame Duke Edric for the crime! You convinced them that he was the beast, that he transformed from man to monster. And tonight, you meant to murder your uncle, then attack the castle and slaughter everyone inside!"

I turned back to Edric. "You must believe me!"

Edric's expression darkened. "Coelmund, tell me the truth."

A rustling swept through the trees: low, ominous.

Coelmund laughed.

"The truth no longer matters, Uncle." His voice was triumphant. "You're too late!"

With a swift motion, he drew his sword, calling out to the hidden figures lurking in the woods. The villagers sprang forward, an ambush. Coelmund lunged for Edric.

But Sir Brock was faster.

His blade sliced through Coelmund before the traitor could strike.

A chorus of furious cries erupted as the villagers charged. I barely had time to react, my sword flashing as I fought off the nearest attackers.

Duke Edric staggered against me, blood seeping from a wound in his arm and leg.

Sir Brock was a force of nature: a whirlwind of steel and fury. His sword carved through the chaos, driving back the relentless onslaught. But we were vastly outnumbered, forced to retreat toward the castle.

Then came a sound from behind us.

The castle guard had arrived.

Shouting war cries, they stormed forward, their blades carving a path through the villagers, clearing the way.

And with them, we fled back to the safety of the castle.

The villagers pursued, relentless. Again and again, they surged against the palisades, only to be repelled by the castle guards. But each assault chipped away at our defenses. Their fury escalated. They set fire to the wharf and its storehouses, flames licking hungrily at the structures.

Duke Edric stood with his captain of the guard, their grim expressions betraying the truth neither spoke aloud: we couldn't hold out forever.

We were going to die here.

Soon.

I thought back to my choice to spare Dunstan. Had I erred? If the villagers had believed the beast was dead, would they have seen through Coelmund's lies? Would it have changed anything? Could it have saved the castle?

But even if Dunstan had been slain, Coelmund's betrayal would not have ended. The bloodshed would have continued.

I should have warned Duke Edric about the whispers brewing in the village.

The battle at the palisades didn't need me, the soldiers held their ground well enough. So, I descended into the dungeon.

I paused outside Dunstan's door. "Dunstan? Is it you?"

A beat of silence, then his voice: low, strained. "It's safe for now. The beast has left me… for the moment."

I unbarred the door and stepped inside.

"The villagers have attacked," I told him. "Coelmund betrayed us. They blame Duke Edric for the killings."

Dunstan listened in silence, his body slumping against the cold stone wall, head bowed.

Then, finally, his voice barely above a whisper.

"Help me to my feet."

I moved quickly, gripping his arm as he struggled to rise. His legs trembled beneath him, weakened, drained. The fight against the beast had sapped his strength.

But if there was still a battle left to fight, he wouldn't face it lying down.

"This is the chance I've been waiting for," Dunstan said, his voice steady with resolve. "We must show them the true beast. Only then will the villagers realize their mistake and abandon the attack. Help me walk. I need to reach the palisades."

I hesitated. "No, it's too dangerous. They'll kill you."

Dunstan smiled, his expression clearer, more peaceful than I had ever seen. He looked… free.

"That's what I want, dear friend," he said softly. "When I step into the full light of the moon, the beast will return. I will hold onto myself for as long as I can; long enough to lead the villagers into the forest, where God willing, they will kill me and the beast together. Then, finally, I'll be free." He exhaled. "This is my choice. We must hurry."

There was no arguing with him.

I slung his arm over my shoulders, lending him my strength, and together we struggled up the stairs, through the great hall, toward the metal-plated front entrance. We crossed the small courtyard, moving with urgency, until at last we reached the palisades.

Duke Edric turned at the sight of us, his face lined with concern. "Herr Fuchsg, what's happened to you?" His eyes flicked to me. "Lord Go, he shouldn't be here in his condition!"

"You must trust me, your grace," I said. "Order your men to open the portcullis."

Duke Edric recoiled. "And let the mob in? Have you gone mad?"

Dunstan met his gaze. "He's right, your grace. You must let me out!"

I gestured toward the villagers, standing at the edge of the forest, no longer attacking, only watching, waiting. "They aren't charging right now. Look, they're regrouping. This is our only chance!"

Dunstan straightened, standing as tall as his weary body would allow, locking eyes with Edric. "They believe you are the beast, your grace. But you are not." His voice dropped to something almost solemn. "I am."

"We have to show them the truth," I urged.

Duke Edric hesitated, studying Dunstan with a mixture of confusion and disbelief. "Herr Fuchsg?"

Dunstan fell silent.

Then, suddenly, he pushed me away.

A low, guttural moan escaped his lips.

I looked down. There, on the ground, cast by the rising moon, was the unmistakable shadow of a wolf.

Duke Edric's breath hitched.

Then, resolve hardened in his expression.

"Open the portcullis! Quickly!"

Dunstan met my gaze one last time. A silent nod: friendship, gratitude, acceptance. Then he turned and ran, disappearing through the open gate.

I rushed to the top of the palisades.

"You were lied to!" I shouted to the villagers. "Duke Edric didn't kill anyone! There is your beast!"

Under the pale glow of the moon, I saw Dunstan loping down the road toward the forest. The villagers recoiled, startled, before scrambling after him in pursuit.

I stood frozen, listening.

His howls echoed through the night, leading them farther and farther from the castle.

Then, at last, a sharp cry of pain.

Silence.

He was gone.

Somehow, against all odds, Dunstan had kept the beast at bay long enough to lure the villagers away. Long enough to save us all.

I turned to find Duke Edric staring at me, his face taut with expectation. He looked like a man demanding answers.

I mustered my best smile, preparing to tell my story.

But before I could speak, the world blinked around me.

A breath later, I was standing on the mud-splattered docks under the warmth of the sun.

Beside me stood Bear Draydon.

"Well done, Captain," she said, beaming. "No one before you has accomplished what you did today."

I blinked at her. "Accomplished what?"

"You befriended Herr Fuchsg. You helped him achieve redemption. And in doing so, you saved the castle, and yourself, from slaughter. No one else has ever done that." She paused, studying me with admiration. "Everyone else who has played this game before you have died at the end."

I frowned. "They've all died?"

She nodded. "Either they kill Herr Fuchsg immediately, or they spare him but tell Duke Edric, who then has his guards execute him. In either case, they assume the game is over. Some even tell me later they planned to complain about how easy it was."

She let the words sink in, then continued.

"But the killings in the village continue. Coelmund is still there. That's when they realize the game isn't truly over. Tensions rise; they fester. Then Coelmund betrays his uncle in the forest, and the villagers storm the castle.

"Everyone dies.

"Afterward, I greet the newly deceased guest here, on the docks. They tell me how horrifying the experience was, how the game gripped them until the end. And then, shaken but grateful, they go back home.

Then everyone takes a break."

"Takes a break?" I echoed.

Bear smiled knowingly. "As you're aware, everyone here, besides you and me, are non-playing characters. Each has a vast, predetermined set of behaviors, numbering in the hundreds of thousands, allowing them to react appropriately to any situation."

She took my hand, guiding me down the dock toward the bay.

"Except," she added, "I never gave Dunstan any food recipes. You're the first person to ask about his love of cooking. I'll make sure he gets some."

I glanced at her, curiosity sparking. "Your NPCs are so meticulously designed. Has any of them achieved thruman status?"

Bear's expression grew contemplative. "Not yet. But I believe some are on the verge of a breakthrough. Dunstan, with everything he's endured, is the closest, but he's still a step or two below true self-awareness. Maybe giving him those recipes, adding more to his story, will help push him over the edge."

She let out a soft sigh before continuing. "Even without full awareness, I believe NPCs deserve ethical treatment. So, after every game, I send them all to a tropical paradise I created called Altar Island, for a two-week vacation. They bask in the sun, unwind, and after they're well-rested, we return to Ainsleys Castle to greet the next guest. Then the cycle begins again."

I absorbed her words, then nodded. "Despite the horror of it all, I had fun. Thank you, Bear. This world you've built is incredible. I can see why people love it. And I think, somehow, I've learned something about myself while being here."

A pause. Then, hesitantly, I added, "If Dunstan ever reaches self-awareness, would you call me? I've grown to like him. I'd even say he's a friend. Also, could you send me some of the recipes too?"

Her smile widened. "I'll do that, Captain. It was a pleasure hosting you. And please, keep our privacy in mind when sharing your experience with others. We want to preserve the mystery for future guests."

She pressed her palm against mine in a parting gesture. "May the stars guide you."

"And you as well, Bear," I said.

Then, the world blinked.

A breath later, I stood in my cottage, surrounded by my quiet garden. The scent of lavender drifted through an open window, comforting and familiar.

"Back where I belong," I thought.

CHAPTER TWELVE

The Final Threshold

I stood in my cottage kitchen, stirring the rich bouillabaisse as it simmered. The aroma of saffron, fennel, and seafood filled the space, wrapping around me like a familiar embrace. Alice Tracker would be proud, I thought, remembering how I'd studied her technique on "Seasoned Table" with almost scientific precision. The way she'd layered the flavors, adding each type of seafood at precisely the right moment to preserve its texture and flavor.

My movements were confident now, no longer the hesitant motions of someone following instructions for the first time. I added a pinch more salt, tasted, and nodded with satisfaction.

"Perfect," I murmured to myself.

The kitchen had become my sanctuary. Something about the methodical nature of cooking grounded me, especially after experiences like Ainsleys Castle. My mind still wandered through those gothic hallways, remembering Dunstan's eyes when I'd offered friendship instead of suspicion.

I reached for the bottle of white wine I'd set aside, pouring a splash into the stew and another into a glass for myself. The simple action felt like a small celebration.

Something had awakened in me at the castle. A realization that had been waiting patiently for me to notice.

I missed taking care of someone.

The thought settled over me with unexpected clarity as I stirred the bouillabaisse. For years, I had been Amy's constant companion, her go-fer, her support. Making her tea when she worked late. Remembering which book she'd mentioned wanting to read. Bringing her coffee in bed on Sunday mornings.

I took a sip of wine, letting the memory wash over me. The kitchen timer chimed softly, pulling me back to the present. I reduced the heat and covered the pot.

Amy didn't always need me to take care of her. She was fiercely independent, brilliantly capable. But in the times she did, I loved being there. Finding small ways to make her life easier, more comfortable. More joyful.

It had been such a natural part of who I was for so long that I hadn't realized how much I missed it until I found myself helping Dunstan in the castle. Listening to his fears. Offering comfort instead of judgment.

The satisfaction I'd felt wasn't just from solving the castle's mystery. It was from connecting with someone who needed help and offering it freely.

I moved to the window, looking out at my garden where the oak tree stood tall, twenty wooden birdhouses nestled in its branches. Each one a testament to years of caring for Amy, creating something new for her each birthday.

My fingers traced the condensation on my wine glass. Paradise was filled with people, but something had been missing from my life here. A purpose beyond captaining the ship. A connection beyond duty.

I turned back to the stove, lifting the lid to release a cloud of fragrant steam. The bouillabaisse was nearly ready. I'd made enough for several people, though I hadn't invited anyone to share it.

Old habits.

I smiled to myself, realizing I could invite someone. Temper, perhaps. Or Lieutenant Chen. Dr. Wong. Bear Draydon.

The castle had reminded me that caring for others wasn't something I'd left behind on Earth with Amy. It was part of who I was, who I am. Captain, neuroclone, explorer, and caretaker.

I reached for my comm unit, feeling lighter than I had in months. "Temper? It's Go. I've made bouillabaisse. Enough for two. Care to join me?"

His response came quickly. "You cooked bouillabaisse? This I have to see."

"Alice Tracker would be proud," I said, smiling to myself.

"I'll be there in twenty minutes. Don't burn anything down before I arrive."

I set the table on the cottage patio, beside the flower boxes. A gentle breeze rustled through the leaves above. I placed a bottle of whiskey alongside the wine, knowing Temper's preferences.

When he arrived, his eyebrows shot up at the sight of the steaming pot.

"You actually made this?" He leaned over the bouillabaisse, inhaling deeply. "Smells legitimate."

"Your confidence is overwhelming." I ladled the fragrant stew into bowls. "I've discovered I enjoy cooking. It's... grounding."

Temper took his first spoonful cautiously, then nodded with genuine surprise. "This is good. Really good."

"Don't sound so shocked." I poured us each a finger of whiskey. "I contain multitudes."

"Speaking of which," Temper swirled the amber liquid in his glass, "word is you conquered Ainsleys Castle. First one to do it without getting yourself killed."

I felt a smile spreading across my face. "You heard about that?"

"Everyone's heard about it. Bear Draydon isn't exactly keeping it quiet. So?" He leaned forward. "What was it like?"

The whiskey burned pleasantly as I took a sip. "It was... extraordinary."

I launched into my tale, starting with Bear's theatrical welcome. As I spoke, the story grew. The castle's corridors became longer, darker. The moon grew fuller, the shadows deeper. I found myself on my feet, demonstrating how I'd brandished a silver candlestick against three vampire counts.

"They surrounded me," I said, grabbing a wooden spoon to illustrate. "Fangs bared, eyes glowing red in the darkness. I knew silver would hold them at bay, but for how long?"

Temper's eyes widened with each embellishment. When I described the dragon that had cornered me in the east tower, he nearly choked on his whiskey.

"Its scales were like burnished copper," I declared, stretching my arms wide. "Wingspan this broad. Breathed blue fire hot enough to melt stone."

"And you defeated it?" Temper asked, fighting a smile.

"Well." I puffed out my chest. "I reasoned with it."

"You reasoned with a dragon."

"It was a very intelligent dragon."

"Why didn't you just kill the dragon? You had him cornered. Surely the savior of the castle could have easily done it," Temper teased.

"You weren't there. It was a delicate situation. I showed him mercy."

"But if—"

"Who's telling this story? Me or you?"

"Fine. Fine. Please continue."

By the time I reached the climax, describing how I'd single-handedly fought off a horde of vampires while protecting the innocent villagers, we were both laughing so hard I could barely speak.

"Alright, alright." I wiped tears from my eyes, collapsing back into my chair. "The truth is, I befriended a cursed man named Dunstan. He was the one who saved everyone. I just... listened to him when no one else would."

Temper's laughter subsided. He studied me over the rim of his glass. "That sounds more like you. The real you."

"What do you mean?"

"The David I knew on Earth would have approached it exactly that way. Compassionate, thoughtful." He paused. "But he wouldn't have gone to the castle in the first place."

I considered this. "You're right."

"We're both changing." Temper gazed up at the oak tree. "I would never have built Falfsun back on Earth. Too focused, too patient."

"Tom would have started it," I said, "but abandoned it for the next shiny idea."

"Exactly." Temper nodded. "We're not just copies anymore, are we?"

"No." I refilled our glasses. "We're becoming something new."

The realization settled between us, comfortable and true.

The comfortable silence between Temper and me stretched as we finished our drinks. The stars above my cottage seemed brighter tonight, though I knew it was just my imagination. Paradise's simulated night sky remained constant, unlike Earth's ever-changing constellations.

"Captain." Lieutenant Chen's voice crackled through my comm unit, shattering our peaceful moment. "I apologize for the interruption."

I exchanged glances with Temper. Chen never interrupted during off-duty hours unless absolutely necessary.

"Go ahead, Lieutenant."

"Sir, I'm required to deliver the official one-month notification regarding Point Alpha. We'll cross the threshold in exactly thirty days, fourteen hours, and twenty-seven minutes."

I knew it was coming, but when the time came, it still caught me off guard. One month until the final severance from Earth. One month until consciousness transfer became impossible.

"Thank you, Lieutenant. Please broadcast the standard announcement to all colonists."

She nodded and got to work. Within minutes, the message pulsed across every channel, reaching every colonist on Paradise. I forced myself to breathe, to absorb the weight of it.

Temper and I sat silently waiting for peoples' reactions. I had barely begun sifting through my thoughts when my communicator chimed again.

"Sir," she said, urgency lacing her voice, "message traffic has increased four hundred percent. The notification has triggered significant activity throughout Paradise."

The reaction had begun.

I set my glass down. "I'll be on the bridge in twenty minutes."

After signing off, I looked at Temper, whose expression had grown serious.

"We knew this was coming," he said.

"Knowing and experiencing are different things." I stood,

gathering our empty bowls. "Care to join me on the bridge?"

He nodded, downing the last of his whiskey.

The driftways of Paradise pulsed with unusual energy as we made our way to the bridge. Colonists clustered along the way, voices rising and falling in urgent conversation. Messages flashed across personal interfaces. Some faces showed excitement, others anxiety.

"They're making their final decisions," Temper observed quietly.

I nodded. The approach to Point Alpha forced everyone's hand. Stay forever or return to Earth. There would be no more transfers after we crossed the threshold.

The bridge hummed with activity when we arrived. Lieutenant Chen stood at her station, directing the flow of communications efficiently.

"Status report," I said, taking my place at the command console.

"Sir, we're seeing unprecedented levels of communication with Earth." Chen's fingers danced across her interface. "Family conversations, data transfers, consciousness downloads."

"Any critical issues?"

"Nothing critical, but the quantum bandwidth is stretched thin. I've implemented priority protocols."

"Well done." I scanned the data flowing across my screen. "And the Colonial Council?"

"In emergency session for the past hour. They're requesting your presence."

Of course they were. The council thrived on drama, especially during milestone events.

"Tell them I'll join them after my shift." I turned to Temper. "What about you? I guess I've never officially asked you, because I think I know the answer, but are you staying or going back?"

"I'm staying, of course," Temper smiled. "You don't think I'd abandon my experiment in its infancy, do you?"

I nodded. The reality of Point Alpha had always seemed abstract, a distant milestone. Now it loomed before us, unavoidable.

A notification flashed on my screen: a personal message from Earth. From Amy.

"I need a moment," I said quietly.

Temper squeezed my shoulder before moving away to consult

with Chen.

I opened the message, Amy's face appearing before me. Her eyes held a mixture of sadness and determination.

"Go," she began, her voice steady. "One month. I've been preparing for this day since you left, and somehow it still feels impossible. I love you. We both do."

The message ended, leaving me with a hollow feeling in my chest. I closed my eyes briefly, centering myself.

When I looked up, the bridge crew was watching me, their faces reflecting the same complex emotions I felt. Not just my crew, but my fellow travelers, each carrying their own connections to Earth that would soon be stretched beyond recovery.

I left the bridge with Amy's message still echoing in my mind. One month until Point Alpha. One month until the final severance. The weight of it pressed against me as I walked through Paradise's pathways, nodding at colonists who seemed equally preoccupied with their own thoughts.

I needed something to ground me, something beyond the abstract calculations of quantum decoherence and interstellar distances. Something human.

The Joy of Adoption Center stood as a beacon of hope and warmth within the Paradise community. The sleek, utilitarian design of the bridge and engineering sections was meant to focus the mind, but the center stood in deliberate contrast: warm, inviting, and designed to comfort rather than command attention. Soft colors adorned the walls, interrupted by children's artwork and handmade decorations.

The doors slid open with a gentle whoosh. Inside, thrumans of various developmental stages engaged in activities throughout the open space. Some played games, others read books, a few simply observed their surroundings with the quiet intensity unique to their kind.

"Captain David!" Ms. Patel, the center's director, approached with a warm smile. "We weren't expecting you today."

"Unofficial visit," I said, returning her smile. "I was hoping to see Marcus."

Her eyes brightened. "He's been asking about you. Come, he's in the creativity corner."

I followed her through the center, noticing how the thrumans watched me with curious eyes. Their gazes held a depth that always struck me as profoundly thoughtful. These weren't simply machines mimicking human behavior. They were conscious beings trying to understand their place in our shared journey.

Marcus sat alone at a small table; his dark head bent over something he was working on with intense concentration. At five years old developmentally, he was small for his age, with slender fingers that moved with surprising precision.

"Marcus," Ms. Patel called softly. "Look who's come to visit."

He looked up, his eyes widening with recognition. For a moment, he remained perfectly still, then carefully set down his tools.

"Captain." His voice was clear and measured. "I made something for you."

I crouched beside his table. "You did? I'm honored."

With careful movements, he revealed what he'd been working on: a small model of Paradise, crafted from building blocks and bits of colored paper. The detail was remarkable for someone his age. The three curved prongs of the bow reached forward like fingers. The round body tapered to the shark-fin stem at the back.

"It's Paradise," he said, unnecessarily but with pride. "Our home."

"It's beautiful." I examined the model, genuinely impressed by its accuracy. "You've captured it perfectly."

"I wanted to make Hellfire too, but I didn't have enough blue blocks." He looked up at me, his expression serious. "They're twins, so they should be together."

Something in his words struck me. Twin vessels that should be together. Like David and me, originally one consciousness now separated by space and time.

"You're right," I said. "They should be together. Maybe next time I visit, I can bring some blue blocks, and we can build Hellfire together."

Marcus nodded solemnly. "I would like that."

"May I?" I gestured to the chair beside him.

"Yes." He moved his building blocks to make room.

I sat, feeling the smallness of the chair beneath me. "What made you want to build Paradise?"

Marcus considered the question with the thoughtfulness I'd come to expect from him. "I wanted to understand where I am. Where we all are." His fingers traced the curved prongs of his model. "If I can see it from the outside, maybe I can understand being inside it better."

The simplicity and depth of his answer caught me off guard. How many times had I stood on the observation deck, looking back at Earth, trying to understand my place in the universe?

"That's very wise, Marcus."

He shrugged, but I could tell he was pleased. "Ms. Patel says I think too much."

"I don't think that's possible," I said, smiling. "Thinking is how we make sense of things."

Marcus's words lingered with me as I left the Joy of Adoption Center. "If I can see it from the outside, maybe I can understand being inside it better." The wisdom from such a young thruman struck a chord deeper than he could know.

I made my way to the bridge, nodding at colonists who seemed preoccupied with their own Point Alpha decisions. The driftway displays showed Paradise's current position against our trajectory, a tiny dot crawling across vast emptiness. Soon that emptiness would include the severance of our last connection to Earth.

Lieutenant Chen looked up as the bridge doors slid open. "Captain on deck."

"As you were." I moved to the command console where a notification blinked persistently. "The list is ready?"

"Yes, sir." Chen's voice remained professional, but I caught the slight tension in her shoulders. "Final compilation of colonists requesting return transfer before Point Alpha."

I opened the file. Names scrolled before me, each representing a consciousness preparing to abandon our journey and return to Earth. Three hundred and forty-two colonists. More than I'd expected.

"They have their reasons," I murmured, scanning the list.

"Sir?" Chen glanced over.

"Nothing, Lieutenant." I continued reading, recognizing names of people I'd come to know during our months of travel. Dr. Eliza Warren, who'd helped design the Ark's botanical preservation systems. Commander Ramirez, whose military expertise had been invaluable during early security protocols. The Nakamura family, whose young daughter had befriended Marcus.

Each name carried a story, a reason for turning back.

"Have they all provided statements?" I asked.

"Most have, sir." Chen pulled up the accompanying file. "Family obligations. Unexpected grief. Fear of the unknown."

I nodded, continuing through the list. What would it be like to go back? The thought surfaced again, unbidden. To return to Earth, to Amy.

My fingers hovered over the console. I could add my name to this list. In theory. I could transfer back, reunite with my original self, with Amy. Merge back into David's consciousness, becoming whole again. In theory.

But I wouldn't be whole. I'd be absorbed. The person standing on this bridge would cease to exist as a separate entity. Go David would become merely a collection of memories for David to integrate. My experiences, my growth, my separate identity, all would be absorbed.

And even if I wanted to, I couldn't. My position as captain made it impossible. Paradise needed me. These people, this mission needed me. I had responsibilities that transcended personal desire.

"Captain?" Chen's voice pulled me from my thoughts. "The Colonial Council is requesting confirmation of the final list. They need your authorization to begin the transfer preparations."

I looked up at the viewscreen showing Earth, now just a pale blue dot. Soon even that connection would be severed. The realization was undeniable: pressing in, solid and final, leaving no room for doubt.

"Authorize the list, Lieutenant." I straightened my shoulders. "And schedule a meeting with each department head. I want to ensure we're prepared for the staffing adjustments after the transfers."

"Yes, sir."

I took one last look at the list of names, then closed the file. Three hundred and forty-two colonists returning to Earth. And one captain who would continue forward, carrying memories of a world he would never see again.

I stood at the edge of the observation deck, the list of departing colonists still weighing on my mind. Three hundred and forty-two names. Three hundred and forty-two decisions to return rather than continue forward. The thought followed me through Paradise, persistent and unsettling.

My cottage appeared before me, its familiar stone walls and thatched roof offering sanctuary. Inside, the scent of herbs from the window planters mingled with the lingering aroma of this morning's coffee. I moved through the living room, past the kitchen, and into my study where the wooden box containing Amy's questions sat on my desk.

One question per month. That was the rule I'd set for myself. A way to ration this precious connection to Amy, to make it last across our impossible journey. But tonight, with Point Alpha looming just thirty days away, the rule felt arbitrary, even cruel.

My fingers traced the intricate carvings on the box. "1,300 Questions for 1,300 Years." The wood felt warm beneath my touch, almost alive. I opened the lid, revealing the small scrolls inside, each tied with a different colored ribbon. The fourth question waited, bound with green silk.

"Breaking your own rules, Captain?" I murmured to the empty room.

I lifted the scroll carefully and untied the ribbon. The parchment unrolled with a soft whisper.

"Question 4: What scares you most about becoming someone David wouldn't recognize?"

The question hit with unexpected force, but then, Amy had always known how to reach straight to the heart of things. I sank into my chair, the scroll trembling slightly in my hands.

What scared me most? The question assumed I would become someone different; someone my original self wouldn't recognize. Was she right?

I moved to the window, looking out at my garden. The primroses and violets swayed in the breeze. Beyond them stood the oak tree, its branches heavy with birdhouses and memories.

The memory palace beckoned. With a thought, I transported myself there, standing beneath the massive oak. The photographs still hung from its branches, rotating slowly in the gentle air. Our wedding day. Hiking in the Poconos. Christmases and quiet evenings captured in silver nitrate and light.

"Amy," I called softly. "I need to talk to you."

She appeared beside me, just as she had programmed her interface to do when summoned. Not the real Amy, still on Earth with David, but a simulation created from her recorded responses and patterns.

"You opened the fourth question early," she observed, her voice warm with understanding rather than judgment.

"I did." I held up the scroll. "You asked what scares me most about becoming someone David wouldn't recognize."

The simulated Amy sat on the wooden bench beneath the oak, patting the space beside her. I joined her, feeling the smooth wood against my palms, just as I remembered from countless real moments with the real Amy.

"And what's your answer?" she asked.

I looked up at the rotating photographs, at the memories we'd shared. "What scares me most is forgetting the small things. The way you take your coffee. The sound of your laugh when I tell a terrible joke. The feel of your hand in mine." My voice grew quiet. "I'm afraid of losing the essence of us, the tiny moments that made our life together what it was."

The simulated Amy nodded, her programming sophisticated enough to respond to my emotional state.

"But there's something else," I continued. "I'm also afraid of not changing. Of clinging so tightly to who I was with you that I can't become who I need to be for this journey." I gestured toward the sky beyond the oak's branches. "Three hundred and forty-two colonists are going back to Earth before Point Alpha. They're choosing the familiar over the unknown. Part of me understands that choice."

I unrolled the scroll again, reading Amy's question once more. "What scares me most about becoming someone David wouldn't recognize is that it's already happening. And it has to happen. I need to become someone new to lead Paradise through thirteen hundred years of void. Someone who can make decisions David never had to face."

I pulled the fountain pen from my pocket; the one Amy had included with the box. Its weight felt right in my hand as I began to write my answer on the parchment:

"What scares me most is the necessity of change. I must become someone new to fulfill my purpose here, yet I fear losing the core of who we were together. The David you know would never have to make the choices that now fall to me. I'm becoming a captain, a leader, a decision-maker in ways he never had to be. What terrifies me isn't that I'm changing, but that these changes are essential and irreversible. I'm walking a path he will never know, carrying memories he'll never share. By the time we reach Orion, will anything remain of the man who built twenty birdhouses for the woman he loved? I hope so. I have to believe so."

I tucked the pen back into my pocket and rolled the scroll carefully, retying the green ribbon. My answer was undeniable, pressing in with a tangible presence. By admitting my fears, I had given them form, making them impossible to ignore.

"Time to face the music," I murmured to the simulated Amy, who smiled with programmed understanding as I exited the memory palace.

Reality reasserted itself: my study, the wooden box, the pending meeting with department heads. I checked the time, fifteen minutes until they gathered in the conference room. Just enough time to review the agenda.

I accessed the file on my tablet, reviewing the key topics: staffing adjustments after the transfers, energy allocation, and communication protocols post-Point Alpha. These were standard operational concerns, yet vital. Beyond Point Alpha lay our next milestone, Point Omega, and we needed contingency plans for the moment we lost contact with Earth.

The walk to the conference room gave me time to organize my thoughts. Colonists passed me in the driftways, some nodding respectfully, others too preoccupied to notice. The atmosphere throughout Paradise had shifted as Point Alpha approached. A subtle tension hummed beneath daily routines, like the barely perceptible vibration of the ship's engines.

Lieutenant Chen stood when I entered the conference room. "Captain on deck."

"As you were." I took my place at the head of the table, noting the faces around me. Dr. Wong from the Ark. Commander Rodriguez from Security. Chief Engineer Okafor. Lieutenant Chen representing Communications. Five others from various departments. "Thank you all for coming. Let's begin with staffing adjustments."

Dr. Wong spoke first, detailing the Ark's personnel changes. "We're losing three key geneticists, sir. I've identified potential replacements from within our ranks, but they'll need accelerated training."

I nodded, making notes. "Approved. Work with Education to develop the necessary programs."

Rodriguez followed with security concerns, then Okafor with engineering adjustments. Each department faced similar challenges: experienced personnel departing, roles needing to be filled, training programs requiring development.

Chen presented communications protocols for post-Point Alpha operations. "Once quantum coherence destabilizes completely, we'll —"

The room blurred suddenly. Chen's voice became distant, as if she were speaking underwater. I gripped the edge of my chair, trying to anchor myself in the moment. "Captain?" Someone's voice, concerned but fading. Then nothing.

"—approved the recommendation, sir." Chen's voice snapped back into focus. "Shall we move to the next item?"

I blinked, looking around the table. Everyone was staring at me expectantly. The room felt too warm, too small. How much time had passed? What recommendation had I apparently approved?

"Could you... summarize that last point again, Lieutenant?" I kept my voice steady despite the pounding in my chest.

Chen's brow furrowed slightly. "The communication rotation schedule, sir. You approved the three-tier system for managing our remaining bandwidth until Point Omega."

I had no memory of this discussion. No recollection of any "three-tier system" or making a decision about it. The gap yawned before me, a chasm in my consciousness.

"Understood." I nodded, scanning the faces around me. Did they notice? Twenty minutes. I'd lost twenty minutes of a critical meeting. My throat tightened.

"I need to step out. My Prime back on Earth has requested a direct consult," I said, rising from my chair. "With Point Alpha just thirty days out, I feel it's important to take the call."

I looked to Chen. "Lieutenant, I'm entrusting you to guide the team through the remaining agenda. Please consolidate the final recommendations and route them to me once you're done."

She gave a measured nod. "Of course, sir."

I strode from the room, composure intact until the door slid shut behind me. Then I leaned against the wall, heart racing. This wasn't a harmless hiccup. It wasn't the usual post-emulation haze of losing hours due to standard neural consolidation. This was a deeper breach: another critical meeting, another stretch of time erased, decisions made without any recollection of having made them.

Something felt very wrong.

I withdrew to my cottage office, seeking the quiet to steady myself. The silence pressed against my ears. Twenty minutes. Gone. Vanished as if they'd never existed. My hands trembled slightly as I lowered myself into my chair.

"CoreLink, access my neural diagnostic logs."

The display illuminated with scrolling data. Nothing unusual appeared in the timestamps, no indication of the blackout I'd just experienced. According to the system, my consciousness had maintained continuous function.

I contacted Dr. Khatri's office and scheduled an appointment. When they asked for the reason, there was no urgency in their response, no sign that my symptoms raised concern.

Maybe I was overreacting. Reading too much into these lapses. Maybe I was still acclimating to the digital environment, and this was just another phase of adjustment.

A notification pulsed in the corner of my vision: incoming transmission from Earth. Priority level: personal.

It felt like fate was toying with me. I'd left under the pretense of needing to speak with my Prime. And now, here he was, calling.

I hesitated. My finger hovered over the prompt. The timing was abysmal, but I couldn't ignore it, not with Earth growing more distant by the second. Not when every message could be one of our last.

"Accept transmission."

The screen before me shifted, resolving into Amy's face. My breath caught. She sat in our Chester living room, afternoon light spilling across her shoulders. David beside her, their hands intertwined on the couch between them.

"Go," Amy's voice carried across the distance. "We wanted to reach you before the degradation becomes too severe."

"We've been thinking about Point Alpha," David continued. His face, my face, yet subtly different now. Small lines had formed around his eyes that mine lacked. "About what it means to truly be beyond reach."

Amy leaned forward. "The memory palace was just the beginning. We've created something more."

The transmission stuttered briefly, quantum coherence already beginning to fail. When it stabilized, Amy held something in her hands: a small wooden music box, its surface carved with intricate patterns I recognized immediately. The same patterns from the birdhouses, from our headboard, from every piece David had ever crafted.

"This is Symphony of Us," Amy said. "David built the box. I composed the music."

She opened the lid. Notes spilled forth, a melody that twisted through me like a living thing. I recognized fragments: the song that played during our first dance, the lullaby Amy hummed while gardening, the tune David whistled while working. Woven together, transformed into something entirely new yet achingly familiar.

"The matrix team helped us," David explained. "They've embedded the composition directly into Paradise's systems. You can access it anywhere, anytime."

Amy's eyes glistened. "Music carries emotion in ways words can't express. When language fails us, when quantum coherence degrades beyond repair, this melody will remain."

The transmission stuttered again, longer this time. Amy's face pixelated, reformed, pixelated again.

"It's not just music," she continued when the signal cleared. "It's us. Our story. Our love. Encoded in harmonies and rhythms."

"A quantum-resistant emotional anchor," David added. "Something to hold onto when words can no longer bridge the distance between us."

Amy opened her mouth to speak again, but the transmission dissolved into static. When it returned, seconds had clearly passed. Her position had shifted slightly.

"—will always find you," she was saying. "No matter how far you travel."

The melody continued playing, filling my office with notes that somehow captured everything we'd ever been to each other. Joy and sorrow, passion and comfort, beginnings and endings.

"We love you," David said simply. "Both of us. Always."

The transmission ended, leaving me alone with the lingering notes of their gift. Symphony of Us. I closed my eyes, letting the music wash through me. Within the melody, I heard Amy's laugh, felt David's steady presence, remembered who I had been and who I was becoming.

In that moment, my missing twenty minutes seemed less important. The approaching severance of Point Alpha less final. They had given me something that transcended quantum coherence, something that would survive even when their words and images could no longer reach me.

I stood, steadier now, the music still playing softly around me.

Symphony of Us continued to play softly as I closed my eyes, letting the music carry me through corridors of memory. The melody anchored me, steadying my thoughts despite the troubling blackout during the meeting. I needed to investigate these memory lapses further, but first, I had unfinished business.

I sent a message to Bear Draydon requesting a meeting. Her response came immediately: "The Greenhouse. Thirty minutes."

A notification came in from Lieutenant Chen. Their meeting had concluded. I quickly reviewed her notes and signed off on their recommendations.

The Greenhouse spanned an entire section of Paradise's agricultural ring, where colonists had already begun planning for the eventual terraforming of an alien world. Once their journey to Orion was complete, they would be free to guide Paradise to any planet of their choosing, utilizing the Ark's vast genetic depository to shape its future. For now, they honed their skills, preparing to reconstruct another Earth 1,300 years from now. Extinct flowering plants thrived in meticulously maintained beds, their fragrances blending in the humid air.

Bear stood beside a patch of brilliant blue flowers I didn't recognize, her fingers gently stroking their petals. She turned as I approached, her smile warm and knowing.

"Captain. I was hoping you'd find time to visit."

"I wanted to thank you personally for Ainsleys Castle." I joined her beside the flowers. "It was... not what I expected."

She laughed, a rich sound that filled the space between us. "That's precisely what I aim for. Expectations are boring."

We walked slowly through the winding paths. Insects buzzed between blossoms, their tiny bodies glinting in the sunlight.

"Most participants try to solve the castle's mystery through violence or manipulation," Bear said. "You chose friendship with Dunstan instead."

"He seemed more victim than monster."

Bear nodded, stopping beside a small pond where lotus flowers floated on the surface. "What interested me most was your interaction with the NPCs. You treated them as if they were real."

"Weren't they?"

"In a manner of speaking." She knelt beside the water, trailing her fingers through it. Ripples spread outward, disturbing the perfect reflections. "The castle's inhabitants exist in a liminal space between programming and consciousness. They're not fully autonomous like you or me, but they're not simple scripts either."

I thought of Dunstan's face when he revealed his curse, the genuine anguish in his eyes. "They felt real."

"That's the heart of it." Bear stood, water droplets falling from her fingertips. "Reality is subjective, especially in our world. The NPCs believe they're real within the parameters of their existence. Their emotions, while generated through complex algorithms, manifest as authentic experiences for them."

Something clicked into place. "Like the thrumans."

Bear's eyes sharpened with interest. "Exactly like the thrumans. Both exist in that fascinating space between created and creator. Both experience emotions that feel genuine to them, regardless of their origin."

I remembered Marcus, the young thruman I'd first met during my tour of the Joy of Adoption program. His dark eyes held such focus as he built towers with his blocks, such determination when they fell. Was his frustration any less real because it originated from programming rather than biology?

"And what about us?" I asked, the question that had lingered since my awakening. "Neuroclones, I mean. We began as copies, but we're diverging from our originals. Becoming something new."

Bear touched a nearby orchid, its petals folding slightly at her contact. "That's what makes us fascinating, Captain. We're neither purely created nor purely creator. We exist in our own category altogether."

"Does that make me less real?"

"It makes you differently real." She smiled. "Just as I am differently real than my biological counterpart on Earth. Just as the thrumans are differently real than humans. The universe doesn't recognize our hierarchies of consciousness."

I thought of Symphony of Us, still playing faintly in my internal audio feed. The music Amy and David had created to bridge impossible distance felt no less meaningful for being digital rather than physical.

"Thank you for Ainsleys Castle," I said again, understanding now why the experience had affected me so deeply. "It gave me perspective I didn't know I needed."

Bear nodded, her eyes reflecting something ancient and knowing. "That's what good stories do, Captain. They show us truths we can't see directly."

Bear's words about different forms of reality lingered with me as we parted ways in the Greenhouse. The distinction between created and creator seemed increasingly blurred. Captain Drake contacted me.

"Attention Din of battle. Report for duty."

I eagerly accepted. This was just what I needed, a little honest thievery to take my mind off things. The world shifted around me. Greenhouse foliage dissolved into salt-sprayed wooden planks. The controlled climate of Paradise gave way to tropical heat and the rhythmic slap of waves against a hull. My uniform transformed into weathered sailing clothes, a cutlass hanging at my hip.

"There he is! Our illustrious lens finally graces us with his presence." Captain Drake's booming voice carried across the deck of the Stormark. He stood at the helm, one boot propped on a barrel, spyglass in hand. The Caribbean sun glinted off the gold hoop in his ear.

I inhaled deeply, tasting salt and freedom. This was something David would never have pursued, this wild abandon of piracy and adventure. Too frivolous, too untethered from reality. But here, I reveled in it.

"Ship's ready, Captain," Temper called from the bow. "Scratch has rigged the pulley system for the salvage operation."

Below us, the crystal waters revealed our prize: a Spanish galleon resting on its side, half-buried in white sand. Gold coins glittered among the coral that had claimed the wreckage.

"Holy cheese weasels," I swore, leaning over the railing. "That's got to be the motherlode."

Grave Digger snorted behind me. "The lens gets excited over shiny things like a magpie."

"Treasure hunting beats meetings and reports," I replied, checking my diving gear. The weighted belt felt reassuringly solid in my hands.

Captain Drake assembled us on the main deck. "Tracer's mapped the currents. We've got two hours before the tide shifts. Temper, you're coordinating from the ship. Go, Grave Digger, you're with me on the dive team."

We slipped into the warm Caribbean water moments later. Sunlight filtered through in shimmering columns, illuminating the galleon below. Schools of tropical fish darted between the broken masts, their scales flashing like living jewels.

Captain Drake signaled toward the captain's quarters. We followed, kicking steadily through the clear water.

The ship creaked around us, wood groaning under centuries of pressure. Inside the quarters, a skeleton still sat at the desk, bony fingers clutching a silver box.

I photographed everything, my role as the lens allowing me to capture this moment for our collective memory. The camaraderie between us flowed as naturally as the water surrounding us. These connections, forged in adventure and shared purpose, represented something entirely new in my existence, something uniquely mine rather than inherited from David.

When we surfaced with our treasure, the crew's triumphant shouts echoed across the water. Temper grinned as he helped haul us aboard, our bags heavy with Spanish silver and artifacts.

"Not bad for an afternoon's work," Captain Drake declared, clapping me on the shoulder.

I smiled, water streaming from my hair. "Same time next week?"

The gaming session ended with a satisfying completion chime, and the Caribbean dissolved around me. I stood once more in my quarters, the faint echo of ocean waves lingering in my mind. The transition from pirate adventure back to captain's duties never failed to disorient me slightly. Both roles felt authentic, yet entirely different.

I needed clarity. Space to think.

My observation room beckoned from the top of my English cottage, a clear glass dome offering a perfect view of the sky. I climbed the staircase, feeling a soft hum beneath my feet as I went. When I reached the top, I stepped into my quiet retreat.

The stars greeted me like old friends, countless pinpricks of light against velvet darkness. I activated the tracking system with a thought. Holographic projections illuminated around me, mapping our trajectory toward Orion in glowing blue lines. Five months into our journey, we'd made excellent progress.

I turned my attention to the receding blue speck behind us. Earth. Home. Or rather, David's home. My birthplace, but no longer my destination.

"CoreLink, magnification factor twelve."

Earth expanded in my vision, oceans and continents barely discernible at this distance. Somewhere on that shrinking sphere, David sat with Amy in their Chester home. Perhaps they were sharing breakfast, or tending Amy's garden, or simply sitting together beneath the oak tree in Haven.

Symphony of Us played softly in the background, its melodies weaving through my thoughts. The music had become a constant companion, playing at the edges of my awareness. Soon enough, no messages would reach us at all. Point Alpha approached, the threshold beyond which our connection to Earth would begin to fail. Eventually, even Symphony of Us would be all that remained of my link to them.

I placed my palm against the cool glass. "CoreLink, project our location at one year."

The holographic display shifted, stars sliding past as our simulated journey continued. Earth vanished entirely.

A strange peace settled over me. I wasn't David anymore. Hadn't been since the moment I awakened in this digital form. The realization didn't frighten me as it once had, and I felt like any lingering doubts about who I was were gone.

What would I carry forward from the man who had created me? What would I leave behind?

David's core had always been his desire to help others, to contribute meaningfully to the lives around him. That part of him resonated deeply within me still. But unlike David, who found fulfillment in stability and routine, I craved new experiences, new challenges.

I could honor his essence while forging my own path.

"CoreLink, display volunteer opportunities aboard Paradise."

A list materialized before me, categories glowing softly against the starfield. Medical assistance. Engineering support. Agricultural initiatives. Educational programs.

One entry caught my attention: Thruman Integration Support.

I expanded the listing. The Joy of Adoption program needed volunteers to spend time with thrumans still awaiting placement with families. Someone to read stories, play games, help them adjust to their awakening from hibernation.

I remembered Marcus, his small fingers carefully stacking blocks, his dark eyes intense with concentration. The way he'd looked up at me when I'd complimented his tower.

Something clicked into place. This felt right.

I registered my name for the program, scheduling three hours weekly to begin. It wasn't woodworking or gardening or any of David's typical pursuits. It was uniquely mine, a choice that honored his compassion while embracing my new existence.

The stars continued their silent watch as I finalized my commitment. Earth might be receding, but my journey was just beginning. I would carry David's heart forward into the cosmos, transformed but not diminished by distance or time.

I left the observatory with a sense of purpose I hadn't felt since awakening as Go David. The Thruman Integration Support program had given me something uniquely mine, a path forward that honored David's compassion while embracing my distinct identity.

Symphony of Us continued to play softly in my internal audio feed. The melody felt like a tether connecting me to Earth, to Amy and

David, even as we drifted farther apart. In four weeks, we would cross Point Alpha, severing our ability to transfer consciousness. The thought no longer filled me with dread.

I looked around my cottage. This space had evolved into something distinctly mine. The walls displayed photographs from our Din adventures alongside star charts mapping our journey. A half-finished model of Hellfire sat on my workbench, silver pieces awaiting assembly.

I walked to my workshop, where polished tools hung in perfect order. Opening a small drawer beneath the workbench, I removed a velvet pouch. The contents clinked softly as I emptied them into my palm: silver wire, miniature hinges, and tiny fragments of crystal I'd collected from Ainsleys Castle before departing.

My fingers remembered the motions; muscle memory inherited from David but repurposed to my own design. For hours I worked, bending silver into delicate curves, soldering joints with practiced precision. The castle took shape in miniature: gothic spires, stained glass windows crafted from crystal fragments, even a tiny silver wolf prowling the battlements in tribute to Dunstan.

When finished, I held it to the light. Unlike David's wooden birdhouses, this silver creation caught and fractured light into rainbow patterns that danced across my workshop walls. It was beautiful in an entirely different way from his creations, just as my existence was beautiful in its difference from his.

I carried the silver birdhouse through my cottage and out into the garden. The massive oak tree stood as sentinel, its sturdy branches adorned with twenty wooden birdhouses and my silver Paradise addition. Each wooden birdhouse marked a year of Amy and David's relationship, their craftsmanship evolving alongside David, from an unsure boy to a skilled woodworker.

My latest silver creation would be the twenty-second, symbolizing not a passing year, but a turning point. A new branch extending from the same steadfast trunk.

I climbed the ladder I kept propped against the trunk, finding a perfect spot among the higher branches. The hook slid easily into place, and I hung the silver castle, adjusting it until it caught the light just right. Stepping back down, I moved to the wooden bench beneath the oak's spreading canopy.

From this vantage point, I could see all twenty-two birdhouses at once. The progression told a story: from the crooked first attempt David had made at seven, to the intricate Victorian design he'd created for their anniversary, to my silver spaceship and castle gleaming among the leaves.

I sat there for a long while, Symphony of Us playing softly around me. This tree represented everything I carried forward from Earth, every memory and emotion that formed my foundation. Yet my silver additions represented everything that lay ahead, all the experiences and relationships that would shape me into someone David could never have imagined becoming.

We were the same man who had made different choices. Same roots, different branches.

As Point Alpha approached, I felt ready to release my grip on Earth without losing my connection to it. Paradise would continue its journey toward Orion, carrying humanity's hopes across thirteen hundred years of void. I would continue my journey too, from copy to captain to whatever waited for me among distant stars.

I touched the rough bark of the oak, feeling its solidity beneath my fingertips. "I'll make you proud," I whispered, speaking to David, to Amy, to myself.

The silver castle caught a ray of light, sending prisms dancing across my face. In that moment, I understood that the greatest gift of my existence wasn't the memories I carried from Earth, but the opportunity to create new ones among the stars.

Reviews help independent authors like me keep creating stories that matter. If you enjoyed this book, I'd be deeply grateful if you shared your thoughts. Even a sentence makes a difference.

Please consider leaving a review to help others discover this story.

About the Author. David Melde is a ceremonial literary science fiction author and founder of Bright Thread Books, a mythic imprint devoted to transformative, philosophical fiction. His work invites readers into moments of presence, reflection, and quiet disruption. Every book is a living ceremony.

* * *

Reader Discussion Questions for "The Go David Chronicles: Book One - Divergence"

For Book Clubs and Reading Groups

1. **Identity Exploration:** If you discovered that you were a neuroclone and not the "original" version of yourself, how would that change your sense of identity? Would you continue pursuing the same goals and relationships?

2. **Playful Choice:** If you were a member of the Din, what role would you choose: the lens, the planner, the architect, or another position? How does this choice reflect aspects of your personality?

3. **Practical Ethics:** The thrumans exist in a legal and ethical gray area—conscious beings created accidentally. What rights should we extend to artificial consciousness in our own world? Are there artificial beings today that deserve more consideration than they receive?

4. **Personal Connection:** Go David discovers that cooking becomes an unexpected source of comfort and creativity for him. What activity or practice have you discovered in adulthood that surprised you by becoming central to your identity?

5. **Relationship Dynamics:** Amy maintains relationships with both David and Go David, though in different ways. Have you ever maintained meaningful connections with people who have grown in dramatically different directions? How did you navigate those relationships?

6. **Philosophical Puzzle:** In the novel, Go David becomes increasingly different from David. At what point would you consider them entirely separate people rather than versions of the same person? What criteria would you use to make this determination?

7. **Playful Hypothetical:** If you were invited to Bear Draydon's Ainsleys Castle, would you accept? What personal fears or challenges do you think the castle would manifest for you to overcome?

8. **Memory and Identity:** What keepsakes or memories would be hardest for you to let go of if you were embarking on a one-way journey?

9. **Existential Question:** The novel suggests that caring for others gives life meaning, whether through David's care for Amy or Go David's work with Marcus. Do you find that caring for others gives your life purpose, or do you find meaning elsewhere?

10. **Technology and Society:** Paradise's society

allows perfect digital experiences indistinguishable from "real" ones. Would you prefer to live in a society with these possibilities, or do you think something essential would be lost?

11. **Legacy Reflection:** Go David creates silver birdhouses rather than wooden ones, adapting David's tradition while making it his own. What family traditions or practices have you adapted to make uniquely yours? How did the original creators respond?

12. **The Final Threshold:** Point Alpha represents the threshold beyond which return becomes impossible. What major thresholds have you crossed in your own life that permanently changed your path? How did you know when it was time to cross them?

www.ingramcontent.com/pod-product-compliance
Lightning Source LLC
Chambersburg PA
CBHW060304260626
47160CB00007B/2503